# SEASONS OF FOUR FACES

**BENJAMIN KWAKYE**

𝒞𝒲𝒫
Cissus World Press
Milwaukee 2024

Copyright © 2024 by Benjamin Kwakye
*All rights reserved.*

No part of this publication may be reproduced, distributed, or transmitted in any form or by any means, including photocopying, recording, or other electronic or mechanical methods, without the prior written permission of the publisher, except in the case of brief quotations embodied in critical reviews and certain other noncommercial uses permitted by copyright law.

This is a work of fiction. Names, characters, businesses, places, events and incidents are either the products of the author's imagination or used in a fictitious manner. Any resemblance to actual persons, living or dead, or actual events is purely coincidental.

Published in the United States by Cissus World Press, Milwaukee, Wisconsin. www.cissusworldpressbooks.com.

Library of Congress Cataloging-in-Publication Data.
Benjamin Kwakye

Seasons Of Four Faces/ Benjamin Kwakye—1st ed. p.cm. African/ Ghana (English) 2. Ghana----Fiction. I. Title
ISBN: 979-8-9889745-9-8

Manufactured in the United States of America
First North American/Worldwide Edition

Cover Image by Dike Okoro

# ALSO by BENJAMIN KWAKYE

### Novels

*The Clothes of Nakedness*
*The Sun by Night*
*Legacy of Phantoms*
*The Other Crucifix*
*The Three Books of Shama*
*The Count's False Banquet*
*Obsessions of Paradise*

### Collections

*Eyes of the Slain Woman* (novellas)
*The Executioner's Confession* (short stories)
*Shimmering at Sunset: New Stories from Africa* (as editor)

### Poetry

*Songs of a Jealous Wind*
*Soul to Song*
*Scrolls of the Living Night*
*Songs of Benjamin*
*Innocence of Photographs*
*Tale of Shadows*

# TABLE of CONTENTS

ALSO by BENJAMIN KWAKYE ......................... iii
PART I ................................................................. 1
CHAPTER 1 .......................................................... 3
    After the Gloaming ........................................... 3
    Finding the Air of the Wind ............................ 7
    Banquet of Death ........................................... 11
    The Dust of Dawn .......................................... 18
    Tears of Festivals ........................................... 22
    Searching for Noon ........................................ 24
    Finding War and Love ................................... 28
    Marching with Dust ....................................... 35
    The War .......................................................... 37
CHAPTER 2 ........................................................ 42
    Embrace of Spirits ......................................... 42
    Echoes of Silent Chambers ........................... 44
    Currencies of Ambition ................................. 49
    A Taste of Eternity ........................................ 54
    Shadows of the Nights .................................. 62
    Breath of Last Gasp ...................................... 65
    Childbirths ..................................................... 67
CHAPTER 3 ........................................................ 71
    Running with Immortals ............................... 71

 Rage of Spirits ........................................... 74
 Breakfast of Despair.................................... 77
 Past the Duel of Serpents............................ 81
 A Song for the King .................................... 84
 Voice of Mountains...................................... 86
CHAPTER 4................................................... 93
 Children of the Nile .................................... 93
 Thickening the Plot..................................... 97
 Archeology of Geneses.............................. 101
 Battling the Unknown ............................... 106
 Tasting Darkness....................................... 110
 Song of the Ghosts ................................... 111
 Singing of Woe.......................................... 118
 Embracing the Clouds............................... 123
PART II ........................................................ 129
CHAPTER 1................................................. 131
 Dancing with Wind................................... 131
 The Arrival ................................................ 133
 A Rendezvous of Spirits............................ 137
 Fire and Fire .............................................. 143
 Weaving Testimonies................................ 146
 Friends in the Forebodings........................ 147
 Favor and Doubt....................................... 153
 Taming the Roaring Lions........................ 155
 Of Tongues, Eyes, and Minds................... 158

Thickening Pathways ................................. 163
Fame and Suspicion ................................. 165
A Great Question .................................... 168

CHAPTER 2 ............................................ 171
Miasmas and Visions ................................ 171
Hope and Glory ...................................... 179
A Portrait of Destiny ................................ 181
Singing Greatness ................................... 185
Life as a Proverb .................................... 187

CHAPTER 3 ............................................ 190
Flirting with Immortality ........................... 190
Eyeing Immortality .................................. 193
Looking for Immortality ............................. 196
Foreign Soils ........................................ 199
Intrigues of Foreign Soils .......................... 202
Invasion of Hope .................................... 205

CHAPTER 4 ............................................ 209
Looking Forward to the Past ........................ 209
The New .............................................. 215
Thickening the Broth ................................ 218
Romancing Fate ...................................... 223
Out of the Shadows .................................. 227
Pushed to Twilight .................................. 233
Beckoning Night ..................................... 238

PART III .............................................. 249

CHAPTER 1 ............................................................. 251
    The Arrival ..................................................... 251
    House of Queens............................................ 257
    House of Ghosts............................................. 260
    The Favor of Stools ....................................... 267
    The Golden Stool............................................ 269
CHAPTER 2 ............................................................. 272
    Conference of Ghosts.................................... 272
    Up the Good Tree.......................................... 279
    Testing the Farmland .................................... 283
CHAPTER 3 ............................................................. 286
    Shading of the Night...................................... 286
    The Fear ......................................................... 292
    Seeing Past Sight ........................................... 300
    Unearthing the Fire........................................ 303
    Wrestling Fear................................................ 309
    A Time for Everything................................... 314
    Fighting the False Shadow ........................... 319
    The Second Conference ............................... 322
CHAPTER 4 ............................................................. 324
    Voices of Shadows........................................ 324
    Touching the Dry Palm Fronds ................... 328
    Staring at Life ................................................ 333
    Staring at Death ............................................ 340
    Fidgeting for Blood ....................................... 345

  Encircling the Python..................................350

  Foraging for More Blood ..........................355

  Howling for Whispers ................................361

PART IV ...............................................................363

CHAPTER 1.........................................................365

  Songs of the Shore ....................................365

  A Homecoming ..........................................374

  The Heart of Embrace ...............................377

CHAPTER 2.........................................................385

  Hooting at Hunger.....................................385

  A Battle with the Sea.................................390

  Song of Wrestlers ......................................395

CHAPTER 3.........................................................399

  Stirring Time Awake..................................399

  Positive Action...........................................407

  Wounds of Freedom .................................413

  A Fight ........................................................417

  The Battle Past Silence..............................422

  A Time for Everything...............................426

CHAPTER 4.........................................................428

  Afternoon Delight .....................................428

  Embracing the Time..................................432

  Water Droplets..........................................434

  Walking the Chasm ...................................437

  Song of Heroes..........................................445

| | |
|---|---|
| Another Look at Time | 450 |
| Shackling the Unshackled | 456 |
| Heart-washing | 463 |
| The Brink | 472 |
| Canoeing Freedom | 474 |
| Fresh Air | 477 |
| Time and Space | 478 |
| AUTHOR'S NOTE | 480 |
| ABOUT the AUTHOR | 481 |

*Once again, with love*

for Sister (Afia), Benjamin (Sr.), Moses, Mama (Abrafi),

and in memory of Ebenezer and Samuel

"All that is not eternal is eternally out of date."

~ **C.S. Lewis** *(The Four Loves)*

"That which is has already been,
And what is to be has already been"

~ **Ecclesiastes 3:15**

# PART I

# CHAPTER

# 1

*"Tonight, your reign ends," said one of the men.*

## After the Gloaming

Her mind was full of threatening characters. She'd woken up, not from the usual nocturia, but from something she could not comprehend. The night of multiple characters became a composite character informing her of imminent death. Its threat deepened, molded into a face with only one message, contorted in the pleasure of the macabre message it announced: You, Madam, are about to die. She had heard of the rumors, some whispered inadvertently within ear-shot, when she had even imagined herself an animal being prepared for the abattoir, a slaughterhouse where she herself had sent many before their time, though in her estimation never out of spite but of necessity. Beyond physical death, she had also often imposed the death of obscurity on those who threatened her prominence. Among them was her stepson.

Was it now her turn to die one of the many forms of death? If so which one?

The worry and the fear.

It was one thing to know that death would come some day and another to face it. In the stifling inner chamber, she looked through the window, but the darkness was as dense as death itself; and she was thick with regret that found twinship with her fear. At the same time the darkness soothed her with the deceit that she would survive.

It was a hard negotiator, this night, in its demand to tease discomfort from her mind into her body. And the strongest comfort she was able to afford at that time was from the images her mind conjured. And she imagined night clothed in a cloak of many layers, each layer singularly dark for a collective darkness transcending understanding, not even by her mind's eye. But as death moved with purpose towards her, it unfurled its outer layers every now and then in false striptease, because each unfurling emitted malodorous smells that her mind's nostrils initially mistook for a comforting breeze until she could fully catch the fullness of the whiffs, causing her to sweat. And her chest bore witness to her fear with the intense motions of her heart's drumbeat.

She took deep breaths and reimagined her fate. She would live and not die. Live and not die. Live and not die. Live and not die. She was as bold as fear and did not fear death. Bold, unafraid of death. Bold unafraid of death. Bold unafraid of death. She allowed the darkness to remain as is, refusing to negotiate it with for any form of illumination. Come, she whispered sotto voce, come death, let's tango and you will lose this round. Come for the ultimate seduction. I know you. I love you. I have fed your insatiable nether parts with many souls. Therefore, come as a lover in the night and let us engage in our illicit affair. We will engage and I, I will leave you exhausted in the quake of my passion.

She danced a slow motioned dance, as death came towards her.

She began to prepare herself for her lover. In the darkness, she could only see herself from memory and in the silhouette of her body in the shadowless darkness. Hatshepsut ran her still nervy, shaking hands over her head, which was hairless without her wig, and down the contours of her face, the broad forehead, down the cheeks of high bones, to the tapering chin, and then up at the aquiline nose. It was a totally naked face, now that she had removed the false beard she wore at times — a queen who would be king.

Death must find her in her true and pure form without the props that helped her wield power, for surely death was not impressed by such paraphernalia. And now, thinking how it would feel like to make love with death and survive as she sensed death so ever present, she let slip the robe that clothed her and, in this state of undecorated corpus, she ran her hand down the body firm in some places but soft in many others, a body tamed by years and illnesses. Come, lover, come, she continued to coo. I am ready for you.

The darkness listened and things got darker both outside and inside.

But she did not imagine the actual manner in which the death she so personified in order to avoid death was actually approaching her, not in a metaphoric representation that she could negotiate with through the interlocution of make believe voices, not in manipulation of her mind, but in the form of living persons who had become at that moment ministers of death.

## BENJAMIN KWAKYE

There were three of them walking towards her, as though emerged from the wombs of the night, and they had only one purpose in mind, bearing the mind of the night, their steps producing ominous staccato sounds, soft but audible. At the moment when the night got darker and darker still, it was im- possible to decipher their features, for they were almost one with it, rendering the hoods that covered their heads super- fluous.

SEASONS of FOUR FACES

# Finding the Air of the Wind

This was their rare opportunity, with Pharaoh Hatshepsut and a small entourage having left the palace to this much smaller replica where she came on rare occasions for rest. Only few people knew of this, the getaway intended to provide her with as much quiet as she needed to relax. Those who approached her could not have had such seamless access to the main palace always full of countless people and with much activity. The secrecy of the getaway was sufficient to assure her, though falsely, as some of those she trusted the most sought to breach that trust.

No one was abroad at that time, only minutes before midnight, or if anyone did, they would retreat like thieves upon seeing the three who continued to move as if they were the night. In fact, the three would not appear to the human eye as human, though human they were, but would be equated with gods in temporary human corpus worn as needed garb to perform a human purpose, after which they would retransform into their godly forms. Evidently these were not to be engaged in any form or manner, for their silhouettes created an aura of utter fierceness and even something diabolical. Such were they, the three as they walked in unchoreographed tandem, near silent steps, shadows too dark to be counted as shadows, merging with the night. If they could be distinguished in the starless night of lunar dullness, it was in height, as tall, medium and short or, depending on the perspective, as tall, taller, tallest. And perhaps gait: coordinated, more coordinated and most coordinated.

One of them hated Senenmut, Pharaoh's chief minister.

When he hoped she would have turned to him, Pharaoh had instead turned to Senenmut, giving Senenmut too much control over the kingdom, in some talebearers' version of events, even offering her body to him as a lover. The night walking man hated this union of bed and state. His piqued hatred for Chief Minister Senenmut would not permit him to consider the possibility of a business, political or platonic relationship and that the rumors might be false. The obscurity he had suffered was a form of death for him, one who craved kingly attention, one who believed that the glow of limelight creates beauty and power (and he wanted both but had been denied both).

One of them, the only woman among them, was offended in particular by the way Pharaoh had depicted and ordered herself to be depicted in statues and paintings as a male pharaoh, with a beard and large muscles. What was she trying to convey with this portrayal? What was she saying to the couple of female Pharaohs who had come before her or those that might come after her? She had herself witnessed Pharaoh in a beard a couple of times when she had been summoned to treat the queen for certain illnesses, particularly her inflammatory skin condition. She was a healer and a giver of life, and to her Pharaoh had crossed a line into hopelessness with her spiritual ambiguity. Pharaoh Hatshepsut could not be healed. But hers was not just that—she also looked forward to the power she would wield with the queen's death.

One of them was a man of war. But rather than wage wars, Pharaoh Hatshepsut had pivoted to trade, and he'd had the ignominy of accompanying her on a seaborne trading expedition to Punt. He deemed this an insult and was not placated that she had brought back gold, ebony, animal skins, baboons, and myrrh trees that were planted in the gardens of Deir el-

# SEASONS of FOUR FACES

Bahri. Was he, a man trained for war, who preferred the force of the wind, to be part of an army as idle as air? This insult could not be healed by her impressive building projects, including pyramids, but particularly around Thebes, such as the grandiose memorial temple of Djeser-Djeseru (Deir el-Bahari). So they each had their grievances which, alone, may have waned over time and become a babble for talebearing, an afterthought for leisurely dinner; but it was the overarching matter of what they had been promised that connected them and calcified the grudges into something as hard as vendetta. And from this common chalice they drank the broth that intoxicated them to action. This, in addition to Pharaoh Hatshepsut's usurpation of power.

None of them had had any quarrel with Hatshepsut's role as regent for her stepson, Thutmose III (at the time when he was a mere infant), when her husband and also half-brother, Thutmose II, died. They were each, however, deeply troubled when she later assumed the title and full powers of a pharaoh. None of them would forgive her for this. Each of them dismissed those who defended her action as a move to forestall the threat to the throne from others who wanted to grab power for themselves, and to save it for her stepson. They instead viewed her as a woman who, having tasted power and become comfortable with its accoutrements, had become uncomfortable with her temporary regency and its tenuousness and had therefore moved to ensure that the throne would be hers. Nor were they impressed that she pointed to her royal lineage, claiming that her father, who preceded her husband, had appointed her his successor.

As they moved forward, the three rarely spoke, each aware of what was at hand, but as if seeking assurance, one of them spoke presently, a male voice that bespoke authority: "We are ready."

The woman among them replied, "I am ready." If use of the singular pronoun troubled her male companions, they did not comment on it.

They kept moving on until they were almost at the door of Pharaoh's rest house. The third person spoke, a manner of sealing the purpose of the congregation of murderers, though they would not have considered their intent as murderous.

"The time has come."

# SEASONS of FOUR FACES

## Banquet of Death

There had been an easy entry, for the one who sent them had enormous power and, having come of age, was not one to be crossed. But the seamlessness of the entry did nothing to assuage the tension mounting to its highest pitch.

Pharaoh, who had imagined death, personified it as a paramour coming for illicit coitus, may have been prepared for one, but she was unprepared for three, whether as imagined personifications of death (or as ghouls or spirits with whom she could wrestle or romance spiritually) or as death's agents in human forms.

She considered calling her guards, but refrained in the obvious knowledge that they were not available, either overpowered or, worse, that they had abandoned her. Their names remained in her throat and she almost choked on her stifled voice as she saw the three enter her bed chamber. At first, the three were close together, giving her a brief illusion that they were indeed one after all and easier to defeat. But they soon separated into their proper three separate beings. She knew them, even in the darkness. These were three of her subjects, each having performed a duty or another for her, each owing her something: the man she had elevated in her army, the healer she had turned to on occasion and therefore burnished as trustworthy, and the man who could have been her chief minister whom she had consulted, even if she had not elevated him to chief minister. None would have been bold enough to appear before her unannounced, except at risk of injury and even death, let alone penetrate the night and override her security detail (now nonexistent, of course) and enter her bed chamber to view her in such total nakedness. Clearly, their intentions were hostile.

She instinctively reached for her cloak to shield herself, but decided her state of nudity was ammunition, perhaps the only one she had, to unnerve them. The Queen of Egypt shivered at the triple threat in her room and sought to fish out courage from her inner will. And even more, she had a voice after all, and she had to use it with all regal authority to her best advantage. It would quiver in her present state, so she needed to sturdy it before speaking. She thought of her ancestors before her who had held the office. They were not mere mortals, but gods, embodying the secular and the spiritual. No mere mortal could dare challenge her authority. One by one, she tried to mentally summon the ghosts of those who had come before her for a conference of spirits. But none responded to her call and her request was like a voice echoing itself endlessly in a large echo chamber without inhabitants. She was on her own and keenly aware she'd always been (though she had enjoyed shrouding her belief with the claim to deity).

She heard the voice of her heart and the peace she had forged for Egypt, if at cost of rendering it less powerful and somewhat listless. She was proud of it. She called on the voice of her mind, with which she had negotiated a reign that survived despite all forms of plots and counterplots against her. She was proud of it. She listened to the voice of her spirit, acknowledging that no matter what happened, the worst fate was death, and with it she would transition to the spirit world of her ancestors before her. In this she fetched a little inkling of boldness. She would try to live, but death was not an end. With these voices egging her on, she finally managed to sturdy her voice.

"This is not a time for promenading?" she said.

# SEASONS of FOUR FACES

"We are not promenading," the woman said.

"We have come on assignment," one of the men said.

"Not on your own behalf," the queen said, "then on whose assignment have you come?"

"We can't tell you," said the other man.

"So what is the assignment?" the queen asked.

"Your life," said the woman.

The queen grunted and asked, "And why?"

"That is not for us to say," said one of the men.

"And what if I don't give it?" the queen asked.

"We are not asking for your permission," said the woman.

"I am Pharaoh Hatshepsut," she said, "and you will obey me."

"Tonight, your reign ends," said one of the men.

"It hasn't ended and you are still subject to my command."

The three approached Pharoah Hatshepsut. She held out a hand to stall them, so forcefully that the confidence of the three was temporarily diluted, their advancement forward halted. For a moment, all parties in the queen's chamber pondered the possibility that this would not end in the death that had besieged their thoughts and saturated her night, that perhaps there was a way this up-to-now seemingly assured march towards death would be halted, even ended, and the queen would live.

But the stalemate was short lived, the steely determination of the three more potent than the threat of regal supremacy or even the questionable deity of the queen. Plus, having exposed themselves this way, failure to kill her would assure their own deaths. The three advanced towards her and only when they were within hand's reach did they remove their hoods, which in the darkness of the room did little to accentuate their identity any more than the queen knew. But it carried a greater sense of foreboding when even the false veil of anonymity was gone, suggesting a do-or-die stage in the unfolding plot of still uncertain denouement. So, though she knew their identity all along, this unveiling did two things, one troubling, the other encouraging. It was less threatening for her to see three uncovered heads, the now unveiled parts of their faces projecting a form of hidden diabolism that she believed could be massaged into compromise. But it was more threatening and much more treacherous to look into their shaded, naked faces which, in the stoicism marking them, reflected nothing but the ambient darkness without even any pretense of mercy that left any room for negotiation.

The queen groaned in frustration, but she would not surrender yet. Where veiled threat of force failed, perhaps appeal to humanity would work. She tried to force her eyes to look into their eyes, each one of the three, which in the darkness revealed nothing but darkness. Eye to eye (could they even see her eyes in the darkness?), she would nudge them towards sympathy. But in the darkness she could not see much but the darkness. Instead, she would say their names, hoping for that personal connection, or a recollection of their previous bond, that would soften their resolve.

But before she could complete the first name, one of the men stopped her. "No names," he said. "No names!"

How soothing it was to her to hear a voice again after the interregnum of movement and gestures and shadows. But if this gave her any respite, it was brief, as from her hand, the woman among the three produced a small gourd, as though it had materialized out of nowhere by some magical gesture.

## SEASONS of FOUR FACES

    The queen took a step back, aware of what they required of her, as the gourd was held towards her, knowing very well the prowess of the woman who had once helped treat her of her various ailments. "I will not drink this poison," Pharoah Hatshepsut said.

    "We are not asking," the woman said. "You will do it voluntarily or we will make you."

    Before she could respond to this, in movements that were as swift as they were deft, the woman set the gourd on the floor, lodged one leg behind the queen's leg and pushed the queen to the floor. Pharaoh would not be so easily overpowered, lunging back up with fury and determination. She leapt at the woman, forcing both of them to fall to the floor, the gourd close. One of the men reached out with both hands and grabbed it, clutching it to his chest like a treasure. The women began to wrestle. At one moment the queen was up, at another time the woman was up; the queen would grab the woman's neck, squeezing it; then the woman would free herself, holding the queen's neck, squeezing it; the woman would put the queen in a chokehold in one moment and in the next the queen would free herself and put the woman in a chokehold. Though the fight was vicious, it also carried an elegant quality, two equally matched combatants, one's sweat hidden or soaked in her robe, the other's sweat slithering over her unclothed body in big beads.

    As equally balanced as it was, this fight may have continued for a longer period, but time was an enemy of the three, for the veil of night would not last long, nor could they be sure how long it would take before someone intruded. They needed to end the dance-tussle. In mid-effort, as the queen was about to turn over the woman, one of the men leapt forward to pin Pharaoh Hatshepsut's arm behind her, while the other man moved equally speedily and did likewise to the other arm. One arm in each man's hand, they first pinned her face down to the floor and then forced her up. The woman stood up and brought both hands around the queen's neck, hands slipping on account of the queen's sweat, before finding a firm grip. Then she began to squeeze. The queen struggled, gasping for air, but the men held her firmly.

"Stop," one of the men said, but the woman was oblivious to the instruction, anger energizing her to squeeze harder. "Stop!" the man said again. "This is not how we are supposed to do it."

This reminder resonating, the woman slowly weakened her grip, the thawing grimace on her face suggesting her determination to kill by suffocation had eased. She took the gourd from one of the men as the other man pried the queen's mouth open. One of the men tilted her head backwards and closed her nostrils, and the woman poured a substantial amount of the gourd's contents into the queen's mouth. Pharaoh Hatshepsut tried to spit it out, but the tilt of her head and the way her cheeks had been squeezed to force her mouth open made it impossible to spit it all out. As Pharoah Hatshepsut swallowed reluctantly, almost gagging, the woman poured the remainder of the contents down the queen's throat. A gurgling sound turned into resignation.

For a brief moment, the queen's body relaxed as the liquid traveled her insides. And then the brawling ballet of death began. Her body convulsed uncontrollably, only prevented from totally thrashing about by the hands that firmly gripped her arms. Her face twitched violently, a facial earthquake, her stomach heaped in quick motions, foam from her mouth traveled down her chin, and her breasts pendulously protested the poison shutting down her system and drowning away her life. Slowly her struggle began to wane and her movements became less violent and then she was still.

When it was all over, the men put her on her bed. Naked as they had found her alive, they were about to leave her naked in her quietus, spreadeagled in death and in her full corporeality, but the woman among them protested. And they clothed the corpse before hurrying out of her room in steely silence.

BENJAMIN KWAKYE

# The Dust of Dawn

The discovery of the body in Senenmut's house (and his subsequent incarceration and shuttering into oblivion), the surreptitious carriage of the corpse under bleak protection of night, and the secret entombment where her body would not be easily discovered, lifted a thick cloud off the new regime and its leader. If anyone had questions or doubts, they were not expressed in the atmosphere of fear that pervaded, fear that it was taboo to question the official version of events that the queen had died of natural causes in her chief minister's company.

Senenmut was guilty.

Why had he not called for help? Why had he not mentioned that the old pharaoh was dead until the new pharaoh's guards got hint and searched his home? Until the old pharaoh's body was found, there was a surfeit of brooding uncertainty. For the would be king, it was not whether or not she was dead. He knew his stepmother was dead: He had been assured of that by the three who carried out the deed. The question that tormented him was who had the body and why anyone had stolen the body after the three left her corpse in her bed chamber. With what motive? Was there some plot in gestation that involved her body? Was it to be used as a weapon of sorts against him? As long as these questions lingered, they were like the bitter aftertaste of sweet medicine, the medicine being her death, the aftertaste her stolen body and its attendant uncertainties. But sweetness reinforced sweetness when he gained control over the body, unleashing him to begin his goal of restoring Egypt to its glory. It would be a campaign of war, many wars, and blood and sweat and pain and gore.

In Tiempo, Pharoah Thutmose III had the ally he needed: the man's bravado (the extent of which many already knew), his fierceness and fearlessness and how he had more recently proven his loyalty, each affirmed the victory, nay victories, that would come. The new pharaoh had made the right decision, not merely elevating Tiempo as a leader in the army, as the previous pharaoh had done, but to the leader (only secondary to the new pharaoh himself). Many of his counselors had cautioned Thutmose III about Tiempo's potential loyalty to the dead pharaoh. She had elevated Tiempo in the army, after all, even if not to the topmost position, they argued, and his loyalty would belong to her. But what did they know of the plot drawn in meticulous care in secret with the three who would become Thutmose III's closest advisors? What did they know about this great secret that bound them together? And then came the hydration of that bond with the discovery of the dead woman's body and the purging of the new pharaoh's enemies.

Amid all this, including his immediate elevation to head of the army, Tiempo was not particularly inclined to at tend Apophis' invitation, but it would be deemed an affront if he refused the priest's invitation. Apophis, the priest, was a friend of sorts, but also prone to such laxity as Tiempo did not approve. Tiempo often wondered how the man, a friend of the new pharaoh since their infancy, had maintained his priesthood. Nor could Tiempo fathom why Apophis would hold a party only ten days after the queen's demise. But he suspected the party had been sanctioned (perhaps even ordered) by the new pharaoh.

He was surprised by the large attendance when he arrived.

But he reminded himself that he ought not be surprised because Apophis, in addition to his reputation as a close confidante of the new pharaoh, was renowned for organizing great parties. Pharaoh himself was not present, which made sense: whether he liked or hated her, he had lost his stepmother. If for no other reason, to be seen at such a public celebration would be untoward.

Tiempo greeted Apophis and his wife Thema and then eased himself into the gathering, a crowd, if you asked him. He looked up, searching for two people in particular. On the far side, he noticed the healer Sharifa and his heart beat harder. Sharifa, who could have been his sister, both of them children of the Nile. But that was a story for another day. On another side he saw the priest Adom, walking around with a slight limp. Behind Adom were two men, one quite massive in size, one whispering in Adom's ear after Adom gave him something Tiempo could not identify. Adom, in one sense a collaborator and in another sense a rival. But that too was a story for another day.

Tiempo soon received with salivating tongue the pork placed before him. On his left, he saw people eating and gulping down beer; on his right, he saw the same. He decided to eat up but forgo the beer. He had hardly swallowed his first bolus when he heard the beginning sounds of the musicians who had gathered. The sound of the harp joined the sound of the lute, and joined the sound of the flute, and together began to produce a harmony that outdid the ongoing repartee around him, and with such assurance that it quieted the expressions of the humans, so that soon the only conversation in the room was between the musical instruments. He was not one to bask in such moments that he deemed as idleness, but even Tiempo breathed easier. And then the servers came with honey flavored pastries that were explosive in their sweetness. And then his nostrils began to take in the melting perfume cones on the heads of the servers who came back and forth dutifully.

Tiempo thrived on the sound of bones cracking under the weight of a hand, flesh opening to the force of a spear or arrow, the macabre, bestial holler of a man in the throes of death, or that guttural yell of pain that could evidence strong wills erased, cartilage and muscle torn asunder. He was used to the smell of blood fresh from a slit throat, intestines gushing out of a split belly, even excreta accompanied by hoarse expressions as men lost control in the pains of battle. But this was asking something totally different of him. Not that he had never been at a party, but he rarely ceded control to his surroundings the way he was doing at Apophis' party after the death of a pharaoh. Was it because of his recent elevation? For a moment he closed his eyes to allow the smell and tastes to blend. And when he opened his eyes, he could see dancers take center stage. There were three of them: tall, taller and tallest; slim, slimmer and slimmest. And, except for the jewels around their waists and necks, they wore nothing. Tiempo breathed hard as the young women began to dance, waists sashaying with impossible speed, done in a manner that caused every part of their bodies to jingle, breasts untagged by age to move with grace, and caused bellies to twitch under practiced control of movement of all body parts. Tiempo inhaled and exhaled, not just with his nostrils, but with every part of his body.

And his body was crying, crying in need, crying for satiation. He had denied himself for so long that he had almost forgotten that there was also another part of the human being that needed to be possessed as much as it sought to possess.

BENJAMIN KWAKYE

# Tears of Festivals

Thema had come to see Tiempo not long after this party and soon after the Festival of Drunkenness. It was not a festival that appealed to Tiempo and he was skeptical of its origins. It was said that the sun god, unhappy with humans for their rebelliousness, had sought their destruction. To that end, he had ordered Hathor, his daughter, to become a lion. And Hathor, full of magical power, was sent down to kill humans. She accomplished her mission by devouring people as she traversed the Nile River Valley. When her father asked her to stop, the lust for blood was too strong and she would not relent in her bloodthirstiness. So the Council of Gods had flooded the fields of the Nile River valley with ocher tinted beer, so that the Nile looked like blood. Enticed by what must have been a picturesque valley of blood in her blood-lustful-eyes, Hathor drank the beer and then fell asleep in her intoxication. When she woke up, she had been transformed into a kinder goddess, lacking bloodguilt. And humanity was saved. Tiempo had wished she'd not drunk the beer so he could confront her, assured he could show her that even if she was a god, he was stronger than her and he would have liked to catch her attention in an agora, and thrust a sword through her blood gorged throat, whether in feline or human form, severed her head, and hanged it in a public place for all to observe. Where was this kinder and gentler Hathor who had allowed herself to be transformed in order to avoid men like Tiempo and only live in the people's commemoration of her ignoble defeat to alcohol by drinking to the point of passing out?

Some years before, Tiempo had once gone to a festival party that Apophis had organized in a temple, where young women, their hairs decorated with floral garlands, their bodies anointed with perfume, served alcohol, some of them calling themselves mistresses of drunkenness. The common talk was that they would be traveling through the marshes, which was to say, having sex. Tiempo refused to drink, afraid that he would lose control, but he had seen how Apophis had drunk to the point of inebriation, how he had made an open play for some of the young woman, grabbing buttocks and breasts. And this was a priest? Tiempo had left, aware that the carousers would eventually awake to the beating of drums, that in between all these events and carousing, many would engage in intercourse, and he had no doubt that Apophis, who had a reputation for keeping various consorts, would be one of those who took the sensual aspect of the festival to its logical extreme. As often as he thought of this, he also repeated the question: And this is a priest?

So when Thema came to see him, Tiempo knew what to expect. It was not the first time she had asked him to advice Apophis to be circumspect and more discreet, knowing that her husband highly respected Tiempo. Tiempo had refused in the past to confront Apophis, reluctant to interfere. But Thema's tears and deep distress this time had been too much for him and he went to see Apophis about it. The priest had smiled and promised to change, but both they both knew that was said to assuage Tiempo for the moment and the moment only. And rumors about Apophis' promiscuity continued.

BENJAMIN KWAKYE

# Searching for Noon

But Tiempo could not dwell on Apophis' philandering. He had more pressing matters ahead, matters that involved the pharaoh. And in his audience hall, the new pharaoh, sometimes calling himself Thutmose, sometimes Ramses, embraced the air with a voice that covered space as if it had a life of its own, carrying the authority of a man used to power, having been bred in the hallways of power, even if he'd had to wait in darkness as his mother—no, correct that—his stepmother, pulled the country down with her unbridled quest for peace, a retreat into a shadow of what once was, with boundaries squeezed narrow like a dried up stream. Now the new king had the opportunity to remake what once was, and to push Egypt further into greater glory. His voice, therefore, carried both power and the urgency of the moment, an urgency he was loathe to betray lest it be interpreted as desperation. He'd let flash a stern smile, brow furrowed, eyes firm, meant to convey seriousness than levity.

The inner circle of three stood with him in that inner chamber of the palace. They were in the limelight (or is it lime-night?) now. Why he'd summoned them in the late hours of night was beyond all three, except perhaps to underscore the seriousness of the occasion. Ever since he'd assumed the throne and made clear to them that he intended to rely on them as his innermost circle of advisers, all meetings had been held in the course of the day, so this night summons must carry special meaning.

The baritone voice continued to dominate the room. "Much time has been wasted," he said "and I don't want to waste any more of it. We must move with haste to beat back our enemies and take our rightful place. Our enemies must once again respect us and know that we are a nation of warriors. So I called you to help me think through certain affairs of state, the wars to fight and the enemies to be vanquished."

Tiempo nodded. "You are right, Great Pharaoh," he said, "our enemies are laughing at us, thinking we are weak. The time of trade expeditions must be a thing of the past. From now on, we trade with the currency of war."

Pharaoh smiled his stern smile again. "I know you are a man of action, Tiempo. I know I can count on you. That is why I have put you in charge of the army, second only to me, even when some said you are loyal to my stepmother, and some of the generals are wary of you. Not to mention the secret that binds us, that binds all four of us here. We are creatures of the night, performing many sacred acts in the night."

Pharaoh turned to the woman in the inner chamber, his eyes fully trained on her. Sharifa stared back at her king, as if ready to do combat with him, betraying her steeliness, but only as far as it would not suggest hostile confrontation, not with the new Pharaoh. "My king," she said, "I am here for you; you know that and I'm ready to support you in whatever plans you have to bring honor to our nation." The healer paused to ensure her expression of loyalty had found good reception before adding, "I only caution that we not move too fast in a way that plays even more into our enemies' hands. Tiempo is better situated to address this than me, but it will seem to me that an army dormant for so long may take some time to whip up into battle readiness."

"You are right, Sharifa," Tiempo said. "I am best suited, except our great pharaoh, to address the army's battle readiness, and I am confident we are ready to face any enemy."

"You are a man of war," said the fourth person in the

chamber. "You will do anything within or even without your power to go to war. Wasn't this a source of tension between you and Queen Hatshepsut?"

"This is the last time I want to hear anyone of you mention her by name," Pharoah Thutmose said sternly. "Never mention her name again! If you must, you can refer to her as that woman."

"My apologies, Pharaoh. My mistake. But I know Tiempo is so bellicose he will fight for any or no reason, prepared or not. He came to Egypt with that posture."

"Came to Egypt with that posture?" Tiempo asked. "What is that supposed to mean, Adom?"

"Don't pay him any mind," Pharaoh said, his stern expression trained on Adom.

"I do not apologize for wanting to bring glory to my nation and Pharaoh," Tiempo said.

"But at what cost?" Adom asked. "Before that woman decided to retreat and sue for peace, the army had suffered several defeats. We can't assume that the army will suddenly be combat ready."

"The defeats you mention were never suffered under my command," Tiempo said, "nor under our new and true Pharaoh."

"A peacetime army does not translate easily to a war army," Sharifa said. "An army fierce in peace is not the same as an army fierce in battle."

"Sharifa makes sense to me," Adom said, exposing stained teeth.

"These are words of cowardice," Tiempo replied, his words directed more at Adom than Sharifa. "I know my men. I know they are ready to wage any war Great Pharaoh plans for them. Under your leadership, Great Pharaoh, we will wage great wars and win them and all glory will be to Great Pharaoh. This is how greatness is constructed, one victory after another, until it becomes an undeniable testament to greatness, an everlasting song of pride."

"Adom is close to the gods but he is not a man of action like us," Pharaoh said, "and Sharifa knows many medicines, but she is not a woman of physical battles like us, Tiempo. They are wise in many ways, and we will always seek their counsel and we will always listen and ponder their words, but when it comes to matters of war, the ultimate decision belongs to men who fight on the battlefield, not those who kill in the quiet of chambers at night."

Pharaoh's words somehow seemed to chill and erase any further dissent or even advice on the matter of contemplated war. And unseen shadows of the room hovered over the three men and one woman, reminding them that there was a history between them they all need not be reminded of. Pharaoh hugged each one, tightly and for long moments, as if reassuring them of a bond that ought not be considered lightly. It was thusly a night of debate (if muted), of reassurance (if unspoken) and of shadows (if unseen) and of unuttered secrets and the talk over war that was already a fait accompli.

BENJAMIN KWAKYE

# Finding War and Love

Tiempo was his man and with Tiempo the new pharaoh would pursue his reforms and prosecute his wars. For many days, Pharaoh consulted with his army commander. Pharaoh and Tiempo. Pharoah and Tiempo. Pharoah and Tiempo. Pharoah and Tiempo. In his chambers they could be seen talking ear to mouth, mouth to ear, forehead to forehead, tete-a-tete, exchanging thoughts, suggesting ideas, eschewing ideas, plotting strategies and stratagems; they were together in the night, during daytime, promenading in avenues, heads nodding in agreement, sometimes shaking in guarded disagreement. Many watched these close consultations between the king and Tiempo in awe, elevating the army commander to godlike status on account of such long and intimate proximity to the god who was Pharaoh.

Those were intense periods for Tiempo, and when he had short breaks at the palace, he would seek out Pharaoh's son Amun and engage the boy. From the audience hall, he would walk to the lower parts of the palace, going past corridors where a number of female musicians and dancers practiced, then walk past green and red columned hallways, before turning left to the prince's residence. In a way, he had become a second father to the boy. And it pleased Tiempo when he remembered how instrumental Sharifa had been to Amun's conception and birth.

He remembered the joy that had come into the household when Amun was born, and the even more joyous celebration that had followed particularly on the seventh day after his birth. Tiempo remembered the gathering of many guests, and it seemed every person of import in Egypt was present. He enjoyed the warm, rich, creamy, and heavy moghat drink and the delicious lamb meal served, singing children holding candles in the background, lighting the way for Nefertiti (who carried Amun). The baby was placed in a big kitchen sieve for his bath, seemingly unbothered even as the sieve was shaken. Amun was placed on the floor and an older relative banged a copper pestle against a mortar, making a clanging sound that Tiempo found needless and irritating—his least favorite part of the ceremony.

It was more bearable when a number of women began chanting commands to the child. Tiempo listened to their various commands asking for the child's obedience to his parents. One of them boldly stated that it was his mother who had suffered to give birth to him, so he ought to obey her, not his father. Though Tiempo had heard variations of this in the past, he thought it exceedingly bold of the woman to say this when the father was Pharaoh. But the king seemed to take it all in levity and laughed heartily.

Then the child was clothed, and a group of women began to burn incense. Nefertiti was summoned to step over her son seven times, each step dedicated to God by the women, as some of them continued to chant. Tiempo remembered the gifts of nuts, sweets, nougat, gold and silver coins. He remembered how Apophis had cried almost uncontrollably in joy as he watched the events.

Tiempo had always loved the child, now growing into a strong boy. They would play wrestling games and Tiempo would always let the boy win, but in the process he would shout a few tips on how to overpower an enemy. They would sometimes play the board game of senet and Tiempo would tell the boy stories of war.

And then Tiempo would resume his consultations with

the boy's father when playtime for man and boy was over, with Pharoah gleefully complaining that his army commander was becoming more of a father to his son than he was.

It was little surprise therefore when the reforms the two discussed were implemented with haste. After such long planning by the gods, how could the implementation not be swift and effective? Pharoah made sure weapons were adequate and modernized: bronze tipped arrows with reinforced wood were made, hammers for each soldier were shaped in case close combat was needed, and wooden wheeled chariots were built. The king and his army commander supervised several training drills, and the king made sure that the army had more than abundant provisions to keep the soldiers content.

And then arrived time to go to their first war.

Tiempo went to see Sharifa the night before he left for war. She stepped outside to meet him.

"You were expecting me," he said.

"I can tell when you are coming to me," she replied.

"You would think we are twins."

"Triplets, if you include Adom."

He didn't like this reference to Adom, so he said quickly, "Shall we go inside?"

"Inside? Of all the good the night has provided us, why would we go inside?"

He would not push. "I am going to war," he said.

"I know."

"I told you?"

"You are not the king's only confidante, Tiempo."

"I should have known."

"Are you afraid?" she asked.

"Of what, death?"

"No, I don't see the fear of death in a man like you?"

"Then why would I be afraid, Sharifa?"

"Defeat, Tiempo. Are you afraid of losing?"

This question hovered with discomforting truth.

"Don't be afraid," she said.

"You are right. I am not afraid to die, although I ponder over how I'd die if I should perish in battle. I do not want any of my body parts cut off as a price of victory by anyone. But if that happens then it happens. Yes, you guessed right, Sharifa. What worries me is that we might lose. Pharaoh has so much confidence in me, in himself, that I worry sometimes that I may disappoint him. After all the advice I have provided him, I will lose my place if we should lose."

"Tiempo, I have great confidence in you."

He made no response, staring into the vastness of the night.

"It will be well," Sharifa said.

"Will you miss me if I do not return alive?" Tiempo asked.

"You should not ask me that question, Tiempo."

"Why? Because you do not like the answer you will give?"

"Tiempo…"

"You know how I feel about you, Sharifa. You have resisted me for a long time, but you have never said an outright no. Why, Sharifa? Why this ambivalence?"

She now looked into the vastness of the night.

"I do not want to get involved with anyone, Tiempo."

"Even at the expense of feelings?"

"Feelings are for mere mortals, Tiempo. People like you and me must master our feelings."

"But why, Sharifa? We are humans, after all."

"Are we? Regardless, a man like you ought to understand

this better than anyone. Here today, gone the next moment. And then what is left but pain?"

"Memories created in moments of pleasure. They are also necessities of life." He could not believe he was the one arguing this position and he realized how so much unlike him this was and perhaps how so much unlike herself she was arguing.

"What if you die in your battles, Tiempo? Where will that leave me?"

"You just said you have confidence in me, Sharifa, and now this?"

"I am sorry, Tiempo."

"I don't understand your reasoning at all. Just let yourself go, Sharifa. That is all there is to it."

"And lose my heart if you die?"

"There you go again."

"I am sorry."

"What if I make a deal with you? If I return from war, you can rest assured that I will not die and you can be free to give me your heart."

"One war does not make you invincible, Tiempo."

"Fair. Name the number of wars I need to win to assure you then I am a survivor."

"The number of wars is not relevant. You could win one hundred wars and die in the next one."

But he would not be denied. "How many?"

"You are not hearing me."

"How many?"

"It's not a matter of..."

"How many, Sharifa?!"

"Eighteen," she said, sighing.

With an equally deep sigh, Tiempo whispered the word

# SEASONS of FOUR FACES

"eighteen" to himself eighteen times, his head bowed as if crestfallen and then in a quick lift of his head, he declared, "It is settled, then. Every time I am on the battlefield, I fight not only for Egypt and for Pharaoh, but for you, Sharifa, for whom death will be an honor, the greatest pain-joy, if it is in the service of your love."

Sharifa smiled.

"But I have one question," Tiempo said.

"What now?"

"What about Adom?"

"What about him?"

"Where is he in all this? I have found the two of you in your room before, you know. And the way he looks at you, the way you look at him sometimes, I wonder if you have affections for him."

"I do have affections for him," Sharifa said.

"That man, full of so many days?"

"He is still a strong, desirable man."

"So you love him?"

"Tiempo! You are prepared to go to war but afraid of competition from one man, one old man as you yourself say?"

"This pains me, Sharifa, that I have to compete for your affections with another man."

"Think of it this way: I am even worth the more fighting for because a man of his stature finds me desirable."

"I hope my quest will not be in vain."

"You have my word. Eighteen."

"And in the meantime?"

"Just wish for the best."

Eighteen! It was not clear to him if that was meant to ensure that he would never have her, considering that he would most likely die in so many wars. But then, it could also be an inspiration to victory after victory.

Tiempo left Sharifa's with nothing but war and victory on his mind.

And the wars began. And they were fought. And fought. And fought. And the Egyptian army, modernized and effective, won. And won. And won. And won. And Tiempo counted. And counted. And counted. And counted. And continued to count.

SEASONS of FOUR FACES

# Marching with Dust

Then came the planning for the most important war.

And Pharaoh called his counselors and diviners for long consultations, with war hanging thick, an engorged raincloud that would bleed red, a forgone conclusion whose outburst was only a matter of time. It seemed all the previous wars were irrelevant or, at best, mere preparations for this one, considering the importance Pharaoh attached to it. When he heard of the King of Kadesh's rebellion, Pharaoh was furious, deeming the revolt a challenge to his reign, perhaps a calculated test of his mettle. That other Canaanites would join the King of Kadesh's rebellion against Egypt made this treachery even more dangerous and called for ruthless quelling, more so because the King of Megiddo had joined the revolt. These vassals could not be lost, considering that the location of Megiddo was critically important as the main trade route between Egypt and Mesopotamia.

For days, men of great importance came to and left the palace, ubiquitous as breath, sometimes whispering in undertones as though afraid that the wind would carry their expressions to the enemy camp, and sometimes declaring their intention of war against Egypt's enemies in loud voices as if that would somehow threaten the enemy into standing down from the posture of revolt.

By the time Pharaoh consulted Tiempo, Sharifa and Adom as a group, there was no doubt that he had made up his mind. The three expressed their support, echoing what others had been saying and buttressing Pharaoh's own conclusion. None of them was as vociferous as Tiempo, whose call for war was accompanied by wild hand gesticulations. He was ready for action, he affirmed, and Megiddo and Kadesh must be taught a lesson. If war could be won by the verbal expression of the bellicose, it would have been won in Tiempo's mouth. For Sharifa and Adom, Pharaoh and Tiempo had won many wars and they could not argue about the rustiness of the army, nor base opposition on any reasonable ledge that would not draw Pharaoh's ire, or worse. Pharoah dismissed the meeting by hugging each of the counselors.

Once decided, the generals were summoned to get ready.

To prepare himself for this war, Tiempo spent some time with Amun, playing the usual games with Pharaoh's son. This relaxed him, especially the boy's unbridled confidence that his father would return unscathed. Hopping from one leg to the other, he lifted both hands and declared his father's greatness. O, the confidence of youth (and perhaps ignorance). After he left Amun, Tiempo went to see Apophis, for what it was worth, to remember them to the gods. Thema greeted him with slumped shoulders, which he attributed to her resignation to her husband's recidivism on matters of promiscuity, and he regretted that he had not done more to pressure Apophis to be more restrained. But that was a matter for another day. Focusing on others' affections was bad for war, all except Sharifa's. He was sure to visit Sharifa as well, to remind her that he was counting down to eighteen. She would be waiting, she said.

SEASONS of FOUR FACES

# The War

With the unhinged hope of Amun and the promise of Sharifa in his mind, Tiempo joined the twenty thousand men comprising the calvary and infantry, which signaled that Pharaoh was leaving nothing to chance. After all, they had heard that the King of Kadesh, with the support of Syria, Aram and Canaan chieftains, had amassed troops numbering fifteen thousand. With Tiempo and his other generals by his side, Pharaoh moved the troops forward to Gaza, a caravan of chariots and bows and arrows, as numerous as they were fierce. They were prepared, equipped and hungry for victory as they marched and marched forward. After a short rest in friendly Gaza, they continued on an eleven day march farther north to Yehem, Pharaoh in inspirational determination, Tiempo in supporting, continuing bellicose talk. If he was or had been warmongering, Tiempo was proud of it, and every now and then he would touch his bow as if it was a talisman of sorts, and then caress it as though teasing some sort of strength from it.

 At Yehem, Pharaoh asked Tiempo to lead a team of scouts on surveillance. With feline stealth they traveled north and with serpentine cunning they slithered a little south, shielded in turn by rocks and dark nights, observing without reciprocating observation. With patience, they discovered that the King of Megiddo had set his forces at the waters of Taanach, in reasoned expectation that the Egyptian army would come through the main route of Taanach via Dothaim into the Valley of Kishon.

 As stealthily as they observed, they returned to report their findings to Pharaoh, noting that they had three options to reach Megiddo. The safer route was the northern one via

Zefti and Tel Yokneam, or the southern one via Taanach. But both were longer than the central route through Aruna. When they heard this report, the generals conferred and concluded that they had to pick the northern or southern routes, their reasoning reasonable, intuitive and logical: though longer, these were safer than the risky Aruna route.

Pharaoh pulled Tiempo aside.

"You hear what the men are saying," he said. "What do you think?"

"We should not do the expected," Tiempo advised.

Tiempo did not need to say more than this.

"We will advance by way of Aruna," Pharaoh announced to gasps. That was too risky, the generals insisted, surrounding Pharoah like desperate suitors of unrequited love, begging him to reconsider. The persistence and vehemence of their pleas betrayed their conviction that this course was madness, but the madness unexpressed in words as a king's folly for fear of provoking the wrath of Pharaoh. He had decided, Pharaoh reiterated. By Aruna they would travel!

So down the tortuous ravine the troops marched forward, a ravine so narrow that they could only travel single-file. The discomfort notwithstanding, the troops moved forward painstakingly, so tortuously that at some point even Tiempo began to question whether he had given bad advice, and also to consider that if their gamble failed and the King of Kadesh was waiting at the tip of the Aruna route, the Egyptian army would be cut down bit by bit in hopeless massacre with little room to maneuver. But he was heartened that Pharaoh himself led the troops, an act of both daring and inspiration. If death came, it would grab him first. This act alone was sufficient to tamper if not totally quell any further babblings.

And the army eventually emerged from this tortuous

pathway into the open with no sizeable force awaiting them. As Tiempo and Pharaoh had hoped, the King of Kadesh had positioned the bulk of his troops on the safer southern and northern routes, not thinking that any army, especially as large as the Egyptian force, would embrace madness and come down that narrow Aruna path. With the advantage of numbers, the Egyptian army had no trouble defeating and moving past the pittance of a force they encountered, which provided an unimpeded route to Megiddo.

That night, the generals who had urged Pharaoh to take the alternate routes voiced their admiration of the wisdom of his ways and that of his chief commander, aware that Pharaoh had consulted with Tiempo amid their clamor. Pharaoh received these words with equanimity and urged his forces to get some rest for they had work to do. That night, he summoned Tiempo and the other generals and began to arrange them under the light of moon that fell with a dark opaqueness that amplified their conspiratorial strategizing. When they were done, the forces stood arrayed in a concave formation, consisting of three wings.

So formed, they attacked the next morning. Pharaoh in his gilded chariot emitted an aura of majesty and invincibility, a transmissible aura that Tiempo, the other generals and other soldiers caught. Tiempo mounted his own chariot, leading the right wing, as he looked over to take in the impressive sight of the other ancillary wing of attack with another general also in his chariot and ready to attack. They were indeed beautiful for situation, impressive for war, and unbeatable in confidence. They attacked, wheels of chariots, hooves of horses, and feet of men. They came like a mighty rainfall, ready to uproot whatever was in its path. Surprised by this sudden show of force, the King of Kadesh's forces were totally unprepared. As his chariot moved forward, Tiempo drew his bow and shot one arrow. He felt the whiff of a weapon, perhaps an arrow, flying past him. But he was undeterred as he charged forward, releasing another arrow, and another. Then he saw the adversarial forces in front of him begin to retreat and he realized that they were not ready to put up a fight. In this he was disappointed. He had hoped that they would standfast and fight, so that he could teach them the lesson he intended to teach, send a message that the Egyptian forces were not to be trifled with. But now sensing that he would not have the chance, he dismounted the chariot and went after the retreating enemy forces on foot, his sword drawn, unable to hear that his mind was telling him to stop and survey. He was indiscriminate, in his hand a weapon of mass destruction, plunging sword into flesh, pulling it back with blood gushing out and then plunging it into the next body as the dead bodies mushroomed around him, with some bodies that had already fallen from what must have been an earlier fight already undergoing skeletonization. He was not ready to take prisoners, but in this singular focus to kill, he did not pay attention to the forces that had fled into the walled part of the city and closed its gates. By the time Tiempo realized this, it was too late and the King of Kadesh had also fled. As he surveyed the battleground, he was buoyed by the number of the slain packed on the ground of war, but regretted that many had fled. Later, when he joined with the other wings of the army, he was made aware that they had captured one hundred and twenty four chariots and two hundred suits of armor. But the closed gates made Megiddo impregnable, and the only option left to the Egyptian troops was to lay siege outside the city. What they had hoped would last days stretched into weeks and months. In that time, the Egyptian forces built a moat and wooden palisade until, eventually, after seven months, Megiddo surrendered.

# CHAPTER

# 2

*"Remember this," she said.*
*"Remember with your body and with your mind, not your eyes."*

## Embrace of Spirits

The paths of treacherousness are best navigated in the dark recesses of the night, Tiempo reassured himself one day (or rather night) after his return from war. He had carefully weighed embarking on the mission in the daytime, and the urge to do so was as strong as the fire that raged inside of him. But the mission would be too dangerous, he thought, in the sanitizing exposure of the day. So he had pined an entire day waiting for the opportune time, breathlessly waiting for the sun to melt over the treetops and buildings in its faded yellowness, a beauty to behold as it scattered moribund beams like bronze colored spit over the earth that was its spittoon, becoming a lover spent, leaving its final masterpiece behind as a faint reminder of the earlier youthful light.

# SEASONS of FOUR FACES

This, a brilliant segue to the moonglow that Tiempo considered the more desirable of the two lights of the heavens, the more deceiving and therefore more brilliant, the light that in its relative weakness summoned the more sinister, clandestine acts of humans. Oh, how he admired its dark canopies that gave cover to all sorts of diabolical acts.

When he set out, therefore, he was in high spirits, first on account of whom he was about to see and second due to the joy of the night itself and being able to roam in it under the opaqueness of moonglow. This, then, was his moment. Tiempo moved on in the night's unconquerable darkness, a quiet darkness only partially wooed by the glow; the night fully out in haunting echoes of what he himself had seen or perpetrated in the night, the night continuing to entice him with the promise of what could be. Oh, night, I love you! The night then had become like a paramour and he hugged it with the memories of his mind and the promise of things to come. Tall and elegant in his movement, the night requited the love, flattering him when all the contours of his face and physique were buried in silhouette, unlike the probing exposure of sunlight. In that marriage, merger into oneness, the more flattering leanness of his body appeared like a serpent in vertical-rise, slithering through the seamless darkness of the night, the quietness of the hour an orchestra of the silent vocals of the instruments of his deeds, past and future. It egged him on and on until his movements became almost a dance because it indeed was a dance of sorts as Tiempo's limbs began to move a little faster than normal, not so much to move quicker but more so to syncopate the rhythms of this mind and its throbbing beats.

BENJAMIN KWAKYE

# Echoes of Silent Chambers

Therefore, the night followed him like a bedfellow who would not be left behind, as if eager to know the aftermath of a cherished romance. It was an expected visit; no pre-announcement was necessary as he entered the building, his heart beginning to beat harder and harder, his chest heaving with the upheaval of a heart in seeming volcanic outpour. But this nervous tumult could not stifle the grin celebrating his arrival. Before he entered the inner chamber, he mentioned her name, not as a means of announcing himself but to sound his presence as a means of endearment. The mention of the name was so softy whispered it was barely audible, and yet it carried the full force of wanting and anticipation that any ear could have heard in the building. Four times he mentioned it, pronouncing it with ease of familiarity and wonder of expected exploration.

Sharifa. Sharifa. Sharifa. Sharifa.

The night that pervaded the atmosphere carried the name like an unending echo. He did not wait for a response, for he believed none was needed. And he stepped farther into the inner chamber, his anticipation rising and rising. He could barely contain himself in search of her in the darkness until his eyes suddenly (question this word, for but for his blind anticipation, he would have noted it was not sudden), adjusted to the sight of two people in the room. Blinking many times did nothing to rid him of the reality that there was another besides Sharifa in the room. The contortion of his face mirrored the disappointment taking firm hold of him, deep in his belly with a burning sensation.

Sharifa remained still, and it was the other person in the

room who moved a pace towards Tiempo. "What is the awake doing in the night of the sleeping?" the man in the room asked.

Tiempo stared a moment at the man and without answering the question turned to Sharifa. "Him?"

"Yes," Sharifa said. "But..."

"If you, why not me?" the man responded.

Tiempo ignored him and again directed his question to Sharifa: "Are you really consorting with this old man?"

"Why do you think I am consorting with him?"

"Why would he be here at this time of the night?"

"And why are you here at this time of the night?" Sharifa asked.

"But isn't that what we arranged?"

"Did we?"

"It doesn't matter. I can come visiting anytime."

"Likewise him."

"For what purpose?"

The darkness in the room had settled somewhat and Tiempo could see the grin on the man's face.

"I need company sometimes," Sharifa said.

"Both his and mine? At this time of the night, Sharifa?"

"The company of us three," Sharifa said. "After all we have been through together, all we have committed together, is it not befitting that we spend a night together?"

"I thought... I thought..."

"Think nothing you have not been explicitly told, Tiempo," Sharifa said.

"I thought you had finally agreed to..."

"Think nothing, as I have said, except what I have expressly said," Sharifa said.

As if he thought himself becoming irrelevant at the moment,

the other man chimed in: "We gather once again as friends in the night."

Tiempo looked hard at the man and forced himself to de-anonymize him (at least in name) realizing that Sharifa might deem him petty for not saying his name. Slowly he let his mouth articulate the name of the man who had invaded his romantic aspirations. "Adom, what do you want here?"

Adom re-registered his grin. "I want what you want."

"You are too old for her, old man," Tiempo said, even as he reassessed the older man's potential masculine wiles.

Adom's mirthless laugh was designed to cause irritation. "If you are such an enticing young man, what does it say about you that I am here on equal footing with you? To think about it, I even beat you to it, arriving here before you. The old man is swifter than the young man. And who knows what we may have done before you arrived."

"What are you trying to say?"

"Trying to say or saying?"

"Don't provoke me, Adom."

"Or else what?"

"Warn your friend, Sharifa."

"I thought he was your friend too," Sharifa said.

"Friend? Just because I have acted in cahoots with him does not make us friends."

"Friends," Sharifa said, "I expect more from you. I expect cordiality, at the least. For all that binds us, we should remain close, plan together, think together, lest our secret be exposed."

"You make sense to me, Sharifa," said Adom, "but I am not sure about this hot tempered soldier who can put everything in jeopardy."

"Why this hostility? Why would I put everything in

# SEASONS of FOUR FACES

jeopardy? Do you take me for a fool?"

"You will have to prove it to me," said Adom.

"I don't answer to you, old man," said Tiempo.

"We answer to one another," said Sharifa. "Listen, we have come very far and we need to stay together to consolidate our gains. See how Pharaoh now draws us into his innermost circles, see how he consults us on critical matters of state."

"He trusts us," said Tiempo.

"And we need to make sure he continues to trust us."

"Look," said Tiempo, "I am his commander of the army, Adom is the number one priest, although Apophis may be a better choice, and you, Sharifa, you are the most trusted healer he has."

"Yes," said Adom, "but don't forget there were others like us that the woman picked. And I will ignore your comment about Apophis."

"Do you think Pharaoh may be thinking of replacements?" Tiempo asked.

"Not yet," said Sharifa, "and I don't want that to change."

"So what shall we do?" Tiempo asked?

"Stay close, keep our eyes keen, keep our ears close to the ground," said Sharifa.

"I have a plan," said Adom,"

"Wait," Tiempo replied, "why are you two changing the topic of our discussion to this?"

"Tiempo, please drop your contention and listen," Sharifa said.

"As I was saying," Adom said, "I have a plan to demonstrate our loyalty. We will need to shed some blood. There is no surer way of proving loyalty than with bloodshed. And this time innocent blood, unlike the killing of non-loyalists after the former pharaoh died. Innocent blood is the purest there is. It will feed the bloodthirsty spirits, including that of Pharoah."

"I don't fear to shed blood," said Tiempo. "You know this."

"Then it's settled," said Adom.

"So your plan," Tiempo said, "let's hear it."

The conspirators huddled closer in the dark chamber, tete-a-tete, and the darkness encircled them, uniting them, darkening even more with each breath, darkening even more with each word of the plot as it unfurled from Adom's fertile mind.

SEASONS of FOUR FACES

# Currencies of Ambition

The blood soaked architectural design formulated in the night was a building of intrigue erected on the foundation of falsehoods, but it was so solid it could not be demolished, whether by implosion or explosion.

If there was no insurrection, one had to be invented.

Following the death of Pharoah Hatshepsut the rumors of wrong play had gained currency. First, there were those who insisted she was not dead—how come no one could find her body? To them, no body meant no death. If she was not dead, then she was still queen, which implied that Pharaoh Thutmose III was illegitimate. Second, after her body was found, there were those who believed it was not her real body. And then there were those who considered her dead but questioned the circumstances of her death, suspecting murder. To the last group, Pharaoh Thutmose III was even more illegitimate, having ascended the throne on the corpse of his stepmother. This belief had more currency, considering that stepmother and stepson hated each other, nor was it lost on them that the stepson had been eyeing full access to the throne for a long time. It stood to logic that he would kill her, the only obstacle to his pharaonic ambition. These currents of suspicion, which had been stifled when the new pharaoh ascended the throne, began to percolate after a while, sufficiently to cause discomfort for the new king, even if it had not erupted into open dissent or rebellion. Pharaoh was conscious enough of them to express his worry to his three confidantes, playing into, in fact, feeding the plan that was afoot.

As his trusted spiritual leader, Adom consulted the gods and informed Pharaoh of where the deities were pointing him to. He revealed this to the king while he was receiving treatment for a boil on his thigh from Sharifa the trusted healer. As she rubbed medicine over the boil, Sharifa noted, "Great Pharaoh should not tolerate those who encourage such vile rumors."

"What do you propose I do?" Pharaoh asked.

"This is where Tiempo comes in," Adom said. "Those the gods point to must be exterminated without delay before their poison spreads."

Tiempo acted surprised when he was soon called to the palace, and when he saw Adom and Sharifa already confabulating with Pharaoh. The ensuing consultation, then, was brief, and the commander of Pharaoh's army put in charge of the operation. Adom had mentioned the names of his targets to Sharifa and Tiempo. The three reviewed and revised the list, which included ten members of the army and two notable seers (who, until then, were tipped as potential successors to the ageing Adom). Adom had wanted to include Apophis in the list, but Tiempo argued against it.

"He is a threat to me, being so close to Pharaoh."

"Exactly why you must exclude him. Pharaoh will not take kindly to it, and he may even begin to question you if he sees his trusted friend on the list. Besides, Apophis is my friend. I know I have brought up his name in the past, but when you really consider it, we all know that Pharaoh is too savvy to consult with Apophis on serious matters. Apophis is too full of irenic instincts on affairs of state, prone to badinage despite his priestly office, too gamesome and averse to matters of blood. Pharaoh likes to keep him close just for the friendship."

"For now, let's exclude him then," Adom said.

Tiempo summoned his most trusted subordinates and marched from home to home in search of those Adom had named. They wasted no time once they seized their targets. One by one, they executed the purported traitors, cutting off their hands after each execution and putting the dead men's hands in a basket. Spear into heart, the killings were that mechanical, devoid of emotion, full of perfunctory precision. They entered the home of the second in command to Tiempo last. Equally renowned for his bravado as Tiempo, he had been mentioned as a replacement should Tiempo falter.

   He seemed ready for them when they entered his house, standing in the receiving chamber with his sword drawn. But valiant and skilled as he was, he was no match for the highly skilled six men who battled him, striking him six times on the upper torso. As he lay on the floor dying, Tiempo raised his sword high, but before he brought it down for the coup de grace, the dying soldier yelled through blood filled throat, "Traitor!" He was about to repeat the accusation when Tiempo brought the sword down with all the force he could muster. Tiempo relished this killing more than the others, as he severed the dead man's hand. "A special treat for the king." He tossed the severed hand into the basket of dead men's hands and ordered his coterie to leave for Pharaoh's palace, when a thought which at first seemed errant for its needlessness, prompted him to look farther than met the eye. "Wait," he said as he entered the slain man's inner chamber.

   It took a little while for his eyes to adjust to the deeper darkness of the room, but then it was soon obvious that there was another body in the room. Who could it be, considering that the man was not married? A concubine, perhaps? Tiempo was about to settle on that explanation when he decided to look closer and closer and even closer, each closer look building to the conclusion that had begun to take shape on second look: lying before him (body mummified but recognizable) was the woman, the former pharaoh, Hatshepsut. Tiempo's thoughts swirling in consideration of the fortuitous find, his knees turned weak, he began to breathe rapidly and he began to sweat. What was he to do? This required more minds than his alone. Still sweating, heart percussing, he sent two of his subordinates to get Sharifa and Adom.

The wait was painful, filled with the fear that somehow he would lose his finding, that some counterforces would come and overpower him and his soldiers before he could figure out what to do next.

He ushered Sharifa and Adom into the inner chamber as soon as they arrived, his agitated voice quelling their intended questions.

Rather than speaking, Tiempo gestured with his head, urging Sharifa and Adom to look down. It took a brief while for them to comprehend the gesture. And they looked.

Adom grunted with surprise and Sharifa covered her lips with her hand to stifle a gasp.

"Is this who I think it is?" Sharifa asked.

"It can't be," said Adom.

"It is," said Tiempo. "Now we have added value, that this man stole the body of the woman after we believed it had been anonymously entombed."

The breathing of all three got deeper.

"What shall we do?" Tiempo asked.

"Pharaoh must know without delay," said Sharifa. "This, even more so than the death of his enemies, will bring him great joy."

"You think he would be glad to know we have found her body here?" Adom asked.

"Yes, he will!" Sharifa said. "We all had no idea the body had been stolen and now look. What was he planning to do with the body? Plan some form of rebellion with the body as totem or emblem? This adds even more credence to our plot, and the king will be forever grateful to us."

"So we tell him and then what?" Tiempo asked.

"Let him decide what he wants to do with the body," said Sharifa.

"But with our input," said Tiempo.

"Our input is to provide the body," said Adom, "and nothing more."

"No," said Tiempo. "I will advise him to burn the body. Her body, like her memory, should be erased forever."

"Tiempo, you surprise me sometimes with your ruthlessness," said Adom. "You loved her once, I thought."

"I remember her for her weaknesses."

"Let us not waste time with talk," Sharifa said.

It was decided. With the home protected by a dozen guards, Tiempo, Sharifa and Adom marched to the palace with the severed hands of those who had been branded traitors and ordered dead by Pharaoh, and the more important delivery of the location of Hatshepsut's body.

It did not surprise them that Pharaoh was more interested in the body than in the severed hands of his enemies. He chose Tiempo's brutal treatment of the body. There was to be no public spectacle of the body; rather, she was to be anonymized in death, and all physical testaments to her erased.

BENJAMIN KWAKYE

# A Taste of Eternity

Soon after this victory, Tiempo and Pharoah prepared for another war together. And Tiempo was counting to eighteen. The first has been easy, particularly because the enemy was picked more for practice than anything else, to weed out any detritus from the many years of the army's dormancy under Pharaoh Hatshepsut. For Tiempo it was one done, seventeen more to go. It seemed endless. And the next war, slightly more difficult but not by much, yielded another victory with no casualties on the Egyptian side. And then the third and then the fourth. At the rate of conquests and the relative ease of each, Tiempo began to salivate, looking towards number eighteen. The next five were more challenging but still fairly easily won, although there were a few Egyptian casualties. Still, his bravery and fearlessness, coupled with Pharaoh's own boldness and battle craftsmanship, were a formidable challenge for any opposing army. They were on course, acquiring a growing reputation as a lethal force of military excellence. Then they had fought at Megiddo, the most difficult yet, and still won.

Ten wars without a whiff of defeat was as enviable as it was fear-inducing. But it was also a recipe for complacency, with too much assumed.

They went in search of the eleventh victory.

The eleventh war, O, the eleventh, when almost at the point of etching another conquest, Tiempo relaxed his vigilance, standing on the battlefield without optical surveillance to ensure there was no enemy hidden from sight. Over-salivating, standing akimbo in self-satisfaction, Tiempo was about to account for the number of hands severed for Pharaoh's ego, when he felt a sharp pain in his lower abdomen. Everything around him began to go out of focus and he yelled as his knees weakened and he began falling. And he mustered every reservoir he could to stay standing, but he could not help his body as it tumbled to the ground. The last image he could register before the world turned totally black as the night in which he had so frequently reigned, was an enemy's face with a sword lifted, about to bring it down.

The involuntary surrender to total darkness lasted four days. He was lying on his back when he regained consciousness, the world, and light, slowly returning to him. He could barely see through the blur of viscous liquid that filled his eyes, forcing him to blink again and again. Similarly, his mind was lost in a fog of meaninglessness, his thoughts like a stranger on an isolated island. It took a while, but slowly the vision returned and slowly the sight returned also.

The face. The face. The face. The face.

He had never seen the face so beautiful, not simply from the radiance of the smile, but also from the seductive strain, as one would look on a dead body with pity and concern, but also with affection that defied any dictional frame of reference or analogy in experience. The face, so otherwise perfectly proportioned, now asymmetrical because this expression was so novel to it that it could not fit without throwing its facial residence into disproportion: twisted on the one side, tightly squeezed on the other; strained on the one end, painfully stretched on the other.

And then the voice. The voice. The voice. The voice.

He had heard it many times, of course; but now, having returned from the brink of something potentially everlasting and unforgiving, a place of stark darkness and uncertainty, he heard the sweetness of the voice as if for the first time. It was the voice of water dripping softly from a rooftop in the middle of a dolorous afternoon, like a counter-voice to the drabness of desiccation. More so, it was the sound of a mighty, skiey river watering the seedlings and plants of his very soul. It was like the Nile itself, bringing life. It was the deep sound of a waking dawn, bringing the promise of a new day.

"Tiempo," sounded the voice, "you have come back. I thought I had lost you."

The voice drew him in to her. He tried to raise himself from the bed, but she stopped him.

"No," she cooed, "Rest. You need your energy."

In the joy of regained sight, he looked at her anew, as she placed a hand on his chest; no gentler hand could have been placed on one human being by another.

"Sharifa," he said. "Sharifa. Sharifa. Sharifa."

And then he was sucked once more into that dark place he had so recently escaped, only this time it was not for days, but only hours. "I told you to preserve your energy," Sharifa admonished, but even then the words, as softly as they were spoken, belied the even softer affection behind them. And so it was, in and out of darkness and light, he journeyed, the darkness weakening him, the light strengthening him, only the light strengthened him more than the darkness could weaken him, until she determined that it was time for him to be on his feet.

In those alternating moments, she apprised him of what had happened, of the wound in his abdomen from the tip of a spear, which fortunately had not struck any vital organs, even if it left a gaping wound.

He had been at the mercy of an enemy, a wounded man who had been presumed dead, but had recovered to launch his attack on Tiempo. He had lifted his spear, on the verge of bringing it down to finish off the fallen Tiempo, when Pharaoh himself, his eyes focused on his army chief, had unleashed an arrow into the back of the enemy. This description about Pharaoh's arrow into someone's back brought over Tiempo a strong sense of déjà vu that perplexed him.

"He saved your life," Sharifa said.

And her words ignited a strong sense in Tiempo that something similar had happened in the past, but he could not support this with any images from memory.

When they brought him to her, Sharifa continued, his pulse was faint, his body seemingly slipping into the oblivion of death. "Save him," Pharaoh had told her.

She did not need to be told to muster all the medicinal powers she could to bring him back from the brink. She wanted to save him for future battles; she wanted to save him for something she deemed more important than military conquests or love. She wanted to save him to have him, not necessarily for romance, but just for the sake of his presence. A presence stronger than love. He had become such an intricate part of her emotional, perhaps spiritual, repertoire, that if he died, she would die too. Not physical death, but a form of death that would totally change her mode of existence. Whether as friend, colleague, conspirator, paramour, or whatever, he had to be there. So she had put all her knowledge and emotions into nursing him. On five occasions, she thought she'd lost him when he was in that nebulous place where life slips into the oblivion of death. But even when other medicine men and women had come to encourage her to let him go, she had refused, cajoling and caressing his body back to life with the gentle massages of her fingers that no other healer could perform but her, coaxing his spirit with speech and song, teasing his spirit back to her.

One time, he slipped into the darkness that fellowships with death, and he saw the ghosts of his many wars singing to him. They were many, even countless and they gathered before him and sang in voices that were diverse, but still unified and coherent:

>We are the groan that spits blood under
the hammer of death.
>    Come, brother, come. We shall hold
hands now and fly together
>    in the chorus of the war dead: our lives
have been snuffed out
>    before its time but we fought for a cause,
good or bad, wise or foolish,
>    and we must accept our fate. We are that
sound of the galloping horse
>    heading into the battlefield, knowing that
flesh and blood will be torn
>    asunder and many will be widowed and
orphaned, that love stories
>    will be unfulfilled because the voice of
love becomes the gasps of the
>    dying with an arrow lodged in his throat.

They sang and sang, even when he begged them to stop. And Tiempo was groaning, tossing this way and that, until Sharifa shook him awake.

Others had visited. Adom had come in and out of the nursing room. He would sit for long periods with Sharifa, sometimes encouraging her to continue, but sometimes encouraging her to surrender to the wishes of the gods. Once or twice he had wondered aloud why he should not choke Tiempo to death. He may have effected these thoughts but for fear that Sharifa would abandon him, never forgive him. Apophis the priest and his wife Thema had also come to see him and they were in accord with Pharaoh: Save him.

Through it all, Sharifa continued to reanimate Tiempo through days that alternated between sunburst and dark clouds, plagued by the uncertainty of what might fall from the sky or strike from the ground, out of nothingness or out of somethingness. Sometimes, it was all a blur, a place of ambivalent promises.

    Slowly, she allowed him to sit, then step one at a time. Slowly she allowed him to walk outside and take strolls, short ones at first, and then longer ones, walking beside him, sturdier in her walk than he, whose height sometimes gave him a bit of less sturdy gait. Then he would return home and rest. Once, in a lighthearted moment, Tiempo opened his eyes and saw Sharifa looking at him with a tenderness he could not have imagined. Smiling, he remarked, "When I recover, I will make sure to get ill all the time so you can cure me."

    And then one day Pharaoh came to see him with Amun. "The boy misses you," he said as Amun held Tiempo's hand, his confidence that Tiempo would live and not die clear in the beaming face that needed no verbal expression. He was waiting for Tiempo so they could play their usual games, Amun said. Pharaoh himself could barely contain the joy of seeing him recovering if still not at full strength.

    "We have suspended all major wars," he said. "We want you to return so we can win wars together."

When they left, uncertainty hang between Tiempo and Sharifa, the uncertainty that was them. Without doubt she needed him. With doubt he did not know in what capacity.

"So what have you decided?" she asked. "Are you going back to the army?"

"Why do you ask this, Sharifa? That is my profession."

"So you will go back." She knew the answer and so did not frame it as a question.

"Do I have a choice?"

"You have nothing to prove now, Tiempo. Everyone knows you are a great soldier, a brave one. You almost died on the battlefield. You may not be so lucky the next time."

She did not sound convincing to herself because a part of her wanted him to return to the battlefield—for Egypt, for himself, and for herself—in recognition of the complexities of the relationship between love, heroism, and danger.

"You want me to leave the army like a coward, Sharifa? How can I live with myself?"

"You will take bravery over life?"

"I have no choice, not to mention that Pharaoh, the man who saved my life, wants me back. You heard him say it. They have suspended major wars as they wait for me. I owe it to him. I owe it to Egypt. I owe it to myself. And I owe it to you!"

"You do not owe me anything."

"But Sharifa, how do I manage to fight eighteen wars if I don't go back? I need to do this for us."

She could have negated the requirement there and then, rescinded the condition for the sake of her affections, reduced the number to wars already fought. But they both knew that she could not. She could not reduce it because it would imply she'd lost confidence in him to survive, or even cheapen herself in his eyes. What had been bargained had been bargained, and one near fatal hiccup could not reverse it. They only had to hope, even if it was threshing hope from possible despair.

And it was in that place of nebulousness, as though in a confusing gloaming, where no one can properly find a seat and sit comfortably because it involves the dynamism of human emotions… it was in that place that their souls began to gel and to communicate, like dead spirits, even though they were both alive, in a language that their physical senses expressed but could not fully appreciate. Or perhaps it was not a language at all, at least not as language as commonly understood, but rather a form of expression that defies comprehension by those still inhabiting earthly bodies.

BENJAMIN KWAKYE

# Shadows of the Nights

Sometimes, my beloved is like the shadows of the night because he so easily blends with it and in this shadow swimming he comes to me; and effortlessly as the wind he comes, opening his heart to the vastness of the waves. I know this because I know him and I have watched him come and I have watched him go, and his footsteps at my doorstep are as false as a deserted heart, because though he leaves, he never leaves: How can anyone leave his heart and still live? Therefore, it's all a pretense of a body in motion, when what really matters is deeper, which is as real as life, but which the eyes cannot see. So when I see the footsteps in the sands pointing towards my door, I smile; and I smile when I see his footsteps pointing away from my door, focusing on what never leaves.

In the courtyards, they are filled with confusion, asking who is her beloved? Her eyes, we cannot read, and her heart is even more closed to our minds. Her tongue is as sweet as salt, but she guards it too much like a treasure of the affairs of life and death. I have heard their whisperings and I have heard their murmurings, but I have not told them. Though sometimes they think my beloved is too corporeal, they only look at the physical, at what they see and not the unstoppable power of the unseen. When the teeth of the grin of my beloved glistens, they do not understand how he burns fire in my heart and some think he has wooed me with some strange masculine wile.

My beloved comes, looking for me in the night, for he is afraid I am not his, he is afraid he will lose me. And he might for the day, but not for the tomorrow. That which is meaningful and worthy does not count its worth today but looks to the everlasting. It endures. It waits, takes chances on the currency of hope. Sometimes it even compromises with the affairs of today. But in looking long term, it knows that what starts as a wedding in love, a marriage of true love, ends also in a wedding of love, rests ultimately in that marriage of true love.

Therefore, wherever you are, whether in the land of the living or the land of the dead, I will be yours and you will be mine. Remember this my beloved in your journeys of many battles and in your journeys of many nations. Look for me always, my beloved, as I sing you this song of love. I say look for me always. I may be that shadow behind you in the dark when you walk the deserts or when night soaks you like a stormy rainfall. I may be that body in the profile of wrapped clothes that disappears around the corner. I may be the voice that haunts your dreams with the echoes of a deep longing that cannot be sated by anyone but me. I may be the hand that stokes your dreams with passion, the shadow now seen, now unseen. I may be the swimmer in a river calling for you. I may be anywhere, or even nowhere, but if I am nowhere, know that I will soon be somewhere, for just as you seek for me first, I will also seek you from somewhere.

My beloved bargains for my love and I have given him the bargain, not because I need the bargain but because, though he does not realize it, he needs it, to be fully convinced that love is not for sale, but is consummated at cost; otherwise, it shatters at the next challenge.

I will say to him when every voice has spoken, that I love him. I will be his vision, urging him on from me and towards me.

## BENJAMIN KWAKYE

When I see him in the courtyard, my heart rolls faster than his chariots of war. So spirit that perches with me in this avian vision, come back to me. You will live and not die. In the cauldron of tension and confusion and the astonishments of affections, we will eat of love.

# Breath of Last Gasp

My beloved is like the breath of my last gasp, for she bestrides the day like the sun itself when she casts her heliotropic glance in my direction, and then to think that she may cast that glance at another. But, though the sun shines as brightly as the glitter of her smile, I prefer to go to her in the darkness, when my competition is not sunlit bodies and their suspicious shadows, but the shadow of the night that reveals itself only at risk of perishing, as there is no one to offer salvation in the depth of night, but those who know it and its deeds.

But though she is the shadow of my thoughts and the sun of my heart, I am afraid that she will slip away like the sand slips through open fingers.

I do not understand all the things she says or all the hindrances in her thoughts and actions, but I know that she is my lifeblood, and if the blood begins to flow out, the body must seek the blood or perish.

She, the idol of my heart, walks the pathways as if she were an ordinary woman, but those are the pathways that can be seen, for she also walks another pathway, where she is invited without condition, admired without criticism, loved without untoward demand. Therefore, if on this pathway, there falls a hindrance, it is just that, a hindrance that lasts a day but will be uprooted tomorrow. Anyone who has had another being walk through his heart will know this, when the heart becomes a nation where only two people can live, and where any other person is persona non-grata. In this nation she has the liberty to walk about with impunity. And I love that she has this license, because it is otherwise too lovely and uninhabitable to anyone else. She has left such deep dents of her footprints that to evict her will also mean cutting off parts of those footpaths, parts of myself that can only lead to death. So if I cannot find her in the night, I will seek her in the day. If the day eludes me, I will seek her where night meets day. If she is in the rain, I will open my eyes to the raindrops and let them wash them until my vision is clear enough to see her in it.

I do not have the words for my beloved, for love, like death, cannot be defined. It can only be demonstrated, and if in that demonstration men are able to find definition, then let them speak. As for me, what can I say to demonstrate my love? If she needs my love demonstrated in the most difficult manner, I will do it. If I must fight, I will fight. If I must die, I will die, for how else can I live with myself? The intestines of my very existence, she takes in, sucks in the nutrients and ejects all wastes. Love without finitude.

SEASONS of FOUR FACES

# Childbirths

They, or their spirits, had spoken to each other. They better understood each other now. What next?

Childbirth. And childbirth.

Known for her prowess, Sharifa was reputed to have helped in Nefertiti's delivery of Amun. With that delivery, her reputation had grown large. Tiempo also knew how deeply she had been involved in Thema's pregnancy. When for a long time Thema could not bear children, she and Apophis had summoned Sharifa to help. Sharifa had prepared concoctions and inserted them into Thema's vagina. And later, Sharifa had gone to examine if Thema was pregnant. With Thema on her back, Sharifa had covered Thema's breasts, arms and shoulders with oil she had specially prepared. Then in the early morning Sharifa had examined her again and announced her pregnant upon seeing her blood vessels strong and fresh. Sharifa had also been present at the delivery, which occurred in a confined pavilion. She mixed kheper-wer plant, honey, water of carob and milk, and placed the concoction in Thema's vagina. Thema then sat on her delivery seat, under which Sharifa placed hot water, expecting the vapors to help ease delivery. To appease Thema for her strong belief in them, Sharifa called upon the goddesses Hathor and Taweret to help with a smooth delivery.

With such and similar successes, Sharifa's reputation had grown even larger, Apophis and Thema, as part of the human trumpets that vouched for her excellence, and she was often called upon when needed to help with various pregnancies and deliveries.

So it was no surprise that she would be called upon to help with the delivery of another child when she was nursing Tiempo, although this time it was a desperate call, a pregnancy she had not been involved with. The messenger who came to call Sharifa told her the pregnant woman, Naunet, had been in labor for a long time and was perhaps even on the verge of death. After checking to be sure Tiempo was doing well, Sharifa hurried with the messenger into the evening. In her absence, Tiempo considered her again, a woman who helped bring new life into the world, in fact many new lives, now asked to assist with another, and also the woman who helped sustain life, and also the woman who was coaxing his own life from death. He was sinking deeper and deeper into that place he would rather not totally surrender to, that place of poetry and not war. How could the comfort of love so soften a man of war and death?

When she returned later that night, Sharifa told him, how so close to death Naunet had been, with the baby's head in the wrong place and how she gently had to turn him around until his head was in the right place where Naunet could push him out even if with ebbing strength. This time, she had forgone the traditional ways of childbirth, such as kneeling, or sitting on her heels or on a delivery seat. Instead, she'd had the woman lie on her back and then with her hands and fingers communicated to the baby to move into the right position.

Newly admiring her, Tiempo asked, "How did you do it?"

"I will show you," Sharifa said.

The shadows in the room were like clothes that they both

wore and they moved sometimes tightly and sometimes loosely over the faces and bodies of their human counterparts. He did not expect a long answer, perhaps a cryptic response about intuition and experience. But as they wore the shadows in the room, Sharifa looked at Tiempo so intensely that he was goose-pimpled. She asked him to stand on his feet. He complied. Then she took a step back, her eyes examining him from head to toe, and then she asked him to remove his upper tunic. He hesitated. She repeated her request. Tiempo complied.

Then she asked him to lie on his back on the floor. He was about to protest when she hushed him with a finger to her lips. Do as I say, she communicated without speaking with words. Tiempo complied. His heart beating hard, he watched her hovering over him. At that moment, she was life and she was death. She could have wrapped her hands around his neck and suffocated him to death and he would not have resisted. Sharifa knelt at the bottom of his supine body and took hold of his feet and slowly pulled his legs apart. Then she moved closer to him until she was kneeling between his legs, where his groin throbbed. Sharifa placed her hand over his belly and asked him to close his eyes.

"Remember this," she said. "Remember with your body and with your mind, not your eyes."

She slowly began to move her hands over his belly, in the process speaking to his belly as if it held a child, saying to the phantom child to cooperate. Tiempo gasped, straining to focus rather than abandon himself. And Sharifa continued to knead and massage and press. And then she moved her hands from the upper part of his belly to the lower part, and Tiempo thought all that was within him that was capable of offering life was being released from his body. "Push," Sharifa said, and Tiempo pushed something that was life out of himself as he yelled gutturally with the release of the pressure that had consumed him.

# CHAPTER 3

*"I have consulted the gods," the priest said.*

## Running with Immortals

When Pharaoh celebrated the Heb-Sed or Feast of the Tail, an event whose name was derived from the wolf god Wepwawet or Sed, the almost fully recovered Tiempo followed every part of the event. Like Pharaoh's shadow. He watched with wide eyes as his king, the man with whom he had fought many wars, presented his offerings to the gods. Then Pharaoh, stern as character, sat on a raised platform, waiting to be crowned. At the moment, sitting so magisterially, he did indeed appear the monarch of all he surveyed, with none to dispute him, even if some would have liked to, or even if he was sitting in the middle of all forms of hidden alarms. With the assurance of a man who knows his place as higher than mere mortals, he received the two thrones of the cobra-goddess: Wadjet of the Delta town of Buto, and the vulture goddess Nekhbet of el-Kabcthe, being the two symbols of Upper and Lower Egypt.

As Adom, Apophis and the other priests carried the statues of the gods and presented offerings, a faint smile crossed Pharaoh's lips, perhaps in appreciation that this was a sign of thanksgiving for past loyalty and for securing strong relationships in the future. In the distance, Tiempo saw two men, one with a massive physique. Tiempo had seen them somewhere with Adom before, but he could not recollect where at the moment. He focused on the event instead, and the retrospective was strong, fortified by battles in which Tiempo was mightily gratified to have participated. Tiempo was pleased to remind himself that these were indeed times of action, unlike those of the previous pharaoh, whose penchant for diplomacy had kept him idle and irritated. And if the past was any sign of things to come, then the future would shimmer well; for him in particular, more wars meant that he would meet his part of the bargain with Sharifa. Seven more to go. Tiempo looked at his monarch and smiled, filled with pride and confidence. He wished he could have replaced Adom or even Apophis in the procession of the priests, envious of the solemnity, and yes dignity, with which they filed past, like demigods communing with gods.

Following this, Pharaoh dressed in a short kilt with a bull's tail in its back. This was The Feast of the Tail, after all. It was now time for him to run the open space between two rows of shrines, a race he did four times alongside the Apis Bull, the ruler of Lower Egypt, wearing a Red Crown, and four times as that of Upper Egypt wearing a White Crown. Running between the two points became a kind of reenactment of the borders of Egypt, a demonstration that he was indeed in total dominion over the entire kingdom. Not only was he dedicating the kingdom to the gods, but he was also demonstrating beyond doubt, not that any had doubted, that he was still physically fit and agile, capable of ruling the country; indeed, he was rejuvenated and reborn. Tiempo admired the man, his strength, the way he seemed to command his muscles to flex and unflex as he did his run, effortlessly, gracefully, royally.

Then came the final part, when Pharaoh was carried in a procession to visit the chapels of the gods, first as king of Lower Egypt to the chapel of Horus. There, he received the crook and flail, a staff that looked ordinary but in his hands seemed something of divine import. The king was elevating everything he touched, and Tiempo wondered if he was the only one who perceived things this way. And then Pharaoh was carried as king of Upper Egypt to the two chapels of Horus of Edfu and Seth of Ombos. There, he was handed a bow and arrow. Pharaoh took the bow and arrow and looked around him, his gaze in its fully pompous glory, and shot an arrow in each of four directions. After this, if anyone held the heretic thought that Pharaoh was unfit to rule or that he had weakened in any way, they were assuredly disabused of it, for indeed the monarch's power and authority was reestablished and reaffirmed in Egypt. And Tiempo was a part of it.

BENJAMIN KWAKYE

# Rage of Spirits

Tiempo, a man soon fully recovered, pulled from the precipice, a man who had seen the abyss and its long, dark emptiness and overcome it, reassured by the reign of a pharaoh who leaned heavily on him, a man who believed he had all to live for, as in death he could not show Adom that he was the better man, demonstrate to Sharifa that he was more deserving, a man with only seven more wars to win. But a man now more careful in battle in the overriding need to stay alive. On the battlefield, he was pulled by two urges, one to continue to build on Pharaoh's confidence as a valiant and skilled warrior, and the other to stay alive for Sharifa. She may have two loves now, but by her own promise, he would be her only love indeed if he met his part of the bargain. With the near death experience, he negotiated his fights on the battlefield in order that he would not be overly tentative so as to invite Pharaoh's suspicion or undermine his confidence in the man he believed to be his best warrior. And six wars later, none of them too difficult or too easy, Tiempo managed to negotiate these urges, which oftentimes seemed in complete conflict, emotionally taxing and even mentally draining. So, six wars after his dance with death, he eyed the remaining one with angst as much as expectation.

"I am almost there," he told Sharifa in the interregnum, when after the seventeenth war he went to see her.

But the expression, or lack of one, on her face created a deep doubt. Why was she not enthused about how close he was? Why had she simply stared at him, her cheeks not ripening into a smile, nor her lips widening into a grin? Was she signaling a form of withdrawal from the bargain? He was afraid to give voice to the concern for fear she might indeed be reconsidering her part of the bargain. So he moved away from it and instead regaled her with stories of war, of the way they fought, he, his king, and his men, of their invincibility on the battlefield, of how they were reclaiming glory for Egypt. She listened without saying much, her questioning limited, this lack of interest goading him to frustration. How could she who had nursed him back to life with care and sweet songs of love grow so cold?

That night, and many nights afterwards, he could barely sleep, tossing, tossing, closing his eyes but living his concerns in his mind, sometimes standing outside when the moon calmed the skies, in hope that this would calm his mind, but without avail. Sometimes he would step away from bed and pace and exhort the gods to come to his aid, but without fruition. He would try to contemplate the numerous wars he had won to build his confidence, not on the battlefield of arrows and hammers and daggers, but on the battlefield of love and emotion and enticing words. But this did not prosper his aspirations of rest. Tiempo was frustrated, deeply frustrated, when he began to have dreams that tormented him even more. In his dream, he could clearly visualize Adom and Sharifa. The moon was their pillow, the heavenlies, their bed. Though they were two, they were one, as they made the earth the cuspidor of their salivation for each other. And the songs they sang of themselves, for each other as well, was as sweet as any song he could imagine, and even sweeter. It was a dream that was as palpable as his own heartbeat, creating a newer and deeper jealousy he had not imagined possible. Never mind that what he had dreamed had, as far as he knew, not been substantiated in reality and therefore was mere shadow-copulating, that the sorrow of the mornings afterwards were only feignedly real because he allowed his imagination to dwell on a reality he was creating for himself out of dreams, in a vicious cycle that continued for days; a dream, a self-inflicted reality that fed the dream and vice versa. It fed his jealousy anger and fed it and fed it and continued to feed it, until he decided he had to act on it or otherwise choke one day on its venom.

## Breakfast of Despair

Full of this jealous anger, Tiempo went to see Adom. The older man was finishing his breakfast of beer and bread when Tiempo challenged him to a duel. "Let it be settled here and now who is the better man," the soldier said. "Fight for Sharifa."

"You may think you have the advantage of youth," Adom replied, as he sipped the last dregs of his heqet beer through the straw inserted in the terracotta vat, doing so noisily as if to annoy Tiempo. "And you may think you can easily win this preposterous fight you are proposing, but you forget that I have longer experience in life and the gods on my side."

"Fight like a man. If you win, I will leave her to you, old man. If I win, leave her alone."

"She will decide, will she not, Tiempo? She is not some property you fight for."

"The words of a senile, old man," said Tiempo, staring down at Adom, who stood only as tall as Tiempo's shoulders, his slight limp deepening the appearance of his inferior physical stature to Tiempo.

Tiempo did not wait for Adom to respond, leaping at the older man. But the older man was prepared for this, stepping aside from the lunge of the warrior, whose zeal and underestimation of Adom exposed his vulnerability. All it took was for Adom to trip Tiempo with a foot. As soon as Tiempo fell face down on the floor, Adom was upon him with such speed as took Tiempo by surprise, and before he could recover from the surprise, Adom had already pinned his hands behind him, sitting on his back and strengthening the hold on him.

The strength with which the older priest held on to his

hands and the tenacity with which he maintained the hold stupefied Tiempo for a moment, more so as he tried as hard as he could to free himself without success. He had been in many such holds and in each instant, he had managed to free himself without significant ado. But not this time. The old man's tightening began to spread a deep pain through Tiempo, first in his arm and then his entire body. Still, the one satisfaction he would not offer Adom was gasp in expression of pain.

"Free yourself now, young man," Adom taunted. "Warrior of Pharaoh's army, free yourself."

Tiempo's anger, fueled further by this taunt, sent a strange surge of strength through him. This was his moment, as he summoned the energy of hunger and avoidance of humiliation into a push, but it was like sending a puffing wind against a towering edifice. Adom's hold would not budge. And then in one quick move he released Tiempo's hands but put Tiempo in a chokehold with one hand. With the other hand, Adom brought a dagger (from where, it wasn't clear) to Tiempo's throat.

One false move and his throat could be slit, but he decided to call Adom's bluff, out of pride than reason. "Do it! Do it, old man. What are you waiting for?"

The older man bought his breath closer, which was quite foul, and whispered in Tiempo's ears, "I could kill you right now, you fool, but I am not as foolish as you are. Pharaoh needs you and Egypt needs you, so I will let you live. Your time will come soon enough and at that time I will kill you, and Sharifa will be pleased."

With that threat established, Adom released his hold and got off Tiempo's back. Slowly, Tiempo stood back up, his body now fuming with humiliation. The two men were proximate,

Tiempo with his hands by his side, his fists clenched, Adom with the dagger pointing at Tiempo. One lunge forward and one would be at the other's throat. Tiempo now knew the older man was stronger, more agile than he could have imagined and another attack was not likely to succeed, and Tiempo could not be certain exactly why Adom had chosen to spare him, despite the reasons Adom articulated. The part that continued to pierce him, to hollow him out like a giant worm eating into his soul, was what Adom said about Sharifa.

"Why will Sharifa understand if you killed me?" Tiempo asked, notwithstanding his heaving chests of anger and his staccato breath of humiliation.

"You are not the only one who has a bargain with her, you know," Adom said.

"Bargain. You have... you know about my bargain with her?" Adom did not respond, prompting Tiempo to continue, "What bargain have you reached with her?"

"I will advise you, young man, to leave. Now! Before I change my mind about letting you live."

"This is not the end of this, Adom. I promise you that."

"It certainly is not, young man!"

On the way home, the usually friendly night for companion, Tiempo could not put his mind at ease, the sense of betrayal that Sharifa had disclosed their bargain to Adom relentlessly hounding him. And clearly Adom had reached some manner of a bargain with Sharifa. As much as he could not be sure what it entailed, if Adom was to be believed, Sharifa would approve of Adom killing him. What did that mean? What manner of potentially diabolical game was Sharifa (perhaps in cahoots with Adom) playing? The anger and humiliation were urging him to go see Sharifa right away and settle whatever needed to be settled that very moment with the night as judge and jury. But he knew even then, past anger and humiliation or perhaps because of them, that he was capable of anything at that moment, that if he did not hear from Sharifa words that would soothe him, he could perpetrate violence that he might regret later. For his own sake and for the sake of the woman who had nursed him back from death, he would suffer with the uncertainty for the remainder of the night and hopefully be able to confront her with a clearer mind and waned anger the next day. But he would not wait any longer than the next day. He would go to Sharifa the next day, or more likely the next night, no matter what.

But it was that very next day that they heard of the arrival of the man named Moses. And they did not know it then, but that man was about to change everything.

SEASONS of FOUR FACES

# Past the Duel of Serpents

Tiempo was aware the man had fled after incurring the pharaoh's wrath when he'd killed an Egyptian to protect a Hebrew, this after the pharaoh's daughter had rescued him from drowning in the Nile where he had been abandoned. That he would forgo the comfort of royal largesse with such recklessness and then run than face his fate, was what Tiempo found foolish and the telltale mark of an ingrate. They had all thought he had died in the wilderness or over time grown old to the point where he had decided to die in whatever land had adopted him. And now he had come, not for recompense, not to seek absolution for his wrong, but to request of Pharaoh that he let the Hebrews go so that they could worship God. His God. What audacity! Tiempo advocated that the man be put to death immediately, together with his brother Aaron. Tiempo would be glad to do it personally and display their heads in Goshen for all the Hebrews to see. But instead Pharaoh had listened to the advice of Adom and Sharifa to ask that the Hebrews work harder on Pharaoh's projects, with less resources but with the same output. And this would teach Moses a lesson? How weak and stupid, Tiempo thought. And he suspected that Adom and Sharifa somehow were teaming up against him to run counter to his advice. If he'd proposed what they had proposed, he suspected they would have proposed what he'd proposed.

His greatest pain was about Sharifa, who had become quite elusive.

On three occasions he'd gone calling on her and on each occasion she had not answered, his only proximity to her being in the presence of Pharaoh, when they had been called to give counsel. And when he had tried to accost her outside the palace, she had taken shelter in Adom's company, sure to be by his side. Tiempo would bide his time, even if he was dying an emotional death each day; and, unlike a battlefield, he did not know how to kill off the enemy this time. Who was the enemy anyway? He sometimes wondered. Was it the rival Adom? Or was it Sharifa, who had become even more of an enigma recently? And the more he wanted and craved to hate her, the more he realized he longed for her. The torment had to end soon, but he did not know how. And now that Moses had come with his demand for freedom, Pharaoh's mind seemed less occupied with the next war and more with Moses. Kill the man and be done with this, he kept muttering, but it was as if he was speaking to the wind, and it was as if the man had something over Pharaoh, whose ruthlessness could be as vast as the Nile.

Worse was the humiliation Pharaoh, and by extension all of them, had to endure in what became a duel of serpents. Moses has asked Aaron to throw down his rod, which turned into a snake. A cheap magician's trick, they all thought, asserting that such magic was for intellectual milquetoasts, except Pharaoh had summoned the great sorcerers of the land to perform the same trick; but they had all seen the humiliation of having the serpent of Moses' rod swallow the rod turned serpents by the sons of Egypt. That had sparked the first itch of respect for Moses from Tiempo: the man's sorcery, at least in some respects, had bested those of the sorcerers of Egypt. He had to give the man some respect for that, and also be more wary of him. He could become more of a nuisance to Tiempo's goal of getting Pharaoh focused on the next war.

## SEASONS of FOUR FACES

In these times of uncertainty, the only person who brought joy to Tiempo was Amun. Pharaoh's son never judged him, was always glad to entertain the soldier and spend long periods with him, sometimes just trading stories. And more and more, Tiempo sought out Amun for comfort.

# BENJAMIN KWAKYE

# A Song for the King

The incident of the swallowed serpents brooded over them all. But amid this humiliation, Apophis began to speak to bolster Pharaoh and remind him that he need not be threatened by anyone. In the course of a meeting of counselors and elders, Apophis decided to raise the spirits of an otherwise forlorn Pharaoh with a song:

> Great Pharaoh, you are the water that fills the Nile and you stand like the tree whose shadows stretch over land, sea and river. Who can compare to you? When your feet touch the sands of the earth, both earth and sky tremble and the air rejoices to know that one as mighty and needed for life as itself is abroad. You are the air of Egypt, Great Pharaoh, and who can compare to you? We have seen the skies grow full with soaked clouds that threaten a deluge, but when the clouds hear your voice, they shed their fullness and run for cover to the dry places of the heavens and your people are spared, for who needs water when you are the water and at your call rain that must rain will rain. Yes, you are the rain and more so, you are the sun, the great light of the day who gives vision to those whose eyes are open and to those whose eyes are closed, for your light shines on all. And in the night, you grow gentle, shining as the moon with a soothing that permits sleep to come after you have vetted its intensions and decided it has not come

# SEASONS of FOUR FACES

to steal lives.

Oh Great Pharaoh, you are that and you are more. Yes, you are the honey of many tastes, the bitter honey that your enemies drink unto death, and the sweet honey that your subjects drink for joy and to life. The eye that sees the hidden parts of the night and that sees the shadowy secrets of day, you are the great eye of the land.

Oh Great Pharaoh, warrior without whom war is but a child's game, but whose arrow brings meaning to battle and determines victor and vanquished, whose bow has eyes to catch enemies in their secret hideouts, whose name makes their hills tremble, whose voice roars louder than thunder and whose flying arrows flash faster and brighter than the lightning that carries light to those who embrace and death to those who oppose. The throat that has a thousand voices, the eye that has a thousand visions, the heart that has a thousand love interests, the tongue that has a thousand languages, the chin that does not shift to the left or right, the hand that carries a thousand lives in one grip, the mouth whose spit fills a thousand rivers, Great Pharaoh, you are the greatest!

BENJAMIN KWAKYE

# Voice of Mountains

Tiempo classified these words as nonsense, although they appeased Pharaoh and gave him joy. But if this offered a brief diversion, the humiliation would only mount soon when Moses threatened and then stretched his rod over the Nile, causing the water to turn red, attributing the feat to his God. That was indeed some feat, as the water became undrinkable, and the fish floated in the river in strange lifelessness. Pharaoh consulted with his advisors and sorcerers, soliciting all manner of opinions, none of which seemed satisfactory to him. He summoned his most trusted, unofficial inner council of Tiempo, Sharifa, and Adom, for counsel.

Tiempo advised again that the man be put to death. He obviously had some magical powers which he would use to dazzle and sow confusion unless he died. "Let Goshen become a sea of blood, starting with Moses' blood," Tiempo advised.

"I have consulted the gods," the priest said.

"Tell me what they said," Pharaoh asked with widened eyes.

In Adom's opinion, after spiritual consultation, the man Moses had no powers at all. The gods had shown him that what happened was a natural occurrence. They had shown him that a desert sandstorm had caused the Nile to turn red. Harpe, the god of the Nile, had been particular about this. The desert sandstorm had stained the river with an algae bloom that caused the water to stain and the fish to die. But Harpe was going to remedy the situation soon. And apparently he did so when in seven days the water returned to normal. Pharaoh held on to this as a sign that indeed Moses was showboating and had no special powers.

## SEASONS of FOUR FACES

He would not free the Hebrews, even when Moses warned him that a second plague was afoot, a warning realized when multitudes of frogs left the Nile. It seemed the water was raining them onto the land, causing nuisance to man and beast. And, again, Adom explained this was the result of desert sandstorms, saying he had seen even deeper into the spiritual realm, speaking about a Santorini volcanic eruption, with its impact on Egypt and on the waters, with a stress that had caused an acceleration of frog metamorphosis from the tadpole stage on account of the lack of oxygen. This acceleration explained the explosion of frogs.

Perhaps he wanted to believe what he wanted to believe, but Pharaoh thanked Adom for his sagacious explanation. He hugged the counselors, a bit reluctantly, and that would be the last time he would hug any of them. He would not let the Hebrews go. Nor would he, even though he came close a few times, when subsequent plagues followed: an overabundance of lice and fleas, and an epidemic which Adom attributed to a lack of green water, not supernatural powers. Likewise when a sixth plague of boils and blisters affected the land, Adom noted that it was all due to the lack of oxygen.

On their sixth summons on the issue, as Tiempo listened to Adom's explanation, he thought he heard the biggest hope he could have asked for, when for the first time, Sharifa asked, "Are you sure about all these explanations, Adom?"

Adom was sure, he said. But it was the first sign of doubt she had expressed and in it he found hope.

His own body itching with a couple of blisters, Tiempo deemed himself lucky, for others had had it much worse, with blisters and boils bathing their entire bodies, and so too the animals. He had gone to see Sharifa, and confessed outside of her door that he needed treatment for his blisters. This time, she had let him in. She examined the blisters, gently, ever so gently, and summoned that deepness of touch with which she had brought him back from the dead. He had to galvanize all his willpower to stop himself from going into spasms of somatic release. As she applied a balm to the blisters, she said, "This will take care of those." But then she asked him to strip. He demurred. She said it again, and he hesitated. "I need to apply the balm to your entire body," she said "as prophylactic; otherwise, you could have it spread on your entire body like the rest of them. Have you not seen the suffering this brings? Do you want to suffer like them?"

"No."

"Then do as I say."

Still, he hesitated.

"Strip!" This time, it was not a request but an order. But was it the order of a physician or of a lover? "Look, Tiempo," she added, "I have done this for Pharaoh. And have you seen any blisters on him?"

He had not, but then he had not seen any blisters on Adom either. Had she done it for him also? If so, had she offered it to him or had he come asking for it? If she had offered it to him why had she waited for him to come to her? Out of pride, he considered rejecting her offer, but reconsidered, considering that if Adom had enjoyed the treatment, then so would he. As she watched him, he stripped until he was standing naked before her. Her eyes stayed on his face as she covered both hands in balm and started applying it. She started with his face, gently rubbing the balm in. And then his neck, then his chest, drawing a slight moan when she rubbed over his nipples, then his hands, then his stomach. She stopped there and asked him to turn around, then she rubbed more lotion in, starting from the shoulders, his back, then his buttocks and then his legs and ankles. She asked him to turn around. This time, she worked his thighs, knees, and the rest of his legs, bending in the process to apply the balm. Then slowly she applied it to his toes. And then when he thought she was done, she took a large portion of the balm and applied it to his loins. Had she done the same to Pharaoh (or Adom) or was this special treatment? It was a question he could not, dared not, ask her. She was slowest with that part, as though she wanted to elicit a response, which he tried hard to withhold, recalling Adom's foul breath, the knife at his throat and trying desperately to hold on to that image. But he could not stay his reaction much longer, exhaling a long groan that was as much a release as it was a protest. Had Pharaoh or Adom also reacted this way? He reached out to touch her, but his hand got only as far as the outer layer of her clothing before she stopped him with one hand. "Don't," she said, as she rubbed the remaining balm into him and he gasped. And gasped. And gasped.

"What are you doing to me, Sharifa?" he asked when he was able to regain his stolen breath.

"I am protecting you," she said, "healing you."

"Like this? By tormenting me like this?"

"This should not be a torment, Tiempo."

"Do you know what your touch does to me Sharifa? And then to know that I can't have you."

"You can, but at the right time. We agreed."

"I know about our agreement, but why did you have to tell Adom about it?" She turned from him, but he did not bother wearing his clothes. And naked, he continued, "Why, Sharifa?"

"I'm sorry, Tiempo. I should not have told him. But... you don't understand... when I am around him, I don't seem to have full control of myself. He makes me say and do things that I don't seem able to control."

"You think he is exerting some spiritual power over you?"

"I don't know… I just don't know."

"He has no power over you, unless you want him to have power over you."

"He is no ordinary man, Tiempo. And you should know that. Did he defeat you in a fight, even though he is full of years?"

"He told you?"

"He did. And he told me you would be asking me about my bargain with him."

"Yes, he mentioned a bargain between you two. And I've been trying to ask you for a while now, but I have the feeling you have been avoiding me."

"I have."

"Why?"

"Because I am afraid to tell you the truth."

"Please tell me. I need to know the truth… Please."

"I can't, Tiempo. You will hate me."

"Please. Sharifa. I can't hate you. I love you."

"All the more reason why you will hate me if I told you—love betrayed harbors a strange kind of hatred."

"Have you betrayed me, then?"

"I am sorry I have."

"How?"

"Please…"

"Do you love me at all, Sharifa?"

"Did I not nurse you when many thought you would die?"

"Do you love me, Sharifa?"

She did not answer.

"Do you love me, Sharifa?"

She hesitated for a moment before responding, "Yes, I love you, Tiempo. I love you. We have sung many songs in spirit and in truth."

"Then tell me. Trust me."

"Very well... I made a bargain with Adom, even before I made one with you. He had professed his love to me, saying he wanted to marry me and I had rebuffed him, telling him I loved you. But then he said that if I really loved you, I ought to put you to the test, have you prove your love. He said that he would put a curse on us if I refused. I should let you promise to fight eighteen wars for my love. I refused at first, but he said he would kill you if I did not agree. And I know he's capable. You have seen how far he can go to get rid of his enemies. He is very cunning. So I agreed. When that day you suggested you would fight to win my love, it was as if Adom had foreseen that moment. He is a priest and seer after all. I think he believed you would not survive so many wars and you would be dead before you finished fighting them. And you came close to dying, but I think our love is stronger than the seer's hope or vision of death."

"I have concluded that seeing into the future does not make the foolish man wise; it only makes the future more dangerous, subject to his foolish manipulation. In blind ambition, even wise men become foolish. But that is a something for another day. He said something about you been happy if he killed me. Why would he say that?"

"I did not say that. I said all those battles would kill you and it might as well be as if he'd killed you himself."

"That night we fought, he had a knife to my throat. Do you have any idea why he didn't he kill me then?"

"Kill you so blatantly and invoke the ire of Pharaoh? He

would not want to risk that. He would rather have you die in battle than by his hands. Of course, if he has no choice and he thinks he can get away with it, he will kill you. That's why I don't take any of this threats lightly. That's why I don't want to get him to a place where he will abandon reason."

"You have made me so happy today, Sharifa. You have no idea how much. But why did you not tell me all this before, Sharifa?"

"What difference would it have made? Tiempo, your temper gets the best of you, and I feared you would have reacted in a manner we both might regret."

"And now?"

"I am tired of all the secrets, Tiempo. Let what will happen, happen. And I get a sense Adom's time may be limited, with all the reasons he's been coming up with about the plagues. It's only a matter of time before Pharaoh gets tired of him. I've heard that Pharaoh may be considering Apophis as a replacement."

"Apophis is my friend, but that will never happen."

"Any why?"

"I have mentioned him as a replacement, but that was only to irritate Adom. Apophis is not serious. Sometimes, I think he is a priest in name only."

"That's true, but Pharaoh may act out of desperation."

"I doubt that. But about this man Moses, do you think he is real? That he has special powers?"

"I don't know what to make of him, but I don't think he's an ordinary man. He possesses something unusual, I'm just not sure what it is."

"So what do we do now?"

"We bide our time and wait. And we go about things very carefully."

# CHAPTER

# 4

*"Listen to reason," Sharifa said.*
*"This is not a fight for us or the gods."*

## Children of the Nile

There had been many days when his path was clear and he knew exactly what he wanted, days when he looked forward to the next war. He was after all, a soldier, with a stubborn caprine-lust for action and resistance, with little use for ovine-idleness or other distractions. He had stood with his king and fought many wars to lift up the kingdom and he would like to continue to fight many more. That was what he was. A warrior in search of the next fight. But also, this did not reflect his perfect face, for he was fully aware that he was a man of many faces, and warlikeness was only one of those faces. The other face reflected that part of him that beheld Sharifa, who teased out his affections when they were lost to emotional stoicism. When he wanted to stay in that hard place, she called him out of it, when he wanted to hear a roar, she whispered. It was not because she was soft. She was not—she had shown him that she could be as tough, caustic and ruthless as any. The softness was rather inside him—his own inner softness responding to her in a way that no one else could draw out. Even in her hardness, he responded to her with softness. And it was this part of him he would have liked to shed so that he would never be so vulnerable, that part that made him cede a part of his happiness, even his very being (or existence) to another. He often wondered if there could be a Tiempo without a Sharifa, or vice versa.

And the more he considered it, the story of Moses began to resonate with him in a way that not everyone knew. As it must resonate with Sharifa. The very story of their geneses, shrouded in mystery, haunted them both. Tiempo had sought the truth, when the woman who should have been his mother had confessed on her deathbed that she was not his biological mother. She had told how she'd picked him up from a little basket-boat floating on the Nile, believing him to be an abandoned baby. She had taken him in as her own. But not only that, she had been with another, a stranger, who had picked up another baby floating from the opposite direction, coming towards Tiempo (just as it seemed Tiempo was going towards her). His mother was barren and, seeing the child, deemed herself gifted a baby by the fertile wombs of the Nile. She would have liked to pick up the other baby and nurse the two of them as twins, but the other woman had gotten to that baby first.

Tried as he would, Tiempo could not remember his childhood. It was as if he had just materialized as a full grown adult. So where was his childhood? His mother would not or could not answer. Where was the other baby? His mother could not or would not answer. It was only when he met Sharifa that he concluded she was the other baby floating on the Nile.

The first time Tiempo could remember seeing Sharifa was when he'd been summoned to Pharoah Hatshepsut's presence; by then he was a full time part of the army. Why had he joined the army? Because he could think of no other befitting profession. For a man whose past seemed a blackness, or perhaps a blankness, into which his mother poured whatever she wished, he had seen the army as his worthy destiny, a place of equal uncertainty as his past, where the next battle could spell death. His strength, adeptness and agility had inspired his quick rise, and Pharaoh Hatshepsut had recognized him as an important general. In fact, as best as he could remember, he had not really joined the army. He had always been a part of it.

When Pharaoh Hatshepsut called Tiempo to tell him that he was being elevated to second in command (apparently on reports of his prowess that she had heard and the recommendation of his compatriots), the queen was seated with arms outstretched as Sharifa rubbed some form of treating ointment into those arms. Their eyes had met and he had felt life leaving him and flowing into her (Sharifa), except he also felt life leaving her and entering into him. He was surprised he had not seen her earlier, a woman so striking. It was not meant to be so, he concluded, and the timing was a matter decided by the gods. In their ensuing conversations, he had been unable to unlock her past, and the only thing he had was the story offered him by a dying woman. He wanted to confirm his intuition that Sharifa was the other baby on the Nile. Did Sharifa's mother account confirm the story? Tiempo had asked. Sharifa would say that her now dead mother had found her on the Nile. This was sufficient information for Tiempo. Beyond that, though, Sharifa said she did not remember anything and, like him, her past was as blank as a dead river. With such a cryptic past, it was little wonder that they were drawn to each other, except she had neither fully yielded to him nor shown she was open to his advances, until he pressed the issue.

And so whenever he examined his life, he felt himself in a place that was impossible to negotiate, sometimes compelled to leave her be and move on with the summons to war and more war. But he could not war forever, and just as the bellicose part was a part of him, the yearning for her love was also a part of him. And more and more, in the periods between wars, he needed her. Could he pluck out his heart and continue to live, or close his nostrils to air and survive? So, more than ever before, Tiempo affirmed he needed Sharifa. And when he allowed himself to yield to this sentiment, he began to redefine his situation, no longer as a dilemma, but as a path, a one way path, often winding, but that must lead inevitably to Sharifa, or to his own demise. He saw no other way when he thought of it this way.

## Thickening the Plot

Amid Moses' threat, Tiempo heard the rumors Sharifa had mentioned that Pharaoh was considering a new confidante on spiritual matters besides Adom, and that Apophis was the chief candidate for the position.

One day, as Adom, Tiempo and Sharifa were leaving the palace, they saw Apophis at the front portico. He greeted them but without his usual bonhomie, and quickly walked past them into the palace. They had seen him at the palace on many occasions, just like other ministers or priests, and never attributed his presence to any other reason than the usual consultations Pharaoh had with different people. But remembering the rumors and seeing Apophis' solemn attitude, this visit seemed different. What was its purpose? None of them broached this as they went to their respective homes. But a few hours later, Adom came to see Tiempo.

This was a rare occurrence, so Tiempo knew Adom needed something desperately.

"You and I have many differences," he said. "And I know we each sometimes hate the other. That is the truth. We have fought each other, physically and for a woman. But we also work well together as Pharaoh's trusted confidantes, even killing together. Nothing binds us more than the common blood we have on our hands. I hope you agree with me."

"Adom, why do you say all this?"

"As you know, I now have a threat that must be eliminated."

"What threat is that?"

"Tiempo, let us not pretend here. You know what I am talking about."

"Let's say that I do. Why are you here?"

"Isn't it obvious? I need your help to get rid of the threat."

"You don't need my help. Whatever you need to do, you can do yourself. I will not be implicated."

"Think about it, Tiempo. If the alliance we have should unravel, all of us will be in trouble. We must stand together."

"This from a man who has threatened to kill me?"

"You have tried to kill me too, Tiempo. Your motivations for survival are no different from mine."

"Listen, Adom, I know you feel threatened, but the threat you see is not as you think. The threat is prone to jest and joy, not reasoned hardness as you. Pharaoh will turn back to you if he ever picked him over you. And Pharaoh knows you know too much to maltreat you. I think you should look at things over the long term. Your long term position is assured. I am not the one who should be telling you this, given how much you have become a rival and a nuisance. But facts are facts. If I were you, I would go home, relax, and let things play out."

"He has been contradicting my account of the plagues to Pharoah. I can't have that."

"Many of us have."

"You are not priests."

"It does not matter."

"So you will not help me?"

"Exactly what would you have me do?"

"You know what I need."

"The only help I will give is the advice I have given."

"In that case, I have no other choice but to follow your advice and wait it out and see how things turn out. But I remain very worried."

"That is normal, but trust me, you will prevail and if he is elevated, your perceived threat will return to where he feels most comfortable: the shadows where he can engage in his trivialities."

"You are saying this because he is your friend."

"So why do you ask me for help, knowing this?"

"You have access as a friend that I don't. You can make things easier."

"Adom, you are worrying too much. As I said, relax."

After Adom left, Tiempo weighed his options, wondering whether to warn Apophis to be more careful, but decided that might start a cascade of undesirable events. If Apophis panicked and took preemptive action that, given his nature, was likely to fail. The man was just not the type to engage in hardcore conflict. Tiempo decided to monitor events and see how they unfolded and only intervene if they became imminently dire.

He did not imagine that two days later Apophis would be found dead in the room of one of his consorts. No one suspected foul play, attributing his demise to his over-exertions. No one except Tiempo. He cried for his friend and for Thema, but he did not know what to do.

He went to see Thema and she was even more devastated than he had imagined, this for a man who had been blatantly untrue to her. But that did not matter because the man was a force of life, an ever pleasant presence, a joy-giver in many ways. No wonder Pharaoh had liked him and always sought his company and the ease it provided, even if he may have ignored his counsel. Tiempo would miss him and if what Thema felt for Apophis was even half of what he felt for Sharifa, then this loss would never heal and Thema would die, spiritually, and her physical death would be precipitated because of the pain. Her deeply bloodshot eyes, tears that would not be stanched, wailing that would not be syncopated with breath-catching, were clear evidences of this. And then Tiempo thought of how Apophis' body of flesh and vitality would be mummified into a dryness that was as still as stone. And Tiempo wept.

# Archeology of Geneses

Tiempo went to see Adom, looking for ways to disarm the priest, anything to gain advantage over him, to get him to admit to murdering Apophis as well as to back away from Sharifa. He recalled Sharifa's advice to wait and bide their time, but it was no longer sound because it seemed Adom had become desperate. He had no strategy, but Tiempo hoped by confronting the older man, he would be able to prevail somehow, that the circumstances of the confrontation would offer their own solutions. Tiempo had tried a physical duel and failed, so he was clutching at anything he could find. First, he would get Adom to admit that the priest had no meaningful connection with Sharifa and should therefore acquiesce and then he would finish off with having him admit to the murder. In his desperation, the only thing Tiempo could conjure was the common story with Sharifa that they were both found on the Nile. "I am a child of life," he told Adom. "I am a child of the Nile. And so is Sharifa. She is a child of the Nile too. We are destined for each other. You are just an intruder, and you don't belong."

"Child of the Nile!" Adom said, adding a throaty laugh totally without mirth.

"You are jealous," Tiempo said.

"That is what you would like to believe and you can believe falsehoods if you like."

Now it was time for Tiempo to reciprocate the mirthless laugh, though his was a little more tepid, for he knew that the story of discovery on the Nile was untested.

"I know it sounds refreshing to hear," Adom said, "but if no one has told you the truth, I will. It's about time you knew."

"What truth?" Tiempo asked.

"If you will be patient enough to listen, I will tell you."

Tiempo opened up his arms to gesture for Adom to continue. And he did:

Egypt had gone to war with its neighbor, Kush, during the reign of Pharaoh Thutmose I. It was an intense fight with neither side victorious; but each side had suffered significant casualties and had significant numbers of wounded warriors to nurse. Both sides began to mutually retreat in recognition of the stalemate, but it seemed one soldier of the Kushites was not prepared to concede to the equipoise. He charged forward with spear in hand towards the retreating Egyptian army, his compatriots yelling at him to return to them. He would not listen. The Egyptians saw the charging soldier with surprise and awe: either he was the bravest man alive or the stupidest, for this solo effort was suicidal. Stunned momentarily into inaction, the Egyptian soldiers continued to watch him advance. And for a glorious moment, with the setting sun in the foreground, profiling his fast advancing body, he seemed invincible, even mythical, capable of executing some heroic act.

He was soon upon the Egyptian forces, thrusting and piercing, and as they now tasted the fatal capabilities of this man, they started fighting back. And there were many of them upon him, the Kushite in the middle still felling the Egyptians with acrobatic moves, eluding them, pushing back, piercing them. For a while, it appeared the entire Egyptian army would succumb to the phenomenon attacking them. Until the commander, standing a distance off, unleashed his arrow. It hit the man in the shoulder and, as he fell, one fist blow to his head thrust him into total blackness.

## SEASONS of FOUR FACES

At that time, the Egyptians thought they had only him to contend with, but then in the next moment another was running towards them, also oblivious to the calls of her people for her to cease her advance. She was unarmed, shouting, "Do not kill him!" Now wiser, weapons were drawn to strike her down, but the commander of the army directed that no one at tack her. As they watched her approach, she said, "I am a healer; allow me to heal him." But at that very moment, the commander unleashed his arrow, piercing her in the shoulder, just like the man, and she too fell.

The Kushites by now had retreated even farther and had not come after the two, probably presuming them dead in the hands of the Egyptians. But the Egyptian commander had noticed the bravery of the two. He was a great marksman and therefore would not have missed; so it was obvious he could have killed them with his arrows, but had chosen to strike with those that did not cause instant death, and to pierce their bodies in places that would not kill them. The Egyptians had carried the two with them and, under the strict instructions of the commander, nursed them back to health, given each to separate women renowned for their healing prowess.

But the strange part of the story, which even Adom could not explain, was that neither could recall their past when they regained full consciousness. And it was not clear why. Had each mind somewhat voided itself of memories on account of the trauma of the army commander's arrows? Did the arrows contain some magical powers that rid them of memory? Had they felt betrayed so deeply in the subconsciousness that their compatriots had not come to rescue them that they had developed some form of psychosomatic amnesia? Had the women who nursed them voided their memories with strange concoctions? One theory held that a medicine woman had given them concoctions to erase their prior memories. Regardless, their bravery was evident and their presence deemed a potential asset to Egypt. When Pharaoh Thutmose I was informed, after consulting with his priests, he agreed that they be kept, but to make them fully Egyptian, no one was to tell them their past. Instead, like Moses, they would be deemed children of the Nile. Anyone who breached this was to be put to death. It was miraculous that no one had breached this order, as it was that neither Tiempo nor Sharifa remembered their past. The magical powers of the army commander, since dead, and the women who nursed them and became their mothers, must have been poignant and total.

"That is nonsense," Tiempo said. "False. Deliberately outrageous and contrived not to be believed but to confuse."

"Your choice, if you choose not to believe the truth."

"And how did you know this?"

"Don't forget that I have been close to the palace for a long time and I have seen pharaohs come and pharaohs go."

"Your story is false," Tiempo said again. "It's interesting, but false. But assuming that it is true, why are you telling me now, breaking the order of silence?"

"You are a brave man," Adom said, "but apart from your bravery, you are not special. I want you to know that. The Nile did not produce you, nor are you some special gift of the gods. And I am old now. All those who know the story are dead or about to die. Those who ordered the secrecy are dead. I feel liberated to tell you."

"So, then," Tiempo said, "Sharifa and I have a strong bond, according to your own story."

"It is not my own story. It is the true story. And, yes, you do have a bond, but that I stand a chance with her should tell you that the bond you have is irrelevant. And I want you to know that. Think about it, Tiempo, if I wanted to lie to you, do you think I would include the part about your Kush kinship with Sharifa?"

"Perhaps it is part of your well-crafted concoction to lend credibility to your story. And no such secret could have been kept hidden for so long."

"You and I are not necessarily prone to such things, but you will be surprised how seriously people take oaths made to Pharaoh, their god, and how the threat of death can keep people silent."

"Even my mother at the point of her death?"

"It is an oath she made to her Pharaoh and the gods; she could not break it on the brink of entering the afterlife."

"How do you explain that both Sharifa and I have forgotten this?"

"As I have said, I can't explain that, but I have given you credible theories. Pick one. In any case, life is full of mysteries we don't understand and can't explain."

So then, which was true? Tiempo had come to do the unarming, but he was the one who had been unarmed. He was so perturbed by this story, even if he tried not to show it to Adom, that he neglected to bring up the death of Apophis.

BENJAMIN KWAKYE

# Battling the Unknown

The hail and fire that fell on Egypt next appeared to be the breaking point, a form of inflexion, as the suffering it inflicted, while not the first or most painful when compared to the previous plagues, seemed to push the people to their limit. The death of humans and beasts became a rallying point for the call to Pharaoh to concede. Many elders petitioned Pharaoh to let the Hebrews go, for Moses was more than normal and his God possessed great power. And Pharaoh considered relenting, asking Moses to petition his God to end the pain in exchange for the freedom of the Hebrews, who so far seemed immune to the plagues.

Pharaoh called his inner circle of three.
    Tiempo told Pharaoh, "You know I am not one to step away from a fight, but this fight is not one we can win. We are not fighting flesh and blood, and if we were, we would prevail as we have won all the seventeen wars we have fought. Please, my king, let the Hebrews go. Apophis would agree, were he alive."
    Adom winced, but Sharifa seconded this: "Egypt will be in a much worse place if you don't heed this call, Great Pharaoh. Look at the harm he has inflicted, and please listen to the voice of the suffering masses."
    But Adom beat his chest in anger. "Great Pharaoh," he said, "this is contrary to my advice and an insult to the gods."
    "Do not bring the gods into this, Adom," Tiempo said. "They are not fighting this battle."
    "Do not anger the gods," Adom replied. "How dare you!"
    "Listen to reason," Sharifa said. "This is not a fight for us

or the gods."

"Great Pharaoh," Adom entreated, "do not let Egypt be humiliated; do not let the cowardice..."

"Cowardice?!" Tiempo yelled. "Where were you when we were fighting on the battlefield? Who are you to call anyone a coward?"

"And you think it is bravery to kill a man? Try warring a god and triumphing. That is what I do all day for Egypt, fighting the gods of our enemies. Where do you think you would be but for my solicitations to the gods any time you go to war? Do you know how many gods I have conquered in the spiritual realm in order that you prevail on the battlefield?"

"The man is full of pride and nonsense now," Tiempo said.

"Enough of this," Pharaoh said. "I did not call you here to fight one another. We have enough of that out there. I need your advice on how we deal with the shame of what just happened, when the voice of the former slave becomes the command of Pharaoh."

"But Great Pharaoh," said Adom, "we don't need to deal with this ignominy. Please hear me out. I know the fear is that we are fighting the God of Moses, a great God who will continue to bring plagues on us if we don't let the Hebrews go. But that is not the case."

"We have heard all this before," said Tiempo.

"Let him finish," said Pharaoh.

"But my king..." Sharifa began.

"Let him finish!" Pharaoh insisted.

"Thank you, Great Pharaoh," Adom said. "I will admit that Moses is a sorcerer and has found an ability to see certain things before they happen. But everything that has happened is due to natural phenomena."

"Then how do you explain the strange hail?" Tiempo asked.

"That is easy to explain. I told you of the volcanic explosion that is causing a chain of reactions. The moisture in the atmosphere forms ash crystals that form hailstones."

"This is nonsense," Tiempo said. "The priest does not make any sense."

"He makes sense to me," said Pharaoh.

"But, my king..."

"No, Tiempo, I have heard enough."

"What would Apophis say?" Tiempo asked.

"Do not bring him into this," Pharaoh said, almost tearing up at the mention of his dead friend's name.

"You will change your mind?" Tiempo asked. "You will not let Moses and his people go?"

"I will take all the advice I have received into consideration and decide whether to rescind my decision to let them go. You will hear of my decision soon."

After this meeting, Tiempo went to visit Amun. It was late, so the boy was almost asleep in his room. The boy was growing so strong, excellent at wrestling, boxing, rowing, and archery, among others. He would make a great king someday, Tiempo concluded, as he left the palace.

As Tiempo feared, Pharaoh reversed himself. He would not let the Hebrews go, engendering an eighth plague of locusts on the land, eating all in sight that the previous plagues had not already destroyed or consumed, bringing weeping and great gnashing of teeth all over Egypt and even greater clamor from the people for Pharaoh to free the Hebrews or otherwise risk Egypt's annihilation. Pharaoh of great victories fumed and ranted, as he again consulted with counselors, priests and gods, sometimes invoking Apophis' name and lamenting that his one sure source of peace was dead. The priests urged him to free the Hebrews—all, except the chief among them, the one whose opinion mattered the most to Pharaoh. Although Adom spoke against freeing the Hebrews, the opposition was so strong that Pharaoh pleaded with Moses to ask his God to end the invasion of the locusts in exchange for the freedom of the Hebrew people in Goshen.

As soon as the plague ended Adom went to see Pharaoh, but he would not grant him audience until Tiempo and Sharifa arrived. "I want them to hear this," Pharaoh said. "You three are my most trusted counselors." And once again Adom provided a natural explanation for the locust invasion: the coldness of the waters had caused a decrease in body temperature that made the insects land en masse.

"Insanity!" Tiempo yelled, but not to Pharaoh, who, as had become his modus operandi, promised to think about the matter and then decide. Despite the numerous plagues and the promise to free the Hebrews, he would not do so. Not then or ever! He was the Great Pharoah; the scion of slaves would not cow him.

# BENJAMIN KWAKYE

# Tasting Darkness

Darkness was the next promised and fulfilled plague. Darkness as palpable as skin. Darkness that could be tasted. Darkness that transcended all experience. Darkness that was deeper than the opposite of light. Darkness that would not wane. Darkness that was much deeper and mightier than the night that Tiempo loved. Echoes as deep as pain resounded from home to home: We cannot take this catacombic darkness anymore. "I will free these people," Pharaoh pledged, asking Moses to petition his God once again. This time, he would truly let the Hebrew people go! But as soon as light came, as soon as Adom could find his voice, Pharaoh was once again willing to listen to the alternative explanation to the divine puppeteering asserted by Moses: The sea water bubbled up and had a major blowout that caused an eruption creating a cloud of ash that engulfed Egypt and plunged it into that tactile darkness. Hold on, Great Pharaoh, this will soon pass, entreated the chief priest, and the people will thank you for standing strong, not succumbing to a bearded, old stutterer with a magician's tricks. Hold on, Great Pharaoh, and forget not how these Hebrews have built the land and the gap that will be left if we no longer have their labor. The people calling for you to free them will then be angry with you. Hold on, Great Pharaoh. And Pharaoh did, holding on in uncertain hope, listening to the convenient voice of his chief priest that soothed his pride and put a scab over his wound. Indeed, he was the Great Pharoah. No one dictated terms to him!

# Song of the Ghosts

Alone with him, Tiempo and Sharifa were hoping that Adom would bring down the erected facade of supernatural confidence mixed with natural wisdom that had so far managed to skew Pharaoh's perception. They, being Tiempo and Sharifa, hoped that they could overcome differences with Adom, real and perceived, as they had done that night when the three of them had marched into the night to change destiny, not only of a queen and a prince, but of a nation. That solidarity had to count for something, that blood of destiny. Power that had soiled their hands, or rather glued them irrevocably together, must now come to their aid, like water in the desiccated desert, to bring about one purpose, if for no other reason, then to save Egypt. From Moses. From his God. So they had picked the night as a symbolic tribute to that other night of destiny and gone to see him.

Adom welcomed them even before they announced themselves. "You have come to apologize for the error of your ways," he said, disarming them for a moment with the audacity of his expectation, or the presumption of it. "You are forgiven, but before you go on I must tell you of the song of the ghosts."

"Song of the ghosts?" Tiempo asked. "What is that?"

Adom narrated that he had heard the ghosts of the land and they had sung to him a song that disturbed him. He spoke as a man possessed of the song he had heard and he began to recite the song in a voice that was at once hoarse and deep, throaty and indicative of something otherworldly. He sang at times loudly and at times softly:

> We are the ghosts of this land and we are not happy. Over our backs the land was built, when the earth cracked, we walked it; when it healed, we harvested from it. We never surrendered to the deception of any time. We were never in despair when the harvest was meagre, only determined, learning and growing. On our backs great structures were erected. We were the giants who roamed it and made it ours. We have fought and triumphed, and even in defeat, we persevered. We never looked away from any challenge. We are the ghosts of Egypt.

If Adom expected applause after this, he was disappointed, for Tiempo simply cleared his throat, his quick sideways glance at Sharifa a furtive gesture for moral boosting authority to speak on their behalf.

She gave it with an equally furtive nod, and ignoring Adom's so called song of the ghosts, said, "We are prepared to apologize for whatever may have caused you offense, but on one condition."

"The beggar does not issue conditions," Adom said.

"We would not call ourselves beggars," Sharifa said.

"Let me hear your condition," Adom replied.

This time Sharifa was the one seeking permission with their unplanned modus operandi for speaking on behalf of the group of two. Permission by nod granted, she proceeded: "We know you are the chief priest and we know you are closer to the gods than any of us. But we are now facing a situation where the very future of the land is at stake, our very survival is at risk. Consider all that Moses has made us endure." Adom's face twitched at the mention of the name Moses, but he said nothing. Sharifa continued, "How much more do we have to endure before you drop this charade?"

"Charade?" Adom shot back. "Why would you call this a charade?"

"Adom, we all want to gain greater favor with Pharaoh. The day we went out into the night at his request to do what we did, that was the height of it. So we know each one of us will do all we can to look good before him, but this is carrying it too far?"

"What are you saying, Sharifa?"

"Adom, stop deceiving Pharaoh that all that has been happening to us has a natural explanation revealed to you by the gods."

"You think he is that gullible? So not only are you accusing me of deception, but you now are calling Pharaoh a fool? You are willing to call the revelations that gods have provided false?"

"No one is calling him a fool, nor insulting the gods," Sharifa said. "We know Pharaoh is wise and brave. But now he is in a very vulnerable place, where a Hebrew who was rescued from among slaves has come issuing commands to him. It is humiliating. All this at a time when he has lost his childhood friend Apophis. And it is obvious that Moses is carrying some form of power that we cannot contend with."

"What foolishness!" Adom yelled. "I warn you, you are insulting the gods, who have revealed things to me. The gods have revealed to me that Moises is just a seer of sorts. And he is taking advantage of that to pretend that he is a great prophet, and in the process intimidating weaklings like you. I am so thankful we at least have a leader who is wise enough to side with the gods."

Tiempo was surprised that Adom addressed Sharifa so

offensively. Had the priest decided he was losing the battle to Tiempo and therefore had little to gain? "Stop this nonsense, Adom," he said. "You are only a prophet of illusions. Either you are making this up or you are not hearing well from the gods. If you heard from the gods, how come they do not stop these plagues until Moses stops them, until Pharaoh appeals to him to stop them?"

"These are nothing but natural phenomenon that Moses is simply taking advantage of."

"Then why have our gods not stopped him, I ask again?"

"The gods act as they wish and we can only supplicate, we cannot command them to do anything. They will intervene when they know it is right to do so."

"You are nothing but a charlatan!" Tiempo said.

"You insult me?"

"I do."

"Have you forgotten whom you are speaking to? I can kill you both if I want to!"

"Go ahead. Do it. I am tired of your threats."

The two men were now closer to each other, almost spitting into each other's faces, sending all signals that a physical fight was about to ensue from the verbal version.

"Adom," Sharifa called. "Adom, please calm down."

"Calm down? Why don't you tell him to calm down? You are now totally on his side, are you not? After all I've done for you, after all we have enjoyed together, Sharifa?"

There seemed too much ammunition in Adom's words and all Sharifa could manage for a short while was mouth gaping without words. But she found her voice again and said, "Fighting won't solve anything at this time, not now when Egypt needs us, not now when our king needs us. We have done much for him together, let us now stand together to help him."

"You are calling for peace, but peace comes at a price," said Adom.

"What price?" Tiempo asked.

Adom's stained teeth glistened in the darkness on account of the false grin that bespoke his proposal. "I know Sharifa has told you of our bargain, just as much as she has told me yours. Let's settle it all now and forever."

"What are you saying?" Tiempo asked.

"Stop pursuing her. Leave her to me and all this will end."

"Adom, you insult me so?" Sharifa asked. "You do not ask me to choose?"

"Let us settle this," said Adom. "Man to man, between Tiempo and me."

"No!" Sharifa said. "I choose whom I want."

"Before you choose," said Adom, "remember choices have consequences and some choices hate their consequences, and whatever you decide will lead to something good or bad."

"Sharifa," Tiempo said, "don't let him goad you."

"I'm getting tired of bargains, secrets and open secrets," Sharifa said.

"Make your choice then," said Adom.

Sharifa stared long moments at Adom, fuming, chests heaving, and then for shorter moments at Tiempo. She sighed. And sighed. And sighed. And sighed.

"One will go to war to win my heart. One will kill the one who will go to war if and when he can. Both are treating me like a trophy, trampling on my emotions. And now one asks me to choose. The other would rather let his bargain play out. And so tonight, I choose. Tonight I choose. Tonight, I choose. Tonight, I choose."

"And you choose which one?" Adom asked.

"I choose neither."

"What?" Adom asked.

"I choose neither one of you," Sharifa said.

"Sharifa," Tiempo said.

"I have decided."

"What about our bargain?" Tiempo asked.

"Revoked when you asked me to choose."

"But I did not ask you to choose," Tiempo protested. "Adom did."

"You went to him to fight over me," she replied.

"You have made the biggest mistake of your life," Adom said. "You are not being truthful, Sharifa. Your decision not to choose is a choice. It's a choice for Tiempo. You love him and will not reject him. I know it. I have been a fool to think that I could change that. All bargains rejected, you want me to spare his life, but by your insult, you might as well have replaced his life with yours."

"What is that supposed to mean?" Sharifa asked.

"I have spoken," Adom said. "This meeting is over. Now leave!"

And he was right. There was nothing more to be said among them. And as they left, Tiempo, tempted as he was to talk to Sharifa, seek clarification, entreat her, knew it would be premature. Hearts were too heavy, thoughts saturated with fiery matters of emotion. These had to cool before conversations of any import. He would have to wait for a later day, comforted by his own belief that Sharifa loved him, confirmed by Adom's words, and that she had said what she had said for expedience, to reduce the tension of the moment that could have exploded, even with fatal effect. So they left Adom's house in silence and, in attention grabbing silence, walked through the loudness of the night that resided within each one of them.

BENJAMIN KWAKYE

# Singing of Woe

In the darkness of a night, where we lay our scene, where ancient fears break to new misery: a night of woes and gnashing of teeth, of tears and anguish; and, a night that held death over each house and opened its nostrils wider, exhaling a vapor of lifelessness over households, a foul, fatal breath, but over firstborns only. It spared no first born, including those of the highest nobility, except those in Goshen. And Pharaoh, if he had held out hope that he could wait out whatever ruin Moses' God wreaked on Egypt, wept on his knees with the death of Prince Amun, his firstborn son. His wailing voice joined those of the rest of Egypt in the dawn hours when the realization, the unblinking reality of death, swept through the land. All of Egypt, except of course, Goshen.

Pharaoh's wailing typified that of his people, and it was as if the land itself wept too, ready to give up its ghost, if indeed it had any to give, for plagues and death had sucked everything out of the land. In the morning hours, in rooms and in alleys, the gloom that sat over Egypt was as palpable as the night that had stolen souls.

When Tiempo arrived at Pharaoh's palace upon a quick summons, Sharifa was already there, sitting in silence with the king, their faces staring downward as in defeat and surrender. Tiempo was used to that look of defeat on the battlefield. He had seen it again and again, when a man's life was on the verge of being snuffed out by another, and a look sometimes laced with the fear of imminent death or the knowledge of surrender, or both. All of which he now traced with his trained eyes in Pharaoh's fallen countenance of tearful eyes and drooping lips, which was mirrored in Sharifa's. Tiempo broke down as he tried to express his condolences, his love for the dead Amun straining his every emotion. The pain was deep, the death of the young man who was almost a son to him. The king acknowledged the expression of condolences in a voice barely audible, hoarse with pain and wailing. Tiempo did not know what to do, or for what purpose he had been summoned, except to surmise that Pharaoh needed counseling. Tiempo acknowledged silently the absence of Adom, hopeful that Pharaoh had deliberately excluded him from the group. Obviously, there was no way the man could explain the recent silent carnage of first born deaths.

Pharaoh stared at Adom when Adom arrived later, a hard stare, an accusatory stare. "What is your explanation now?" Pharaoh asked.

Tiempo wanted to yell out with every vocal energy possible that the chief priest had none and that nothing he could concoct this time was worthy of any moment of consideration, this craving to speak restrained only in consideration of the solemnity of the moment, the palpably aching spirit of Pharaoh. "Great Pharaoh," Sharifa ventured, "if I may speak."

"You may," Pharaoh said.

"If I may humbly say so, I do not think the man has any good word for us. It's his advice that has led us all to this point, Great Pharaoh."

"What are you saying, Sharifa?"

"Great and wise Pharaoh, I think we can safely say that the chief priest is a false priest."

"My king..." Adom began to protest.

"Do you realize what you are saying, Sharifa? If true, his

only worthy punishment is death. Should I put him to death?"

"Your punishment, Great Pharaoh, your punishment of him, I leave to you, but we should no longer allow him to claim the voice of the gods."

"My king..." an agitated Adom began to protest.

Once again, Pharaoh stopped him. "And you, Tiempo, what do you think?"

"I think Sharifa has spoken wisely. Adom has led us to this with his false explanations. This can no longer be allowed to continue."

"My king," Adom said, "please hear me out."

"The way they are accusing you, your own compatriots think I should put you to death," Pharaoh said. "And I don't see why I should disagree."

His body twitching, Adom said, "Great Pharaoh, please, I beg of you, hear me out."

Pharaoh waited a long moment before saying, "Very well, I will give you a hearing. But it better be good."

"Great Pharaoh," Adom said immediately. But then it took him a while to continue, in obvious stress and strain to pick the perfect words for his defense. "What happened tonight has a perfect natural explanation..."

"Not again!" Tiempo interjected.

"Let him finish," Pharaoh said.

"What happened was from a fog of bad air. It is the same type of air we exhale. We inhale good air and exhale bad air. This time, because of the Santorini volcanic eruption I mentioned before, the bad air escaped from the rivers in a large quantity and flowed on to the land and then into rooms, suffocating the sleeping and then escaping and dissipating into the air."

"So you expect us to believe that this bad air does not kill us and yet kills our firstborns?" Tiempo asked.

"When we breathe, we breathe out such small quantities that it causes no harm. But in this case, it came in a large, condensed form that is fatal," Adom said.

"Even if so," said Sharifa, "how is it possible that it only killed the firstborns? Everyone breathes air in the night, even when sleeping. So how is it that others did not die?"

"Where do firstborn sons sleep, Sharifa?"

"What?"

"Just answer the question?"

"Everyone knows they sleep on their beds low to the ground."

"Exactly! The air was flowing at a low level as it moved through houses, causing death to those at lower levels, the first born sons, and then it left without lifting to higher ground, sparing those sleeping at higher levels."

"Unbelievable," said Tiempo.

"And how do you know all this?" Pharaoh asked.

"The gods revealed this to me," Adom said.

"And what do they say we do know?"

"My king," Sharifa said, "there is one more question I would like to ask Adom. How come the firstborns of the Hebrews did not die?"

"The bad air did not reach them. It's a matter of location."

"This is impossible to believe," Tiempo said.

"So, I ask again, what do the gods say we do now?" Pharaoh said.

"Great Pharaoh," Tiempo said, "there is only one thing to do now. Let the Hebrews go and leave us in peace."

Pharaoh ignored this entreaty and asked Adom again, "One more time I ask, what do the gods say we should do?"

"They have not told me yet," Adom replied.

"You are a god too, Great Pharaoh," said Sharifa. "You can decide this on your own. Let the Hebrews go."

"I do not doubt you, Adom, that you believe that the gods have revealed these things to you, and for that I will spare your life," Pharaoh said. "But you have said yourself that the gods have not given you direction on this matter, and so I will decide this time."

"Great Pharaoh, sometimes we have to be patient as we wait for the gods to speak and give us direction."

"I do not have time! Our people have suffered enough. I cannot wait for all of Egypt to perish. I will let his people go!"

"Great Pharaoh..." Adom began.

"It is final. So shall it be done!"

And so it was issued, the decree to free the Hebrews, and not only that, but also for the Egyptians to provide them with gold. The humiliation was uncensored and total and the response of the Egyptian body politic was of murmurings at the same time as it was of relief, great relief.

SEASONS of FOUR FACES

# Embracing the Clouds

For Tiempo, this was a period of monumental uncertainty. Having a sluggish Egypt pained him, for he was a man of war, but the country was in no mood for war. They could only hope that they were not attacked. Tiempo could command the army, but the tattered morale of the force might be their greatest weakness—men who had lost so much, including many who had lost their firstborn sons in the cruel stealth of the night. And then there was the unbalanced relationship with Sharifa. The night weighed heavily on him. His thoughts were suffused with the many deaths at his hands, many on the field of battle, some in their homes, and one in her own bed chamber. He would not admit it to anyone, how their ghosts haunted his many dreams of gore and blood, until they had become part of his nocturnal landscape and soundscape. With such despair in the land and in him as he looked to a future, at least in the near future, all seemed bleak, except if he could find a way to repair the breach with Sharifa.

As these thoughts turned heavy, his eyes closed and he kept them closed for a long time, hoping he could slip into the oblivion of a dreamless sleep.

And then suddenly he felt something tactile on his neck. And for a very brief moment of uncertainty, he thought his thoughts had moved from the mentally graphic to a psychosomatic realm where they were beginning to choke him. But in the next immediate moment a smell, primal and earthy and acrid, was penetrating his nostrils. And then he realized this had nothing to do with his mind or imagination. When he opened his eyes, the man whose massive hands were choking him, with an ovate torso, seemed to be smiling as he proceeded to say,

"Die, traitor."

Tiempo saw a second man behind this one, dagger in hand, apparently ready to use the weapon in aid of his colleague. Their first mistake was not using the dagger as the first means of attack, but these were men, he reckoned, who enjoyed the slowness of the death, the joy of slowly squeezing the life out of an adversary. But with this opening he brought every energy in his warrior body to bear, every survival instinct and focus, and he moved his hands up, surprising the attacker who must have imagined that he had weakened Tiempo past any possibility of a meaningful reaction. Seizing the man's surprise to his advantage, Tiempo managed to pry the man's hands a little loose and then take second advantage to punch his attacker in the face. As the man loosened his hold to touch his bruised nose, Tiempo freed himself totally, seeing the man with the dagger lunge forward for the plunge. Second mistake, for his body now free, he used the first man's body as shield, and his compatriot's dagger found him. Before either attacker could react, Tiempo was completely off his bed, standing across it from the man who had the dagger, which he pulled out of the other man's body, the latter now writhing in what would turn out to be the throes of death. And then in a quick movement, Tiempo kicked the dagger out of the man's hand, too far for either man to reach it without turning his back on the other. Equally unarmed, they each lunged forward, body against body, head butting head, limb slithering in trying to escape from a hold. It was an arm to arm combat as familiar to Tiempo as air, but for a long time, it was balanced. Breathless, the men had one short moment apart, when Tiempo, out of somewhere deep in memory, put disparate images together. "I know you," he said, "as he gasped for breath from the exertions of the fight. The images of the past prevailed, coming closer and clearer under the focus, into what was becoming familiar. Images here and there of a man behind Adom, a man whispering to Adom, a man taking something from Adom.

"Adom sent you," Tiempo said. "He sent you to kill me, didn't he?"

Like a man whose camouflage unexpectedly betrays him, the man started to say something and then seemingly unnerved by the exposure, dashed out of the room. Tiempo considered going after him but decided against it, for at that moment the concern that seized him like a fever was Sharifa. If he had been attacked, would Adom not go after Sharifa as well? So instead of chasing after the assailant, he ran, faster than he could ever have imagined, to Sharifa's house.

He had easy entry as all the doors were open, forcing a chilling foreboding. He didn't want to consider it, but the word dangled before the eyes of his mind.

Death.

He rushed into the rooms that were as hollow as vacuum. Where was Sharifa? Tiempo recalled the death of Hatshepsut. Had something similar happened to Sharifa? Tiempo shivered with fear, but he could not dwell on the fear and he rushed to Adom's house, and found it like an echo of Sharifa's: totally devoid of human presence.

What had happened to Sharifa? Where was Adom?

Tiempo could not organize his thoughts as he went home, nor did he have any success when he sat down, his mind focused on the possibility that Adom's man or men might return and on the possibility, even probability, that Sharifa was dead. When his mind calmed a little, he became aware and accustomed to the presence of the corpse in his room, the man who'd been stabbed by his own compatriot. Tiempo went and sat next to it, as if by that act he was claiming some triumph over Adom, that he held authority over the dead man's body and over his soul and transition into the next life. But then other thoughts began to enter his mind. What if Adom was also dead? What if someone else had sent those men to kill him under camouflage that Adom had sent them? What if that person wanted all three of them dead? But who would that person be? Much as he hated to reach the conclusion, he could not escape the probability that it was Pharaoh himself. He had the motive, did he not? What if he blamed all three for his predicament? After all, they had all been there when Adom advised him, and though they had protested at times, especially at the end, had he found their protests too weak? And even beyond that, did Pharaoh not have another reason to kill all three of them? They who had obeyed his request to kill so that he could ascend the throne, was he now, in his utmost point of vulnerability trying to erase any possibility that they might reveal the secret, and perhaps plunge his popularity even lower than where it stood, pressured by the humiliation of Moses and the of the gold of Egypt?

At that moment, Tiempo believed, truthfully or falsely, that Pharaoh wanted him dead, that Pharaoh had killed both Sharifa and Adom. If this was true, then he was living on borrowed time, for if the modest attempt had failed, the next one word be bolder and designed to succeed at all costs. So what was he to do? Remaining in Egypt was suicidal. He reflected on the story of Moses, who at some point had lost favor with the pharaoh and had therefore fled, only to return to claim a victory none would have imagined. That seemed his only choice. With Pharaoh against him and with Sharifa dead, his only chance of survival was to act as Moses did and leave the land. Perhaps someday he too could return to etch a victory as Moses had done. Tiempo looked at the dead man in his room and wept for him. He wept for all the men like him who had died for a cause, sometimes so nebulous that its essence was in the fight itself rather than any grand cause the victory served. He too could have died, in fact had nearly died, in the service of the victories for Egypt.

But now that he had lost so much, he questioned the cause for which he had fought.

Sharifa.

Why hadn't he been more forceful, more passionate, more forthcoming? Tiempo pulled himself forcefully from his mental ruminations in the abrupt break from them he needed in order to make his bold move. His friend the night was waiting to carry him to his next destination. Uncertain where the pathways and uncharted ways would lead him, Tiempo stepped into the dark openness of the night, the new life (or death) awaiting him unknown.

# PART II

# CHAPTER

# 1

*"That is all you see because you don't have greater sight,"*
*Kouyate said.*

## Dancing with Wind

Mansa Musa wasn't sure what to make of the account whirling like a great wind. He had not heard of such combined cheekiness, valor and strength in a long time, if ever, and as the accounts grew more intense he began to ponder whether it was a creation of human imagination, this uncommon strength that defeated so many, this human who seemed to have the energy of a god. From time to time, he reckoned, there emerged a mortal of such uncommon characteristics that he or she deserved to be distinguished from others and, sometimes, the description of god, lesser only to Allah, was merited. Was this man worthy of that status? He had pondered this question in the three days since he heard about the man in vivid terms from multiple sources, and Mansa had become so restless that the accounts mutated into a haunting image that followed him everywhere. He would have liked to call it a rumor, except it would be erroneous to call it as such, since rumor connoted hearsay, but the men who told him swore they were firsthand witnesses to the man's prowess. In the daytime as he negotiated his various responsibilities and activities to the nighttime when he retired to bed, accounts about the man became both a bright shadow in the noontime and an obscure presence that shadowed Mansa Musa in the night and walked the pathways of his various dreams.

SEASONS of FOUR FACES

# The Arrival

The accounts did not vary. The man had arrived at the marketplace, at first an unnoticed solitary figure, out of focus on the fringes of a busy market day, skirting the outskirts of the market, until he walked forward into focus and notice. The tall, muscular frame gained attention just by walking into the market center but then became a kind of force when he asked for some dates from one of the traders, without offering anything in return. When she refused him, he grabbed a handful and another, eating them down in quick time. Onlookers' attention deepened when they noticed this lopsided exchange of nothing for something. If they would have admired him at first glance by virtue of his stature, this unfair bargaining with his body's menace and nothing else caused that admiration to dissipate. A nudge here and another there, a word whispered in one ear and another in another ear, and the anger of one meshed with the anger of many, noting that such brazen taking could not be countenanced. If it was stealthy thievery they could so accuse him, but there was nothing stealthy about his actions, no attempt to hide anything. Could such bold taking be described as theft? Not only that, this man, despite his actions, exuded dignity, both in his physical stature and manner of movement such that it was not easy to classify him a thief. It just didn't fit him. So all they could deem fitting to call him was Taker.

Five men first asked him to return the food he had taken. How? he asked when he'd already consumed the dates. Then he should give something in return, they asked. He had nothing to give in return, he said. Except himself. How would he give of himself? they asked. The anger of the five vented its force when one of the men defied any threat to himself (but perhaps taking safety in the support of the other four) and slapped the Taker's right cheek.

The slap, though delivered with the power of anger, did not stun the Taker, who did not even flinch. Instead, he starred at the slapper with an insouciance that should have warded off another attack, except this stare inflamed the attacker and he delivered another slap to the other cheek. Even then, the Taker did not hit back, rubbing his cheeks gently in what was even cheekier than his lack of a physical response. The Taker then seemed to chew down the last bits of dates in his mouth, as if to say a physical response was beneath him. Words were spoken and even more words, each fierier than the previous, until the wordy weapons against the Taker solidified into a circle of men that formed around him in an attempt to pierce his nonchalance. The Taker did not fight until they attacked him, twenty men, a phalanx ready to defend the honor of the one he had disrespected with nonreaction and the woman whose dates he had taken. The attack was in unison, but the response happened so fast, as if in an eye wink, that when the dust stirred by feet and bodies in motion settled, twenty men lay on the ground and only one man stood in their midst unscathed.

One by one the men stood back to their feet, but this time only about half of them moved forward to attack the Taker. And their second falling was even quicker, less than in an eye wink. As the men lay on the ground, some inspecting the swelling of body parts, the Taker walked away, many wishing that it was the last time they would see him, hoping that he was a passing sojourner.

But he would resurface the next day. This time, he was offered food when he asked for it, and none stalked him. On the third day, however, many were prepared, waiting for him on the outskirts of the market. Forty men. No exaggeration, Mansa Musa was told. Forty men, many holding daggers. They confronted him as he approached and asked him to leave Niani or die. When he refused, they all attacked at once. But it was as if they were fighting a deity with uncommon power. He would slip between men or slither under or even between bodies, and dagger holders would inadvertently stab one another. Then and now, he banged heads together, kicked a weapon from someone's hand, and punched a face or stomach. Then and now he escaped an attack with an impossible acrobatic somersault. This time, the fight took more than the blink of an eye, considering the more formidable number of people and weaponry he was facing, but in perhaps thirty or so blinks, not one attacker was standing, half of them lying in all manners of posture on the ground and half of them having bolted in wise recognition that they were bound to lose the fight. And he stood, no sweat broken, let alone dropped.

News of the results of the latest fight having preceded his arrival at the marketplace the next day, many eagerly offered him food with nervous hands without being asked.

Some would resort to surveillance after the fiasco of the latest attack. And they would discover that even darkness could not shield them from the Taker. Prince of the Moon, some would label him when a bunch of them trailed him throughout the day as he walked about Niani, seemingly tirelessly until late into the night when all of a sudden he dropped down behind someone's house and fell asleep on the ground, apparently oblivious to the elements and not in need of any comforts of a sheltered home. They waited until they were assured he was asleep, then they advanced, daggers drawn. They could not, would not, fail. And yet it seemed the man had an invisible warning system. Before they could reach him and bring their weapons down, he was up and upon them. Knowing his capability, they fled from him, rather than engage in battle.

SEASONS of FOUR FACES

# A Rendezvous of Spirits

After haunted moments, both by day and by night, and after consulting with Inari Kunate, his senior wife, and with Suleiman, his dyeli, Mansa Kankan Musa appointed a group of men to wait for the Taker at the marketplace. The next time they saw him, they were to tell him that Mansa Musa wanted to see him at the royal palace. What if he resisted? they asked. He would not, Mansa said. "From the reports I've heard, this man has only fought in response to attacks by others and he may have wounded many, but he has killed none, even when it seems he has the ability to do so." The question they did not ask and which Mansa Musa knew they wanted to ask was, what if he caused Mansa Musa harm? Clearly, he seemed unstoppable, so far unscathed by sword or word, fist or fury. If he was brought to the palace and attacked Mansa Musa, could anyone really stop him? To ask that question was to diminish Mansa Musa's stature, render him fearful of another, a stranger at that. And certainly, they expected that Mansa Musa had contemplated this possibility. But he would not fear anyone. And both Inari Kunate and the dyeli agreed with Mansa Musa that this was not a man intent on causing harm. And even if the risk existed, Mansa Musa had to see this phenomenon for himself and not allow him to grow into a potential threat.

And as he expected the man, also called the Taker, obeyed the summons, putting up no resistance in word or deed when he was informed that Mansa Musa wanted to see him.

The men escorted the Taker to the courtyard of the palace, the sun beating on them on the way. At the palace, the guards were careful with him, obeying orders not to irk him. A large number of people had already gathered in the courtyard. Removed from the crowd in the forecourt sat Mansa Musa, focused on certain petitioners as they presented their dispute to him. His golden skull cap sat firmly on his head, matching the tunic with its gold coloring around the neck area. The sandals on his feet were barely visible from the flowing tonic that reached his ankles. The Taker was immediately impressed by the grace with which Mansa Musa sat on his massive black ebony throne with big ivory tusks projecting on both sides. A man holding a kora sat at the king's feet. Beside him, someone stood on the platform on which the throne sat, holding a silk umbrella that covered the king, protecting him from the heat of the sun. Two others stood on either side of Mansa Musa, fanning him. Standing behind the king were several guards, holding long spears and shields. And several horses stood at the back of the forecourt. The Taker's breath strained under the impressive scene.

The guards told him to wait until Mansa Musa was ready for him. They did not leave his side, as he waited and watched while Mansa listened to a dispute over stolen cattle. Mansa Musa gave his orders and his dyeli shouted them to the disputing parties. The Taker had not been privy to the full debate, but he heard Mansa Musa's decision to divide the number of disputed cattle in a manner he deemed fair to the parties. More parties were brought forward to argue their disputes, some over land and some over salt and gold. Each time Mansa Musa issued his orders through the dyeli, the crowd around the Taker murmured their approval of his wise judgments.

Then when this was over, it was time for entertainment and education and the dyeli, Suleiman, who had the same name as Mansa Musa's brother, summoned a man forward and asked him to recount the Epic of Mali or portions of it as he deemed fit and as time would allow. As the man stepped forward, the man who sat at the feet of the king began to strum on his kora, producing a rhythm from the long necked instrument of twenty-one strings in the setting sun such as soothed the Taker.

The man who stepped forward, as the Taker would learn, was Ibrahim, considered a great griot and carrier of the story of Mali. His boubou was green, his skullcap white as his long beard. He began the tale of the Mandinka people of Mali, after clearing his throat several times as though he wanted reassurance from his vocal cords that they would not be an impediment to the great story he was about to dramatize solo with nothing but his voice and hand gestures and facial expressions, the intonations of his voice like a great river, sometimes at high tide and sometimes at low tide.

The griot told of the great story of Sundiata, son of the mysterious Sogolon, the hunchback, and her marriage to Maghan Kon Fatta. He told of the day a king sat under a silk cotton tree, his kinsmen surrounding him, when a man dressed as a hunter told of the men who would come with a woman, a hideous looking woman with a hunchback, whom the king must marry to produce a great heir. The king had listened and married the woman Sogolon as prophesied. The griot told of how difficult it had been to consummate the marriage, for Sogolon had repulsed his efforts until the king was exhausted, wondering whether she was human, considering how when he visited her for consummation her body was covered with long hair, as though they had sprouted like grass on her skin overnight. It took the king seeking mysterious signs in his hunter's war bag and a great confrontation with his wife before he managed to consummate the marriage and then conception of their child.

The child would be named Maghan, like his father, and also Sogolon Mari Djata. But the son was not attractive, with large eyes inside a big head he seemed unable to support. Taciturn and content to sit in the middle of the house, he did nothing; this in contrast to the lively Dankaran Touman, son of Sassouma Beret, the king's first wife. Worse, Mari Djata would not walk. He and his mother Sogolon would fall out of favor with the king and then back in favor, all this while Sassouma would not lose any opportunity to mock Sogolon and her son. Then after the king died, the council of elders picked Dankaran Touman as king, and the triumphant Sassouma Berete was even more cruel to Sogolon and Mari Djata. Then, one day, Mari Djata picked up an iron bar he had asked for and with its help stood up on his feet. Then dropped the bar and took a giant step as his griot, Balla Fasseke, cried:

> Room, room, make room!
> The lion has walked;
> Hide antelopes, get out of his way.

And with that, Sassouma Berete turned even more vicious, as Sogolon Mari Djata gained in popularity. Sogolon Djata in the Mandingo language became Sundiata, full of strength and authority at ten. Afraid that her son would lose his throne to the ever popular Sundiata, Sassouma solicited the help of nine witches to pretend to steal gorgon leaves from Sogolon's vegetable patch. But rather than chastise the nine witches and give them a basis to cause him harm, Sundiata filled their gourds with leaves, aubergines, and onions, asking them to return and stock up anytime they needed condiments and to do so without fear.

## SEASONS of FOUR FACES

Afraid for their lives, however, Sogolon fled with her son. After much travail, they ended up in Ghana under King Soumaba Cisse and later went to Mema to the court of his cousin Moussa Tounkara, a great warrior. There, Sundiata would embark on war campaigns, and it was Moussa Tounkara who would give Sundiata half of his army to free Mali after it fell under Soumaoro Kante, the king who wore robes of human skin, a man capable of appearing and disappearing at will.

Griot Ibrahim cleared his throat and mentioned how, meeting at Negueboria, with a war cry Sundiata moved against Soumaoro. Under a brilliant sun and to the sounds of trumpets, drums and bolons, Sundiata, distinguished by his white turban, came face to face with Soumaoro. Sundiata hurled a spear at Soumaoro, but this fell off Soumaoro's chest. And then Soumaoro caught Sundiata's arrow in flight and showed it to Sundiata, as if to taunt him. As Sundiata charged forward on his horse, he realized that Soumaoro had disappeared, only to see him on a hill on his black coated horse. And then he disappeared, the man who was said able to assume sixty-nine shapes.

This would be followed by a series of skirmishes and maneuverings on both sides and a war of words, including many triumphs by Sundiata. Sundiata would say that wherever he passed, death rejoiced, and so he would make death rejoice at the death of Soumaoro. But Sundiata was exasperated and unclear as to how anyone could kill the mysterious Soumaoro, until the secret was revealed to him. Nana Triban, sister of Dankaran Touman, and therefore half-sister of Sundiata, came to him and told her story, of how Dankaran Touman had forced her to marry Soumaoro. She had pretended to love him, all the while holding her admiration for Sundiata as a form of shield that kept her going and believing that Sundiata would one day return to Mali. Nana Triban had ingratiated herself with Soumaoro, becoming his confidante and managed to get him to reveal his secret. Armed with the secret, Sundiata had a deadly arrow of magical powers prepared, its tip containing the spur of a white cock.

Urged on by his griot, Sundiata went in pursuit of Soumaoro. As Soumaoro fled from the ensuing battlefield, the pursuing Sundiata threw his arrow, which flew in the air past all impediments to graze the shoulder of Soumaoro. This time, the fatal arrow performed its function, just as Nana Triban had revealed, and Soumaoro fell, his powers leaving him, gazing towards the sun as a great black bird, the bird of Krina, flew overhead. Soumaoro managed to mount his horse and take flight on horseback. When Sundiata caught up, Soumaoro entered the gaping cave of Koulikoro, connected to a river. The sorcerer king had met his end. And his city of Sosso would be razed to the ground, its fetishes and sorcerers with it, so that it would in the aftermath become a place for guinea fowls and partridges to take dust baths.

And then Sundiata would embark on numerous conquests culminating in his eventual return to Mali, and to acclaim as the villages carpeted their streets with multicolored pagnes, children holding leafy branches to welcome him, majestic on horseback in his smock and tight trousers, his bow across his back. And with his return and consolidation of power, he would rebuild Mali into a place of peace and justice. And the father of Mali would reign, feared and loved.

SEASONS of FOUR FACES

# Fire and Fire

When the griot ended the story, a palace guard told the Taker to wait until the king departed the courtyard on the back of one of the horses that had stood in the forecourt. It was only then that the Taker was taken to the inside of the palace. Standing before him, Mansa Musa could see why the man could inspire fear in many: tall, sinewy, slim. But as the Taker stood facing him, Mansa Musa (with many guards around him) did not detect any animosity from the man; and he trusted himself able to discern people, just by observing them without even speaking. It was a skill that had served him well. So for a long time he stared and studied the stranger. And even before either man spoke, both knew that they were each respectful of the other, that something promising would be harvested from this meeting.

Then finally Mansa Musa spoke, but with a smile, "So you are the man who has been terrorizing my people?"

The Taker moved forward, just by a step, and though Mansa Musa himself did not flinch or budge, the guards standing behind him drew their swords, whose use were rendered unnecessary when the man prostrated himself before Mansa Musa. After Mansa asked him to get up, the Taker, noticing the sparkle in the monarch's eyes, realized that this had not been an act of debasement but rather empowerment, that he had won over Mansa Musa. He said, "Great ruler of the great people of Mali, I have not intended to terrorize your people. If any of my actions have created that impression, I humbly ask the Great Mansa to forgive me."

Taking his time to weigh this response, Mansa Musa did not speak for a while. "I have not seen you in Niani before now," he said to break the silence, "and none of us know you. From where have you come?"

"I have come from very far, Great Mansa. Very far. I have had many journeys, walked many deserts to come here."

"And this faraway place, this place from where you have come, does this place have a name?"

"I believe it does, but it has been so long that I cannot remember its name."

"How am I to believe that you, a grown man, cannot remember the name of the land of your origins?"

"I mean no offense, Great Mansa, but I do not remember."

"You do not remember or you do not want to tell me?"

"Great Mansa, it is as I have said, that I do not remember."

Mansa Musa's pause was long. Still not detecting any hostility from the man, he finally said, "So I have heard them call you Prince of the Moon."

"It is an honor that they will call me by that, Great Mansa."

"And I have heard them call you the Taker."

"That is a name I would rather not bear, Great Mansa."

"So, tell me… What is your mission here in Niani?"

"Great Mansa," said the Taker, "I give of myself. As anyone who would take me in, I give of myself as they would lawfully have me do."

"And if no one takes you in?"

"I will continue with my journey and move on to the next place where they will have me and there I will dwell until the time comes for me to move on."

"Move on? So it seems you are not going to settle in any one place permanently?"

"If I find what I am looking for, I will have no reason to move on."

"And what are you looking for?"

"Impossible to put into words, Great Mansa."

Mansa Musa paused for another long time. "These stories I have heard about how you've fought and defeated so many, are they true?"

"I am sorry, Great Mansa, but I have had to defend myself."

"Against as many as forty men?"

"I did not take count, Great Mansa."

"Are you capable of beating forty?"

"As they have said, I am Prince of the Moon."

"You speak in riddles."

"I speak as best as I know how, Great Mansa."

He was looking at a man who could be an asset to the kingdom, Mansa Musa realized. He would not let him leave; at a minimum, he needed to test him and then, if he proved himself worthy, employ him to the benefit of Mali.

"One more question, a question I should have asked at the beginning of our conversation, Prince of the Moon: What is your name? Or have you forgotten that too?"

"No, great Mansa, I have not forgotten my name."

"Will you tell me?"

"Tiempo," he said, "my name is Tiempo."

BENJAMIN KWAKYE

# Weaving Testimonies

Mansa Musa's orders were clear and Tiempo was grateful for the gracious manner the king requested that he stop harassing the people: With a faint smile hinting at friendship, the king asked him not to go to the market foraging for food, and then as if as an afterthought, Mansa Musa added that Tiempo was not to attack anyone, even though this must have been said to appease those who were aggrieved by the defeats Tiempo had inflicted, as it was clear to all fair minded observers that Tiempo had never initiated any of the attacks that earned him notoriety, except if they deemed his taking of food without permission an attack. And in fairness, Tiempo reckoned it was indeed a form of attack, even if explained by the ravishing hunger that had spurred him. As Mansa Musa rendered judgment, his dyeli Suleiman beside him, the attending guards squeezed their faces (outside Mansa's sight) as though to register their disapproval. Aside from the order, the rest of Mansa Musa's pronouncement was elevating: Tiempo was to be under the care and observation of one of the most trusted men in Niani, a friend of Mansa Musa's. Kouyate was to house Tiempo, provide his needs and make sure that no one harassed him, this in addition to Mansa Musa's reiterated verbal edict that no one was to attack Tiempo and anyone who defied this would be answerable to Mansa himself.

# SEASONS of FOUR FACES

# Friends in the Forebodings

And so it was that Tiempo was released into the care of Kouyate, whom Tiempo found to be man of very simple tastes. A friend, and a trusted one at that, of Mansa Musa could have ridden that favor to personal wealth, but he had not, by all appearances, his modest four chambered house a testament. He lived alone, had no wives or children, and apparently ate little. But he was not averse to Tiempo's large appetite, which he met with the supply of food that was provided bountifully by the surrounding families. Why? Kouyate shrugged when Tiempo asked. Why were they so generous, providing for his small appetites but also the bigger one that Tiempo brought with him to Kouyate's house? He had simply told his neighbors he had a new guest and with that they were sure to provide for the increased need.

"Could it be because they want to find favor with Mansa Musa and your friendship brings them that favor?" Tiempo asked.

"It could be," Kouyate said, and shrugged.

The adjoining neighbors who took the most interest in the guest were Ibrahim and Mariam, a young married couple who would come over often to chat with Kouyate, and by extension Tiempo, now that he was part of the Kouyate household of two. Ibrahim usually brought his kora with him and would sometimes strum on it for several minutes as the four of them relaxed in many afternoons' dolorous hours. Sometimes he brought his bamboo flute instead, piping tunes that, though piercing, carried such gusto that Tiempo enjoyed listening and watching Ibrahim's effort. Ibrahim liked to intimate that life was to be lived in the moment, not being a form of corrigendum to be added after the living. In a few days after Tiempo's arrival at Kouyate's, Ibrahim brought a carving of a tall, muscular man with a long spear in hand and presented it as a gift, noting that it was his impression of Tiempo, whom he envisaged a warrior. It was then that he divulged to Tiempo that he was both a musician who played at the palace at times and also an artisan who sold his carvings to supplement what Mariam brought home from her days at the market. Taking note, Tiempo realized how closely Ibrahim resembled Kouyate: tall, lithe, nose extremely flat in the middle but spreading wide at the nostrils. Eyes, ever wide. Were they brothers? Yes, they said, but not biologically. They'd known each other for such a long time that they were as siblings and trusted each other completely. They could have been twins, Kouyate said, except Ibrahim was much younger, Kouyate's graying hair a sharp contrast to Ibrahim's pitch dark hair color.

And then there was Mariam, who carried her ebullience like a wind that charged the atmosphere with energy whenever they came to visit. She stood just below her husband's chin in height and, though slim, carried many curves, even showing in the flowing boubou that she liked to wear. She was always chewing on a cola nut and explained that it was to help with the nausea of her pregnancy. This would be their first child and she wanted a girl but Ibrahim wished they would have a boy. Occasionally, Tiempo visited them and was treated to the same treatment of music and conversation, and Mariam would muse over the baby she was going to have.

The rest of the neighbors who brought meals to the Kouyate household were friendly but not as welcoming as Ibrahim and Mariam. Tiempo thought them all extremely generous; but he soon uncovered what he suspected was the true basis of their generosity and even reverence.

One night, about month after he'd been staying with Kouyate, Tiempo woke up and reckoned he'd been sleeping very deeply and satisfyingly. His eyes peered into the darkness of the room. The self-consciousness was for a brief moment, as Tiempo thought he was beginning to dream and in his dream he could hear a familiar voice seizing the deep night, a voice that was human but also seemed more than human. He could not place the voice, although it sounded so familiar. And then it became more and more familiar, but the more familiar it became, the more unfamiliar it seemed. He could not fathom this contradiction for a while until the dreaminess passed and he realized that the voice was coming from the adjoining room and that it was Kouyate's. Tiempo did not want to eavesdrop, let alone intrude, but he could not resist the voice that was familiar yet so novel. The voice was soft but he could hear every word of it, with every syllable distinct, in a language he did not know.

Tiempo got out of bed and tiptoed intruder-like into the adjoining room. And what he saw... What did he see? No. It could not be. It could not. Tiempo was numbed, unable to move his body, totally immobilized at the sight. If his body failed him, let him try to use his voice, if only to convince himself that he was alive. But that too was dead, temporarily beyond resurrection at that moment when he needed some form of movement or sound to remind or rather confirm to him that he was not looking at the dead in the land of the living. Transfixed, Tiempo had no option but to observe and observe and observe because he could not even close his eyes to the spectacle.

But what did he see?

Kouyate stood in the middle of the room, naked from the

waist up, his upper torso glistening with crisscrossing sweat, the pupils of his opened eyes non-visible so that only their whites showed, shadowed by gray eyebrows, his tongue flipping in and out of his mouth with reptilian resemblance (even if it still carried a form of dignity), his arms stretched out as if he was offering something at the same time as it appeared he was receiving something, his body trembling ever so slightly. And surrounding him were at least four (they were hard to number, as they seemed to be one but separate; or, now one, now separate), and they had bodies but their bodies looked transparent and they made sounds, though they were not sounds Tiempo had ever heard or could describe. Now they moved around Kouyate, now they stood around him, now they touched him, now they moved away from him. And this went on and on and on. And then they began to fade ever so slowly until there was a nothingness where they had been. Or perhaps they had not been there at all and it had all transpired in a certain fertile portion of an imagination that Tiempo did not know existed.

Kouyate's countenance changed, the pupils reappeared and he brought his arms back to his side, then he looked at Tiempo and said, "You saw. They must have wanted you to see them."

Tiempo's self-presence returned at the moment Kouyate spoke and he could move again, and he could speak again. "Who are they?" he asked.

"Come with me," Kouyate said, as he led the way outside. Once outside, Kouyate spread out his arms as if pointing to and embracing the universe at the same time. "Now tell me, Tiempo," he said, "what do you see?"

A puzzled Tiempo said, "See?"

"Yes, what do you see?"

"The skies, the moon."

"Is that all you see?"

"I see buildings. I see some trees. I see you."

"That is all you see because you don't have greater sight," Kouyate said. "There is more than you can imagine around us, only we don't see them. I can and I do."

"So those I saw with you, they are real? I was not imagining them?"

"They are as real as you and me. Just because we don't see them, many don't think they are here with us."

"So who are they?"

"Call them spirits. Call them the departed. Call them what you will."

"They are spirits of the departed?"

"You can say that, sometimes. Sometimes I think they are more than that. Spirits that never lived like you and me. They just are."

"And they come to you at night?"

"They visit sometimes when I haven't called them, but usually I call them and then they make themselves visible to my eyes."

"And what do they tell you?"

"It depends, I can't tell you everything they tell me, but they have warned me of bad things to come; and sometimes I have asked them for protection."

"And your neighbors, they know this?"

"They know I have powers, as I have foretold things to them that have come to pass."

"Is that why they hold you in such high regard?"

Kouyate shrugged and said, "It could be."

"And Mansa Musa?"

"He ascribes it to a gift of Allah."

"Do you agree?"

"He believes in Allah. I have different beliefs. I look to our ancestors and a god who sits on top of the universe, but I don't subscribe to his beliefs."

"And he has no problem with that?"

"That is one of his great attributes, Mansa Musa, he doesn't impose his religion on me or on anyone."

"But about this night, I have never seen anything like it."

"As I have said, you are not a seer. You see but you do not see. I am a seer. I see and I see."

"So how come I was able to see them?"

"As I said, they may have wanted for you to see them. And sometimes even people who don't carry the office of a seer are able to see into the otherwise invisible for reasons I don't know."

"Are they the same every time?"

"Sometimes they are the same and sometimes they are different."

When Tiempo went back to bed, he could barely sleep, his mind on the strange happenings, wondering if Mansa Musa had placed him in the care of one who had something Tiempo could not counter with physical force. Did Mansa expect Tiempo to uncover Kouyate's gift and in so doing tame any inclination Tiempo may have of rebellion? He could not mull over this much as the next day he was asked to come to the palace in the early morning.

SEASONS of FOUR FACES

## Favor and Doubt

"Kouyate informs me that you are a man of great wisdom," Mansa Musa said as he sat amid a number of courtiers.

"He did?"

"Why, do you doubt your own wisdom?"

"It is an honor to be deemed wise, Great Mansa," Tiempo said.

"If you are as wise as he says, perhaps you can address a matter at hand."

"It will be my honor, Great Mansa."

Mansa Musa smiled. "I have asked my wise advisers to tell me a story that never ends. But no one has been able to do so. Some have said that there is no story that never ends, but others, including Kouyate, disagree. When I asked Kouyate to tell me such a story, he said he can't but he believes you can. So that is why you're here today. Are you able to tell me a story that never ends?"

Tiempo chuckled.

"You find this amusing? This is a very serious matter."

Despite his expressionless face, Tiempo suspected Mansa Musa was himself amused and that this was simply a matter for his amusement, or to gauge Tiempo's range of humor or assess how he would react to silliness dressed in seriousness and, if so, then this test was not so much in what he said but how he reacted.

"No, Great Mansa, pardon me if my reaction has created that impression," Tiempo said. "All of the kings' advisers are wise and I believe they have each spoken from knowledge and experience, each response tailored to their own history."

"You speak with the bearing of a man of regal experience."

"I'm honored to be so highly regarded, Great Mansa."

"But the matter at hand... Are you able to tell me a story that never ends?"

Tiempo did not reply immediately, waiting for effect, enjoying the suspense as Mansa Musa and the courtiers looked at him. "I can, Great Mansa," he finally said.

These were whisperings in the room, even several frowns betraying bemusement.

Tiempo detected a slight furrowing of Mansa Musa's brow. "Go on then," the king said.

"Yes, Great Mansa," Tiempo paused to clear his throat as he had observed the griot, Ibrahim, do, then he began, "Not too long ago, on one of my sojourns, I came to a land full of insects. Hungry and in need of a place to sleep, I visited the home of one of its inhabitants. The man, his wife and four children were very gracious to me. They gave me food to eat and a place to sleep for the night. I was sleeping well when all of a sudden I felt an insect bite me on my cheek. I swatted at the insect but then I felt it land on my other cheek. I swatted at it and then I felt it land on my forehead. I swatted at it. Then I felt an insect land on my shoulder. I swatted at it. An insect landed on my other shoulder. I swatted at it. An insect landed on my thigh. I swatted at it. An insect landed on my knee. I swatted at it. An insect landed on my foot. I swatted at it. An insect landed on my toes. I swatted at it. An insect landed again on my cheek…."

This story of landing and swatting continued through the afternoon into the early evening, and Mansa Musa moved from curiosity to irritation to where he had started: amusement and perhaps even admiration. With a broad grin, he said. "Enough, Tiempo. You have told a story that never ends!"

SEASONS of FOUR FACES

# Taming the Roaring Lions

And so it came to be accepted that not only was Tiempo strong, but that he was also a man of wisdom, or to those who would begrudge him this, that he was at least a man of great cunning, capable of any challenge, not just of brawn but also of the mind. And with the passage of time, he gained the admiration of almost all who knew him or knew of him. Even those who withheld bestowing on him encomiums would become more accepting of him. It was therefore not surprising when Mansa Musa summoned him to the palace one day to consult on a matter Mansa described as of great import to Mali. Mansa Musa dispensed with prolonged pleasantries, moving to the matter as soon as he had inquired of Tiempo's health, intimating that he'd consulted his dyeli Suleiman and other trusted counselors, including Kouyate, but before making up his mind, he wanted to hear what Tiempo had to say about the matter, the matter being about gold miners in the south, whose pagan practices Mansa found abhorrent. Normally, Mansa Musa explained, he was content to have others practice whatever religion they wished, but these people seemed godless and he had to intervene to prevent them from becoming a corrupting influence. He had ordered them to desist from their pagan ways, convert to Islam and thereby adopt its tenets, a religion that had come to the region many centuries earlier when Berber and Tuareg merchants had brought it south. They had refused and slowed down their production of gold, which was critical to Mali's economy. If the slowdown continued, Mali's economy would be badly impacted. At the same time, Mansa Musa could not countenance their paganism or rebellion. What should he do? Mansa asked.

"This is not an easy matter," Tiempo said.

"That is why I am deliberating over it."

"And what have your advisers said?"

"I want to hear from you. I know what they have said and I will consider their counsel. But you, teller of stories that never end, Prince of the Moon, what do you say?"

Tiempo had decided on his response, but given the intensity of the Mansa's gaze, he needed to show that he was contemplating the matter hard with all the resources of his mental faculties, so he wiped his hands over his face and squinted as if those strained eyes would unveil the answer somewhere in the atmosphere. After a prolonged silence in which he goaded the king's impatience, Tiempo said, "Great Mansa, in my humble view, the best way to handle this matter is to leave them alone to practice their beliefs and way of life."

"Leave them in their pagan ways?"

"Yes, Great Mansa. Forced religion is false religion. If they find Islam attractive, you do not need to foist it on them. In fact, they may have an outward pretense of conversion when in their hearts they believe something else. Such deception would be an affront to their own dignity as well as to Great Mansa and Islam."

Mansa Musa took a deep breath and his ensuing sigh was as much a signal of frustration as it was of relief. "And allow their insubordination to go unpunished?"

"Some may see it that way, but I would not call it an act of insubordination when a people want to continue to practice their way of life. And even if it is an act of insubordination, I will ask the Great Mansa to weigh the matter and see which weighs heavier. On one side, Mansa is highly respected and revered. Letting this go will hardly change that. On the other side is to risk a prolonged slowdown and, as the Great Mansa has indicated, potentially wreak havoc on the economy of Mali."

Mansa Musa thanked Tiempo for his advice and noted that he would consider it, alongside all the other advice he had received on the matter, and then decide.

Then the next day, Mansa Musa summoned Tiempo again and asked him to join a delegation to the south to inform the people of Mansa's decision that they could revert to the old way of life.

On this trip, Tiempo became acquainted with the great commander of the southern army of Mali, Soukar-Zouma, whose great bearing was a camouflage for the grace with which he spoke with Tiempo, saying, "I sense a man of many wars in you. You are no ordinary man." These were words that the delegation would hear and relay to Mansa Musa.

The delegation itself was a success in that the joy with which the news of Mansa Musa's decision was received would bear consequences to Mansa Musa's delight, as the southern miners' output of gold suddenly increased, erasing his concern of a long term impact on the economy.

"You are becoming a trusted counselor of Mansa," Kouyate said. "Be careful, not everyone will take kindly to that." This warning resounded loudly in Tiempo's mind, but he did not know how he could guard himself against any lurking danger (if indeed any existed).

Perhaps Kouyate could look into the future and warn Tiempo of any impending danger? Yes, if he foresaw anything, he would let Tiempo know, Kouyate promised, but he did not always see things. All he could see concerning Tiempo were great forests, a great war, great waters and a resolution out of darkness. But what those meant, he could not tell. "Be circumspect," he advised.

# BENJAMIN KWAKYE

# Of Tongues, Eyes, and Minds

And Tiempo resolved to be careful. And the only times he allowed himself to be carefree were when he was with Kouyate or Ibrahim and Mariam. After his trip back from the south, they took him with them to the market one day. This time many were willing to offer him food gratis and not out of compulsion. And this time the marketplace was not like a dense fog through which he had to forage for survival. He was now the friend of people in high places, and he took it in with the keen eyes of the privileged.

A market with a taste, where the tomatoes seemed to spill their guts from the garlands that were the baskets holding them, licking the basket bottoms with red juices and rolling for landing in arachnid crawl on the soil. Yellowish mangoes, some with skins singed in burning sun, also stained the bottom of baskets, reaching out with succoring aromata. Bulging potatoes, groundnuts, millet, onions, bananas, lemons, arrayed in a battle for attention in plain sight. Mingled colors of sun, earth, seeping sepia. A sea choked full of stalls in zigzag formation, a labyrinth for a soul and odorous composition of food and garbage, all amid vociferous bargaining. Hagglers, sellers, sweating a trade. Together, a hard smell afflicting the giant, afflicting the fly, a smell to be tasted, a smell to be eaten; a hard smell as tasty as the smell of the sea filling the depths of veins, felt in nostrils and felt in the mouth, also the smell of perfumes corrupted by fusty smell of sweat. Through the air it gathered its smells, modified them through the smut and laid siege to the marketplace.

Next, Ibrahim asked Tiempo to come with him on a trip to

Timbuktu. Ibrahim tried to go up once every year to visit an uncle who lived there. He would usually make the trip with Mariam, but with her pregnancy she was not up to making the trip. He would be greatly honored if Tiempo would come along. Tiempo was about to turn down the offer when Mariam pleaded with him to go with her husband. Ibrahim was easily bored and Mariam could think of no better companion than Tiempo. With this urging (and flattery), Tiempo accepted the invitation, and they set out on a canoe on the River Niger. Being on this River of Life was more exciting than Tiempo imagined, this great river that was indeed a major artery, the heartbeat of trade, which facilitated the trade of goods, especially gold from the south and salt from the north.

"What do you see?" Ibrahim asked Tiempo.

"Why, water," Tiempo replied.

"Isn't it soothing?"

"Absolutely so."

"That is the point, my friend. Water. Sometimes we have need of stone, but we should also never forget the refreshing water can bring. Just like human beings. We have in us water and we have in us stone. We don't have to be stone all the time. Stone crashes and kills, hard and brutal; water nourishes, soft and gentle. But remember that even water can kill sometimes. You don't always need the stone; sometimes you need to reach for the water in you. You can think of it in different ways, song and insult, for example. Sometimes you need to sing the song to lull rather than insult to provoke."

Tiempo remembered his first day at the market and the ensuing encounters and wondered whether Ibrahim was alluding to that, or if it was in reference to Tiempo in general, his countenance and general disposition.

Amid conversation and river gazing, Tiempo enjoyed the

journey more than he had expected. And when they arrived in Timbuktu they walked a long dusty pathway, past a series of mosques, and eventually arrived at a tall building. Ibrahim announced himself and was welcomed by a young man in a blue boubou. He greeted Ibrahim pleasantly, obviously glad to see him, and then led them indoors, past a passageway to an inner chamber, where an older man in a white boubou was seated, reading a book. Tiempo found out the man was Boubacar, a marabout of sorts, who was a teacher at one of the nearby madrassas. Behind him were several worn out books. The younger man who had let them in seemed a famulus of sorts. His name was also Ibrahim, perhaps explaining the joy with which he received the older Ibrahim.

They sat down to a long conversation, and Boubacar, projecting a man used to much lucubration, was more interested in intellectual discussions than small talk, dispensing with frivolous conversation after he had inquired about Mariam. Although he spoke at great length, Tiempo judged him to be a reserved man who only discussed things he was deeply passionate about and, despite the paraphernalia of bookishness, he spoke in simple language and without much inkhorn diction. He mentioned how he was hoping to help transform Timbuktu into a great center of learning, the foundation having already been laid by its strategic location where the camel meets the canoe. Great people were already influencing its thought and more great scholars would definitely come to Timbuktu. He also envisaged Timbuktu flourishing as a great metropolis of commerce and scholarship. Boubacar spoke of other subjects, including the importance of the Mali constitution as one of the fulcrums of stability in Mali. He explained how Sundiata had gathered a number of wise men, chiefs of various clans, at the Kurukan Fuga, to formulate the Kurukan

## SEASONS of FOUR FACES

Fuga Charter, the constitution of Mali, containing a preamble and seven chapters. He spoke with relish of how it established constitutional monarchy with the Gbara, or Great Assembly, to advice on matters of state, and spoke to a wide range of matters covering social peace, the sanctity of human life, equal rights to all, including slaves, the right to an education, food security, and self-expression. It ensured law and order in a manner that was fair and devoid of whims. The only challenge was, since the constitution, though codified, was not written, only few people knew of its nuances. In his view, the more people learned of the constitution, the more they would be inclined to respect its institutions.

That night Boubacar treated his guests to a delicious meal of grilled capitaine fish caught that very day from the Niger River. The accompanying hibiscus drink was refreshing as the men, mostly Boubacar, talked. Ibrahim would later confess to Tiempo that he needed this annual trip for intellectual refreshment. It was not so much for his uncle's company, as his mind.

When they returned to Niani, Ibrahim and Mariam invited Tiempo to their house again, round shaped just as Kouyate's, with a grass domed roof, unlike the more recent ones that were flat roofed. He loved their walls, their ocher look, the adobe plaster over the mudbricks, and the large wooden support beams that jutted out of the walls on the outside always gave him a sense of assurance and support. They served him bouille that morning, a porridge of grounded millet, tamarind and sugar mixed with milk and millet made pancakes. Mariam had missed him, she said.

Tiempo observed his friends, always unnerved by their generosity. Ibrahim spoke proudly of the son they would have, as Mariam countered that she was the mother and knew they were going to have a girl. The son would have to wait. Tiempo observed how beautiful and ebullient she looked, fully dressed in a loud yellow pagne tunic and a neatly wrapped green wrapper around her head. There were stirrings of longing inside him as she looked at her, how so attractive she looked, and his groin hardened, so strongly he had to look away from her for fear that he might betray this desire, as natural as he felt it was perverse. He spent most of the time in their house that morning looking into the food or in the direction of Ibrahim as he ate, trying as much as he could to avoid looking at Mariam.

# Thickening Pathways

Then one day soon afterwards, Soukar-Zouma, the commander of the southern army came calling, recalling the joy he'd had when Tiempo visited the south on Mansa Musa's mission. He conferred secretly with Kouyate for a while and then beaming, saluted Tiempo as though he was a colleague before announcing that he had come to take Tiempo on a trip up north. He needed to consult with his northern compatriot, Farim Souro, and he'd be delighted if Tiempo would come along. Tiempo's hesitation was brief, considering that Kouyate, who was standing behind the commander nodded his assent and also that it would be disrespectful to turn down the honor. Good! Soukar-Zouma shouted. They would set out the next day.

And the next day, Tiempo went to Mansa Musa's palace as they had agreed, and together with a few other soldiers, they left for the north, an uneventful journey for the most part, except for Soukar-Zouma's bonhomie. Now and then, he would declare that they would have Tiempo join the army soon because he would no doubt make a great soldier.

Then they met up with Farim Souro, who was a bit more formal than Soukar-Zouma, but welcoming. The two commanders needed to confer separately, so they left their retinue by themselves for a while. In their absence, a man of heavy bearing came towards Tiempo and announced himself as Oumar, second in command to Farim Souro of the northern army. Tiempo did not like the way he announced himself, his chin lifted high as he sat on his horse. The man then dropped his chin and stared hard at Tiempo, wearing the strains of this thoughts in the furrows of his face, his eyes squinting, though the sun posed no threat at that time to warrant it, his lips pursed. He had heard about Tiempo, Oumar said, and Tiempo would hear of him.

    Later, some of Soukar-Zouma's soldiers told Tiempo that Oumar was a reliable assistant of Farim Souro, very much respected for his prowess and heavily relied on also to help collect taxes from the traders who came from the northern countries to trade in Mali, most of them bringing salt. On the trip back to Niani, Tiempo thought of Oumar with a shudder and he felt unsafe even in the man's absence. The vice commander had been needlessly hostile, Tiempo thought, and he was happy to return to the home of Kouyate, where he was safe and respected, even if the proximity to Mariam now troubled him.

# SEASONS of FOUR FACES

## Fame and Suspicion

The next summons Tiempo received convinced him he needed to be even more circumspect. His reputation for wisdom and physical strength were opening more doors to those sitting highest in Mali's political echelons, but this was different, the summons to the home of Oumar, second in command of the northern army, especially so soon after their uncomfortable meeting.

With a couple of spear toting guards behind him, Oumar studied Tiempo as before, only this time sterner and longer. "You are becoming very famous in the land," Oumar finally said.

Tiempo responded with a nod, studying the commander and concluding that, though he did not carry the same authoritative presence as Farim Souro or Sauker-Zouma, he carried something more dangerous: impulsiveness, perhaps irascibility.

"You have nothing to say to that?" Oumar asked, frowning.

"I take you at your word, but I have no interest in fame."

"Then how come you are doing all these feats that I keep hearing about? If you are not seeking fame, then I would expect you to keep a low profile, especially for a foreigner."

"I do not question the sources of your information, but what they may not have told you is that everything I have done, I have done in response to what others have asked me to do or done to me."

"I do not deem going to the marketplace like a king demanding food as doing something in response to what others have done."

"On this, you have a point, and I am guilty, but even so, I only took what I needed to feed my hunger."

"Hunger for food or hunger to impose yourself on others?"

"I was hungry and took some food. Nothing more."

"And even more perplexing to me is that you will not tell where you came from."

"I have travelled many journeys. Memories fade."

"I am not fooled by this, Tiempo, if that is in fact your name."

"It is in fact my name."

"Mali has its enemies, and there are those who would want to do us harm. A man of your prowess does not just journey around without aim."

"I do have an aim."

"And what is that?"

Tiempo argued peace as a manifesto of love: "To find peace from love," he said.

"And there is no peace or love from where you came?"

"There is always peace and love, even in the middle of hatred and war. But sometimes the peace and love of a certain place eludes some and for them they must decide whether they can find what they are seeking elsewhere."

"You are not making any sense, so tell me instead who sent you."

"No one sent me."

"I ask again, who sent you?"

"No one sent me; or, if someone sent me, I don't know who."

"So you admit someone sent you?"

"As I said, if someone sent me, I don't know who that would be."

"You speak to cause confusion. So who sent you to do what?"

"I have no ill intentions. I am not here on a mission to harm anyone."

Oumar's frown deepened as he paced back and forth, the guards behind him watching intensely. Oumar seemed on the verge of issuing some foul instructions as he lifted his arm and pointed at Tiempo, his frown even more intense, but it was at the moment that a woman entered the room, fully covered, her face veiled, except for a small opening that exposed her eyes. The entrance was as thin as a whisper, for just as suddenly as she entered the room, she left it, as if she had entered it by accident and concluded she was intruding. She did not speak or gesture in that whisker of time. But it was enough time for both Tiempo and Oumar to turn from their conversation to look at her.

And Tiempo...

Tiempo nearly fell down, suddenly weakened in body, as if he had been hit in a vital part of his body, in fact all over his body, blows that not only touched body but also reached within his core, totally deenergizing him, and it took him enormous focus and strength to stay on his feet. His body shuddered and goose pimples covered his skin. He worried he was at the point of transformation, like a death of sorts, or perhaps a birth, or perhaps rebirth. Oumar observed Tiempo and the impact of the woman's brief visit was not lost on him, his frown ever present, if more stressed. But he did not comment on it; rather, Oumar abruptly dismissed Tiempo and remarked that the conversation would continue on a later day.

BENJAMIN KWAKYE

# A Great Question

What obsessed Tiempo as he left Oumar's home was not the concern that the second in command of the northern army mistrusted him and even possibly meant him harm. Rather, it was the woman who had come into the room and left it as though the entry was in error, a form of trespassing. She was the one who occupied Tiempo's mind. The woman whose face he hadn't even been able to see. This was the woman who came to him again and again, like a shadow in the dark, a profile at night, eyes looking out of a face veiled. He did not know her and yet he felt he knew her. Tiempo was perspiring badly, more agitated than he had ever been under physical assault.

"Has someone attacked you?" Kouyate asked, observing the man who entered the house. "I knew you were not safe. Where are they? Did you see their faces? We need to report this to Mansa Musa. This is a violation of his orders…"

"No, Kouyate, no one has attacked me."

"Then why are you sweating like this?"

"Can you keep what I am about to say between us?"

"You can trust me, Tiempo. Who doesn't?"

Tiempo was not sure he could think his way through the decision to confide in Kouyate, so he did not even try. "Who are the women in Oumar's household?"

"But what kind of question is that?"

"Do you know the women in his house?"

"Why are you asking me such a strange question, Tiempo? I have been to his house a number of times, but how can I number all the women in his palatial house?"

"Very well, let's start with his wives. Do you know his wives?"

"Tiempo, I ask again, what kind of questioning is this?"

"Please, answer me. Do you know his wives?"

"Yes. I have met them. Of course, except his most recent wife. I have not met her yet."

"Do you know their names?"

"Yes, except the most recent."

"What are their names?"

"Aminata, Hawa, and Bintu."

"Those are all of their names?"

"I told you I don't know the name of the most recent wife. And of what interest is that to you, anyway?"

"Please, do you know her name?"

Kouyate shrugged. "How many times need I tell you I don't know her name?"

"Will you find out?"

"Not until you tell me why you are asking me all these strange questions about another man's wives."

"You won't understand, Kouyate, but when I was in his house a veiled woman entered the room very briefly. I hardly got to see her before she left the room, but it's strange that she is all I can think about. I can't explain it."

"This is very bizarre. Are you telling me that you are interested in a woman you barely saw and that this woman is having this profound impact on you?"

"I don't understand it myself, Kouyate, but you yourself have seen how I was sweating when I came in. I need to know who this woman is."

"Now you are treading on a very dangerous path, Tiempo. Not only are you talking about another man's wife, but also the second in command of the northern army."

"Please help me."

"Listen to yourself. Have you gone mad?"

"Please help me."

"Oumar is a very powerful man, and also very dangerous."

"Will you help me?"

"Tiempo, go to bed and get some rest. Let's talk about this tomorrow."

"So you will help me?"

"Let's talk about this tomorrow!" Kouyate said with finality and authority. And Tiempo knew he could not break the man's resolve. So he would wait and bring up the matter the next day.

And through the sleepless night, all he could think about was the woman he'd encountered at Oumar's home. But his hopes of discussing the matter with Kouyate were soon doused. The next day he realized that Kouyate had left the house early. For a short while he intended to ask Ibrahim or Mariam if they knew Oumar's wives, but he remembered Mariam's weight on him previously and amended his intention, and more so considering that he might be opening himself up to danger by broaching such matters with more people, no matter how much he trusted them.

Before he could contemplate much further, a messenger from Mansa Musa told him he was wanted at the palace, where he was informed that had been picked to help plan a royal pilgrimage to Mecca, and that he would be an important part of Mansa Musa's security detail, and with all the preparation it would entail, he would be required to stay at the palace until the journey.

# CHAPTER

# 2

*Mansa Musa turned to Suleiman and said,
"I told you he has a sweet tongue to match that sharp wit."*

## Miasmas and Visions

The next few days, which became weeks, which became months, were a miasma of activity of preparation, so intense, with everyone occupied, including Mansa Musa's head servant Farba, that it was no use trying to keep track of time, for it would have been an exercise in frustration for Tiempo, on the one part tugged by the responsibility placed on him by Mansa Musa and on the other part by the woman of obscure appearance, who continued to taunt him in images, sometimes with face fully unveiled, only it was full of such light he could not decipher the features of the face. And then at other times her face was as he had seen it, veiled with a tiny opening for the eyes only but shaded by even darker contours. At one time she was calling to him, like one who was imprisoned and needed to be freed, and when she would point to her chest Tiempo imagined that she was indicating her shackles were emotional. Then, again, at other times she was dancing, jerking her body in different directions in a carefree manner that suggested total freedom. The enigma was alien as she was familiar. And Tiempo could not fashion a way to free himself from her.

His only salvation in this ongoing chameleonic appearance was that Tiempo was so preoccupied with helping plan the trip for Mansa Musa that he could not wrestle with the images on his mind for too long, and when at the end of the day he collapsed into sleep, he could barely manage to keep his conscious mind active for long before he fell asleep. Now and again, he would wake up with the echoes of memory in the middle of the night, sometimes sweating and sometimes sweatless, sometimes anxious, and sometimes totally calm. Now and again, he was tempted to leave the palace in search of the woman, but Mansa Musa's orders were clear: he was not to leave the palace, unless in service of the project he had been entrusted with. So he soldiered on and helped select the security guard, all the while also observing the other elements of the trip coming together in one of the most grandest, if not the grandest, planning anyone could imagine, as people came in and out of the palace to confer, as he went with the head of the guards to help pick strong people, as he consulted with Farim Souro, head of the northern army, and Sauker-Zouma, the head of the southern army, who always beamed at seeing Tiempo and pronounced how proud he was of him and reassured that Tiempo had been chosen to help keep the king safe on this important trip.

Between the intense planning and preparation, Mansa

# SEASONS of FOUR FACES

Musa was sure to organize feasts and entertainment from time to time. Sometimes acrobats performed feats of incredible human body gyrations, sometimes drummers played percussive rhythms that were on some occasions loud and on other occasions soft and slow, sometimes flutists joined in, and sometimes all of the performers came together in a massive ensemble of artistry. He had hoped Ibrahim would perform at one of those events but he hadn't. Perhaps the organizers wanted to leave him alone to tend to his pregnant wife.

One evening after a great, if orchidaceous, performance that seemed to particularly please Mansa Musa, even with the palace still astir with motions of busy limbs that were tireless like time itself, he called Tiempo to one of his inner chambers, Dyeli Suleiman by his side.

"I am very pleased with your willingness to join this planning, Tiempo," Mansa Musa said.

"It is my honor, Great Mansa; my deepest honor."

"You are a part of us now, you know that?"

"Indeed, Great Mansa, and I would have it no other way."

Mansa Musa turned to Suleiman and said, "I wonder if anyone has told him of my uncle."

Suleiman said, "Your history is well known and I am sure he has heard it."

Mansa Musa said to Tiempo, "It is not the same when you hear it from others."

And then assuming that Tiempo had not heard, Mansa Musa told the story directly to Tiempo. He recalled the day when he stood on the beach with his uncle, the waves beating gently against the shore, the horizon telling nothing of whether it was a graveyard or a carrier to new life. Several men loaded the two thousand assembled ships with food, gold and other paraphernalia that would be needed for the trip. "Like me, my uncle was excited about his expedition. It was not enough that he was Emperor of Mali; he was very passionate about exploration, and he would not be denied this trip to feed the long yearning of his to see what lay after the ocean." He had previously sent four hundred on a like mission. Then after a while one ship had returned, the captain claiming that the ships ahead of him had been lost. This time, my uncle would go himself. It was not lost on him that this could lead to his doom, or to fame and fortune. He could be lost on the sea forever until death overtook him. Or he could find a land of hostile people. He didn't know. But whatever lay on the other wise, he was committed to finding out.

Then the Emperor of Mali turned to Kankan Musa, his sister's son, telling the younger man that if he did not return, Kankan Musa would become the next emperor.

"Given that my uncle never returned, do you think it foolish that I would embark on this pilgrimage?" Mansa Musa asked Tiempo.

"Not at all. Your uncle must have known that his journey was dangerous, and yet he did not shrink from the challenge. And from what I can gather, this was not just a random journey, but a journey borne of expectation and the mystery of what was out there, the quest to find the unknown. That lies at the heart of human endeavor, this quest that leads to discovery and greatness. It can be a quest to feed a wanderlust, to find love, to acquire territory, to get closer to God. They are all legitimate in my view. And even when the quest fails, it puts down a marker for others to follow, to pick up. To do otherwise would not only be an act of cowardice but of smallness when great people must reach for great quests and bigness."

"Even those so perilous?"

"Especially those so perilous, for only the great and the bold can dare venture."

"So you think my trip is comparable?"

"In many ways, yes, in its daring and bravery, though less perilous because this is a journey that has been done before. But the bravery lies in the enormity of the group, the unprecedented preparation. Generations yet unborn will sing songs about you."

Mansa Musa turned to Suleiman and said, "I told you he has a sweet tongue to match that sharp wit."

"And in this you spoke wisely, as you always do," said the dyeli.

Mansa Musa smiled and held Tiempo at the elbow, ever so gently, and said, "Come, let's join the rest before I am accused of partiality."

In the months of preparation, Kouyate had come to the palace a number of times, but they never had time to themselves in a way that would allow Tiempo to broach private matters deeply, depriving Tiempo the opportunity to inquire if he had found out anything about the woman of wonder. Kouyate told him that Ibrahim and Mariam were always asking about him. And Tiempo realized how the stirrings for Mariam had so quickly been replaced by the thoughts of the woman at Oumar's home. Mariam's impact had been strong; therefore, it was perplexing that it would be so forcefully pushed out of his forethoughts to a place where his remembering of her was out of a distilled place of fondness rather than physical desire. But the evening before the trip, Tiempo could wait no longer. As the royal staff discussed last plans, he reckoned none would miss him if he went to see Kouyate. With the chatter around him, and the bodies of many occupying the palace, he slipped out when no one was watching. And into the night he went, looking this way and that, his heart beating rapidly as if it would escape his body. Mansa Musa would not be pleased if he found that Tiempo had disobeyed his orders. Once or twice Tiempo quickly moved behind a tree when he thought he saw someone familiar. Every now and then he looked down when he thought someone called his name. So monitored by his own fears, he finally arrived at Kouyate's. His host did not act surprised.

"I have missed you," Kouyate said.

"And I you," Tiempo said. "But I am sorry I can't stay long. I will be missed at the palace."

"You have come for a last supper with an old friend," Kouyate said with a smile.

"Let me get to the matter for which I came…"

"But what other matter, Tiempo, except to see your old friend before you leave on a long journey?"

"Kouyate, please, I don't have time to waste. And by the way, I am surprised Mansa did not ask you to come along with him on this trip."

"Why do you say this now?"

"The time is now so near and it's weighing on me that I will be going on this long journey without you."

"He needs eyes and ears behind while he is away."

"Very well, but now to the matter… Have you found out more?"

"About what?"

"O Kouyate, why do you torment me?"

Kouyate shrugged.

"What have you found out?!"

"Not a lot."

"But what little have you found?"

"The only thing of importance is that I have confirmed that Oumar has a relatively new addition to his household. He has a new wife, as I told you before, and from what I have gathered so far he keeps her away from the public or any public appearance."

"Why?"

"I don't know."

"What else do you know?"

"I hear she is very beautiful."

"Is that why he does not want others to see her?"

"I don't know, Tiempo."

"Have you seen her yourself?"

"No, it's just what I have heard."

"Do you know her name?"

"I have asked, but I have not been told."

"This is very strange to me, that Oumar has a secret wife."

"It's strange, I agree."

"Do you think she is the woman I saw when he summoned me?"

"Tiempo, my friend, are you losing your mind? How will I know that?"

"You are a seer. You are supposed to see things."

"You are truly losing your mind."

"I'm sorry; it's just that I find this very unusual."

"As I do too."

The riddle was worse, and Tiempo regretted that he had even gone to see Kouyate, except the refreshment of having seen his old friend once again free from the crowdedness of the palace. But now he would have to pay the price of the deepened mystery hanging over his head the entire trip. He considered asking Mansa Musa to excuse him from the trip, but it was an insane thought he refused to nurse long, as it would be highest act of ingratitude and even impudence, not to mention insult to Mansa. Therefore, he would bear the emotional strains, which were still senseless to him, for as long as it took. The one thing he knew was that Oumar was not going on the trip. For that reason, there was no chance any of Oumar's wives would be on the trip.

The angst was so palpable that when he returned to the palace a couple of people asked him if he was sick. He was well, he said, just sad that he was leaving the land that had received him so well and which he so loved. This was a sacred trip, they reminded him, and he should count himself fortunate that Mansa Musa had handpicked him personally to embark on the journey. This was not lost on Tiempo, of course, and as much as he suffered through the night, the thought of the sights and pomp of what lay ahead cheered him somewhat.

SEASONS of FOUR FACES

# Hope and Glory

The next morning a motley group of sixty thousand people, ambulatory like a motional village, gathered at the palace, ready to travel to Mecca. It took a little while for the entire caravan to assemble: here (eight thousand soldiers); there (twelve thousand in brocades or silks from Persia, five hundred carrying ornamental staffs made of gold); there (members of the royal family in ornate attires); here guides; there governors; and, here, hundreds of horses, some with strands of gold woven into their manes. Tiempo observed in awe, not only the overall impressive number of sixty thousand, but the colorful dressing of bold cottons, fabrics embroidered with gold or silver, and also awe inspiring, the camels carrying food, water, tents, tools, clothing, cooking utensils, with eighty of those camels carrying nothing but gold, three hundred pounds each. Then the griot, Ibrahim, came through the crowd to inform Tiempo that Tiempo was helping write a new Mali epic. He was now a true son. Then he walked away.

There was such excitement in the atmosphere, such expectation, that for a moment, and for a brief moment only, Tiempo could think of nothing but the significance of the occasion, the glory of Mali, its history. He gazed in greater awe at the assembly and foresaw the marking of a great time in the history of the world, for very few, if any, could match such variety, such technicolor of attire, such brilliance of wealth. Perhaps it would become a watershed moment, a touchstone for what it meant for kings and queens of majestic bearing to travel. It was a moment when his own yearnings were insignificant, lost in the grandeur of the whole, even if he realized that the grandeur of the whole was only momentary and that at some point or another he would have to focus on the micro, even if still in the presence of the macro. But the breathtaking assembly, its novelty and beauty and the audacity of it, was enough to hold him still, hold his mind, hold his very being to a place that demanded that ovation of the heart that was not expressed with hands, but the glitter of eyes, the fast beating of the heart and even the weakness of the knees.

Then by late afternoon, when everything was ready, Mansa Musa emerged, riding on the back of a black stallion adorned with solid toppings, wearing a wide pair of pants, wide at the seat and narrow at the leg. A great cheer greeted Mansa Musa, ready to cross nine thousand miles to Mecca, most of it desert. Like his uncle or some would say his brother, Mansa Abubakari II, before him, this was a chance to engrave his name in placards of history, or perish, perhaps to be forgotten, eaten by the sea of sand.

# SEASONS of FOUR FACES

# A Portrait of Destiny

The joyous excitement infected (or perhaps infested) just about everyone in the impressive caravan as they set out on this well-crafted trip to Mecca, the perilous session over dry, arid land not expressed, the sense of fanfare complemented by the shimmering beauty of Mansa Musa and all who were accompanying him, the glitter of gold, embroidery and decoration of man and beast sufficient to draw any depressed heart up into heartiness. The people and animals and scenery provided such a picturesqueness Tiempo knew he would forever hold in his memory, and he wanted to capture as much of it as he could.

As they moved forward, the grasslands of Mali unfolded and unfolded, lush in view and refreshing to walk on. Tiempo had stationed enough guards with Mansa Musa and to guard the camels carrying the valuables, including the gold, that he was relieved to go back and forth to ensure that no one felt under threat. And none seemed to feel under any threat, whether from within or without the caravan, leaving him to take in the scenes.

The herds of elephants they encountered on their way strolled past as if in boredom, seemingly oblivious to their human companions, so too the giraffes, some straining to drink from nearby streams, and so too the gazelles that dashed back and forth across the grassland. The fields were like seas of plants and animals—goats, cotton and peanuts bore testimony to the fortunes of Mali, not just the gold but the array of flora and fauna. And then the sight of the setting sun softly shimmering yellow over the River Niger was like a transformation into a spiritual world where spirits and humans interacted in harmony. Tiempo watched these as much as he kept his attention on Mansa Musa, who occasionally galloped away from the caravan on his horse to explore sights he found fascinating. Because of such behavior, Tiempo resolved not to stray too far from the king, even though the assiduous guards were always alert. When they decided to rest for the night, the caravan spread out like the sky itself, the empyrean shelter like a generous parent watching over his children.

At that moment, Tiempo was exhilarated to be free from the confines of the palace, despite its luxuries, in a way that he thought perverse, though he could not fathom why it was perverse. He hoped that distance from Mali would enable him to put distance between his thoughts and the images of the woman who now usually occupied them.

The cooks who prepared dinner primarily of tiguadege na (peanut butter stew with lamb) were the toast of everyone. After this, the caravan enjoyed meni meniyong sesame-honey sweets. Then the night entertainment began. The king and his wife watched as drummers talked with their drums, interspaced by scatting, and accompanied by the dancers, who beat their feet into the ground in such dustbathing that made the earth from which they teased out the brown powder become a part of their bodies, and who moved in trained rhythm that seemed unrehearsed in a way that drew the audience's admiration, content after a delicious meal and anticipating a restful night in the open. The night passed uneventfully after the entertainment, as tents were set up and the caravan went to sleep.

For Tiempo, the night was not of full rest as his mind and even his dreams roamed and would not stay still. At first, he tried to think about the many days ahead and what it would take to keep Mansa Musa safe, but also the rest of the caravan for which he felt personally responsible. That was enough burden to keep him awake. But inevitably–he could not ward this off for too long, as he had deceived himself into hoping– the thought of the obscure woman at Oumar's returned with stubbornness. Tiempo rubbed his head many times, as though he could massage her out of his mind, but if it had any impact, this gesture rubbed her more into his mind, and his memory was resurrected to that moment when she had entered the room, seizing it for that one instant of appearance. Why had she so quickly withdrawn? Why had she not said anything? Why had that moment become so meaningful to him that he could not shed it from his mind? How was it possible that she had created such strong cravings in him when he had scarcely seen any part of her beyond her clothing? Tiempo fought this unrelenting tug, still hoping that somehow it would leave him alone to focus on the trip ahead.

Sleep only came when his total tiredness overwhelmed his mind so that he fell asleep without willing it. And even in his sleep she continued to come to him as she had in previous nights, shapeshifting, calling and then rejecting him, leading him into the light of the sun and the darker glow of the moon and the dark belly of the night, as well as the drowning depths of the sea. There was no logic nor reason nor rhyme nor rhythm to any of this. It was draining in the absence of her physical presence and it was also reinvigorating in the vivacity of promise.

He was tired the next day, but he had work to do and could not allow his frame of mind (or body for that matter) to influence his responsibilities. Assured that all was in order, he allowed his mind to rest a little as the caravan continued. They had days of relative ease, until they entered the desert phase of the journey. The heat was unrelenting as it toasted sand and warmed skins, but they trudged on, sure to replenish their water supplies anytime they came to an oasis. Because of the repetitive nature of the journey and its activities, it became arduous with time, the eat, move on, rest, eat, get entertained, and then move on, all this while, or for a large part of the day, while fighting the cruel sun.

A respite would come when halfway or so through the journey they came to the Tassili n'Ajjer Plateau, a remarkable thing to behold, a breathtaking view of its covering of eroded rock formations and caves and steep-sided gullies. But even more eye catching were the various paintings of artists limning life with their rock paintings: a shepherd bent over as if in search of lost sheep as other sheep followed him; a fallen warrior, his bow by his side; a dancer whose rhythmic movements were captured in the static form of a painting with arms thrown from the body; elephants, rhinoceroses; life and death captured in various states, thought Tiempo. Which part of it would they end up on? Life? Death? Something in between? At that moment when they still had miles and miles of endless desert ahead, notwithstanding that they had prepared so well for this journey, it was not farfetched for Tiempo to consider the possibility that they, or some of them, might perish on the journey.

And then soon they would come across a most moving sight, where a man had made the shade of a baobab tree his place for weaving cotton clothes. "The man in the tree," Mansa Musa said, as if this was one of the greatest wonders he had ever seen. But who could blame him for embellishing every sight if only to keep spirits up?

## Singing Greatness

One evening Tiempo was ushered into the presence of Inari Kunate, her maids at her side. "How are you faring?" she asked.

Tiempo stammered to respond. It was not the first time he'd seen her, but she had always looked at him without speaking, except the occasional "How are you?" And now she was standing face to face with him and seemingly expecting a response, not a rehearsed and perfunctory "I am well." Yet, in as much as he wanted to say something profound to this simple question, he could not find anything witty to say, so he fell into the cliched response: "I am well." The same "I am well" that was insufficient for the occasion.

"Yes," she said. "I know you are well, but how are you?"

This time it would be an insult to answer the same way. "It has been a great privilege to come on this trip with the Great Mansa and you and the people of Mali," he said.

"I have seen how you take pride in going about your job. Keep it up."

"Thank you. It's always my honor."

"You must know that I very much care for my husband and anything that concerns him concerns me, just as anything that concerns me concerns him. You are a brave and strong man. You have demonstrated that. And I know that my husband has called you for advice sometimes. But like I said, anything that concerns my husband concerns me. And I am concerned that you seem a little distracted lately."

"Distracted?"

"When you stare into the air rather than eat your meals at dinner time, when you sit for minutes during leisure hours, paying attention to no one, I know you're distracted."

"I did not realize that you were paying attention."

"My husband likes and values you, so I make it my business to observe. It may not be my eyes, but I have other eyes besides my own. You understand?"

"Yes."

"So if there's anything bothering you, you will let us know, won't you?"

"You are very kind; yes, I will."

"Good, and thank you."

Tiempo asked Suleiman if he had reported to Inari Kunate that he'd become absent minded, but Suleiman denied this. How did she know, then?

"If she is calling you herself to talk to you, then she must like you. I tell you, Mansa Musa will do everything for her. He loves her that much, so count it a great fortune that she likes you. If ever you're in any trouble, she will be your advocate. That, Tiempo, is power."

From then on, though Tiempo's preoccupations were as strong as ever, he was careful to hide them, conscious not to seem to be aimlessly daydreaming or distracted, which placed an even greater burden on him. And the dreariness of the long journey was telling on others as well and it was difficult to move on, but they had to, as returning was not an option. They would take frequent rests and move on and on and on and on…

The dyeli spoke often with Tiempo to check whether Tiempo was faring favorably. But even he sometimes appeared deflated despite outward appearances to suggest otherwise.

SEASONS of FOUR FACES

## Life as a Proverb

They continued to move on and on and on, puncturing the monotony with entertainment as frequently as they could, though even the singers and musicians and acrobats seemed to tire, apparently bereft of new performances, so that their repetitions began to add to the dreariness. So one night Suleiman took over, performing the Epic of Mali like a great griot, holding the ears of the audience, Mansa Musa and Inari Kunate at rapt attention as he gestured, gesticulated and emoted, and then as a grand finale, he began to sing Mansa Musa's praises:

Mansa Musa, your life is a proverb and when future generations mention your name, they will explain the meaning of this proverb and they will smile many smiles and laugh many laughs, all with pleasure and pride when they understand the meaning of the proverb, though you will still remain a riddle that cannot be fully solved because only the ordinary can be fully understood and the mighty and complex are better contemplated than fathomed. Indeed, you are the mystery none can unravel because you are the color of shadows, shadows that reflect the height and width of your people, shadows that have a life of their own hovering like a good bird over the people he oversees, the shadow that is brighter than the sun. You, Great Mansa Musa, are like the breath of your people, knowing, everywhere, shadowing to protect and comfort. Great Mansa Musa, yes, you are shadows.

But you are also light, not the light that blazes the skies carelessly but the careful light that picks the deepest moods of sorrow and hopelessness and shines into it joy and hope. The light that fades when the joy glitters so the joy can find its own light. Unselfish light. Light that gives, ever burning like fire, but also understands the light of great waters. You are the light of lights. You are the light of great waters.

Like the sea. You are the sea, Mansa Musa, you are the great sea. The sea that knows when to dance, dance like a wave or dance with the ripple of low tides, when to lie calmly in sleep, even when to merge with the moodiness of the moon at night, calmly humming for the soothing release of the early dawn, and when to rise like the storm that demonstrates to the shore who is king. Inhalant for the infauna, exhalant for the epifauna. You are the great sea. And who knows better when to brew love than the great sea? Oh great sea, whisper casting its long wings onto the sands, supervising the beach. You are the storm-roar of the great sea.

But not just the sea, your might is like great land, the land of sand and the land of trees, and nothing grows without you, nothing passes from here to there unless you permit it. The land that opens its arms from one people to others, that offers its sands for dust baths and its waters for water cleansing as it pleases, as the seasons that sit on your wise head dictate. One word from you and we dance like the leaves of a great storm. You are the sea of valleys and the clouds of mountains. That is to say, you are what we cannot comprehend. Mansa Musa, you are a great land.

But more than that, sea and land, you are a mighty tree. Mightier than the baobab, you offer your wings with the heart of a father, the bosom of a mother, for your people, indeed all people, to test and nest in. The tree that withstands all mighty winds, the tree that is mightier than all storms, storms of water and storms of dust. The tree whose leaves are tastier than the sweetest fruit to all who come in peace, but more bit ter than bile for those whose eyes are evil. The great spear of Mali. You are the great tree that bows to no wind. Great Mansa Musa, you are the air itself. Who can live without you? Mali breathes you. Your people breathe you. The world breathes you, Great One who is the color of shadows!

The applause was spontaneous and instantaneous and long, hearty and enthusiastic, and the performance was a form of refueling. And then the caravan continued to move on and on… and at some point the reverberation of the griot's performance also waned, but the pilgrims moved on and on, and at some point, a few began to wonder if the guides had gotten their bearings wrong and whether the caravan was lost in the sea of sand, reigniting (if not vindicating) Tiempo's concern that some of them would die. And also concerning, though he had pushed this aside as much as he could, was that he was returning to Egypt.

# CHAPTER

# 3

*"From now on, trust no one," the dyeli said.
"We will be sure to keep an extra eye on you."*

## Flirting with Immortality

**B**ut they moved on until Cairo came into view. The exhaustion of the trip at the moment was lost in the beauty of the city waiting for them like a patient lover, its contours defined in the empyrean light as the descending sun sprayed a waning glow over the city's outline, creating a sense of calm, that twilight feeling that things are about to come to rest, even if temporarily. And seeing the city lose its horizon-like elusiveness, the sense of exhaustion turned into relief, and then the relief into excitement, which sparked joy, and then the joy and excitement provoked something even braver: Energy.

And Tiempo's nervousness increased at approaching the

land where he had once lived and found love, the land that had given him so much, the military conquests and great standing with the pharaoh at the time, at the same time as it had taken away the most important person in his life. But his anxiety was drowned in the ovation around him and the almost unanimous loud proclamation of joy and perhaps awe at seeing Cairo in sight after such a long journey.

The city (or a part of it rose like the glorious sun itself), though soon black in silhouette, outlined by the ever so gentle pink and yellowish glow of the sun that was sinking in the sky with brilliant but fading power like an ancient artifact. If they could leap over the short distance between themselves and the city, they would have seized that option immediately. But it required one hundred or so steps for Mansa Musa, Inari Kunate, Suleiman, the front guards, Tiempo, and a few others to finally enter Cairo, followed by the large caravan of human beings and animals in that ostentatious display of tenacity and wealth.

They were like an invasion of sorts, the group of sixty thousand in a city of one million. And everyone who saw the motional town stopped to watch in awe, the caravan that paved a way like a force of nature in the middle of a crowded street. Many came to line the streets, in a moment of the animate and inanimate lined up in spontaneous homage to the caravan, the animate represented by people (including peddlers and vendors), and camels and donkeys and the inanimate represented by the unending shops and markets.

Not long after this august entry, representatives of the Sultan of Egypt (Al-Malik an-Nasir), who knew the Mali caravan was on its way and now heard of its welcome intrusion, sent representatives to meet Mansa Musa to invite him to the sprawling quarters that had been prepared for the group. But now seeing the sights and sounds and flora and fauna of Cairo, Mansa Musa was highly curious, wanting to take in more of the city's soundscape and landscape. And he did a little of that but reckoned there would be opportunity for more of it in due course; so for now he, and the rest of the colossal retinue, needed to take a good bath, rest and recreate themselves.

(And so it was that the caravan came to a standstill for three months in Cairo.)

# SEASONS of FOUR FACES

## Eyeing Immortality

The Sultan's invitation to Mansa Musa was as welcome as it was expected by protocol, except Mansa Musa and his retinue had underestimated how grand it would be. On entry to the Sultan's palace, one of the sultan's men approached Mansa Musa before he could get close to the seated Sultan himself and noted that Mansa Musa was required to bow before the Sultan before he would be allowed to sit. On first hearing this, Mansa Musa squinted in surprise and asked that the request be repeated in order to dispel his disbelief. The request was repeated: he had to bow before the Sultan.

Taking deep breaths, Mansa Musa retorted, "How can it be that I am being asked to pay homage to a man? Am I not on my pilgrimage? I have come to praise Allah and only Allah."

He would not bow, creating a stalemate that was as odious and threatening as death itself and it appeared the event would end in ignominy before it started, and many in Mansa Musa's entourage were crestfallen, their glances cast downward as if in shame, while on the Sultan's side there were murmurs and expressions of anxiety.

At that moment, as if by some telepathic means of communication, Inari Kunate looked in Tiempo's direction, and Tiempo caught her eyes. Was she expecting him to resolve the impasse? Yes, he was sure she was saying. But how? He could not afford to disappoint Inari Kunate, even if her expectation of him was unrealistic. He looked at the Sultan, seated in his glory, a man assured in his expectations. Tiempo considered walking up to him and asking him to relent, to respect this glorious Emperor of Mali and waive the request to bow, but that would be a breach of protocol, Tiempo knew, and even if the Sultan agreed, which he most likely would not, Mansa Musa himself might not take kindly to such a brazen intervention.

And then a thought came to him.

Tiempo moved closer to Mansa Musa and whispered in his ear, asking if he could venture a suggestion. Mansa Musa asked him to proceed. Speaking softly, Tiempo suggested that Mansa Musa not bow but instead kiss the ground, a recognition not so much of the Sultan, but an act in honor of the land that was hosting them. Mansa Musa's countenance brightened immediately as he whispered to Tiempo, "This is why I brought you along, for moments such as this," and then proceeded to do just as Tiempo had suggested. Immediately after Mansa Musa performed this act, the Sultan spoke above everyone else and asked his august visitor to take the seat next to him. And the men entered into a lengthy conversation.

This is what most would remember, not the great food or entertainment, but how the men got along, except, of course, the enormous amounts of gold that Mansa Musa gifted to the Sultan.

And the ensuing days would be replicas of sorts of this generous gesture: the ample giving of arms randomly in the streets of Cairo, the overpayment of gold for goods in the marketplace and the general provision of gold, at times to all and sundry without discrimination. In those three months of their stay, Cairo witnessed Malian generosity in a manner no other nation had demonstrated, so much so that the price of gold fell significantly and there was a sudden inflationary pull on prices as, on account of the sudden influx of gold, demand outpaced supply.

## SEASONS of FOUR FACES

A grand moment indeed in Mali's impact, which enamored the Malian people to the Egyptians, which both pleased and amused Tiempo. As he strolled the streets of Cairo, he wondered if there was someone, perhaps a progeny of someone long, long dead, that he could somehow recognize, one of his soldiers' offspring perhaps.

BENJAMIN KWAKYE

# Looking for Immortality

One day, when he managed to free himself from the rest of the group, Tiempo tried to retrace his steps to his previous house. On broad boulevards and pathways, he walked past many markets and bazaars and mosques and colleges, and hospitals. But all these sights were an irrelevant backdrop to the one building he wanted to see. But it was not there. In its place was a farmland instead. Let his habitation become desolate or otherwise fruitful. Did it matter? He had moved on in many ways, except in other ways he had not. But there was one other house he hoped desperately, if unrealistically, would still be standing, one house he hoped would have withstood the erosions and demands of time, weather and humans, or at least to have left some remnant he could latch onto in homage and remembrance of the only woman he had loved, or would ever love, except he also shuddered to think that he could be losing his grip on this singular love, considering that the obscure woman in Oumar's household was contending for a part of him he did not want to give away.

So it was with some trepidation that he walked over, slowly and slower still to where Sharifa's house had stood. It was not there; instead, a large tree grew in its place. Tiempo thought a part of him had been uprooted and buried in a dark, dank tomb; and he cried, as he knelt down and, like Mansa Musa at the Sultan's palace, kissed the ground, tasting dust the way a snake eats dust. The dustbathing of his lips at that moment thrilled him because he was loving the soil where Sharifa had lived, but the strangeness of the serpentine thought was not lost on him and it was in anger that he allowed it to feed his mind, considering what he considered the serpentine treachery that had caused the demise of Sharifa and his own exit from Egypt.

He returned to his new people desolate, and Suleiman questioned why he was so sad in a period of joy and rest, reminding him that Inari Kunate would not be pleased to see him like this. Yes, but how could anyone understand what it meant to love and lose that love and then be condemned to live through generations in the experience of that loss and to believe that it was a love that could never be replicated? For on his many journeys, through bush and elsewhere, over many lands, fertile and barren, desert and oasis, he had experienced much, seen life and death, pain and joy, and hatred, but for himself never again the love that he had found for Sharifa. Was there a fate worse than death? Surely, the dyeli would not understand this transcendental love and how the nostalgic stairs of returning to the land that had initiated the love had torn anew a hole within him, springing forth a kind of pain that was so palpable it could fall many, as if death had taken residence in him, but would not kill him.

And that night, perhaps realizing that Tiempo was tormented and needed cheering, Suleiman sat with him for a long time, reminding him how he had become such a respected part of Mansa Musa's inner circle, how he was now a big part of the Mali family of great warriors and griots. He was home now, Suleiman said, and he ought to be happy that he was loved and respected by so many, including Mansa himself, and Inari Kunate. Whatever was bothering him, it could not, ought not, detract from the fact that he, Tiempo, was a part of this grand new family. The man was repeating himself and rather than this, Tiempo considered asking the dyeli about Oumar and his wives, but he refrained, as he had not developed that trusted intimacy with Suleiman that he had with Kouyate.

"I think your stature will only grow and grow," Suleiman said. "You are making some of us so jealous, Tiempo, but it's a good jealousy because it makes all of us want to get better."

These were some of the kindest words Tiempo had heard since he arrived in Niani and for a brief while the weight that had so strongly fallen on him lifted and he was able to enjoy the night's festivities. And someone whispered in his ears that Inari Kunate was immensely proud of him and would see to it that he was amply rewarded when they returned to Mali.

He tried to enjoy the rest of the stay in Cairo.

And soon the time came for the caravan to move on to Medina, cross a desert (again), the long and narrow one between the River Nile and the Red Sea.

SEASONS of FOUR FACES

# Foreign Soils

The time in Medina and the subsequent trip to Mecca belonged to Mansa Musa and most of his entourage, but Tiempo chose to stay in Medina. Having come this far with him, Mansa Musa hoped that his trusted companion would make the final leg, but he respected Tiempo's decision not to go along. So while most of the caravan was in Mecca, Tiempo roamed, pondered and wondered what to do when he returned to Niani. He suffered alone without the distracting sounds of many around him, and the hope that the relative solitude would help him contemplate his way to a solution, that the shedding of the façade of stoicism required of him in guarding Mansa Musa would ease his inner tensions, proved futile. It was a thought pattern with the same motif. And Sharifa would come to him in the tightest embrace ever. And they would roam lands and seas, lose each other and then find each other, and they would, in those times when they were apart, find counterfeits of each other who monetarily appeared to be who they were not. And in all this, the unnamed woman at Oumar's was a part of the backdrop, there and not there, visible and invisible. And when the caravan returned, he had found no solution to the brooding predicament.

Most notably when Mansa Musa returned from Mecca, having now become a Hajj, were the number of people he gathered to return with him to Mali, including the poet and architect from Granada, Abu Ishaq as-Sahili, also known as the Moor. It seemed Mansa Musa's magnetism had served him well in the manner he was able to convince such men to journey with him back to Mali. In addition to the Moor, he convinced a number of scholars to return with him, as well as four shurafa (who were descendants of Mohammed) and their families, this after great negotiation with Mecca's Grand Sharif.

What a great feat, many in Mansa Musa's retinue remarked. Mali would indeed be blessed by the scholars and the shurafa and was on its way to becoming renowned in the world, not only as a land of great wealth, but also as the epicenter of great learning and of Islam.

Tiempo noticed how excited Mansa Musa was to have the scholars and shurafa with him, how much he was engrossed in conversation with them and how difficult it was to pull him away from them. In particular, noting how he engaged the scholars, Tiempo remembered the vision of Ibrahim's uncle, Boubacar, about turning Timbuktu into a metropolis of great learning, and he wondered how fascinating it would be for the two men to talk, the philosopher and the king and how complementary that would be. He imagined the two men seated in deep conversation over the future of Mali, about spreading the knowledge of the Malian Constitution, about capitalizing on Timbuktu's location as a place where canoe met camel. As Tiempo imagined it, this would be a conversation of equals, the charismatic king and the somewhat introverted scholar, one spewing thoughts and the other implementing them in solutioning for establishing Mali's future as a great land and bridging internal fissures that might threaten that future.

But for the moment, the caravan would have to return to Cairo and buy supplies for the trip back to Mali.

Back in Cairo, many were worried about the nine thousand mile return trek to Mali, such that the joy of arrival in Cairo

## SEASONS of FOUR FACES

the second time did not match that of the first. Still, Tiempo and others tried to cheer the rest that they could look forward now to returning home, with the pride and comfort of having conquered the desert and putting Mali among the respected nations of the world, particularly with the showcasing of wealth and the elegance and pomp with which they had done so. For generations to come, song makers would compose songs about this trip, scribes would scribble great words about it, griots would weave elegant phrases, and cartologists world draw Mali with its glory, the only hiccup being that they ran out of gold, embarrassingly, and Mansa Musa had to borrow from the merchants of Cairo (later repaid with a handsome interest).

BENJAMIN KWAKYE

# Intrigues of Foreign Soils

Two nights before the departure from Cairo, Tiempo went to bed under the weight of his anxieties over the woman at Oumar's palace, but surprisingly fell asleep immediately. But his sleep did not last long.

Tiempo was gasping and gasping for breath, hoping that the dream would pass, except this hope was not materializing, indicating that he wasn't dreaming. Indeed, the hands on his neck were tactile and firm, such that he opened his eyes to the realization that he was going to die and that the death was by mis-virtue of murder. Thoughts rushed through his mind when he recollected a similar, though not identical, assault many, many years before in Egypt, also in the depths of the night, which in slow motioned recollection became even more sinister. As he tried to move, he realized that these were two people in the room, for his feet were held down, and that these were strong men, although the dark room's darkness made it difficult to see their faces in full.

With all the energy he could muster, summoned from years of warfare and combat, Tiempo lifted one hand and brought it straight to the solar plexus of the assailant whose hands were squeezing his neck. This caught the man by surprise as he staggered back, loosening his grip. The other man holding his legs down said, "He was supposed to be too weak to resist." Seizing this opportunity of surprise, Tiempo tried to lift himself from the bed, but realized he didn't have much energy. So he yelled as loud as he could:

MURDERERS!

The men seemed startled by this and froze briefly. They soon heard approaching voices, and the assailants fled from the room. When a couple of men entered the room, Tiempo was lying on his back. The men helped him to sit up and he told them about the attack and asked that they pursue the assailants. One of them left, rousing others to go along in the search. But they would return later saying their search had been futile.

The next day, when news of this reached Suleiman, he wanted to inform Mansa Musa to ask for help with the Sultan of Egypt to find the assailants, but Tiempo dissuaded him. He did not want to bother Mansa Musa, and besides, they would be departing Cairo the next day and would leave this behind them, though both men knew they would not leave this behind them, for they discussed the likelihood that whoever attacked Tiempo had help from the inside, helping provide easy access to Tiempo. And the admission by one of the assailants, who must have thought Tiempo did not understand his language, that Tiempo was supposed to be weak, suggested as much. It wasn't clear to Tiempo, though, exactly how he was supposed to be weak. Had someone attempted to put a soporific agent, perhaps, in his food? He had indeed felt weak at the point of sleep, when sleep had come suddenly. Was it a form of soporific poison that worked slowly? And he had was lethargic the next day. But if they wanted to kill him, why had they not brought a weapon that would have finished the job faster? Say, a knife? Or did they want it all to appear as someone who had died in his sleep? And, above all the questions, who would want him dead and for what reason? Was it someone on the trip he had offended in his first days in Mali whose grudge had matured to the point of murder? Was it someone he had otherwise offended on the trip itself? Was it someone jealous of his position with Mansa Musa? His questions were hard and ferocious but unanswered.

"From now on, trust no one," the dyeli said. "We will be sure to keep an extra eye on you."

The guard guarded?

# Invasion of Hope

Tiempo was glad to leave Egypt not because he was leaving the threat behind, in fact he believed he was traveling with the threat or even going into it, but because it would be harder for anyone to try to kill him in the course of the journey. He slept lightly as if with one eye open and he walked around carefully as if with an eye at the back of his head. And he made sure he watched his food, eating only when others had eaten and making sure he was present at the point when the food was served. With such caution, he moved on with the caravan on the return trip to Mali.

And on and on and on they traveled in the déjà vu drudgery of the desert, until it came to a point when Mansa Musa's wife, Inari Kunate, made magic happen in the desert, when one day, begrimed and frustrated, she said to her husband, "Kankan, I am weary, and I can't sleep. My body is covered with dust and grime. How I wish I could splash about and swim carefree in the river as I did at home."

Mansa Musa the Great summoned his head servant Farba and said, "I've been able to give her everything she's wished for, but only Allah could create a river in this barren place. What do I do now?"

Farba, like many others, had developed great confidence in Tiempo through observation and proximity, so he consulted with Tiempo and, after much discussion, they found a way. They gathered a number of men and dug a trench along a thousand foot line, throwing up a wall three times the height of a man, then the trench was lined with gravel and packed with sand for its entire length. On top of the sand, they placed blocks of wood rubbed with oil of khartie nuts. Then with a flaming torch they made the melting oil fill in the crevices to form a smooth channel. Several servants, in the thousands, were sent to an oasis to fetch and fill the canal with water. At sunrise, Inari and her five hundred women were led unsuspectingly to the canal. Seeing it, with utmost joy and shrieks, they ran and jumped into the water.

A canal in the middle of the desert had brought so much joy to Inari Kunate and many of the women and to Mansa Musa himself, but it also caused a delay in their progress and he was determined to make up for lost time by taking less frequent stops. Once again, Inari Kunate was sure to tell Tiempo how much she appreciated him after she heard of his part in granting her wish. It was a moment of joy in the otherwise monotonous routine. And on and on they went….

But then, just as unexpected as the appearance of a canal in the desert, they saw someone approaching, and they could not determine whether he was friend or foe. Tiempo got close to Mansa Musa, ready to draw sword if necessary. Unnecessary, for the man prostrated himself before Mansa Musa, announcing that he was a messenger of good news. Gao had been captured and Songhai was defeated and the king of Songhai was ready to surrender to Mansa Musa. This news jolted Mansa Musa into a celebratory mood and he ordered the caravan to make a detour to Gao, where he would receive the king's surrender and dictate the terms of the surrender.

Tiempo was heartened for Mansa Musa, knowing how important this victory was to him. But his joy was severely tampered by two things. First, if he had fought in this battle, for whatever it was worth, it would have been his eighteenth. But in his absence, the battle had been fought and won. And second, it would take even longer to return to Niani, prolonging further the still unformed plans that he had for the obscure woman of Oumar's home. As he brooded, Suleiman came and sat next to him.

"You look very sad for a happy moment for Mali," said the dyeli. "Don't disappoint Inari Kunate. What is causing this sadness, anyway? Is it the attack in Egypt?"

"That is part of it."

"If that is not all of it, what is the rest?"

Tiempo thought about this question for a long time. He had kept many secrets, but this one was so pent up he was afraid it would erupt into an untoward act if he did not unburden himself to someone. How he wished Kouyate, so far his only real confidante in Mali, had come on the trip.

"You will not understand," Tiempo said.

"I am your friend," Suleiman responded. "I will understand. Tell me. If it warrants help, I will help you."

"Why?"

"To me, you are family. You are an asset to Mansa Musa and Inari Kunate. That much is obvious to anyone. It saddens me to see a man as you so down. Tiempo, I know Mali; if there's anyone who can help anyone who is a part of this kingdom, it is me."

"This... it's too private a matter."

"That is why you only need to tell it to a friend. Unburden yourself or it will kill you, my friend. Tell me and free yourself."

Already decided to tell the secret but still not totally sure and hoping to ride time a little, Tiempo said, "It's a secret. Someone else might hear."

"I think we are out of everyone's earshot. No one will hear."

"Can I trust you?"

"Do you now want to insult me, my friend? If Mansa Musa can trust me, I think you can too."

"Very well, but you must never tell anyone this," Tiempo said, as he drew closer to Suleiman. And then in very soft whispers he told of his meeting with Oumar, the obscure woman's entry and exit, and how he couldn't get her out of his mind.

"Very strange," Suleiman said.

"I knew you would not understand."

"That is not what I said, but this is very dangerous territory. Yet, as I said, I will help you. But I don't know exactly how."

"Can you arrange for me to meet her?"

"First we must find out who she is," said the dyeli.

"Kouyate hints she might be Oumar's new wife."

"The wife that Oumar has been hiding? So Kouyate knows of your interest?"

"Yes, he is the only other person I have told."

"I can now understand why you did not want to tell me. And now that you've told me, you must be careful not to tell anyone. This is what I can promise you. When we get back to Niani, I will do what I can to get you a private meeting with her. I don't know if she's the same woman you saw, but once I get you together, you can find out."

"Thank you, my friend."

"May the heavens help you."

# CHAPTER

# 4

*"You are a very strange man, Tiempo," she said.
"What I offer you, many men would have seized, but you show such disinterest. Are you not a man?"*

## Looking Forward to the Past

The Great Mansa Musa had every reason to be joyful, having achieved great victory in his absence with the triumph of his army over Songhai and, having achieved great victory with the journey itself, stamping Mali's name into the annals of world history as a great, powerful, sophisticated kingdom, a shining light with a great leader. He had every reason to bask in these triumphs. When he rode into Gao on his bejeweled black stallion and in his white attire, Mansa Musa had the world at his feet. But, even though he dictated the terms of surrender to the king of Songhai, he had been careful to accord the Songhai leader all the courtesies worthy of a king. And then, in such diplomatic and military glory he had returned to Niani, his reputation expanded, greatly expanded, his mood booming, and thankful to all those who had helped make it so, from Inari Kunate to Suleiman to Tiempo, and he ensured that the welcoming festivities highlighted these men and women of his glory and Mali's great moment.

Nor had Inari Kunate forgotten her promise to Tiempo. The very next day after they returned, she summoned Tiempo to her presence, her maids standing beside her. She thanked him once again, emphasizing that he was now a full son of Mali. Whatever he desired, she would make sure that he received. And nothing was too much. Be careful, he spoke in his mind, for what I desire may come at a very high price. He would think about her offer, Tiempo said, and he was humbled to be so honored, he said.

But Inari Kunate wouldn't release him yet. "What do you desire at this very moment?" she asked.

"To spend time with my old friends again," he said, "Kouyate and Ibrahim and Mariam."

"You will, but what else do you want for yourself?"

"I am happy to serve the Great Mansa Musa," he replied.

"Gold?"

"I do not desire gold."

Inari Kunate's maids looked at one another in frowns. "You may not desire it, but you will have gold," she said. "What else?"

"Nothing else."

"Do you desire a wife? That can be easily arranged, you know."

You know not what you say, Inari Kunate, Tiempo said silently. Aloud, he said, "I do not desire a wife."

Inari Kunate's maids looked at one another in deeper frowns.

"Why, a man of your stature? But perhaps this is not the appropriate time to bring this up, so we will let it rest, but a beautiful woman of our kingdom you will have for a wife. You do not desire gold or a wife, but those you will have. Do you desire a house of your own? You have been staying with Kouyate for a while now. I think it's time you had your own house."

"I do not desire a house of my own," Tiempo said.

"You are a very strange man, Tiempo," she said. "What I offer you, many men would have seized, but you show such disinterest. Are you not a man?"

"I am, but I suppose just a different type of person."

"Very well, a house of your own you will have, though you do not desire it. These things I have promised, I will make sure you receive in due course. But for now, I want you to enjoy the celebrations."

While he participated in the palace's celebrations and accompanying joys, Tiempo's focus was elsewhere. And he was unshackled when he was released to return to Kouyate's (although Inari Kunate's promise of a place of his own echoed in his mind and he wasn't sure he liked it, worried that his return to Kouyate's home was supposed to be temporary). Although Kouyate had come to the palace to bid Mansa Musa welcome, it was not the same greeting his friend in the company of many and being with him alone, his attention singular. They both grinned with the joy of the proximity without other company, Kouyate bemoaning how lonely it had been without Tiempo, and Tiempo complaining about how he missed the times with Kouyate. For a while they talked about the trip, and Tiempo provided all the details in as much graphic description as he could, aware that to get to where he wanted to get to, he first had to sate Kouyate's vicarious wanderlust. There was not much Kouyate could say about events while Tiempo was away. So Kouyate listened and asked questions and, with great patience, Tiempo continued to feed Kouyate's hunger for knowledge of the trip.

After a while, Kouyate said, "You know, as impressive as this trip has been, I fear that Mansa Kankan Musa has done great damage to Mali."

"What?!"

Heresy of heresies!

"Think about it, all the gold spent, don't you see how this has drained Mali's coffers? Would we not have been better served if it had been spent here?"

"But think of the great impression he has made in the world, the admiration and the goodwill."

"And think about how he has marked Mali as a land of gold. Soon, the vultures will be coming to seek Mali's blood."

"So why didn't you say all the before the trip, Kouyate?"

"Like everyone else, I was caught in the glamor, but I have had time to think about it and also to consult."

"Consult with whom?"

"You know of whom I speak."

This conversation had not evolved the way Tiempo had expected and he tried to put it out of his mind.

As anxious as he was to broach the topic most important to him, Tiempo had to see his old friends, and in a way put himself through what he believed was a test of Mariam. So he went to see them immediately after he had exhausted the tales of the journey with Kouyate.

# SEASONS of FOUR FACES

    Ibrahim's excitement was so effusive, Tiempo was embarrassed by how the man went on and on about how much they had missed him. And Mariam's would have been no less colorful, but her pregnancy was weighing more heavily on her. She was heavier than Tiempo remembered, especially and obviously in the belly region, and her face was swollen and she chewed on her cola nut and spit on the floor again and again. And Tiempo realized that, even though her features were somewhat distorted by the pregnancy, she was no less attractive than the last time he'd seen her, only the urgings he had before were not as strong, he believed by virtue of his preoccupation with the woman at Oumar's home. For no other reason, if these were to be his friends, then Mali was worth it, Tiempo concluded as he left their house.

And then the moment came, when he believed he had fed Kouyate as much as he could and in fact exhausted any reservoir of memory or recollection of the trip. No more respectful of tact, Tiempo said, "Now I have to ask you an important question that has been itching my heart?"

    "I can guess."

    "I am sure you can. So have you been able to find out more?"

    "That, I am sorry I haven't. I have tried to ask, but in these matters, as you know, I have to be extremely discreet. It seems Oumar is very protective of her."

    "That is disappointing, but I am thankful that you tried."

    "Sorry, my friend."

    "Is there a way you can get me to Oumar's house?"

    "That won't be hard. I just have to find a good reason for you to get to meet Oumar again. I am sure I can come up with a good reason."

"No, no, no, Kouyate... I don't want a meeting with Oumar. I want a meeting with her."

"You have gone even madder than before you left on the trip. If you are suicidal, I won't help you achieve death."

"No one is going to achieve death."

"In any case, we don't even know with certainty who she is. And if she is the person we think she is, she is so well kept in the palace that I do not see how you can get to be with her."

"There has to be a way."

"Perhaps she will appear again when you get in front of Oumar, and then I can see what happens next. One small step at a time."

SEASONS of FOUR FACES

# The New

About two days later, both Tiempo and Kouyate were woken up in the middle of the night when Ibrahim rushed into the house, yelling that Mariam was dying and needed help. Could the seer help? Tiempo and Kouyate labored to calm him down in order to coax more information from him: Mariam was in labor and try as the midwife would, the baby would not come. Mariam had been at it for hours and she was losing blood and energy. He was afraid she would not survive. Tiempo considered it a desperate act to ask a seer for help with delivering a baby, but both men accompanied the agitated Ibrahim back to his home, if only to offer him support.

They heard Mariam's moans, the strained moans of an exhausted woman in pain, moans so soft in tone that, although the sounds travelled through the house's passageways to reach them in the outermost room, it signaled a surrender rather than a fight. Ibrahim was crying now, tears running down his face.

"Do you mind if I try?" Tiempo asked.

"You?" Kouyate questioned. "What do you know about midwifing?"

"I have experience in this," said Tiempo.

Ibrahim looked helplessly at the older man for guidance. "If he says he can help, let him do it," Kouyate said.

"Come then," the weepy Ibrahim said as he led Tiempo and Kouyate down a passageway to the room where Mariam lay on her back, her legs wide open, the midwife urging her on but apparently helpless herself. The midwife, her back to the men, turned to look behind her. "He will take over now,"

Ibrahim said.

The bewildered woman asked, "This is not a man's business."

"I will do it," said Tiempo.

"This is not a place for you," the midwife said.

Faintly, Mariam murmured, "Listen to him. Do whatever he says." It wasn't clear if she was referring to Ibrahim, Kouyate or Tiempo, but it did not matter, as the midwife moved aside and Tiempo knelt between the legs of the laboring woman. He studied Mariam, the disheveled hair, the stains of tears on her cheeks, what seemed remnants of saliva around her lips and chin, her exposed breasts full and heavy and falling to her sides, her body covered with sweat. He noticed the blood and feces. How is it that a thing of beauty is born in such indignity? Tiempo wondered as he closed his eyes and remembered.

And he became Sharifa.

He remembered that day when she guided him to give birth, not of a baby but of himself in a manner over which he had no control. Then he put both hands on Mariam's belly and began to knead and massage and caress. Slowly but assuredly he worked, coaxing the baby until he was certain it was ready at the bottom of the birth canal. Mariam was breathing heavily. Ibrahim was breathing heavily. Mariam was sweating. Tiempo was sweating. Tiempo took deep breaths, continuing to work on Mariam's belly as he spoke to the unborn. Sharifa's unseen shadow was breathing deeply too and speaking as well. And then he started speaking to Mariam, softly but confidently, saying, "The baby is now ready and you can push again." He asked the midwife to hold her hand for comfort and then he asked Mariam to push harder, as he continued to knead her belly gently. And then as she pushed, she expressed a guttural sound of pain as he had rarely heard, not even on the field of battle when soldiers succumbed to weapons thrust into bodies. But with this expression of pain came the protruding head of the baby. As the mother took her breath to regain energy, Tiempo urged her on, that it was almost over. As difficult as this was, she should give it one more push. And she did, this time her expression of pain lost in the weakness that engulfed her with the effort. And then Tiempo reached in a bit and pulled the baby out and then as the cry of the new baby pierced the air, Tiempo remarked, "Mariam, you are a warrior, but Ibrahim is the seer, for you have given him his wish for a baby boy." And Ibrahim's body collapsed to the floor in relief, muttering the words, "Tiempo. We had picked a name for him, but after tonight, his name will be Tiempo."

And Mariam whispered the name, Tiempo.

And Tiempo whispered the name, Sharifa.

BENJAMIN KWAKYE

# Thickening the Broth

That was a night of relief and joy for Tiempo, especially the honor of having the baby named after him. But his mind was now on his own affairs. Could Kouyate not see how this thing was consuming him? There had to be a way. He began a long period of contemplating how he could steal into Oumar's house, but he could not put anything concrete together as actionable. He had no deep knowledge of the soldier's house, let alone where the woman would be. Tiempo was on the verge of accepting Kouyate's proposal as better than nothing when he remembered his conversation with Suleiman and the promise to help. What did he have to lose? Off to the palace Tiempo went to seek the dyeli, who guessed what Tiempo had in mind before he asked it.

"I knew I would see you soon after you had recuperated from the long journey," Suleiman said.

"You can tell I am here."

"I have not forgotten the promise I made to you, and I intend to fulfill it."

"Intend, but have you done anything about it?"

"I have found out her name…"

"You have?" said Tiempo, leaning forward. "What is it? Tell me."

"You are so impatient," Suleiman said. "Her name is Fatima."

Fatima was not the name of anyone Tiempo deemed close.

Suleiman continued, "I have initiated inquiries and I know of certain patterns of Oumar, his comings and his goings, when he travels for duty. I know where Fatima sleeps. I can get you in to see her on one condition."

"You can really do that?"

"Not so fast, Tiempo. I said I can do it on one condition."

"What is your condition? Name it, whatever it is, I will do it."

"If it were that easy. It's not what you can or need to do. It's what she wants to do?"

"How do you mean?"

"Isn't it obvious, Tiempo? She has to agree to see you."

"Why? I will just go in there and talk to her."

"Listen to yourself. You can't just walk into her room and talk to her. What if she doesn't want to talk? What if she raises an alarm?"

"So how are we going to solve this?"

"Leave it to me. I will talk to her. I will tell her there is a great man who wants to see her. I won't tell her who it is, of course. But if she agrees, then you will have no problem. I can't guarantee anything. But I will try. If she disagrees then we will have to find another way for you to meet, perhaps on some public occasion when Oumar finally brings her out in public."

"How will you get to see her?"

"Like I said, I know when Oumar is home and when he is not. I have close contacts in his house. When you are Mansa Musa's dyeli, you have influence in many places."

And so it was settled. Suleiman would see if he could convince Fatima, if she would be willing to meet with a great man who had taken an interest in her. The waiting period was extremely painful for Tiempo, and at night he found himself moaning in pain, except he did not know where in his body he had any pain. And he would wake up at times aware that he had been muttering the words, "Fatima, let me in, please." He was afraid that his sudden somniloquism would alert Kouyate that something stealthy was afoot, or that the seer might see into his machinations with Suleiman. But that didn't happen and a few days later, the dyeli reported that indeed Fatima had agreed to meet with him. The dyeli had convinced her that one of the visitors to her home had noticed her and just wanted to talk. She had seemed hesitant at first, but she'd been flattered that a great man wanted to meet with her and also by a sense of curiosity as to who the great man was. What were this man's intentions? she had asked. Why did he want to see a married woman? His intentions were honorable in that he only wanted to become acquainted with her but her lack of public exposure had made this impossible, and he did not want to arouse undue suspicion hence the need for secrecy. Nonsense, she said. It didn't make sense, but still the mystery of this man was sufficient to warrant the meeting. She was only agreeing to meet him as a favor to the dyeli and she would only meet with him once. He would forever be in her debt, he had said.

"I think we both know that this is a game. She is no fool, I can tell, and she knows that your interest is not just platonic. She must know that you're more interested than that. No one would go to such secrecy and extent just for a platonic interest. But she is content to save face with the pretense. So let's give her that room."

"Should I worry about any palace guards?"

"There are two stationed outside, but from what I know they sleep when Oumar is not home. She says you need not worry about them."

"Can you describe her?" Tiempo asked.

"She was veiled. I only saw her eyes."

Suleiman had suggested that meeting in the palace was too dangerous so they should arrange for the meeting somewhere else safer. But she had rejected this idea. She would feel safer in her home. Instead of a secret rendezvous, he should come to her. She knew of a day when Oumar would be traveling for duty. On that day, he should come to her in the late night to her wing of the house, when the maidens were asleep. If he was there in the late night, she would let him in if it was safe. If not, if he waited a little while and she did not come out to let him in, he should leave knowing it was not safe.

"Did she ask my name?"

"She has asked, yes, but I have told her to ask you herself when she sees you."

"And she is content with that?"

"She is content to leave it at that."

So it was settled. And Tiempo waited for the day when he hoped to rendezvous with the wife of the second in command of the northern army of Mali. Yes, it was fraught with danger, but he was the husband of danger, and wherever he passed, danger rejoiced; so he would not let danger stop him from meeting the obscure woman, who cast such a long amorous shadow, who now had a name. Fatima. In fact, danger would rejoice to encourage him. But, as he waited, he was ridden with guilt as he was betraying his past, but at the same time he could not help himself, and it was though destiny was beckoning him, that in Fatima he would find something that would answer many questions, because there was no other explanation for why he would risk so much, why a woman he didn't know, whose face was as clear to him as a distant shadow hidden in a veil, would continue to chase him in his thoughts and dreams. But the danger was now also shared by her, for she too was risking much. Why? There had to be something that defied reason pulling them to each other. He would find out the reason when he saw Fatima.

SEASONS of FOUR FACES

# Romancing Fate

At the appointed time on the appointed day, Tiempo, dressed in black, stood outside Oumar's house in the strong darkness, waiting in deep anticipation. As promised, the two guards were asleep, seated with their heads resting on their bent knees. They must be there for needless deterrence, Tiempo concluded. At that moment, however, the once warrior could not find the shield to ward off the attack of nervousness; and he shook like the leaves of the tree under which he stood, his body wet with the expression of sweat that seemed in protest to the strain to which he had subjected his body. Husband of danger indeed, the bad part of his mind teased him; look at you now. He rehearsed and rehearsed the words he would say and even tried to say them sotto voce into the night with a voice that shook like the man himself. Prince of the Moon, this is your hour, he said. As his heart continued to stammer and beat against his chest, he kept looking at the door where he expected Fatima to appear, hoping that it would be sooner than later, at the same time as he wished she would not appear, somehow spare him from the strain of actually meeting her. The husband of danger had succumbed to the product of himself and his bedfellow (strain), for this time he had not been able to overcome the fear he knew so well, on battlefields of wars and human interactions.

This time it was as if he was totally unshielded and unarmed. He could not do this, he decided. It was just too difficult. He would leave, and when the dyeli asked, he would say she had not showed up at the appointed time and, as agreed, he had left. This was a painful defeat, but he reasoned it was a better one than going through with the rendezvous and punishing his body even more with the defeat to something deeper than fear he could not name.

But just as he was about to leave, he saw a figure appear at the back door (to the wing of the house where he'd been told Fatima resided) open, away from the front gate with the sleeping guards. The figure was barely visible in the dark, being dressed in all black. But she was there, totally garbed in a robe from her head to her feet, her face almost fully covered. As he gaped at the reality of her appearance, she lifted her right hand in his direction and gestured for him to come to her. Now was the do or the die. His fear wanted the die, but he could not now dishonor her so blatantly by leaving. Besides there was another part, equally now matched with the fear, though not defeating the fear, that wanted him to pick the do. It was also an obscure part of him, a place sweeter and more promising. A place powerful and encouraging. So he picked that part. And he did the do. The closer he got to her the more she seemed to pull alive certain aspects of the past within him, an intense sense of deja vu. And then when he was within a few steps, she turned her back to him and entered the building, leaving the door ajar in invitation for him to follow. He did. Then as he entered, she walked on, her back still turned to him, but moving slowly enough as a signal for him to follow. He did. And then they entered a room, which he guessed to be her bedroom.

He knew her.

He knew this woman, Tiempo knew this, even though he had not seen her face.

And the goose pimples that bathed him confirmed that this was—or would not be—an ordinary rendezvous. She closed the door when he entered the room, a room almost totally dark. But they could still see their profiles in the revealing darkness, now standing a couple of steps away from each other. There was no mistaken it now. Tiempo wanted to reach forward and take the clothing that partially hid her face, embrace her and tell her many things as much as he wanted her to tell him many things. He had known this all along but had not given it too much leeway for fear of disappointment. So he ought not to be so surprised. Still, this seemed so unreal, so unlikely to be happening, that the thoughts and emotions in his mind and body respectively stalled him, crippling him into inaction, perhaps shock. Then the lady who had been named to him as Fatima moved to one side of the bedroom and lit a lamp, all her movements slow and deliberate, as if she wanted to prolong every moment as he looked on with gaping mouth.

And then she said his name: Tiempo.

The world seemed to end, as he went deeper into a statis of shock. His chest was heaving so badly that he merely gasped horribly when he tried to speak. He wanted to speak her name but only bursts of incoherent air came out. Then as slowly and methodologically as she had lit the lamp and brought light between them, she removed the part of the clothing covering part of her face, so that now he could see her face. Tiempo collapsed, his body unable to control the whirlwind, the brutal blend of shock and reality that seized him. But though his body fell, he did not lose consciousness. She mentioned his name again. And it was the tenderness with which she said it that brought him faith that this was an opportunity that took its root in history and now reality. That she was not an apparition intent on causing him harm. It explained to him why he could not rid himself of her after that day when she had entered the room when he had audience with Oumar. It explained why he had so desperately wanted to meet with her when it seemed so foolish and even dangerous. Slowly, like a fallen soldier finding a new incarnation, Tiempo stood to his feet and, looking at her, face to face, he uttered her name, her real name, like it was his last breath, with the tenderness of shared, sweet knowledge, and the assurance of history. Not Fatima.

    Sharifa.

SEASONS of FOUR FACES

# Out of the Shadows

He knew it was her and she knew it was him. Still, after so many years, what were they to say to each other? What were they to do? The next act was one of total abandon, caution thrown to spontaneity, even though the impossibility of it still teased him. The embrace was of total surrender, each to the other, the kiss even more so. They had been so interluded for a long time, that the interlock was long and took them to a place sweeter than they could have imagined, better than their individual lives could summon apart, but together became a great and mighty river. Like the River Nile offering life and giving of itself and giving and giving as a place where only those who learned to swim its waters enjoyed its waves and its tides to the sweetest summits, a place where the rest of the world is like a forgotten shadow, a place where the sun shines bright and brighter yet without singed consequence, a place where the moon glow is like the noonday's glow.

    In the exhaustion of the embrace, they were also aware they had to face the aftermath with knowledge, so she led him to sit on her bed and slowly he told her of his many journeys. From Egypt to Kush, where he had stayed a while, its pyramids and elaborately laid out cities looking very familiar, like something he had seen before. Then one day someone called him traitor and threatened him with death for treason. He had not asked for an explanation or waited. He had moved south to the land of the Zulus, an itinerant without hope, just moving on and on, worried he had lost her forever. But wherever he went, he was unfulfilled, something was missing. He would move on, looking for that missing link. Perhaps her pull was what had brought him to Mali, where he hoped he could find fulfillment at last? And then that day when she entered the room, the heart disembodied, cut into two, had to recognize its other part, he said, and he now understood why he could not find rest until he met her, when reason, both his and others', wanted otherwise and even questioned his sanity. If only he had known that she had not died or where she was, his search would have been more focused, and certain.

Then she also told. No, she had not died in Egypt although she'd been almost killed. Adom had sent some men to her house to warn her that her life was in danger and he wanted them to protect her because he expected she would be attacked before the night was over. So the men had stayed with her, five of them, and just as was forewarned, they were attacked that night by a group of soldiers. Their surprise and disadvantage was that they had not expected her to be so protected and her guards took advantage of that element of surprise to repel the attack. But they knew the men would return with reinforcements and so they took her with them, to Adom's. But they were too late, for when they arrived they found him killed, his throat slit, with none of his guards there. Fearing betrayal, they had taken the body and moved to a secret hideout.

It was a treacherous time and no one could be trusted. They had stayed in the secret hideout for many days until they decided they could not do so for much longer. It would only be a matter of time until they were found out and killed. So they left the rotting body of Adom there, and went separate ways and she felt like she was being separated from so much, as if a knife was cutting through the finely wrought tapestry that had been her life in Egypt. She had joined a group of bandits for a while, who gave her protection in exchange for certain favors. She had stayed in Abyssinia for a while, but had become restless, like him, unfulfilled. She had traveled many lands, including Libya and Morocco and eventually joined another band of bandits who plied their trade across the Sahara and further south. On one of their escapades, they had encountered a group of men from Mali, led by Oumar, who were charged with rooting out the bandits who were becoming a nuisance to Mali's trade routes. Totally defeated after a brief skirmish, her compatriots were put to death, but Oumar stared at her, and frowning, expressed his admiration of her beauty and decided to spare her.

    He had brought her to the palace and asked to know more about her. Where was she from? She said she could not remember. He said she was not being truthful. What was her name? Fatima, she said, a name she just made up. He would call her by that name, but he had been suspicions of her veracity. He would have killed her, he told her, but he was smitten. Would she marry him? She would, if he so wished, but did he think it wise to marry a bandit? Would his family take kindly to her? That was his problem to worry about, he said. She agreed to marry him, a way to find some rest from her travels and to find temporary grounding, but the marriage had not been welcomed mostly because she was not Muslim and also that she was a suspicious figure, especially to Oumar himself, who therefore kept her indoors and did not want her fully visible "until he could trust her," he said. "If you hadn't won over my heart," he would say "you would be dead." And he would also say that he could not justify her before others, and that for the fact that he was so highly favored by Mansa Musa and feared by others, they would not have countenanced his marriage to her, which most deemed illegitimate. When he begged him to give her some public exposure, he said it was too risky and besides, she was "too beautiful for public expression," whatever that meant.

And then one day one of her maids had mentioned in a casual conversation that an unusual stranger had come to town and been summoned to see Mansa Musa, but he would not divulge his origins and called himself Tiempo. The name shuddered her heart. At first, she'd believed it to be mere coincidence, for how could he still be alive after so many years? But then she thought about it. If she was alive, why not him? If he was time, she was space. Where one stood, the other stood also. She wondered if this could be her Tiempo. So she had discreetly asked her maid about this new stranger and she had described him for her, increasing the belief that he could be his Tiempo. She had to find out for sure, but considering that she hardly had the chance to leave the house, except if she could do it without Oumar's knowledge, she decided to bring him to her. She had gone to Oumar and riskily, and asked him to summon Tiempo to the palace.

"The maidens speak of a strange man who is gaining great favor with Mansa Musa. As second in command to the northern army, if some stranger suddenly comes to your land and finds favor with the king, shouldn't you know him?"

That was the only seed she had to sow. Oumar had later told her that he had summoned Tiempo to the palace and he would find out what he wanted in the kingdom. So, knowing that he would be at the palace, her brief appearance was on purpose. If it was her Tiempo, once he saw her, even in disguise, even if brief, he would come after her. And that is exactly what had happened.

So now reconciled, what next? They would have to find a way out, although the path would certainly be treacherous. He wanted to stay longer, but she urged him to leave. She would tell him when next to come. Little by little, they would think about a solution. As difficult as it was to leave her that night, she was correct. And so he left, but would return again and again, exactly when she told him to.

It was a time of great risk in that there was always the looming danger that they would be caught. Whenever he set out in the darkness of the night, Tiempo was torn in two directions, one being the sheer joy he could not describe whenever he was with Sharifa, better felt than described, and the other being that sense of spectral doom. But if there was doom awaiting, this was worth it. If he had risked life and limb to fight many battles where death reigned, then he could risk life and limb to go to the place were love reigned. The most difficult part of this being eluding Kouyate, and sometimes telling him that he was needed at the palace for consultations, risking the possibility that the man might suspect or doubt him, or even see something with those his seer eyes. The guilt of lying to Kouyate was subsumed in the truth of his love. And it was on such occasions that he wished Inari Kunate would speed up the process of acquiring a house for him. All the fear and guilt was as good as nothing whenever Sharifa ushered him in. Those were moments that, like his love, defied vocabularic capturing. The closeness, the intimacy, the sharing of histories, even the mere presence of the other… those were beyond magical, and speaking of magical, they started to discuss ways they could escape their situation, including slipping Sharifa out of Oumar's house and leaving Mali for another kingdom.

    They realized that it would take something magical to accomplish this. Tiempo considered that the only way they would be able to do so would be to pick a moment when everyone's guard was compromised, so that they could make enough headway before their absence was discovered. Sharifa confessed how often she had thought of escaping when she first came to live with Oumar. But she had realized that escaping was easy; the challenge was to do so in a manner that would render it impossible for Oumar to recapture her. He had created circumstances that made it impractical for her to have any trustworthy friends, or even any friends at all, except perhaps her maids. Who would help her escape from the clutches of this powerful man in a way that would ensure she would elude capture? She had not been to find that magical trick and so had stayed. Now as they planned what she thought she could not accomplish alone, they realized it would take utmost secrecy and tact. And very careful planning. In the meantime they continued with their modus operandi.

Until one night, about two moons after his first visit.

The bedroom door was suddenly pushed open and in the doorway stood Oumar, two of his guards behind him, glaring at Tiempo and Sharifa in flagrante delicto. For a brief moment he stood there akimbo, clearly as a posture of offense, and even though a distance away, Tiempo thought he could hear the sound of his breathing, quick and deep and angry, foreboding something bad and evil. The darkness that silhouetted him in the doorway made his posture even more ominous. Oumar's frown was filled with desperation and anger.

## Pushed to Twilight

In his jail room, Tiempo had plenty of time to reflect. He recalled the look of horror on Oumar's face when he stepped farther into the room so that the features of his face became more visible, as he looked upon Tiempo and Sharifa, the face so tightly squeezed it seemed at some point its features would no longer fit on his face, the eyes widened, popped open by shock, and the exposed stained grimacing teeth. Then he ordered his men to seize Tiempo. Tiempo did not resist, although he could easily overcome them, including Oumar. But in quick thinking he asked himself what good that would do. Attacking Oumar and the guards without any means of a viable escape would only expose Sharifa to harm, or greater harm if he tried to abscond with her at the risk of pursuit by the other guards of the palace. And so he had not resisted as they seized him, his only words to Oumar, as they took him away being, "Please do not harm her. She is not at fault. I am solely to blame." He ordered him to shut up, and he did, more for her sake than his, Oumar trying to establish an authority that had been severely dented or even lost, if temporarily.

"What are you going to do?" Sharifa asked.

"Be quiet!" Oumar ordered, his ominous frown deepening.

"Please," Sharifa said, as she threw herself against the guards who moved forward to arrest Tiempo.

Oumar brought a heavy hand down, slapping her cheek and knocking her backwards on to her bed.

The moment called for utmost restraint, for as much as he was ready to take all pain and assault, he could not bear to see Sharifa under such assault and he almost avenged that slap there and then.

After the guards seized him, they pushed him out of the room with his hands held behind him. He looked back at Sharifa and saw a face that almost brought tears to his eyes, a look of confusion and disappointment, even horror. As he locked the door behind him, Oumar said, "I will deal with you later."

The guards holding his hands, Oumar behind them with his sword drawn, they led him outside and walked him around the corner through a bypath. As they walked him on, he considered what he would do if they tried to kill him. Should he overpower them and fight to the death? But then what would it mean if he killed the second in command of the northern army? Would his connections to Mansa Musa and Inari Kunate and Suleiman and Kouyate help him, or would it be an act too egregious for pardon? He saw life and death dangle before him like a poisonous fruit that he would be forced to pluck and consider the consequences later. But he was not forced to make that choice, as they took him to an isolated building and threw him into what would become his jail room. He knew guards were stationed outside, for he could her them speak from time to time. (And he knew they changed and brought different guards at different times, as he heard different voices from time to time.)

Inside, the room was bare, with nothing except a floor of sand.

All this while, his biggest worry was what would happen to Sharifa, his greatest regret that the joy they had found or rediscovered had been so soon truncated. Whenever he thought of her he shuddered miserably to think that they might kill her. Tiempo so desperately wanted to get word to Oumar to plead her case, to kill him instead of her. Whatever price was required he would pay it, the only one too high to pay was to live again in the knowledge that she'd been killed. He wondered who else knew. Did Kouyate know? Did Dyeli Suleiman know. What about Mansa Musa and Inari Kunate? If they knew, what were they doing about it?

Tiempo shouted a number of times from the room, asking the guards what had happened to Sharifa. They did not respond or even acknowledge him. After the first two days of trying, he stopped.

For days they fed him nothing and he got weaker and weaker.

Some of his questions were soon answered when Suleiman came to see him four days after he had been jailed. Suleiman embraced Tiempo, which he thought was a kind gesture, considering he hadn't washed for a long time and he must have been emitting foul smells. At that moment, Tiempo could barely move, starved into even greater weakness, and his every word was almost a whisper.

Suleiman noticed this, saying, "I can see they haven't been feeding you."

"Thank you for coming to see me, my friend. I haven't tasted food or drank water in days."

"Don't strain yourself," Suleiman said. "I will be back soon."

He left immediately and returned soon. Shaking his head, he said, "The guards won't let me bring you any food. They said they are under strict orders. This is madness."

"Once again, thank you for coming to see me," Tiempo said. "I didn't know you knew I was in here."

"Fatima managed to get word to me," Suleiman said.

Tiempo's heart skipped and pulsated. "Is she alive?"

"She is," said Suleiman. "It seems Oumar loves her too

much to kill her, although I am told that he severely beat her. I am also told that he is keeping her under great scrutiny."

"Can you get word to Oumar not to blame her but to put all the blame on me? Whatever anger he has he can direct it at me. I will bear any punishment he wants to mete out, including death. I only want him to leave her alone."

"That will do no good, my friend. If anything, any word from you will only infuriate him."

"So what does he intend to do?"

"I am not sure. I think he would have killed you long ago but for fear that killing you will infuriate Mansa Musa. He must also be aware of how Inari Kunate has become fond of you."

"So the Great Mansa knows?"

"He does. I told him, hoping he would order Oumar to release you. I also told Inari Kunate."

"And what does Mansa Musa and Inari Kunate think?"

"I can tell you that he is very sad about the situation. He is disappointed that you were caught in the inner chamber of a married man's wife. He considers that alone a great offense against man and Allah, and it does not help that Oumar is also a trusted commander and tax collector. And though he has asked Oumar not to kill you yet, he is also not able to order him to release you. Inari Kunate is distraught. She has asked Mansa Musa to order your release, but the king can't find a good justification to do so. I had to prevail on Mansa Musa to ask Oumar that I be allowed to visit."

"I am so sorry I disappointed them."

"They are sorry to see you here, believe me, and this deeply hurts them."

"You can tell them I am very sorry and that I will give my life to save Fatima's."

"Is she really worth all this trouble, Tiempo? A woman you hardly know?"

"You won't understand."

"That is what you have been saying all along."

"I wish there was an easy way I could explain it to you, but trust me then I say it's all not easily comprehensible except between Sharifa and me."

"Between you and who?"

"Never mind."

"All I can say is take heart. If we can find a way out for you, we will."

"Thank you. You have been a good friend. Can I now ask you one favor?"

"For you, my friend, yes."

"Please tell Kouyate what happened, and if you can, please get approval for him to visit me."

"I will."

BENJAMIN KWAKYE

# Beckoning Night

Suleiman kept his promise. And Kouyate came to see him the next day. Alarmed to see how much weight Tiempo had lost and how weak he had become, Kouyate left and, like Suleiman before, returned in despair. "They won't let me bring you food. It seems they want to starve you to death or punish you by depriving you of food until you're on the verge of death."
"It is so good to see you again, Kouyate, even if the circumstances are not so good."

After pacing for a while, Kouyate told Tiempo he would be back shortly. It took almost the rest of the day, but when he returned, Ibrahim and Mariam were with him, Mariam carrying the baby Tiempo. He explained that the guards would not let Ibrahim and Mariam in and Kouyate had to get Suleiman to bring pressure to bear from the palace on Oumar for the additional visitors to be allowed. If the three had argued with the guards outside, Tiempo had not heard it, as he had been sleeping most of the time, his weakness worsening. Despite his condition, and the foul smells he must have been emitting, they showed no hints of discomfort. And then as Tiempo lay on the floor, weak and unable to garner strength, he smiled at his friends and said, "Thank you."

Ibrahim and Mariam looked at Tiempo with furrowed brows. Ibrahim whispered into Mariam's ear and she nodded. Then Ibrahim said, "We hear they won't let anyone bring you food, so we have come to feed you."

Tiempo could not find the joke in this remark, considering that they carried no food, but he managed to force a weak smile.

But he had misjudged them. Mariam gave the baby to

Ibrahim and slowly lowered her body until she was kneeling next to Tiempo. Then she lifted her tunic, exposing her breast engorged with milk. Mariam pulled out the breast until it was dangling before Tiempo. Then she leaned forward and pressed the nipple to Tiempo's lips. He could not believe it, but as much as it seemed unreal, he could feel the nipple, tactile, pushing against his lips.

"Drink," Mariam said.

"Drink and be strong," Ibrahim said.

In his weakness, Tiempo looked up at the woman leaning over him, her reassuring face, even smile. He looked at the breast, remembering the night when she delivered, how they lay on her chest carelessly as though bereft of life. Now they were alive, engorged with milk, the nipple elongated, the aureoles themselves full. She must have sensed his hesitation and so she lifted the nipple from Tiempo's lips and squeezed her breast until a trickle of milk fell out onto Tiempo's parched lips. His hesitation faded as she pushed the nipple back on his lips and pushed harder. The other men in the room stood helplessly, wishing they could help but incapable of doing so, their usefulness at that moment peripheral. And Tiempo gave up all resistance and opened his mouth and sucked and sucked, feeding from her.

This would continue for a number of days until Tiempo regained strength. The guards would search the visitors to ensure they were not carrying any food whenever they came to visit, and then the three would walk into what had become Tiempo's jail room and Mariam would breastfeed Tiempo. When Tiempo needed to urinate, the guard told him to do so in the room, once when he needed to defecate they had him wait until nighttime and then they took him outside the building, all the while with one of them aiming a bow and arrow at him. Among themselves they wondered how he was so strong and even able to defecate when he had not eaten in so long.

When Kouyate came to see him alone next, realizing that Tiempo had regained considerable strength, he was not as accommodating as before. "What you did was very stupid," he said. "I refused to help you any further with this madness of yours, but you persisted and went behind me. And now look where it has brought you."

"I am deeply sorry, Kouyate. You have been my only true friend in Mali. You and Ibrahim and Mariam. And Suleiman."

"Suleiman? What makes you think he's your friend?"

"He has been good to me, Kouyate. He has been very kind to me."

"Is that so?"

"Yes, he has, and you know it."

"Who knew of your visits to Fatima?"

"He did."

"I knew you were leaving the house at night, but you never told me where you were going, so if anything I could only guess. I had my suspicions, but I concluded that you are a grown man, so I should let you be, though at times I wanted to interfere. Suleiman is the only one who knew for sure."

"What are you saying?"

"What is the dyeli's job?"

"Why do you ask? Everyone knows he's a trusted counselor to Mansa Musa."

"That's right, so who stands to lose the most if Mansa Musa turns to someone else to be his trusted counselor?"

"I suppose he would lose the most."

"And from what I hear Mansa Musa had been saying great things about you, including when you were before the Sultan in Cairo, or when you helped create a stream in the desert. And not only that, Inari Kunate had also become very fond of you."

"What are you implying, Kouyate?"

"Think, Tiempo. If anyone wants to get rid of you, who would it be?"

"No..."

"Were you not the one who told me you were attacked in Cairo?"

"Yes, but..."

"Who would have the influence to be able to do that?"

"Are you saying Suleiman ordered the attack?"

"You must leave Niani tonight, or you will be killed."

"But Suleiman told me Mansa Musa has ordered Oumar not to kill me."

"Please stop believing what he has told you. I'm not sure Mansa Musa knows, and this is too delicate a matter for me to raise with him. After all this while, I am sure he would have asked about you and they would have told him what they want him to hear. In fact, they won't even let me get close to him lately."

"That doesn't make any sense. Why would Suleiman tell you to come and see me if he is behind all this?"

"Perhaps he wants you to have your guard down."

"And you told me you asked him to put pressure on Oumar to allow Ibrahim and Mariam to visit me."

"He and Oumar are close and that is what I exploited. But I made it appear I was asking him to go through Mansa Musa for help."

"It doesn't make sense at all."

"To me it makes senses. Like I said, he may be goading you to lower your guard to make it easier to kill you."

"So you are saying Suleiman wants me dead?"

"Don't underestimate the power of envy."

These words pulled Tiempo's memory back to a night in Egypt when Suleiman has said: *You are making some of us so jealous...* And Tiempo became more receptive to Kouyate, who continued, "I have ears on the ground. I have heard things. Suleiman commands fear; I command loyalty, and those close to him have told me things discreetly. As they did in Cairo, your dinner tonight will be poisoned. Now, knowing how beloved you are in the palace, they do not want to just kill you with sword or arrow. And I think they are afraid that it will be difficult to kill you and hide your body, that somehow your body will be found. So they were hoping to starve you to death and then they would find a way to convince Mansa Musa that you had died of some strange disease. Oumar would tell Mansa Musa that he found your emaciated dead body on his way to the north and tried to save you but it was too late. And, perhaps he is hoping to be rewarded as the one who found you and tried to save you. But clearly that has failed, as they did not anticipate or know about Mariam's breastfeeding. But tonight, they will try something else. They will bring you poisoned food. When they bring it to you, they expect it to weaken you. And then while you are sleeping at night they will come in and finish it off by hand. But this time they will not take any chances. The poison itself may be enough to kill you off, the ones who come in at night are just to ensure that you are dead, and if not, to finish the job."

"But if they wanted to kill me, why have they waited this long?"

"Are you not hearing me? You survived their effort to starve you to death. How many can perdure past three days without food and water? You are stronger than most and so you survived until we were able to help you. But they are desperate now. So when they bring you the food do not eat it."

"And what next? What about Fatima?"

"I have managed to get word to her. She said to tell you to do all you can to escape."

"Escape where?"

"Wherever. She said wherever you go, she will find you. She said you have been doing all the pursuing but this time she will be the one pursuing you, whatever that means. She said you should not worry about her and she knows you will say you won't leave without her, but she says to tell you she knows how to take care of herself and that she will be fine, that all these years she has survived as you have and that is because it is meant to be so."

"But doesn't she know too much? Won't they kill her?"

Tiempo could not leave Sharifa behind to be fossilized in the regrets of his memory.

"She was worried you would say that. She said you shouldn't worry. She said she has escaped a great king before, whatever that means, and that she can escape a mere assistant commander."

"But to leave without her?"

"Tiempo, for what it's worth, listen to this seer. I have seen into the future and I see her finding you in a metropolis. I don't know where or when, but I have seen it. The most important thing is to keep you alive."

"And you? After all that you know, are you safe? Won't they try to kill you."

"Many have tried, none has succeeded. I know how to take care of myself."

The men hugged a long time.

"Be strong," Kouyate said.

"Thank you," Tiempo said.

Kouyate cried. And Tiempo almost cried.

The story Kouyate had told seemed too intriguing, too contrived, and Tiempo doubted that it was true. What if Kouyate was the one plotting against him? What if he was acting in concert with the dyeli and Oumar? He could not tell whom to believe at that moment. And as he considered this, extreme tiredness overcame him and he could not repel the sleep that swept over him.

And in that deep sleep he dreamt. Someone came to the room, an unannounced, unexpected visitor covered in a black cloak and wearing a long beard. But even before she spoke and took off the false beard, Tiempo recognized Sharifa.

"You," he gasped.

She hushed him, whispering they did not have time. He was to do exactly as Kouyate had suggested. She was on borrowed time, having disguised herself as a palace hand in order to get to him, with the help of a few sympathetic guards.

"Do not worry about me," she whispered. "You must listen to Kouyate and leave tonight."

"How can I abandon you?"

"Love, it is the only way; otherwise, you will perish and if you perish so will I."

"I can't."

"You must. Do this for me, if not for yourself."

"I don't know how I will live without you now that I have found you again."

"I will find you. It's my promise on our love. No matter how long it takes. I will find you."

They did not have time so they embraced that moment with all they had, on the altar of a goodbye which they did not know how long it would last. They dug deep and deep to a place past night and darkness, to a place of inexhaustible sunlight, of palm trees and various flowers, a place of greenery and life, where birds chirped and winds soothed. Past quick exhaustion, they were reinvigorated to begin again, and reluctantly disengaging in the hope that the farewelling was temporary, to be falsified soon in a future reunion.

When he woke up, hoping the dream was real, he searched for the false beard but could not find it. But he could hear the voice from the dream as clearly as he could hear his own breath:

"You must listen to Kouyate and leave tonight."

"I will find you. It's my promise on our love."

And then he was no longer in doubt.

As Kouyate had warned, they brought him the meal he was supposed to consume. "Courtesy of Oumar," the guard said. "He has decided to pardon you. Tomorrow, he will release you. He is doing this out of generosity and because he loves Fatima. He has heard her pleas and decided to release you, only you must never come near Fatima. This is his gesture of goodwill. But first, you must finish the meal quickly. I will return soon for the bowl."

Tiempo took the meal. The guard's mistake: leaving him alone with the food. Tiempo wondered why he would not watch Tiempo eat to be sure. But then again, how would he know what Tiempo knew? Plus, while he had developed some sort of anosmia on account of his familiarity with the execrable stench in the room, few could suffer it, and only those whose interest in him was borne out of love had withstood it. The guard must have found it unbearable to stay in the room. Alone, Tiempo dug a corner in the room, now seeing the earth on which he had slept all this while as a blessing.

He poured the contents of the food into the hole and covered it, careful to soil his hands with some of the food, before wiping it with sand. Then he called the guard moments later and, licking his lips gave the guard the empty bowl.

The guard took the bowl and peered at Tiempo, as if suspicious of him. "Have you finished the meal?" he asked.

"Yes, it was very delicious and fulfilling. So much so that I'm beginning to feel tired already. Eating so much food after a long period must be taking its toll. I think I need to get to sleep."

This seemed to satisfy the guard, who glanced about the room in one quick inspection and then left.

Then in a short while Tiempo pretended to be asleep.

It took a while, but that night, from the corner of his eyes, he could see the door opening and people peering into the room, apparently to ensure that the poison was doing its work.

But forewarned, he was prepared for them when they came. The fight with the three men was swift, for indeed they were no match for Tiempo. As they lay on the floor writhing, he took one of their bows and arrows, which he released as the outside guards came at him. Then Tiempo stood outside in the darkness, and Sharifa's oneiric voice urged him on: "I will find you. It's my promise on our love."

An inner voice told him he ought to wake up from his dream, but another replied that it was a dream from which he will never wake up until it was fulfilled. And then the first voice asked him to make the dream a vision, saying dreams die but visions live.

He no longer hesitated and began to sprint into the night. He had no choice but to stand on those words and believe that she would live, just as he must live, and so the important thing for him was survival.

The night was dark, darker than he could ever remember it, exactly what he needed to make his escape. He was about to leave when he reconsidered and went back and stripped the attire from one of the guards, hoping that it could come in handy as a form of disguise. And now he took a deep breath, inhaling the fresh air of the hour. Tiempo looked around him to take in what was most likely the last sights he would have of Niani. Memories rushed through his mind quickly, of Mansa Musa and Inari Kunate, of Suleiman, of Kouyate, of Ibrahim and Mariam and the young Tiempo who might have called him uncle one day and considered him a father figure. He replayed the time with Boubacar, and he remembered Soukar-Zouma, the commander of the southern army who might with time have become a close friend. He remembered the gift Ibrahim had once given him, the carving of a tall, muscular man with a long spear in hand, reassuring him that he was indeed a warrior, the spearer of all obstacles.

Tiempo took in a couple of deeper breaths and he began to run into the night (or an observer might say he was running away from the night). He ran and did not look back

At some time they would discover the bodies of the guards and that hope of victory would mutate to the bitterness of defeat. Oumar would be enraged and would come after him, perhaps even organize some form of posse comitatus if he could convince others of his cause or failing that marshal as many of the forces of the army at his disposal as he could to pursue Tiempo. And failing that, he would not be surprised if Oumar rode horseback alone in pursuit of Tiempo. His only hope was that, by the time the alarm was sounded that the prisoner had escaped, Tiempo would have made significant headway on his exit and Oumar and whoever came along in the pursuit would be pursuing him into the night of which he, Prince of the Moon, was so familiar.

# PART III

# CHAPTER

# 1

*"And I am told they put you in the hut of ghosts," she said.*

## The Arrival

The forests were as dense as night, even though it was noon time. The wawa and other trees were as an umbrella, shading the angry sunrays. And the shaded grass was like a lowered hispid palanquin, bearing his body as he lay spreadeagled in seeming exhaustion. Though the body was immobile on the grass, the way it reposed provoked thoughts of something regal. And yet, there was nothing dignified about the millipedes and other worms that roamed around him, some fearlessly climbing and descending his body as if it was an anthill they could play in or on with impunity; never mind that the rising and falling of his chest was a clear signal that he was alive. How much alive, that was not so clear.

But if these little arthropods were bold to dance on the body of a large man, the bigger beings were not so blatant, content to observe the man from a bit of distance. Suffer the little animals to come to me, for theirs is the body of man for pleasure, the scene would suggest. Ruminants peered for a while and then scampered away. Pigeons perched on an orange tree directly above him tarried a little and flew away to be replaced by braver hawks that came closer with flapping wings, without getting too close, and even they circled but for a while and left the scene. In the distance, the battling sounds of such birds formed a chorus, whether in welcome serenade or a form of dirge was not yet clear. Would the man live or die? If he would die, some of these animals appeared to want nothing with his death. The grass cutters came and the rats too and departed, where the hedgehogs would not even approach. And all this while the man lay on his back in a vulnerable position, not stirring to the songs of the birds or the bellowing of larger beasts, not moving to the tickling of the worms or the shuffling of wind inspired movements of leaves, some of which attached to his body after the wind had carried them to him, creating a patchwork of little wigglers and larger leaves.

He did not stir even when there was a brief interlude of rain showers, which for a short while separated the dense leaves and branches and tapped on his body—ta ta ta—as if wishing to wake him up, as if to tell him that this was just a deep, long sleep, not some sort of prelude to death. Then after a while, after the rain stopped, the remnant of water left on the treetops and branches and leaves fell now and then to replace where the wetness had lost its fatness. Through all this, he did not stir. Not even when the sun that returned after the break of rain began to descend, discoloring the yellow brightness above the treetops that yielded to a gray.

It was at that time that a group of women came across the man. There were ten of them. At first they thought it was one of the townsfolk, perhaps a lazy farmhand who had decided to take a nap on his way home, although the time and place would be unusual choices. And they might have walked past him had not one of them taken a second look and, despite the encroaching opaqueness of the hour, noticed that this was not one they were familiar with. She prompted her compatriots to stop and look, pointing at the body. They did, startled to see the man, muscular and unclad from the waist up, his loin cloth soaked, revealing the outlines of impressive genitalia under the wet layer of clothing. Whether for salacious purposes or on account of stirred maternal instincts, they could not move on. Who was he? They asked one another without expectation that any one of them would have the answer.

Futile questions and answers floated. What did he want? Why was he lying there so vulnerable to human, weather and beast? Where had he come from? He was a lost stranger, some said. He was a warrior of sorts, others said, judging by his angular muscles. The only question with practical relevance was the one asked last: Does he need help? He did not, not for a man of his size and physique. But others rejoined that he may have been hurt by something. After a little debate they concluded he did, but the what and how became the question. After a little more consultation they hastily left to fetch others from nearby farms. Let the men deal with the man. But even after seven heftily built men arrived, they hesitated on seeing the unusual sight, not just of a man lying down, but a man of impressive structure and sculpturing of muscles, in a pose at once vulnerable, but threatening (in the possibility that if startled he might spring forward and seize whatever was in front of him).

But eventually they approached him, if carefully, until they had surrounded him, their farming cutlasses drawn to face any threatening eventuality. But they did not know how to rouse him from what now appeared just a deep sleep, and seven alert men with ten alert women behind them stood in silence around one unalert man.

The question remained: What should they do?

But soon they no longer needed to act, as he helped them by opening his eyes, eyes which initially stared up into the open as if trying to draw nonexistent sidereal inspiration before darting to the left and then darting to the right. The men held their cutlasses tighter and pointed at him, a couple of them taking a few steps backward, furtive steps for fear the others might label them cowardly.

There was a short stalemate, as the stranger stirred awake and those around him upped their guard, until one of the men waved his cutlass and asked, "Who are you?"

The waking man blinked and continued to blink and it seemed he would not stop blinking. When he opened his mouth, all he did was lick his lips.

"Can you hear me? I said, who are you?"

Still, the man did not speak. "Do you understand me?" The speaker pointed with one hand to his chest (while another pointed a cutlass at the stranger) and said, "My name is Addae." He then pointed to the cutlass holding man closest to him and said, "Karikari." Then pointing to the stranger with an unarmed finger, he asked, "You, what is your name?"

Slowly, as if his tongue needed to adjust to his mouth to find the power of speech, the man on the ground said, "Tiempo."

For a man who had just stirred from what seemed a deep

sleep that was hardly distinguishable from death, the clarity of his deep, commanding voice, was surprising, briefly stunning the men around him. They weighed his response in the pause. And then the one who had spoken asked, "I have never heard that name before; from where have you come?"

"From very far, across many lands."

The man spoke their language with ease. Was he one of them from a neighboring village? The women among them in particular murmured their approval of this development.

"But where?"

"No name. I can't say."

"What does that mean?"

"What I said."

"Man from land of no name, with a strange name, what is your mission here in Ejisu?"

"I would very much like a place to stay."

Karikari, like Addae, coevals and bearing little scarification mark on both cheeks, now asked, "How can we give you a place to stay when you won't tell us where you have come from ? Who sent you?"

"No one sent me. I only want a place to stay and work to do."

"What shall we do with this riddle?" Addae asked.
"What if we killed him?" Karikari asked. "He could be Aboakesie."

"He's not as big as Aboakesie," Karikari said.

"Perhaps he's Aboakesie's son," said Addae.

"Let's kill him, I say," Karikari said.

"You can't kill me," Tiempo said.

"You are a very bold man to say that when you see all these men with their cutlasses," Addae said. "You may be a big man, but we are strong and fearless and we have weapons."

"I know what I am saying," Tiempo said, as he sat up.

"Stay down!" Addae yelled.

Tiempo stayed in his sitting position and said, "You will find that I am a very hard worker if you give me the chance."

"I say let's finish him," Karikari said. "He looks like a murderer."

"No," Addae replied, "we can't shed the blood of a stranger without just cause? Karikari, what has entered your head?"

"Why don't you take him to Nana and let her decide what to do with him?" one of the women said.

"Fosua has spoken wisely," Addae said.

"Why would you bother Nana?" Karikari replied. "We should deal with him ourselves."

"Something tells me there's something good about this man," one of the women said.

"Something says something for nothing," Karikari said. "He won't tell us where he is coming from, which to me creates enough suspicion to finish him. Have you not heard it said that when you find the spider you should kill it, else it will turn into a tarantula and bite you?"

While Tiempo sat and watched, the group debated his fate for a short while and the majority agreed that Fosua had spoken wisely. They all stepped back and Addae ordered Tiempo to stand to his feet. Then Addae asked him to walk ahead of them on the pathway he indicated as the group followed, their cutlasses always at the ready as they yelled orders at Tiempo, where to turn, how fast he should walk.

SEASONS of FOUR FACES

# House of Queens

Nana Yaa Asantewaa was seated in her front yard with her daughter Serwaa in the early dawn of dusk when the party arrived with Tiempo. If she was fazed by the way they briskly, if also brusquely, marched into her courtyard on an evening when she hoped to relax in conversation with her daughter, she did not show it. Just by looking at her, Tiempo concluded she was of great importance. It was not by virtue of size, for indeed she was slight in physical stature and looked worn by many years. He noticed that she was darker in complexion than most around her. It was also the way she sat and listened and observed, exuding an undeniable dignity and power. After she inquired about their business and they apprised her of developments, she looked at the stranger for a long time. All this while, Tiempo, head bowed, put both hands behind him, as though they were shackled together.

"Stranger," Nana Yaa Asantewaa said, "Can you look up?" He complied. She nodded and said, "By looking at you, your countenance and composure, you strike me as a man of importance, perhaps even someone's royal son."

"Didn't I tell you?" Fosua said.

"You did not; shut up and let Nana speak," someone yelled.

Nana Yaa Asantewaa continued, "I must ask you where you have come from."

"From very far, Nana."

"What place is that?"

"I can't say, Nana. Please forgive me."

"Is it in Asanteman?"

"No, Nana."

"But so far you have been speaking Asante very well."

"I learn languages very easily, and by roaming the farms these past few days and listening, I have picked up the language."

"Stranger, that is a story I cannot believe. You are not God to be able to speak a language so easily, but it seems to me that circumstance, perhaps a strange circumstance, has brought you here. Perhaps the past is just too painful for you to reveal to us. After all, as much as you are a stranger to us, we are also strangers to you. But it is difficult for me to decide on what to do because you have told us so little. We are a hospitable people, and we deal well with strangers, but we could also be allowing evil into our midst."

"Isn't that what I said?" Karikari remarked.

"Shut up and let Nana speak," the same person who had yelled before echoed himself.

"Stranger, I am sorry some of my people can be rude sometimes," Nana continued, "but as I was saying, you could be a man of evil intentions. Not everyone loves us. So, tell me if you were sitting in my place, what would you do?"

Tiempo bowed first, but then what he did next drew gasps of surprise as he knelt down before Nana Yaa Asantewaa and prostrated himself before her. And then he lifted her leg and placed it on his neck, the last act causing a few men to move forward in fear that he was about to do harm to the queenmother. But she quickly stretched out her hand to stop them. Then Tiempo returned to a kneeling position and uttered these words: "Nana Yaa Asantewaa, today, I announce my total loyalty to you. I am at your service and total discretion. Do with me as you deem fit. If by volunteering to serve you I am worthy of your trust, then put me to work where you need workers. But if my presence here causes you to deem me worthy of death, then put me to death. Whether for death or for life, your word is my command. I am tired and I just need a place to stay, but if you choose that I should die, I will not resist or blame you."

There were whisperings and murmurings among the gathering, some suggesting that the stranger's show of obeisance was just that, a show, and that he had ulterior motives; and others suggesting that he had shown sufficient humility and deference to be accepted.

"Stanger, what did you say your name is?"

"Tiempo, Nana."

"Tie... ti... Tiempo, that is not a name that fits well on my tongue but if it's your name then I shall say it. I may regret this. The normal approach would have been to isolate you and purge you and then slowly weave you into the society, but I will not do so with you. We will give you a place to stay. If you are well intentioned, you will find this place welcoming. But our eyes will be watching you very closely. Any false move and you will regret it. Is that clear?"

"Nana, it is very clear."

"Good. I will ask some men to take you with them and find you shelter and give you food to eat. Come back when you are rested and I will put you to work."

"Thank you, Nana. You will not regret your kindness."

"For your sake, I hope not."

She called four men and spoke softly to them and they, in turn, nodded vigorously, and asked Tiempo to come with them. Together, they left the compound.

# BENJAMIN KWAKYE

# House of Ghosts

Four men went with him: Addae and Karikari, and two others he found out were named Anane and Manu. Evening had advanced, though the darkness was tentative in that friendly hour before deep darkness. The hut they approached was engulfed in the gloaming, standing by itself with no companion huts near it, mango, lime and pawpaw trees hovering over it and whistling the wind's tunes. If he could give them voice, he would say the trees were even hollering over the hut. Several strides before they got to the hut, the men accompanying him stopped and pointed. Tiempo stood with them in a moment of uncertainty.

"Go," Karikari said. "This is where you will be staying, until Nana changes her mind about you and we come and get you to bid you farewell to the land of the ghosts."

Tiempo acknowledged this with a nod, waiting for further instruction.

"I said go," Karikari said. "Go to your new home."

"Thank you," Tiempo said, as he separated himself from the other men and moved on to the hut. He heard the men chuckle, for what reason he couldn't fathom at the time, although he would soon guess why. They did not offer him any food as had been instructed and he siphoned the idea of asking for nourishment out of his mind. It would only offer a reason for them to register even more hostility toward him than was already evident, he concluded. He entered his new home, opening its one door without any resistance. The room was bare, almost totally dark, with two tiny windows on each side of the spherical one-room hut. When he came out again after briefly examining the vacuumous room, the men were gone and he was left alone for the night. Tiempo went behind the hut, plucked some pawpaws and broke off a few leafy branches off the mango tree. Back in the room, he arranged the branches and leaves on the bare floor of the hut for his bed, then he ate the pawpaws. They were unripe and not filling, but they offered some energy. He listened for the sound of a stream or any water in motion and, hearing none, concluded that bathing would have to wait.

Tiempo sat alone in the hut, left with his memories across lands and times, of love found and lost and of his ongoing search. The long sleep he'd had in the forest sustained him for a while, such that it took him a while to fall asleep, as alone with his thoughts and seducing as well as assaulting memories he embraced the darkness while it deepened all around him. He heard sounds, some he guessed (crickets) and some he could not be sure of, perhaps an owl howling in declaration of its ownership of the night.

Even when it finally arrived, his sleep was short.

He realized he was not dreaming when his eyes flew open and he saw flashes and images amorphous in appearance, fluid in form and shifting in shapes. He observed what he soon concluded were a parade of ghosts concerting right before his eyes. He tried to move but realized that it was extremely difficult to do so, and if these were ghosts of malevolent intent, then he was at their mercy. And then he thought he heard some of them speak in what sounded like deep throated groans: This is our home! Leave our home!

And though he found himself immobilized, he realized it was not out of fear. What it was exactly, Tiempo could not tell. Was it deference, just a psychosomatic reaction to something (or beings) so novel that his body was just not ready to react?

After watching them moving about in the hut, the reaction he could summon at that moment, which must have been a form of antidote to their harassment, was a wide grin of insouciance, for just as soon as he flashed that grin, the beings disappeared, losing their shapes into nothingness like water bubbles bursting. At that moment, Tiempo concluded that the men who had bought him there knew exactly that the hut was haunted, hence the chuckle, a thought that lulled him to sleep. He told himself that they had not realized that he was the air of the day that became the wind of the night, fiercer than anything living or dead. Did they think the ghosts could torment him? In fact, at that moment he told himself that "Memory is harsher than ghosts." It was memory and its elusive promises that he needed to worry about.

So when the morning birds woke him up the next day, Tiempo had registered a form of victory over Karikari, Addae, Anane and Manu. The sun rose earlier than usual, and the cocks crowed in the distance, joining their coco-croo-coos in a form of harmony as had not been heard in the town of Ejisu in a long time. As the town rose earlier than usual, its newest inhabitant stepped out of the hut that had roofed him overnight. He walked out with that extra buoyancy as he went in search of Nana Yaa Asantewaa's home to request work. He had little difficulty retracing his steps from the previous evening.

There were a number of young girls sweeping the compound when he arrived, their brooms spreading out in practiced formation, clearing litter and creating an airy dust as they covered the compound. He asked that they tell Nana he had arrived to receive his orders for the day. When she came out her first words were to applaud his sense of duty. Yes, she had promised him work but had not expected he would seek one so soon. Then she asked that he wait while she summoned a few men to take him to her farm, instructing that they show him the grass-overgrown portion behind her planted yams that needed to be cut. The men took him to the farm as instructed, gave him a hoe and a cutlass, and showed him what portion needed work. Then they left him.

Tiempo stood looking around him, the vast farmland and the parts that needed work. He was not daunted by the size of the workload as he went to work immediately, back bent with cutlass in hand as he cut grass upon grass. The fog of morning was thieved into the rising heat, and things got clearer and clearer, and then the sun rose higher, and Tiempo worked and worked; past praying mantis, worms, ants and so such, Tiempo worked through blades of grass until the sun stood directly overhead. When he stood up to wipe away the sweat from his brow, he noticed two women approaching him. He squinted through sweat soaked eyelashes until the women came into clearer view, one of them carrying a basket. And he recognized them from the previous day, as part of the group that had surrounded him and accompanied him to Nana Yaa Asantewaa's, in particular the one who had spoken on his behalf.

"Stranger," the one carrying the basket said, looking around to inspect his work. "Well done."

He nodded

"I know you can talk, stranger."

"My name is Tiempo."

"I know. I heard you yesterday. But it's not a name I'm used to."

"And you, what is your name?" Tiempo asked.

"They call me Fosua. Didn't you hear them call me by that

name?"

"And you?" Tiempo asked the other woman.

"Mansa," she said, "My name is Mansa."

"I can see you have been working extremely hard," Fosua said. "Nana asked us to bring you this."

She offered him the basket.

"What is it?"

"Why don't you look inside and see?"

Tiempo took the basket and looked inside it: a bowl of boiled plantains and kontomere stew. "Thank you," he said. "This looks delicious."

"Eat well," Fosua said, "we will come back for the basket and bowl later."

It was one of the best meals Tiempo had eaten in a long time, and it galvanized him to work even harder.

Fosua and Mansa returned later in the embers of the afternoon to collect the basket and bowl.

"Who prepared the meal?" he asked them.

"We did, together," Fosua said.

"Are you sisters?"

"No, but we might as well be sisters," said Mansa. "Fosua and I are very close."

"You are excellent cooks," Tiempo said. "This was delicious. Thank You."

When evening came and the world around him got quieter, Tiempo listened again. This time harder and harder until he could hear the sound of water; and his trained senses led him to a stream several strides from where he had been working. It was a small stream, but he plunged into it, letting the coolness of the water cleanse his maculate body. Despite the long day's work, he was much more refreshed when he left the stream than when he'd arrived that morning. When he got to Nana Yaa Asantewaa's home that evening, she offered him clothes she said she had gathered for him. After thanking her, he returned to the hut.

And so it continued for about a week, a well-established routine he was getting accustomed to and comfortable with: the morning arrival at the farm, the work, the meal brought him by Fosua and Mansa, the dip in the stream, the stroll back to his hut, the lonesome night, and the occasional visitation of ghosts, although they never again threatened him to leave—perhaps having realized that he did not fear them, they had decided to cohabit with him. And things were quite tranquil until one day while taking a stroll he saw people running with abandon. When he inquired, he was told that Aboakesie has been sighted.

"I have heard that name before," Tiempo said. "Who is Aboakesie?"

No one answered him then until later, when it was confirmed the sighting was false and it was safe, when someone explained to him the legend of Aboakesie.

Aboakesie was said to be the biggest person ever to live. No one knew where he had come from. As far as they could remember, he was there. He would come to town once in a while and take whatever he wanted. No one denied him anything, for the consequences were dire and could include severe beatings that once or twice had proved fatal. He was said to have uprooted a mighty tree once with a finger, brought down a huge hut with a single blow. One time, it was rumored a group had organized to fight him with bows and arrows and spears. They weapons failed to penetrate his body and all who attacked him had died. Who would not fear such a man? So what he wanted, whether food, or flesh, he got, no questions asked. He took and then he disappeared to a place no one knew, to return at a place and time unannounced. Whenever there was word of an Aboakesie sighting, everyone run and sheltered their homes as best as they could, hoping that they would not be victim to his visit. If he visited, the best approach was to cooperate with him in order to preserve limb and sometimes life.

SEASONS of FOUR FACES

# The Favor of Stools

Nothing eventful happened after this false sighting until one day Nana Yaa Asantewaa sent for Tiempo to return from the farm earlier as she wanted to speak with him. For the first time since his arrival he was afraid. Had he done something wrong? Had he offended her? Had he broken a protocol he wasn't aware of? The one who knew little to no physical fear suddenly worried that some harm was about to befall him. So he bowed a bit too long when he arrived at her compound, where she was seated alone. After greeting her, she asked him to sit on the stool next to her. He hesitated, wondering if he had misheard. She repeated her request, and even then he sat a bit tentatively. She asked him to be at ease.

"I have seen the good work you have been doing on the farm," Nana said. "Fosua and Mansa and others have told me, but early yesterday, I went to see it for myself. You have done the work of ten men. Well done."

"Thank you, Nana. I take pleasure in the work."

"And I am told they put you in the hut of ghosts."

"Hut of ghosts?"

"That's what they call it. I thought someone would have told you by now. It used to belong to a young man who died in there. They say he was poisoned, and that ever since he died his spirit won't rest and he and other restless ghosts haunt anyone who sleeps there. No one wants to go there alone, especially at night. Even Okomfo Fofie has vowed never to venture there. I have to say I was angry when I found out. I had expected one of the men to take you to his home. It is our custom to be accommodating to strangers we let into our midst. Your case is a little different, I must admit, as you have not told us much about where you came from. Still, that is no way to treat someone who has done you no harm. And to think that I picked four of my closest confidantes. But then I said to myself that if you had survived and thrived despite the ghosts, that was the best payback for the bad thoughts of those who put you there. I berated them, but then after some thought, I asked them to leave you there. I want them to see you and marvel at your bravery."

"I'm afraid Nana speaks too kindly of me."

"I can read people, you know. You don't get to be my age or thrive in my position for long if you're not able to read people. You are quiet, but strong. As the elders say, it is the calm and silent water that drowns a man. I have met many strangers and determined their character after very short contact. I'm hardly wrong. And in your case I have no reason to think I made a mistake."

"I thank Nana for reposing such confidence in me."

"I detect greatness in you. I know you don't want to talk about it, and I respect that. Sometimes greatness is so rooted in pain that the great don't like discussing. We have seen plenty of it ourselves, the pain, and we have built a great Asante nation partly on that pain. I just hope we are able to keep it."

"How do you mean, Nana?"

"Hmm, I can tell you don't know a lot about my people?"

"If Nana will teach me, I am willing to learn."

"There's a lot to learn, Tiempo. Your name is still difficult for me, but I have tried to say it properly."

"I am so honored, Nana."

"But about our people, where do I even begin? Perhaps we can start with the Great Nana Osei Tutu."

SEASONS of FOUR FACES

# The Golden Stool

Her eyes were misty when she began to recollect the story of Nana Osei Tutu and his friend and high priest Okomfo Anokye, her words flowing like a stream, coming steadily and ceaselessly, as she told him of the day the Golden Stool had come from the sky, bearing supernal glory. She was so vivid in her description Tiempo could easily create mental pictures as she spoke.

The chiefs of the as yet ununited Asante land gathered, seated in a semi-circle, as Okomfo Anokye, the priest, clad in his raffia skirt, with his whisk in hand, chanted incantations that none could understand, a language for gods. Then in language they understood he translated for them that he was going to conjure a stool from the skies and that the stool would land on the lap of one of them and that person would be their king, the Asantehene. And they agreed. How could they disagree when he was speaking on behalf of gods and great spirits? How could they not agree when he embodied so much power, when he was not there as a mere mortal, but as the representative of deities? His chant pierced the atmosphere, met the creative genius of gods, and shook the clouds to bring together nuggets of gold into a stool that would embody the spirit of the Asantes. And so the priest chanted and the Sika Dwa Kofi or Golden Stool fell from the sky and came to land on the lap of Osei Tutu. It was to be repository of the Asante spirit, the spiritual fulcrum of oneness, at the very core of Asante existence. If the result had been rigged because Osei Tutu was the priest's friend, then it had been rigged by the gods and by the heavens themselves and therefore it was not a rigging at all. It had been decided: Nana Osei Tutu I would become the king of all the Asantes. The united Asante Kingdom was born and they would have their first paramount king! Asantehene Nana Osei Tutu I.

"It is a history of greatness and of conquests," said Nana Yaa Asantewaa. "As to our origins, the elders say our ancestors just appeared from holes in the ground. We just were. Some say "Asa," which means war is combined with "nte," which means because of, and so Asante means because of war or those who make war. Others say it comes from the word "asan," which means clay and "te" means dig, so that Asante means those who dig clay. In former days Asante was a vassal state to Denkyira, providing slaves and paying tributes, including red clay, which was used to paint buildings. It became untenable for the Asantes to be under vassalage, and Nana Osei Tutu had to fight Denkyira in the Battle of Feyiase to break Asante free. Asante has since grown strong. We have fought many wars and we were growing stronger until the white man interfered. In battle, our strategies worked perfectly to our advantage.

"In addition to using the sound of drums and shouting to make ourselves bigger and intimidate the enemy, we were very well organized, with bodyguards, followed by an advance guard, then the main body with the army commander, and then we had columns to the left and to the right, and then the rear guard. The goal was to draw the enemy in into the middle while the left and right wings encircled it with no means of escape. Of course, we also went to war with our Esumankwafo, the medical person who treated wounded soldiers. Our strategy won us many fights, including the Battle of Nsamanko, which the Asante won and beheaded the British leader, Sir Chares McCarthy. We still parade his skull in

Kumasi during the Festival of the Yams. The Segrenti War is what proved our undoing, when Sir Garnet Wolseley advanced to Kumasi after the Battle of Amoaful. Kumasi was deserted and there was internal strife in Asanteman. We were forced to sign the Treaty of Fomena and Asante lost many of its vassal states. Eventually Nana Prempeh had to accept the protection of the Queen of England and, in a humiliating manner, Nana Prempeh and our queenmother prostrated themselves before Governor Maxwell in Kumasi. The British appointed Captain Donald Stewart as British resident in Kumasi and built a fort at his residence. So you see Asante is under siege, and the white man wants us to come under his rule. As if we are not capable of ruling ourselves. What were we doing before he came? We have fought him and defeated him before, but we have been forced to compromise after the Treaty of Fomena. I am very worried over some of the requests he has been making lately."

She went on to explain the pressure being placed on the Asantehene to accede completely to British rule. "And you, I think you were brought here for such a time as this."

The night engulfed them before Nana Yaa Asantewaa excused Tiempo, but not before telling him he would be fully paid for his services. Tiempo was elated, but winning the confidence of royalty had not always boded well for him. Even more troubling was Nana's concern about the demands being placed on the Kingdom and on the current Asantehene, Nana Prempeh, to embrace total British rule. Was war imminent in the Asante Kingdom?

# CHAPTER

# 2

*"The search is the living," added Kouyate*

## Conference of Ghosts

He wanted to invite the living and the living only, the ones he had seen alive and hoped to see alive again, especially the woman most recently referred to as Fatima. He wanted her, rather than the ineffectual ghosts, to visit him and there and then end his search, and his loneliness. He had to rethink it often to comfort himself (if only for moments) that, until he saw her again, his aloneness was never loneliness. When he had thought her dead, he had managed on the sustenance of memory. The thought of her death had been exactly that: thought. It had never sunk into his soul. So he had built in his mind a city of many streets with many thoroughfares and many mansions and rivers and flowery gardens, in which he would roam in darkness until he found her in a brightly lit mansion. But the city was not needed when he knew with certainty that she was not dead. The search was more real now and he would have to perdure, keep on until he found her; or, as she had promised, she found him. So his hope was almost tactile and his wish was for her physical manifestation and the end to the aloneness, for whenever he now thought about her and that she may be in physical danger or roaming some strange place or land, his aloneness worsened.

First, though, he had to dispense with the perfunctory visitation of the ghosts of the hut. Then when they had left, he had a strong sense that somehow Sharifa would appear in the room and announce that her search, just as his, was over so that they could live together happily forever and ever. The desire to conjure the living was as strong as his heightened breath, filling him with great anticipation, which was even rendered more palpable when the room lit up right in the middle of the darkness. Tiempo rose from his face-up-back-down pose and sat up, legs crossed, looking, indeed peering hard into the light, the name Sharifa on his lips. And then when the outlines of a human being began to appear us the middle of the light, he blurted out the name in his heart:

Sharifa.

But the figure that formed when its features became fully visible was not Sharifa, but the one he believed long dead whom he had not encountered alive since leaving Egypt.

Brow pulled into a frown, Tiempo asked in disbelief, "What is the dead doing in the land of the living?"

"The dead have their story too, Tiempo."

"Adom, you are dead. Stay with your own."

"Do you still hold grudges, Tiempo? Am I still unwelcome even in my death?"

"I do not fear you."

"I don't expect you to fear me; just talk to me."

"And for what purpose?"

Another figure began to take shape in the light and its full features transformed from a glob to a more definable presence.

"What are you the living doing in the light of ghosts?" Tiempo asked.

"I am not a part of the living anymore," said the new appearance. "Have you forgotten how long it has been?"

"Forgive me," said Tiempo, "but sometimes it seems so recent."

"I don't blame you, considering you are still searching for Fatima."

"Sharifa!" both Tiempo and Adom said.

"Sharifa it is."

"Yes, Kouyate," Tiempo said. "Her name is Sharifa. And I am looking for her. And I know that she also is now pursuing me."

"Can you be sure?" Adom asked.

"Ever the doubter, Adom, don't tell me she is with you," Tiempo said. "I know she is not."

"And what if she is with me, will you continue to pursue her?" asked Adom.

"What use would that be?" Tiempo asked, more for purposes of making an argument than in reflection of his inclinations. "Pursue the dead?"

"Did you not pursue her when you thought she was dead?" asked Adom.

"Thinking and knowing are different things."

"Then you are a fool," said Adom. "Whether she sits with you in the darkness or with us in the light is irrelevant. You pursue no matter what."

"That sounds foolish," said Tiempo.

"Do you think you can let her go?" Kouyate asked. "Dead or alive? This linkage that transcends time and space?"

"This attraction that does not belong in any one dimension?" Adom said. "I competed with you in one dimension, but you both escaped me. I was so narrow minded then, despite the spiritual power I thought I had at the time. Now look at me, I sit in the light of death and you are in the darkness of life."

"How am I in darkness?"

"I know so, but not because it needs to be so but because you have not opened your eyes," said Adom.

"Don't let a death, even if it's not yours, close your eyes to the light," said Kouyate.

"And how do I that?"

"You are a master of darkness. Perhaps you should be a master of light too," said Kouyate. "Query the past and let the past guide you and then move from it, using it as lever."

"Can you explain?" Tiempo asked.

"We can't say everything," said Adom. "Search."

"The search is the living," added Kouyate.

"Have you come to speak to me in riddles that have no value?" Tiempo asked.

"You know what we have said has great value; you just don't like it because it is not what you wanted to hear."

"I still don't follow, but at least your visit can be of some value, this conference of ghosts."

"Of ghosts and the living," Adom corrected.

"This will be of some value if you will at least tell me one thing."

"And what is that?" Kouyate asked.

"Tell me, where is Sharifa?"

"How can we tell you?" Adom asked.

"You are ghosts; you know everything," Tiempo said.

"False," said Kouyate.

"Just tell me," said Tiempo.

"We can't tell you," said Adom.

"You can't or you won't?" Tiempo asked.

"You should understand this more than any," said Kouyate.

"Not all answers can be given," said Adom.

"And why not?"

"Ask yourself that question, Tiempo. Why have you not told all to Nana Yaa Asantewaa? Why did you not tell all to Mansa Musa, or to me when you lived with me in Niani?"

"You know I couldn't, Kouyate."

"You could, but circumstances did not make that the right course for you."

"So you know and are just not telling me?"

"Perhaps we know or perhaps we don't know."

"This is not helpful at all."

"Seek. Think. Act." Kouyate said. "That is all we can say."

"So what really was the purpose of your visit?" Tiempo asked.

"What is the purpose of any visit?" Adom asked. "For companionship? We have given you that. For discussion or conversation? We have given you that. To relieve boredom? We have given you that. For food? In a manner of thinking, we have given you that. Of course, not in food for the stomach but in food for the mind."

"Listen," said Kouyate, "if Sharifa is alive, you have every reason to look for her. If she is dead, you still need to look for her, for that will give you purpose, especially knowing that the dimensions we think are so separate are not so separate after all. You will not be seeking the dead. You will be seeking the one whom you love, and even if you never find her, you will find purpose in the seeking."

"That bears no fruit?"

"What do you mean?" Adom asked. "Would she be no more if she is dead? Would you give up on her if she is dead?"

"But how can I find her if she is dead?"

"You find her in your heart," said Kouyate. "Or it's up to you... You can find her as you find the living, even if she is dead. Do not profane your love with doubt."

"This is foolish talk. The talk of ghosts. Leave me alone!" Tiempo yelled.

"As you wish," said Adom.

"We came as friends and we leave as friends," Kouyate said.

And then they were gone and with the departure the light in which they had been spotlighted diminished and then disappeared altogether until the room was plunged into its state of default, the darkness of the night that permeated the room. Tiempo had attempted to stop the total disappearance of the light, he who prevailed in the darkness, and he had leaped forward with one hand, an action that even he realized was foolish and futile, the attempt to grasp a piece of the light that had brought a portion of his past to him. As he expected, although in futile hope that it would not be so, he grasped at air instead. Just as he seemed to be grasping for air in the long search for Sharifa, or in the long wait for her to find him. Face down on the floor of the hut, tasting dust, Tiempo wondered if it was worth the effort and wait, this journey of seeming endlessness. And he was caught in an endless back and forth. What if Sharifa was dead? What would be the purpose of continuing? But then again, even if there was the remotest possibility that she was alive, he would have to seek her or position himself in a way that could help her find him. And still, the thought that she might have died haunted him in the darkness. But even if dead, he would continue… because otherwise life was not worth it. Was that what the ghosts meant? Was he, even if knowing that she had died, to pretend she was living? Or perhaps it needed no pretense at all. Just as they, a part of his past, had resurrected in the light of his room, could he in the search be able to resurrect himself in her world or her in his? Not just in the city of his mind, but in every aspect of his life. In the voice of the next female acquaintance, in the heaviness of his breath, in the rustle of the leaves, the chirping of birds, practicing (or poaching) her presence in a way that would render her as real as anyone else living. Therefore, whether Sharifa was alive or dead, Tiempo would seek her and embrace her, whether in physical presence or in that presence that abides so strongly it is just as or even more powerful than the physical presence. What a prolonged, convoluted way to arrive at this conclusion, which now seemed so prosaic. But once he reached it, Tiempo was able to close his eyes to the night and fall into deep sleep.

# SEASONS of FOUR FACES

## Up the Good Tree

Nana Yaa Asantewaa included Tiempo on her trip to Kumasi to celebrate the festival that some had dubbed the Yam Festival in the Asante capital. It was to be part of his embrace into Asante society. She quoted a saying of the elders: "It is when you climb the good tree that you are pushed, and you have climbed the good tree." He was one among a few, including Serwaa, Addae, Karikari, Anane and Manu. Nana warned the men to be on their best behavior. She reminded them that this was an important festival, during which the Asantehene would perform the needed rites pertaining to the first harvest of yams, the ambrosia of the gods, before mortals could eat the newly harvested crops.

    Privileged to be invited and overjoyed to observe, Tiempo took in every scene he was privy to. He saw Nana Prempeh leading a procession to the marketplace. Tiempo strained to catch a glimpse of the Asantehene, glorious and fierce in his black helmet, his face decorated in black and white stripes. As he led, others followed, the beauty of his wives in full display, their bodies covered with white clay, the gold earrings from their ears jingling, the neck adorning gold necklaces sparkling and the bangles around their wrists and the rings around their fingers adding resplendence. As the wives passed, Tiempo also took note of the chiefs who followed, including Nana Yaa Asantewaa, herself sparkling in her batakari attire. He heard them singing war songs, some raising their fists as though they could envision a fierce battle about to ensue right there and then. These were the ones Tiempo admired the most, the war songs resonating with him, reminding him of times past and of great victories on the battlefield, creating a niggling nostalgia. His body moved spontaneously as one warming up. And then he noticed the executioners in tow, and what a fearsome image they projected, with jaw bones hanging around their necks and loins. Their ebony skins were a sharp contrast to their fierce eyes, as if intentionally dyed a deep red for the occasion. Even Tiempo felt a surge of fear when he saw them. The rattling of those jaw bones alone was enough to scare even the strong hearted. Behind them, others shepherded a large cow to be presented as a gift to the Asantehene. When they arrived at the marketplace, Nana Prempeh was presented with a knife, as mighty men with muscular pomposity held the gifted cow down as though it were an easy feat. Then the Asantehene bent over the cow, knife in hand, and slit the animal's throat, and blood gushed out like projected red spit. Then the Asantehene placed mashed yam on the stool that was brought to him, an act that paved the way for humans to eat. That evening, as guests of the Asantehene, Tiempo and the rest of Nana Yaa Asantewaa's entourage were treated to a meal of eto: mashed yam mixed with palm oil, and eggs.

Tiempo was not witness to the washing of the stools event the following day, as only chiefs, nobles and those specifically invited were allowed to the event that occurred before sunrise, when the Asantehene and those allowed, went to the Dra stream. Nana Yaa Asantewaa told him of how the accompanying chiefs washed furniture and stools, gold and silver plates, and brass that held magic medicines. She told of how Nana Prempeh went farther down the Dra stream to wash himself. Then twenty sheep were also washed in the stream to prepare them for sacrifice. Then a goat and a sheep were sacrificed on the bank of the stream. Priests dipped leaves into brass basins and sprinkled the water on those in attendance for purification. Then back at the palace the twenty sheep were sacrificed to the stools, and the entrance to the palace was smeared with their blood. A white lamb was killed and its blood smeared over furniture in the bedrooms, windows and doorposts.

But Tiempo was able to attend the later parade of the skulls of important chiefs who were killed in battle. First came the abrafo, the young executioners, to perform. With the Asantehene observing, they began to dance as if they had no bones, with corybantic gyrations and somersaults performed at a frenetic pace, not to be attempted by the rigid bodied. As though this was not enough, they danced with their faces also, not in a manner designed to be graceful but to elicit fear with contortions and grimaces at once frightful and impressive. Then came the elderly executioners, the abrafo-adumfo, carrying skulls strung on medicinal plants. Tiempo tried to guess which one might be Sir Chares McCarthy's. As muskets were fired, this group of elderly executioners marched past Nana Prempeh.

The serving of drinks the next day was not the favorite part of the festival for Tiempo, considering that he did not like to drink, but it was license for Addae and Karikari to overindulge, Anane and Manu being more temperate in their quaffing. It was the day that the Asantehene provide rum in brass pans and had them placed in various parts of Kumasi for the people to imbibe. Out of curiosity, Tiempo accompanied those who were tasked with placing these drinks in such locations. And at each location, by the time they arrived, there were already large numbers of people waiting, calabashes and pots in hand. As soon as the drinks were placed for their enjoyment, they attacked, filling calabashes, pots and drinking again and again. Tiempo noticed that some used their hands as bowls to gather the drinks, while others lapped the drink with their mouths and tongues. It was no wonder that Kumasi was filled that day with drunk people, some lying in stupors in the streets.

For their part, Addae and Karikari became so inebriated that they seemed to have lost any sense of proprietary, and approached the Asantehene's harem, a no go for anyone who valued his life. They were brought to Nana Yaa Asantewaa as she was retiring for the night and told to hold her subjects in check. They had brought them to her out of courtesy and respect for her; otherwise, they would have faced stiff punishment. "Look at them," she said, "grown men behaving worse than hyenas and goats." When they were sober the next day, on the way back to Ejisu, the two were the subject or her ire. "Why can't you be more responsible like Tiempo?" she asked of the two, whose heads remained bowed in shame.

SEASONS of FOUR FACES

# Testing the Farmland

Tiempo returned to farm work the next day, a job that he had come to love even more. At first it was only about duty; now it was a duty of love. He loved the relative quiet (except the sounds of a few farm creatures) and solitude (again, except the company of those farm creatures, recently including simian ones who perched in trees and seemed content to observe him). As they came to see him, as they usually did since they had been sent to bring him food (which had ranged from ampesi, apapransa, fufu, to akapinkyi and more), Fosua and Mansa arrived at the farm with a basket full of food. But this time, they did not leave Tiempo as he ate, watching him chew down every morsel, even each bolus that traveled down his throat. Each gazed at him intensely, their eyes focused singularly on him as if he would otherwise disappear from sight. He in turn went about the business of consuming the food, and if he felt he was under scrutiny, Tiempo put up a great show of meticulous, slow chewing for this audience of two that had become over the months a part of his world, sisters of sorts who helped sustain him with their delicious nourishments.

    Why they chose to watch him so intensely was beyond him (or perhaps he was pretending, preferring to remain oblivious to their escalating interest), but he would show his appreciation by signaling how much he enjoyed their handiwork, widening his eyes now and again as though in wonderment over their cooking skills, smiling as he chewed the plantain and garden egg stew, nodding to signal approval of the food's taste, and licking his fingers repeatedly. When he was done, Tiempo thanked them and expected them to collect the bowl and basket and leave. But they lingered and for the first time he thought he saw coyness and even flirtation as they squinted their eyes in a manner he had not witnessed before, or had pretended not to notice before. He thanked them again, hoping that would serve as an act of dismissal, but they lingered. Not wishing to offend the two who had so often fed him, Tiempo kept his silence rather than tell them he needed to attend to his work. As they continued to linger, the aura began to feel awkward, even uncomfortable, for Tiempo. He had stared down the faces of many combatants in battle, wrestled many in physical warfare, but never this kind of silence, not sure what he ought to label it. Silent what? Tiempo was nervous and began to ooze copious sweat. "You are sweating," Fosua said, stepping closer to Tiempo and wiping his face with her scarf. Tiempo sweated even more, and Mansa joined the effort in sweat wiping. He ought to tell them to stop and leave but he couldn't muster the presence of mind to do so.

"Do you like that we bring you food?" Mansa asked.

"Ye... yes..." Tiempo stammered.

"And that we are wiping the sweat from your body?" Fosua asked.

"Thank you," Tiempo answered.

"That tells me that you like us," said Mansa.

"I... I am... I..." Tiempo stammered again.

"You like our food. You like us being here with you wiping your sweat," Fosua said.

"But..." Tiempo could barely speak.

"All you have to do is say so," Mansa said.

"And of course come see our parents," Fosua added.

Tiempo could not speak.

"What do you say?" Mansa asked.

Finally able to retrieve his voice, although now significantly softened, Tiempo asked, "What are you saying?"

"We are not the ones to be saying this," Fosua said. "You are the one who should be telling us what you will do."

"But it seems you are a quiet man and perhaps we need to nudge you a little," said Mansa. "So now that we have given you the hint, the rest is up to you."

"But don't waste too much time," Fosua added.

"You know there are many who are interested," Mansa said.

Tiempo could not respond. If the earth could swallow him, he would have gladly allowed it to do so, so that he would not have to face this proposal, so boldly expressed by two women he had come to admire. He pretended to cough, but the raspy sound from his throat was so obviously false that no one was fooled. The women smiled. Fosua stood there in her green wrapper that clothed her from her chest, right under her armpits, to her feet. And the equally gorgeous Mansa's dressing matched Fosua's with a lighter shade of green. Dimpled smiles, both of them, sandwiching high cheek bones; almond shaped eyes glittering wide to observe him. They realized his struggle and, smiling, left him in his dumbfounded state.

# CHAPTER

# 3

*She smiled as she invited him, saying,*
*"As the elders say, it is the water that loves you that enters your earthenware pot."*

## Shading of the Night

Tiempo could barely work after they left him that afternoon. What a predicament. He should have known something like this would happen, but why had he been so blindsided? With hindsight for a vision, he retraced all the time they had come to see him at the farm, the way they giggled as they left him, the way they smiled, the apparent selflessness of bringing him food without asking for anything in return, until now. He knew or should have known. He should have taken steps, whatever steps he could, though not clear what, to dissuade them from any hint of interest other than the purely platonic: frowned, refused to eat, something. What was he to do? He could not construct any solution to the predicament and hoped that time would help him with answers.

But they would not give him time, as they came to see him that night as he was about to retire to bed. They entered the hut like old acquaintances, displaying no sign of discomfort.

"Why are you out so late at night?" Tiempo asked.

"We thought we would remind you of what we mentioned earlier," said Fosua.

"If the day's message was not clear, then perhaps the night's will be," said Mansa.

Tiempo sighed and, refusing to think or rather overthink the situation, said, "So you are asking me to marry you both?"

"Yes," said Fosua.

"Why you both?" asked Tiempo.

"Why not? Fosua and I are like sisters. We do everything together. And we both like you."

"But are you not jealous of each other?"

"No," said Fosua. "As Mansa has told you, we are like sisters, like twins."

"But even sisters can be jealous of each other."

"Not us," said Mansa.

"So we are expecting that you will do the right thing," said Fosua.

"What is that?" Tiempo asked.

"Come and see our parents," Mansa said. "What else? Didn't we already tell you this?"

"If you don't have the bride price, we can help you get it," Fosua said.

"It's not that. Why me? I am a stranger. You don't know anything about me."

Mansa replied, "Yes you are, but that does not matter to us. If Nana Yaa Asantewaa trusts you, so do we."

"Your parents don't know anything about me."

"If Nana Yaa Asantewaa likes you, they will like you."

"But you don't know anything about me…"

"You already said that," Fosua noted, "and as Mansa has told you, we don't care. We know enough. We have observed you for a long time. Do you think we don't have eyes to see? Do you think we don't have ears to hear? You, bold to inhabit this hut of ghosts, so great that Nana treats you as a son."

Tiempo stammered his way through his response, totally without any coherence. He could barely construct sentences and the women seemed to have mercy on him when they excused themselves, bidding him a temporary farewell.

Tiempo could barely sleep and it was in a state of fatigue that he went to work the next day, the productivity at work very low. Fosua and Mansa did not broach the matter when they brought him food that afternoon, nor did they wait for him to eat, nor did they linger when they returned to pick the bowl and basket. And on account of that, Tiempo began to harbor hope that he had done enough or perhaps in his incoherence cohered enough to persuade them to drop their pursuit. It was in such hope that he prepared to sleep that night.

At first what he heard outside was like a scampering, as if someone or something was rolling over dry fallen leaves on the ground outside. Tiempo was startled and alarmed when he found out it was Fosua, who entered the darkness of his room before he could stop her.

"Fosua," he murmured.

"Yes, it's me."

"Where is Mansa?"

"She did not come with me."

"But, but you two are always together."

"Not tonight."

"Twins of day only." His attempt at a joke fell flat. Tiempo's voice shook badly when he asked, "Why have you come alone?"

"Perhaps if you don't want to deal with the two of us at the same time, you will prefer to handle us apart."

"Fosua, it has nothing to do with whether you are alone or together."

"Then what is it? Do you not find me desirable?"

"I do... I mean..."

"Then do what you must do. If you must taste first, then taste."

"No, Fosua, this is not right."

"With you, what is not right is still right."

"No, Fosua I can't do it."

"Why not? What is wrong?"

"Nothing is wrong."

"Then let's do as we should."

"Fosua, please."

"I rescued you on that day when we found you in the forest. I was the one who asked that we take you to see Nana Yaa Asantewaa. From that very day I knew there was something special about you. My own behavior shocks me, Tiempo. I have never approached a man like this. Ask around, if you must, but both Mansa and I are highly respected and desirable in this town and we have many suitors. But we want you, Tiempo. So tell me why you are behaving like I am some disease?"

"Fosua," said Tiempo. "This is very complicated and is not something I can easily explain. Please, in due course I hope you will better understand and things will get clearer."

She still did not understand what was wrong, she said, but she would give it a little more time.

And Tiempo thought he had bought himself considerably more time, but the next night was just as the previous visit, as he heard the rustling of leaves, much unlike the wind shuffling of leaves he was used to, and then a female entry that was too late to stop.

"Mansa," he said.
"Yes, it is me," she replied.
"Why have you come?"
"Am I a disease that you recoil from me?"
"I have not recoiled from you."
"Then come and embrace me and let's be together."
"I can't do that."
"You can. And tonight, you will."
"Mansa, please."
"It is not good for a grown man to beg."

Mansa did not seem interested in dialogue as had Fosua. Rather, she moved forward toward Tiempo in a movement so fast it took him by surprise, as her hands reached out and held his loin cloth, attempting to loosen it. Tiempo forced himself to recovery, to bring his mind into the presence of the moment and the difficult reality of what was unfolding, eventually prying her tenacious hands from his slightly loosened cloth. But that did not deter her as she came at him again, except this time he was prepared, moving back before she could reach him. And for a short while they were like this as she tried to reach him and he tried to avoid contact, circling the dark room, their bodies like mismatched wrestlers in height, muscular angles and even the projection of strength and energy, except this time she was the one projecting the strength and energy and he was the weak and lethargic one. He realized that there was no escaping this, either he repelled her in the most forceful manner or surrendered and granted her request. Just as Tiempo was about to pick between these two options, a third, the most obvious that he had so far been oblivious to, opened up to him. Tiempo ran from the room and fled into the nearby forest.

BENJAMIN KWAKYE

# The Fear

The forest was dense, as if someone had deliberately covered it with a torrent of darkness. Tiempo heard what sounded like the voices of children. He looked to his right and then to his left, but there was no one in sight. He attributed it to the darkness around him that created auditory illusions. And then when he looked to his left, even in the darkness, he saw a pot overflowing with gold nuggets, shining brighter on account of the darkness. He stopped and looked at it and the gold glittered even more, and then he heard a noise, a voice, though he could not see anyone, and the voice said, Gold for you. Tiempo said under his breath, Who would leave all this gold here? It's a gift for you, the voice said. Tiempo turned around, looking for the source of the voice, but still he found none. Who was playing games with him? Come out, he shouted. But he heard no response and it seemed the voice had gone silent. So Tiempo assumed the owner of the voice had left the scene and he was alone with the gold. He took a couple of steps towards the pot, preparing to take, when it occurred to him that it was not his to take. He should have known this all along, but with a ruffled mind, had suppressed the simple axiom not to take what does not belong to you.

And what if this was some sort of test? He stepped back. And then the voice returned and told him not to be a fool. Take the treasure. Tiempo did not listen to the voice. Not all gifts are free, he said. Fool, every gift is free! Tiempo took several steps back and started walking away. Then he turned to look back and under the appearance of sudden moonglow there was no pot of gold but instead a brush of bush. He did not believe this. His vision had not deceived him. He retraced his steps to make sure. And indeed, there was only a brush of bush where the pot of gold had stood.

He considered that someone was really playing pranks, and he decided to move on. But as soon as he had taken seven, maybe ten, steps forward, he saw, again in the moonlight, what looked like a ball of grass rolling by itself on the pathway and it was rolling away from him, although he had not noticed it before. Tiempo started running after it, intent on gathering and inspecting it. But the faster he ran the faster the ball of grass moved, even though there was no wind to move it along. He stopped running after it, this time worried that what he was experiencing may not be from natural influences. So he began to walk back home, determined to leave the forest as quickly as he could. He would rather face Mansa than this. Then suddenly a big wind began to blow and in it he heard whistles and some words that sounded like catcalls.

He had not ever experienced the weight of raw fear that covered him at that moment, a fear that had come as a thief, and he was terrified that something diabolical was afoot. Then from the nearby bushes, he heard a voice. Again. The same voice he had heard before, urging him, Come. Tiempo wanted to run, but found that he could not run. Then as he stood rooted to the pathway, a boy who reached no higher than his knee approached him. His hair fell in long locks to his shoulders and he had stout features and, as he got closer and the moonlight revealed more of his features, Tiempo realized that he was not a boy at all but a man. He was bare chested and only wore a raffia skirt from the waist down to his knees. And Tiempo noticed that he was holding an egg. The wind blew hard.

When he was closer to Tiempo, he offered the egg to Tiempo without speaking, only gesturing for Tiempo to take it. Tiempo did not take the egg, afraid of the man and fearful that this was not a benign offer. The man brought the egg to his mouth, to demonstrate to Tiempo that the egg was for the eating, then he offered it again to Tiempo, who was now totally bathed in goose pimples. Still, the one thing Tiempo believed he had was his choice and he decided he would not surrender it to the man by taking the egg. The wind ceased blowing and Tiempo realized that he had not noticed the sound it had been making through the rustling leaves. As the wind quieted, a total silence fell. Tiempo wondered how long this stalemate would continue.

As he so wondered, he heard noise come out of the forest to replace the silence. It was like a strained song, at once coarse and sweet, sang in a language he had never heard before, and the forest was abuzz with it; and, though he did not know the language he could somehow still translate as: Come with us; come live in the habitation of the dwarfs of the forest. Come. Come. Come.

But he had decided that he would not go, not by choice. And so, with every energy of the remnant of boldness left in him, in recognition that the longer this continued the more likely he would be overcome, Tiempo reached into the innermost part of his belly for strength and yelled: No!!! And then it was as if this had surprised the forest, for the song ceased immediately, and the man who had offered Tiempo the egg began to walk away. It were only then that Tiempo noticed that the man's feet were pointed backwards. And then as he walked into the short distance, the short distance swallowed him, and where his body had been, there was nothing but air. And then Tiempo found his energy returning to him. And he did not wait. He fled from the forest with the speed of one fleeing from a famished lion.

# SEASONS of FOUR FACES

Tiempo slept outside his hut that night and the following night. In the nighttime, he wished the day would come, saying, "Night, night go away; come again another night." In the daytime he wished the night would come, saying "Day, day go away; come again another day." And he was caught in confusion. He did not go to work the next three days. On the third evening, he returned to his hut, and a messenger from Nana Yaa Asantewaa came to see him. The queenmother wanted to see him immediately.

Nervously, he went.

She was seated in her compound with her daughter Serwaa. After they exchanged greetings, she asked why he had not been to work lately. He had not been feeling well, he said.

"Not feeling well on account of the affections of two young women?"

She told him to be careful how he handled the matter: It was not in her place to tell him how to conduct his love life, but he ought to realize that both Fosua and Mansa were highly previous to her. Serwaa asked him not to act with haste in rejecting such beautiful, resourceful women.

As he was walking on the path back to his hut, Addae and Karikari approached him. They were both frowning and Tiempo decided this was not a time for pleasantries.

"Stay away from my sister," Karikari said. "You think you are better than Mansa?"

"Stay away from Fosua," Addae said. "She is my future wife."

"You can have her," Tiempo said, "I am not interested in her."

"So you choose to insult the pride of my heart?" said Addae. "You are not interested? Why, is she worthless? Are you better than her? Who do you think you are, stranger?"

"Be careful," said Karikari, "or else your days here will meet with an abrupt end."

And with those words, they left him. And Tiempo walked home alone as the night began to fall, even engulf him, and he thought of a hoard of vultures encircling in anticipation of the kill.

He needed relief.

He was relieved when Nana Yaa Asantewaa decided to take him with her again on a trip to Kumasi as part of his education and assimilation into Asanteman, to make him an Asante in mind and spirit. She smiled as she invited him, saying, "As the elders say, it is the water that loves you that enters your earthenware pot." This time, it was to celebrate the Big Addae festival that would consecrate the relationship with the spirits of the ancestors. The entourage arrived four days before the festival, again including Serwaa, Addae and Karikari, the latter two included so that they would learn to behave, and to help atone for their bad behavior the last time there were in Kumasi. Anane and Manu went along as well.

Around sunset that Saturday, the day before the festival, they heard drumming from the Asantehene's palace announcing the beginning of the festival. As the sound of the big drum filled the air, Nana Yaa Asantewaa warned Tiempo in particular, considering that he was new this, not to venture outside, because there would be terror on the streets of Kumasi. But what kind of terror was beyond him? The more he thought of it the more he considered it a challenge to him, the one who had conquered many. Was he to fear a little terror? Filled with defiance (against the challenge, not against Nana Yaa Asantewaa) and spurred on by a deep curiosity, he stole outside when he was assured all had fallen asleep.

The darkness was familiar and welcome. After all, he was the Prince of the Moon, master of the night. When he had gone a little distance, he saw a motely group fleeing from something or someone. He called after them, asking why they were running. Were they afraid of terror? They did not respond, but rather ran faster and soon disappeared. And then there was a quiet that would have been eerie to many of faint heart, but not Tiempo. He walked on, seeking the terror he had been warned of, if not to experience it, then to see it. It did not take long for him to get his wish, for a few steps forward, he suddenly saw six bare chested men approaching, bushy haired and covered with dark charcoal so that they were well blended into the darkness, each holding a machete. When he looked behind him, he saw another six of them.

"You there!" one of them yelled. "Stop!"

Tiempo stopped.

"What is your name?"

"Tiempo," he said.

"Of what clan?"

"I don't have any," Tiempo said, "I belong to all of Asanteman."

"Seize him," the questioner said.

And then the men approached Tiempo, their weapons pointed at him. He would be captured or killed. But this kind of action was exactly what Tiempo had missed in a long time, and he was ready to put his skills to use. And his acrobatic maneuvers around and between them as they came for him stunned the men, but they would not give up, as they continued to come at him. He did not want to cause any harm, but if he didn't fight, he would die, And so he fought. He fought them together as they came and he fought them one by one or two by two, however the attack came, until all the men were writhing on the ground, except the questioner who had not joined the fight.

"Who are you?" he asked. "Are you some sort of spirit?"

"I told you, my name is Tiempo."

"A god dressed as a human? There is no way an ordinary human being can put all these trained executioners on the ground."

"I am no ordinary person."

"What is your mission here?"

"I am a servant of Nana Yaa Asantewaa."

By this time some of the men on the ground were beginning to rise to their feet, but were now wary of attacking Tiempo. One of them said, "If he is who he says he is, then we should leave him alone."

The questioner said, "Come with us to the palace."

"As you wish," Tiempo said.

So while some of them continued on their mission, four of them took him to the palace and asked him to wait in a room. A man came to see him, querying his relationship with Nana Yaa Asantewaa. After Tiempo explained, the man said the executioners were highly impressed with his skills. They had sent someone to check with Yaa Asantewaa, wary of disturbing her sleep, but this being so important that they could not wait. After a short while, the man left the room and came back to indicate that Tiempo's story had been verified. Four of the executioners then escorted him back.

He found Nana Yaa Asantewaa pacing, beside herself with

worry and anger, which she unleashed on him, the first time she had done this. She was angry with him for his recklessness, she said. How could he not heed her warning? Didn't he know he could have gotten himself killed? But unlike Addae and Karikari who had simply bowed their heads when she blasted them for their indiscretions, Tiempo knelt before her and begged her forgiveness. This gesture softened her anger and she asked him to get up, but to be more circumspect the next time.

BENJAMIN KWAKYE

# Seeing Past Sight

Tiempo was woken up very early the next morning. There were some men talking to Nana Yaa Asantewaa in hushed tones when he was ushered into their presence. Then they informed him that Nana Prempeh himself had heard of his bravery and had asked that he be brought to the palace. Nana Yaa Asantewaa told Tiempo he had his permission and that it was a deep honor to be so summoned.

He would not get to meet the Asantehene face to face, but the king's spokesman, the Okyeame, escorted him to join a group of people that accompanied the king to an ancestral sanctum near the palace, where the Asantehene chanted a few words. And then twenty sheep were killed, blood flowing from their bodies like water. Tiempo was then released to return to Nana Yaa Asantewaa, who told him that the Asantehene himself had had word sent to her that Tiempo was one to be well kept as an asset to Asanteman. Despite his error for venturing out, she was so proud of him.

Later that day, they went to the palace, where the Asantehene sat in court, receiving chiefs and dignitaries who had come for the occasion. He provided lots of copious amounts of palm-wine and Tiempo noticed that Addae and Karikari were more judicious in their consumption. After that, Yaa Asantewaa's entourage left. But again Tiempo was summoned to the palace that night.

He was told that he was being made privy to a ritual process, because he was going to be groomed to be an asset to Asanteman. So he became part of a ceremony that started from the palace cemetery. Men bearing fire-brands led the way in the dark, followed by those to be sacrificed, their hands tied behind their backs. Tiempo thought of the earlier ovine slaughtering. There were others in procession, clothed in war attire, while the Asantehene was dressed in modest mourning clothes. And then there were those who carried exhumed skeletons of dead kings. Behind all of them was the Death Drummer, who would every now and then beat solemnly on the drum slung over his shoulder.

They arrived at a place where the skeletons, joined together with gold wires in coffins filled with gold, were placed in various cells. In each cell stood a table, chair, dish, water jug, sword, musket, sandals, and personal favorite items of a departed king. The Asantehene entered each cell, poured libation and invoked the spirit of the king in the cell, including enchanting words of his prowess and history, and asked for the departed king's blessing. Tiempo did not see it, but he was told that people were sacrificed in each cell, though he did not hear or see any resistance. He realized that he could have been one of those if he had been captured earlier. No wonder Nana Yaa Asantewaa had been so angry with him. It was almost dawn by the time the Asantehene finished visiting all the cells. The Asantehene then chewed cola nuts, and ordered the Death-drummer to beat his drum for death.

Tiempo took it all in, disturbed, not by the shedding of blood, for he had himself shed plenty of blood, as every society had its way of shedding blood, no matter how sanitized. But he was concerned with the lack of resistance of those being sacrificed, the quiet (and even dignity) with which they accepted their fate. Why had he not heard or seen any resistance? It was a kind of restraint that must have taken a lot of energy.

Before Tiempo was released from the scene, the Okyeame

told him that he had seen too much to ever betray Asanteman. Any such betrayal would result in death. And Tiempo believed this, not a death at the hands of humans, but a death at the hands of spiritual forces with powers he could not fight. And Tiempo had no intention of ever betraying Asanteman.

# Unearthing the Fire

There were two or three false sightings of Aboakesie that tensed up the entire Ejisu. But much more disturbing was how tense the atmosphere around him became, as dense as the forests into which he had escaped, only this time it was not only personal but societal as well, and the societal helped to relieve the personal. It was little comfort, though, considering the stress that it brought upon all. Aside from their post in Kumasi, the British had come before, twice to be precise, with a big mission, and now the emissaries came again from the coast, again to offer Prempeh protection. As he had done before, Nana Prempeh rebuffed this offer of protection. Where he had hoped that the British could be partners or even friends, the British, who had supported him in the struggle for ascendancy against Yaw Atwereboana, were not looking for friendship or partnership but lordship. They wanted Asante as a protectorate, a sure way to quell Asante ascendancy and ensure British supremacy of the Gold Coast. Nor was the governor in the Gold Coast pleased that Nana Prempeh had sent a delegation led by Kyidomhene Kwame Boaten and Oheneba John Owusu Ansah, Jr. to London to state the Asante case, a mission that proved as futile as attempting to douse the sun with a bucket of water.

As these developments were reported, Nana Yaa Asantewaa became increasingly disturbed, and many evenings, she would summon her advisers for consultations, discussing the increasing demands of the British for Asante acquiescence to British protectorate. This was an insult, she declared. Had the Asantes not ruled themselves before the British arrived? Had the Asante Constitution not been well established before?

Was it not this Constitution of laws that helped establish the Asantehene as foremost of the ahenfo or chiefs, and regulated aspects of Asante ethos to ensure a well-organized and united Asante that ran well from the days of Osei Tutu and Okomfo Anokye till now, even if there had been the occasional if inevitable internal friction that besets all great kingdoms? Then she averred how arrogant the British were, that they would come asking for total Asante submission. As she debated these matters, she made sure that Tiempo was present, if even in the background.

From time to time she would ask him what he thought. Tiempo only had one thought: from all he had learned, the Asantes were a great people and there was no need to allow such foreign intimidation; he hoped for the day when the threat would be stifled so that the Asante nation could breathe its own sweet fragrance again. On account of the somberness that had engulfed Nana Yaa Asantewaa and by extension most of Ejisu, and because she often summoned Tiempo, he had little time or mood to confront the demands of Fosua and Mansa. And indeed they also had sensed the change of the zeitgeist and the blowing winds of imminent war in the air such that they seemed content (or at least did not push their case hard) when Tiempo told them that this was not the time for love matters.

And this somberness world turn worse when the British, rebuffed one more time by Prempeh, who was also unable to accede to their demands with respect to payments under the Treaty of Fomena, arrested the Asantehene, who himself asked for his chiefs to vow not to fight back, afraid that British military superiority would cause irreparable damage to the Asante Kingdom.

The one sore point to the British was the refusal to hand over the pride and spiritual embodiment of the Asante: the revered Golden Stool.

## SEASONS of FOUR FACES

When news of the arrest of the Asantehene reached Nana Yaa Asantewaa, she was apoplectic, as angry as could ever be, heaving and convulsing in revulsion that the audacity of the British had taken such a bold turn and that the great warriors of the land had allowed this to happen.

But even worse and personal was the news that her own grandson Nana Afranie, the king of Ejisu, had also been arrested and taken to the coast with the Asantehene, leaving her now as the de facto ruler of Ejisu. Nana Yaa Asantewaa wailed when this news reached her, unafraid to show her emotional turmoil, even with Tiempo and others present. The worst had happened in her mind, the great Asante Kingdom disgraced, and her own grandson humiliated. What would the Great Nana Osei Tutu think? What would the Great Okomfo Anokye think? Where were the brave men of Asante? Where was the spirit of sacrifice even to the death upon which the Asante Kingdom stood? Had the night turned to day and the day to night?

And indeed at times it seemed the day had indeed become the night and the night had become the day. Tiempo walked in these changed times with uncertainty, at times, despite his resolve to stay loyal, not sure whether to leave the Kingdom or stay (and possibly fight for it as Nana Yaa Asantewaa often hinted to him was his duty). Why should he stay and get involved in any of its affairs? This was the best time to move on and continue his search. It was now evident that Sharifa was not in Asanteman and he doubted that she would come find him there, especially a land standing on the precipice of confrontation.

He had to move on and away from this land of trouble and away from the unrequited romance offered by Fosua and Mansa. But the more Tiempo pondered it the more he returned to the certainty that he ought to stay, rooted in the realization that he could not abandon the land at this time, the land that had been so kind to him and showed him its underbelly. And in such moments, the offense of what the British had done and the impunity of their injustice infuriated him. He agreed with Nana Yaa Asantewaa. How any such foreign force would arrest the king of such a dignified people in such a humiliating manner was beyond pardon. How he would love to face any of them or all of them in combat, especially hand to hand. How he would love to kill all of them, one by one until every bit of impudence was rooted out of them, each one of them, including their so called queen who resided in her castle far away and without knowing the strains of combat, issuing orders to foolish underlings. They all needed to be taught a lesson.

So, on balance, as Tiempo debated these matters, he was drawn more to the call to stay and fight when needed. This was even more buttressed when in the middle of one night he woke up in sweat with only one thought is his mind, which he realized had tormented him in a dream, that he had not fully fulfilled the side of his bargain with Sharifa, that he had not as yet fought his eighteenth fight. Over the years he had come close, but never done it. She had not raised the matter when they had last met, but was it still in her mind? Was that why after all these years she had not found him as she had promised? Was that last battle what he needed to finish to ensure that nothing, and absolutely nothing, stood between them? If this was not the case, why had this particular thought come haunting him at the very time when he was debating whether to leave Asante or stay and potentially fight? His last and firm conclusion: He needed one more war to fulfill his bargain, so that next time they met there would be no lingering impediment between them, even if she did not raise or remember it.

Tiempo would stay.

The next day when he went to see Nana Yaa Asantewaa he reminded her of his act of outward fidelity on the day when he prostrated himself before her. He reminded her of how he had been led to her and how she had allowed him to stay and offered him work, how she had been good to him by getting him so close to Asante royalty. Therefore, let it be known that he was prepared to do anything she asked. If she asked him to fight, he would. If she wanted him to journey to the coast to fight the British who were holding Nana Prempeh, Nana Akwasi Afranie and the other prisoners, he would not hesitate to do so, even if it meant death.

"You are a true son of Asante," she said, her eyes misty. "I have not heard such words of fidelity and bravery in a long time. You shall be known as a great son of the Kingdom."

But a number of those present disagreed. "How can you say this, Nana?" one of them said. "You must remember he is not one of us."

"He is now. Tell me, who is the son of Asante? He who stands idly by while others humiliate us or he who is ready to do battle?" She turned to Tiempo and asked the gods of Asante to protect him.

When he left to go home that night, Tiempo's resolve was certain. Let war come so that he could get closer to his love. He remembered all the wars he had fought alongside Pharaoh and the tactics they had employed and the victories they had achieved, now ready to be deployed when called upon on behalf of Asante. Now more than convinced that war was inevitable, he became a happier man.

When Karikari and Addae confronted him the next day

asking about his intentions, he smiled at them. "I have a war to prepare for," he said. "I don't have the time for anything else."

"You have Nana Yaa Asantewaa thinking you are a brave and faithful man," said Addae.

"But I know that at the first drumbeat of war, you will be the first to run away," said Karikari.

"Perhaps you are speaking for yourself," Tiempo answered.

"Are you calling me a coward?"

"Those are your words. You have called yourself."

At this, Karikari, who all along had been walking beside Tiempo hurried to the front to face him, forcing Tiempo to stop, the two men facing each other.

"I don't care who you think you are or have others thinking how brave you are. Today you have to face me."

"I am not interested in fighting you," Tiempo said.

"Fight!" Karikari yelled. "Fight, coward!"

Tiempo sidestepped Karikari to walk away, but Karikari hurried and stood in front of him again.

"Let him go," Addae said. "We can all see that he is afraid to fight you. Let him go."

His chests heaving, Karikari wagged a finger at Tiempo and said, "Watch yourself."

Tiempo did not answer with words, instead sidestepping Karikari one more time and walking away.

# SEASONS of FOUR FACES

## Wrestling Fear

Tiempo had unfinished business with the forest that had caused him to flee. He, who had shed the blood of many on the battlefield, stared down ghosts, repelled the attacks of skilled executioners, seen many wonders with his eyes, traversed many lands and dwelt in forests with beasts without fear of zoonoses, how could he fear the mysteries of the forests and those who identified themselves as dwarfs? He had to settle this once and for all before he joined the imminent war. How he would do this was not clear to him; but he believed he must return to the place he had fled. Although his heart skipped at the very moment when he reached this conclusion, he decided he would not overcome the forest with his mind; he would do so with his inner person, that indomitable self that had experienced and overcome so much. So when Tiempo stepped out to visit the forest he was no longer thinking. He was feeling, and he was feeling confident. The mind would have told him he was being foolish, but the spirit would have told him, as it did, that he was being brave. He entered the forest. As he stood in the narrow pathway of the forest, on his sides were tall mahogany, wawa, silk cotton and other trees, sitting in a sea of overgrown grass. There was for a while a very strong silence that seemed sacred, a silence not to be broken, or to be broken at risk of death. Tiempo looked to his right and then to his left. There was no sign of animal life for company, neither bird, nor worm, nor four legged beast. Tiempo was alone, felt that he was being isolated for a purpose, and the purpose was not going to be in his favor. Therefore, this was his chance to leave the forest and spare his life. He rejected this thought immediately it arrived in his mind. He would not shrink from whatever challenge awaited. He moved on deeper into the forest.

And then a great visible wind gathered momentum in the distance and, as he watched, rushed forward towards him. He could see it as a cloud, loaded with much weight. And it was coming closer and closer. And because he had already firmly rejected fleeing, he stood his ground and spread out his arms, saying, Here I am, come and get me. As the wind of cloud came closer, he felt a chill over his skin, a strange chill that made him think someone was touching him. But he did not budge, clenching his teeth and waiting. Then the wind got closer and closer and when he expected it to hit him with the full weight of its force, it suddenly disappeared and then it was no more.

Before Tiempo could catch his breath, he saw a fire on his left and another on his right, and both fires were raging and, like the wind, they were ambulatory, approaching him. As the ambuscading fires got closer, just as with the wind, a chill tormented his body, when he would have expected heat. And then when he looked closer, he saw that the fires had taken a strange shape. Both alike. There wore a head, no, four heads, each head with four horns. The eyes were a darker shade of the fire and from each fiery mouth protruded four serpentine tongues, flipping in and out of the multiple orifices. The cracking fires had the shape of giant snakes and they were slithering as it were through the air and trees and grass, coming closer and closer. And then they were so close he could have touched them if he tried. But he stood still and watched and they stayed close, although it seemed they could not cross an unseen demarcation into the pathway. Tiempo looked at the fires of serpentine form and smiled, and with that smile, he knew he had won this battle, for the fires were immediately doused, leaving no trace of burnt grass, nor shrub nor tree, nor of embers nor of smoldering.

Once again, before he could catch his breath, he saw the short bodied man he had encountered previously coming towards him. And this time Tiempo was filled with rage, a rage that he had allowed himself to be intimidated by the man in the earlier encounter, a rage that buoyed his confidence. He would be the aggressor this time. Tiempo started walking towards the man. The man stopped advancing towards Tiempo, further engorging Tiempo's confidence, and then Tiempo started running towards the man, who began to retreat, initially walking backwards, and then he started running from Tiempo. But as fast as Tiempo chased the man, he could not catch him, which was strange to Tiempo, considering how short the man was. He noticed that the man's backward pointing feet seemed not to touch the ground as he moved. But Tiempo would not give up and he continued to pursue the man. The chase continued for a while, until Tiempo began to tire and limp slightly. He realized he could not continue for much longer, so he decided to stop, deeming that he had won this battle just by virtue of the pursuit.

Just as Tiempo stopped, he noticed that the man had disappeared and appearing to his right side was a clearing, a huge clearing with a few trees. And then Tiempo was inside the clearing. And he saw a snake, an unusually large python, the size in width and length of at least four grown men. And as soon as he saw the snake, he noticed that it had moved towards a full grown man who seemed to be trying to escape from it. And then in an instant the snake had encircled the man, who was immediately immobilized. And then the snake completely coiled itself around the man, further immobilizing him. And then unwinding itself, the snake began to swallow the man. Tiempo expected this to take a while, but no—the swallowing occurred in a remarkably short time. And the snake seemed content and rested under a tree with the body of the full grown man inside it.

What happened next made Tiempo realize that this was just a show, but an opening act to demonstrate to him what was intended for him, to unnerve him into submission, for he realized that another python the same size as the other one had suddenly emerged in the clearing, and it was coming towards Tiempo at great speed. Tiempo stood his ground, but at full alert. The python then darted forward, intent on stinging him. Having anticipated the snake's move, Tiempo darted to the side so that the snake stung the air instead. Then the snake came at him again and Tiempo avoided its sting again. But the unrelenting python would not give up, coming at Tiempo again. This continued for a while as man and serpent danced inside the clearing and around each other. Tiempo began to tire even more, having expended much energy earlier pursuing the short man. Something had to change soon, for the snake did not look to have lost any energy or its intent to immobilize him. With quick thinking, Tiempo leapt high on to the other python lying content, itself immobilized by the weight of the human body within it, and used that python's body as leverage to jump up on to the tree under which it was resting. Then he was sitting in a tree bough. Tiempo quickly broke off four tree branches and jumped back down.

The snake appeared infuriated by this and came at Tiempo once more, extending its neck for the sting. This time Tiempo moved backwards with an impossible bending of body and the snake's head hang just above his own, and then in a quick move, and with as much energy as he could, he brought two of the branch sticks hard into the python's eyes, plunging them in deep and leaving them in there. He had never heard hissing so loud as the snake's head fell down heavily, Tiempo having moved from under it. But this did not deter it, as it slowed down but came slithering, although this time without aim, blinded, but perhaps detecting the heat of Tiempo's body.

Taking advantage, Tiempo goaded it with the tapping of the sticks on the ground, getting it to move in the direction he wished, its sibilance louder. It would move and lash forward, lifting its eyes-pierced head in search of Tiempo's body. In one such move, Tiempo plunged the third stick into its underside, right where its head joined the rest of its body, and then he buried the fourth stick next to the third. When the snake's head fell, the sticks went even deeper into its body, and then it lay on the ground, its body twitching.

Tiempo left the clearing and found his way back to the pathway. He stood for a while to catch his breath and his bearings. Then he began the long walk back home.

# BENJAMIN KWAKYE

# A Time for Everything

The pre-war party: that is how Tiempo saw it. Nana Yaa Asantewaa was determined to provide a moment of enjoyment before full hostilities began. She had been in a solemn, melancholy mood for a long time, but her daughter Serwaa had suggested to her to bring some cheer to the people around her. "Shall we not sleep because we will die?" she had asked her mother, quoting a common saying of the elders. The queenmother had pondered her suggestion for a long while, and then ordered that ten goats be slaughtered for the occasion, those tough goats with smelly foreheads that made soups smell so good.

On the day of the party, Serwaa supervised the sweeping of the compound, so meticulously swept that not one scintilla of litter could be found anywhere. Then she supervised the boiling of plantains and yams. On account of the number of expected guests, she asked Tiempo, Addae and Karikari to help pound the fufu.

Tiempo was coached on how best to pound the boiled plantains and yams by a teasing Manu, who said real men were born knowing how to do it. Like no one teaches the child God, he said, no one teaches a man how to pound fufu. Tiempo ignored his words while he observed how it was done, then he took over the pounding of the fufu. Tiempo held the pestle and brought it down the piece of boiled yam placed in the round mortar by Fosua, who sat on a low stool behind it. Pu! Tiempo heard the sound of the mortar as it hit the plantain, flattening it. He raised the pestle and brought it down again, Pu! Fosua added more yam and then plantain.

Pu! Pu! Pu! Tiempo pounded as Fosua used her hand and

fingers to turn the piece of pounded yam and plantain around or to bring them together for more pounding. Now and then she would look up at Tiempo and smile, coquettishly, saying nothing but, "You are doing very well." It was a hot afternoon and Tiempo worried his sweat would drip into the pounded yams and plantains. Fosua told him not to worry about that. It happened all the time. It made the fufu taste better.

When they had finished pounding the fufu, the men sat on the compound, breathing in the smell of the palm oil soup being prepared by the women, the fragrant prekese or galbanum mixing with that of the various meats to produce an enduring aroma. They all inhaled deeply.

Then as guests arrived, the food was served in apotowia or earthenware pots. Fosua brought Tiempo's and set it before him with a smile, while Addae and Karikari eyed him, and Anane and Manu remained nonchalant. But Tiempo waited for her to bring them theirs before he started eating. The fufu lay in the middle of the pot like an island amid a sea full of goat and duiker meat and tilapia and snails and mushrooms. He dipped his fingers into the bowl and cut off a piece of the fufu, gathered some soup with his closed fingers and brought the morsel and liquid to his mouth, swallowing in one go without chewing. By the time he was done, Tiempo felt heavy, like an overfed python, and would have preferred to go to sleep. But acknowledging that would be rude, he sat and listened to the idle talk of the men around energized by the consumed food.

It was at that moment that he paused to admire Nana Yaa Asantewaa in her resplendent kente cloth, sitting a distance away on the compound, speaking with a few dignitaries, including the adinkra clothed Amponsah, one of the elders she liked to consult from time to time on important matters.

And then palm wine was served, which Tiempo declined, but not Addae, Karikari, Anane or Manu. With calabash to mouth, they drank copiously, if not as much as that day in Kumasi. And then a group of drummers arrived and began to drum: ken-ke-ken-ken, ken-ke-ken-ken. As they drummed, Serwaa stepped into an opening in the compound and began to dance the adowa. Gracefully, she moved her body, her head ever so slightly to the left and to the right, her feet one short step here and another there, her body in mellow sway in response to the drumbeats; but her arms were the most graceful as they moved and wove patterns with her hands, one on top of the other, the other on top of the one, all these movements harmonized into one graceful dance.

And then she invited Tiempo to join him.

Tiempo was sweating with nervousness, not knowing how to do the adowa dance. But how could he say no to Serwaa herself without causing offence, and doing so before everybody gathered for the occasion, including Nana Yaa Asantewaa? He had seen the dance many times, so he stood up and closed his eyes and recalled every move he could in his mental eye. And then he took one tentative step forward, mind communicating to body and then he took another in the same manner, not allowing anything else to come between this communication. And what started as a tentative dance gained in confidence and Tiempo was moving his big body, molding his movements into grace and rhythm, hearing the sounds of the drums and mixing their beat into his steps, into his body, into his hands, until it seemed there was no distinction between drumbeat and human movement, just as Serwaa had demonstrated.

And then Tiempo could hear shouts of encouragement. He opened his eyes and saw Nana Yaa Asantewaa and she smiled at him, a smile of total encouragement and approval, and she lifted her right hand and opened two fingers into a V sign. And then Serwaa smiled at her dance partner and said, "Well done. We have made you an Asante indeed. When you go to battle, you will be fighting as an Asante to save your people and to save yourself; not as a foreigner, but as an Asante."

Before he could respond he realized that they were surrounded by a crowd of admirers and they too started to dance. He saw Fosua and he saw Mansa. He saw Addae and he saw Karikari, although they seemed so inebriated that their movements, which might otherwise have been graceful, were awkward. But no one seemed to care at that moment, because it was meant to be a moment of joy and levity, a moment of surrender to the group of which they each were just a part. They all danced for a long time, until dusk fell and people began to leave and then the drummers also left.

Nana Yaa Asantewaa asked a few to remain, among them Tiempo, Addae, Karikari, Anane, Manu, Fosua and Mansa. She then told them to gather around her. It was time to tell stories.

"We shall tell some anansesem," she said. "Ananse sem se so," she began.

"Se sem se so," the rest responded.

Nana Yaa Asantewaa told the first Ananse story of the night and ended saying, "So this story that I have told, be it sweet, be it not, I place the next storytelling on Serwaa's head." Then Serwaa began in like manner and this way they went around, each telling a story. When it came to his turn, Tiempo did not know what story to tell, so he decided to go back in time to when he told a story to Mansa Musa, but now to transform himself into Ananse, become the trickster spider himself. Once upon a time, he said, a king asked if anyone could tell a story that never ended. The price for telling such a story was to gain the hand of the king's daughter in marriage. Many came forward and failed, until Ananse had his turn. Tiempo told of how Ananse started by saying he had gone to visit his in-laws in a land infested with mosquitoes. He told of how the mosquitos would land on one part of his body and another and on and on until the king conceded Ananse had told a story that would never end and had given his daughter to Ananse in marriage.

"I have never heard that one," Karikari said. "It is not an Ananse story."

"Have you heard every Ananse story?" Serwaa asked.

"It does not matter," Nana Yaa Asantewaa said. "If it did not belong before, it now is a part of the Anansesem cannon."

As Tiempo walked home that night, he had never felt so close to the Asante Kingdom. He had witnessed its glory and its blemishes, some deeply disturbing. But he had fallen in love with the place and he had never come this close in his total belief that it was a kingdom worth fighting for.

SEASONS of FOUR FACES

# Fighting the False Shadow

Then the next day news reached them that Aboakesie had been spotted on a nearby farm, approaching Ejisu. With helter-skelter all around him, Tiempo rushed to meet this myth that he had heard so much about, even though a number of people tried to dissuade him. He would not be pulled back. A large group of people followed, but careful to keep a distance behind him. Then they got to an area, an expanse of low grass. And they saw Aboakesie approaching.

Tiempo moved forward.

Aboakesie stood much taller than him, at least by two head lengths, and he was massive in every other body part. His head was at least twice as big as Tiempo's, his biceps and triceps no less than thrice the size of Tiempo's, bulging hard even when he had not flexed them, and his exposed chests were like slabs of concrete. His massive thighs were complementary to the huge calves of his legs and it would have been impossible for his feet to fit into any human made shoes. His loincloth strained to contain him.

The men faced each other and, for the first time since they had known him, the people of Ejisu present at this encounter gasped in surprise that Aboakesie did not immediately threaten the person before him. He frowned, his massive cheeks straining to accommodate the novel challenge. They would have liked to cheer on Tiempo, but they knew they would pay the price if (or as many believed when) Tiempo lost the imminent fight. So they remained silent, breaths held in tight, strained. Then Aboakesie growled and the sound was so loud Tiempo could have sworn it shook trees and other nearby stanchions. A huge louse (that seemed to suffer from a version of arthropodal gigantism) crawled out of Aboakesie's unkempt, hirsute head, and Aboakesie grabbed it, put it in his mouth and chewed it to the gasps of onlookers. Then he pointed at Tiempo saying, "You are the who? Don't you know that I cough through my anus? Don't you know that I snore through my anus? Approach if you are a man."

Tiempo did.

And the silence of the moment was as chilly as death, a precursor of death as well. If an instrument could capture the heartbeats in their speediness and project them, they would have deafened ears across lands and generations. Then the two men charged towards each other. The birds were not singing nor the trees whistling. A death would soon be sang and the dirge would be for the one the town favored to win the fight but was convinced would lose. Reality was suspended as it seemed everything was happening in a realm outside of what they could reduce to time or space. And then as the onlookers readied to express their horror over Tiempo's demise, something happened.

Aboakesie tripped over a log on his path. And then he fell. Heavily. Throwing dust into the air and creating a rain of dust. Before the onlookers could recover from the dust fall, Tiempo had taken advantage of the unexpected fall, and he was pummeling every part of Aboakesie's body, hitting, striking, kicking. And for a while it seemed all that was useless, that Aboakesie was unmoved and would stand to his feet to fight. But what happened next surprised all, including Tiempo. Aboakesie stood to his feet in a quick instant, but instead of fighting Tiempo, he ran, apparently abased by what had happened. He ran away into the forest, blurting curse words as he disappeared into nearby trees, which shook with his movements, likewise the grass around them.

# SEASONS of FOUR FACES

The townsfolk stood still. Stunned. Had Tiempo defeated Aboakesie? If he had not even done so in a clear arm to arm combat, he had managed to scare Aboakesie off. They would conjecture as to why. Aboakesie had not fathomed that any mortal would ever stand up to him and, used to the cowering of others for so long, been simply unprepared to deal with the challenge. The fall and Tiempo's beating so humiliated him that he had been stripped of the will to fight.

Amid all this, they could not cheer, the shock numbing them and the lingering worry that Aboakesie would return to take revenge tormenting them into silence. But as Tiempo walked away from the scene, the dust fully settled, he looked at the eyes trained on him, the faces around him, and he could detect nothing but admiration.

BENJAMIN KWAKYE

# The Second Conference

Hoping that Aboakesie had disappeared forever, one more time, before he went to war, Tiempo wanted to call a conference. It was a conference of ghosts, of lovers and of haters, of fools and of kings. He did not wish to discriminate, because in all his travels and travails, he had reached the conclusion that indeed they all mattered and could contribute to the conversation. And he needed them, a lookback in order to prepare for the look-forward. Such was the state of his mind, inescapably linked to the past for assurance that as he moved forward, even if he perished, he had company and could mock the lethal embrace of time.

So he called Hatshepsut and Thutmose III for dialogue, and at the table he set before them he could see that they were still accusatory towards each other, one for usurping the power of a stepson, the other for killing a stepmother.

They went on and on in a dialogue that would not end, so he called on others from his various journeys. Adom explained that all he wanted was to be human and he had pursued what was in front of him in achieving what was expected of him. And then Dyeli Suleiman spoke in support of Adom, though Kouyate and Ibrahim demurred, arguing that human life and love were more important than human ambition. Some, like Mansa Musa spoke of fame and recognition and wealth, and some of the characters of his journey, whom he had not deemed worthy of much through also came and sat at the table and spoke, their stories reflecting that which the larger characters told, their motivations similar and even identical in some cases, except it was acted on a smaller scale that had not drawn attention.

# SEASONS of FOUR FACES

Their voices were at times soft and at times loud, and when they were loud they were an annoying cacophony. So Tiempo wanted to end this party, for the concert of ghosts that he had hoped for had become instead a war of ghosts, and the taking of sides, as was the case with history's large conflicts. He decided it was not his place to question motivation any longer but to understand it and tailor his response accordingly. He wanted to summon one more person: Sharifa. But he could not summon her as a ghost. He could only summon her as spirit. So she came as spirit, and all she could say to him, which would stay with him a long time was:

"Tiempo, no longer ask who you are or what you are. Ask, why are you?"

"Why are you?"

He was not sure he fully understood what she meant, but if he were to ask why are you, then why not say he was in Asanteman at that moment to fight. That, at the very moment, was why he was. He did not know if he would change his mind, but this question and the way he had answered it was one more assurance for his participation in the coming war. From all the mysteries and knots of the past that he still could not disentangle, this assurance of why he was at that moment in time was like moving from the tentativeness of ellipses to the firmness of lacunas.

# CHAPTER

# 4

*"Tomorrow, ghost widows would get husbands,"*
*Nana Yaa Asantewaa said.*

## Voices of Shadows

The intensity of the wait for the British to arrive was as painful as it was exciting. It was now only a matter of time before the ultimate confrontation to surrender the Golden Stool or face the full wrath of the British governor, presumably backed by the Crown in England. Governor Frederick Hodgson had first sent troops with only one purpose: find the Golden Stool. They had searched everywhere looking for it, even beyond Kumasi, as informers provided specific targets. Why else would they come to Tiempo's hut?

It had been an unexpected and shocking visit, when they called him out in the middle of the night, his name pronounced with unmistaken clarity.

"Tiempo, come out!!!" The unfamiliar voice shook the hut, the words spoken with the assurance of someone used to exercising authority and receiving obedience. "Come out now!"

Curiosity, more than fear (in fact, he was not afraid) prompted him to come out of his hut. Coming out, he had not expected to see what looked like apparitions. If anyone should be able to identity and be comfortable around ghosts, it was him. But what he saw did not offer any comfort. Four gun toting men, one white, stood outside, pointing their guns at him. He stood staring at them, not ready to ease the tension with dialogue, for their intentions (obviously) were not friendly.

"Give us the Golden Stool," one of them said.

Tiempo's surprise at this request rendered him speechless for a moment.

"Bring us the Golden Stool!" the man said again.

The absurdity of the request! He smirked. "Show me where it is so that I can retrieve it," Tiempo said,

"Are you mocking us?"

"Are you mocking me?"

"Do you think this is a joke? You think we are playing?"

"Obviously, you are not playing or you would not have your guns pointed at a man in the middle of the night whom you have roused from sleep."

"Then you know we are serious. Bring us the Golden Stool!"

"You keep telling me to bring you the Golden Stool. How can I bring you something I don't have?"

"We have good information that you have it."

"Who would tell you such a stupid thing? That I, a stranger in the land, would be entrusted with keeping such a sacred symbol of the Asante people?"

"Are you calling us stupid?"

"You have named yourself."

The man, apparently their spokesperson, moved forward, as if to inflict some sort of bodily harm on Tiempo, but the white one (who seemed to be the one with ultimate authority) stopped the advancing man with an outstretched arm. The white man then gestured with his head towards the hut and two of the men went past Tiempo and entered it. They returned shortly and reported they had found nothing, but the white man proceeded to enter the hut himself to verify this for himself. He came out shortly shaking his head.

The spokesperson then asked, "Where are you hiding it?"

"I have told you I don't have it and I am surprised that you would come all this way looking for it here."

"We hear you have close relations with Yaa Asantewaa."

"Nana Yaa Asantewaa. Yes, I know her."

"So if they trust to get you so close to her, why wouldn't they give you the stool to protect, knowing you are such an unlikely suspect that no one would think to come here?"

"Someone has really worked on you. Don't you appreciate how sacred the Golden Stool is?"

"Exactly what they said you would say."

"Who are they?"

"That is for only us to know. So I ask you one final time, where is the Golden Stool?"

"My friend, do whatever you want to do, but I tell you one more time, I don't know! And even if I knew, I would not tell you."

"Quiet!" the men yelled. "I said where is the Golden Stool?!" Tiempo did not answer. "Can't you talk?"

"But you just told me to be quiet."

The man turned to the white man and said, "Sir, I think

he's of no use to us. Let's just finish him off and go our way."

The white man stared intently at Tiempo, who returned the stare with nothing but the highest form of contempt telling in the intensity of the frown he effected. Whether this frightened the man or he had orders not to kill Tiempo, Tiempo could only conjecture, but the man ordered the rest of his crew to leave, obviously leaving the spokesperson in discontent, expressed with a contemptuous smirk.

That entire night, Tiempo was awake, alert in the suspicion that the men, or some of them, might return to finish the unfinished job. And in his alertness, he recalled the encounter and its patent absurdity. But then he suspected they would not have wasted their time unless their source was credible. So who could that be? As much as he tried to think of who would have asked them to come to him, the only names that came to mind were Karikari and Addae. Anane and Manu just didn't seem to have what it took. He suppressed the high urge to confront them. They would only deny it and he risked antagonizing them, this time with cause, if it turned out that the accusation was false. But, despite that small, lingering doubt, he could find no one else to bring under plausible suspicion.

A few days later, he heard that the search parties had returned to Sir Hodgson without the Golden Stool. The lull before the next move was filled with intensity: meetings of chiefs and counselors, concern over what would happen next. Nana Yaa Asantewaa fumed at the attempted grab at the soul of Asante unity, the ongoing insult upon insult. But they could only wait. The next move was not theirs to make, and Hodgson did not disabuse anyone of this belief when he sent word for the chiefs to assemble. He wanted to meet with them.

# BENJAMIN KWAKYE

# Touching the Dry Palm Fronds

Sir Frederick Hodgson arrived with his coterie when the chiefs gathered as he had requested, seated in a semi-circle. He was in his all white military uniform with its golden aiguillette, his head covered by a white helmet, face stern with a frown and sterner still on account of his bushy imperial moustache. Then he stood under an awning as the assembled constabulary provided him with a royal salute. Nana Yaa Asantewaa had asked Tiempo to come along as her counselor and guard and he observed the august display with amusement. After this, Governor Hodgson did not waste time with prolonged pleasantries past the usual protocol of handshaking, which Nana Yaa Asantewaa did not offer him, and she was the only ones among the chiefs who offered this rebuke. Governor Hodgson tried unsuccessfully to hide his surprise, and he frowned as he walked past her to sit under the awning in front of the chiefs.

He began to speak through an interpreter. He noted, among other things, that Asante (which he, and those of his ilk pronounced as Ashanti) had not paid any of its financial obligations under the Treaty of Fomena; and he affirmed that Britain was entitled to call upon the Asante people to perform communal labor and government projects, and that the exiled Asantehene would not be returning to Kumasi. And then he pronounced these fighting words:

"Why am I not sitting on the Golden Stool at this moment? I am the representative of the paramount power; why have you relegated me to this chair? Why did you not take the opportunity of my coming to Kumasi to bring the Golden Stool and give it to me to sit upon?"

# SEASONS of FOUR FACES

At that moment, it was as if every insult and humiliation had acquired a human form and become embodied in the person of Frederick Hodgson. There he was in the full authority and impunity of the British Empire, in the middle of the land of another empire that also deemed itself dignified, proud and majestic, forced to face many humiliations at the hands of this force that respected no limits or the sacred beliefs of others. If he embodied a humiliating power, he also at that moment embodied power unafraid to express itself, an audacity that immobilized the tongues of the chiefs, who looked at one another in surprise but with little else to offer by way of response.

But as tongue-tied and emasculated at the chiefs of Asante had become in the presence of British power, one woman was about to demonstrate pride and uncommon valor. When Nana Yaa Asantewaa stood up to speak, the men, including the governor, all seemed surprised that she would even dare stand up, all except Tiempo (who would have lunged at the governor without regard to limb or life if she had given him the order). And her opening words was the salvo he anticipated.

"Foolish white man!" she declared as mouths came ajar like doors, the shock of her audacity daunting. Tiempo held high his head with pride, tempted to embrace her with love and admiration. In his mind, he repeated the damning phrase.

But she had only begun.

"Who are you to demand the Golden Stool?" Ask again, Tiempo said with his mind's tongue, his pride higher in the buoyancy of proximity and relationship to this remarkable woman. She continued, "The Golden Stool is the property of the King of Asante and not for people like you. Do you belong to the royal family? Where is our king? Go and bring him to show you where the Golden Stool is kept. He is the sole custodian and he knows where it is hidden..."

Governor Hodgson replied that the Asantehene had been exiled to Seychelles and would not return to Asante.

"Tomorrow, ghost widows would get husbands," Nana Yaa Asantewaa said. When Tiempo later asked her to explain, all she said was, "The elders say that we speak to the wise in proverbs, not in ordinary language."

It must have been a calculated decision at that time not to order the arrest of the queenmother, or perhaps like the visit to Tiempo earlier that ended in no arrest or death, the governor thought it wise on balance not to take any rash measures. Yet he must have marked her down as one to be contained, or worse, as his venous demands hang in the air, including the demand of higher payments under the Treaty of Fomena. When the governor and his coterie departed, the chill of his demands and insult of the request for the Golden Stool abided, but none was prepared to take any action.

But, as the elders have said, one head does not hold council, so that night, the chiefs met to deliberate. A number of chiefs were not prepared to fight, infuriating Nana Yaa Asantewaa even further, leading her to ask a series of questions. Had they been so easily deflated? Was it because Nana Prempeh and the other chiefs had been exiled? Did they not know that the elders had said that the rain beats a leopard's skin, but does not wash out its spots? To ask for the Golden Stool? They must show Britain that Asante was angry beyond placation, that if nothing had touched the dried palm frond, it would not have made a sound. She went on:

"How can a proud and brave people like the Asante sit back and look while white men took away their king and chiefs, and humiliated them with a demand for the Golden

Stool? The Golden Stool only means money to the white men; they have searched and dug everywhere for it. I shall not pay one predwan to the governor. If you, the chiefs of Asante, are going to behave like cowards and not fight you should exchange your loincloths for my undergarments."

Demonstrating the saying of the elders that wood already touched by fire is not hard to set alight, she seized a gun from one of the guards present at the gathering, intensifying the atmosphere as some feared she might begin to fire at some of the chiefs she had just labeled as cowards, if only to fire some bravery into the rest. But if not of fatal consequence yet no less dramatic, she fired the gun into the air, Tiempo reading this as a clear signal that Nana Yaa Asantewaa would settle for nothing less than war with the British. A number of the chiefs were still unprepared to fight, but a number of them noted their willingness to defend the Golden Stool.

And Tiempo hoped that all the chiefs would answer her call, for how long would they cower while the British continued to treat them with such impunity? In his many travels he had once observed some people dancing the limbo, each time going lower and lower until one of them broke his back. He did not want the Asante nation to continuing limboing, the British bar going lower and lower until Asante's back was broken. He reasoned that even in defeat, they would still be proud that when a foreign threat encroached, they did not throw up their arms in hopeless surrender but had fought for their sovereignty, fought for their dignity and pride, fought for the ability to face posterity with confidence, and for him, fought the war for Sharifa. Death was not the worst fate, except for the coward, he reasoned.

So Tiempo began to prepare for the inevitably of war, and

though there was still resistance in Asanteman, those around Nana Yaa Asantewaa knew it was taboo to oppose her summons to war. Even Fosua and Mansa totally abandoned (or perhaps postponed) their calls on him, whether by voice (as in the past) or gestures (as in more recent days), knowing that all energies must be devoted to the coming war.

    This is my moment, Tiempo said repeatedly to himself.

## Staring at Life

But with the looming war, some, including Anane and Karikari were becoming more inclined to settle personal matters before the actual fighting began. Tiempo could find no other reason why, at a time when the queenmother was amassing troops for the war effort, the two of them came to see him, even abandoning the protection of night. Belying the tense atmosphere, the afternoon was full of dolor when they came to the hut, each clutching a cutlass. He did not invite them inside, preferring instead to engage them on the outside.

"Why have you come?" he asked.

They did not suffer niceties, not that they were prone to protocol anyway, but this time they were even more brusque. They wanted to settle the matter once and for all, and the moment was now. If they were to die in battle, at least they would have died knowing that they had stood for themselves. There was a disarming poetry to their logic, consistent with the way Tiempo himself had reasoned his way to fighting to protect Asanteman and the Golden Stool, and for Sharifa. As he listened in begrudging admiration, they announced that he should defend himself, defend the honor of the women he was interested in. How many times did he have to tell them he was not interested in the women? They did not believe him, they said. No man could plausibly deny interest in them, such beauty paragons. Or was he an eunuch? They could call him an eunuch if that would satisfy them, but they should just leave him alone, Tiempo insisted.

"Here is our proposition. If you beat us, we leave you alone. If you lose, you leave them alone." Karikari pointed his cutlass at Tiempo.

"They are not property to fight for."

"You are saying they are worthless" Karikari asked. "You are saying they are not worth fighting for?"

"Look at me," Tiempo said. "Do you really think you can beat me?"

"We don't fight with size," Karikari said. "We fight with intelligence and the love that brings us to this fight."

Tiempo tried one more time to dissuade them. "But this is not a fair fight. There are two of you and only one of me."

"I will fight you first. If you beat me, then you can fight Anane."

"You are really determined to fight? This is not the time for this. Nana Yaa Asantewaa needs us all, fit and able and totally committed."

The next move was not Tiempo's, though he anticipated it, given the posture of words and physical stance Karikari had assumed, with cutlass now dropped (presumably to level the playing or fighting field), his body slightly bent at the knees, followed by a lunge forward. But indeed it was a total mismatch, for all Tiempo did as Karikari lunged forward was to step to the side; and as Karikari was falling, Tiempo struck him in the belly with a blow as soft as he could manage, intending to send a message without causing harm. But that slight touch caused Karikari to writhe when he fell on the ground. He tried to get up, but Tiempo pushed him back down. Tiempo kicked the cutlass closer to Karikari and said, "Use this if you think it will help you."

Still grimacing in pain, Karikari stood up, picking the cutlass and brandishing it. Several times he tried to lunge at Tiempo to slash him, but each attempt was futile as the cutlass only danced with the wind, Tiempo's swift movements eluding the attempts.

"This is getting nowhere," said Tiempo. "Addae, if you wish to join him, please do so?"

And Addae, who had been standing on the alert, did so, realizing that neither he nor Karikari could match the prowess of this man alone. Never mind their earlier bluster now that he had demonstrated his ability. They tried to get to him, and he eluded them each time, making mockery of the dual power they brought against him. He seemed to be playing with them, moving forward, moving backward, moving to this side and that side, all the while the limbs and cutlasses of Addae and Karikari slashing the air, until the duo began to tire. And then in a couple of swift movements, Tiempo reached out and seized the cutlasses, his assailants at his mercy.

As they cowered in defeat and in expectation of death, Tiempo threw the cutlasses to the side and said, "I am not your enemy. Please. If you need to fight anyone, fight the British; if you need to convince anyone or people about love, it should be Fosua and Mansa. For one more time, I say it again, I see them as sisters and sisters only."

Heads bowed as they left, Tiempo felt sorry for them, seeing their heroism in the service of love so shamefully ended. Desperate to assure them, he yelled as they walked away. "I am your brother. I hope you will remember that."

And he hoped they would, as this could spell life or death, given that they all had joined the army, even as Nana Yaa Asantewaa continued her recruiting effort, urging more to join her with all manners of entreaty, including invoking the wrath of the gods on those who refused to join and asking wives not to sleep with any man who refused to join the war effort.

Slowly the shape of the army began to concretize and war was drawing even closer and closer. It was now only a matter of when. And the when would soon come enough, but old wounds needed healing.

Anane and Karikari returned to see Tiempo, at the urging of Nana Yaa Asantewaa's daughter, Serwaa. She is quite close to us, to Mansa and Fosua, and she knows that all is not well between us, they informed Tiempo. It is not good for men so divided to join in battle together, she had said, reminding them that, "It is to blow the dust off each other's eyes that two antelopes walk together." So they had come to offer their friendship. They were not doing this solely at the urging of Serwaa, though. They had deeply contemplated the matter, the way he had handled their last attack, his offer of fraternity, the way Nana Yaa Asantewaa had taken him in as a confidante and protector, and decided that at such a time as this he would be part of the Asante army, and it behooved them to put all selfish considerations aside. If he would forgive them, they were prepared to become his friends. Tiempo listened, still not fully believing that they were sincere in this offer.

But the coming days changed his mind, as they would come often to visit him, sometimes with smoked bush meat (grass cutter, duiker, etc.) as a gift. Serwaa's influence on them must be powerful, Tiempo concluded. And then one evening they came carrying a pot of palm wine. Although tempted to reject the offer to join them in the drinking, Tiempo realized that the men had done all that anyone could realistically expect to make amends. The path towards friendship had indeed been widely paved, and paid for with humiliation and now some humility, and he ought to walk on it with them or it might regrow with old habits. So he joined them as they sat outside and drank the sweet but intoxicating beverage. They continued to chat and drink as evening turned to night.

Then Karikari asked, "So Tiempo, why won't you tell

anyone where you're from?"

"Does it matter?" Tiempo asked, aware that the liquor had impacted his speech, so that his words were slightly slurred.

"I suppose it doesn't," said Addae, "You are Asante now and that is all that really matters, but we are just curious."

"Some say that you are a child of the rivers, unborn, tossed by the waters. They say you just appeared and will disappear one day," Karikari said. "On my part, I say that you have come from a very far land."

"Yes, you could say I have come from a very far place."

"Where?" Addae asked.

There was a certain level of levity that the liquor was causing that tempted Tiempo to say more; plus, he was deeply moved by their show of friendship, which had come so unexpectedly he relished it deeply. He was tired of the secrecy and the way it was bottled up inside him. "You won't believe me even if I told you," he said after a long wait.

"And why not?" Karikari asked. "Just tell us."

"If you want to know, I will tell you," Tiempo said.

Karikari and Addae drew closer to him. And he told. He told of the days with Pharaoh, the wars they fought together, of Adom and Sharifa, of the days of his wanderings, his time in Mali and with Mansa Musa and his brief time with Sharifa, of his additional wanderings and eventual arrival in the Asante Kingdom. When he was finished, both men unleashed a period of prolonged, mirthful laughter.

"You have a very active imagination," Addae said. "You are a great story-maker."

"I told you, didn't I, that you would not believe me?" Tiempo said.

"I know sweet ears attract lies, but you don't have to

concoct such a story just to throw us off. Whatever is hidden in your past that you don't want to reveal must be really grave," said Karikari. "It must be so sore that you will come up with such an elaborate tale."

"It is true," Tiempo said.

"My brother, so you want us to believe you have been in all these kingdoms and lived all these years and are still alive?" Addae asked. "Are we small boys to believe such a Kwaku Ananse tale?"

"It is true, Addae; that is all I can say."

"Very well, Tiempo, just forget we ever asked," said Addae. "You don't have to tell us if you don't want to. It is still well and we are still your brothers. In any case, the elders say that the pestle will find the elusive palm nut so long as it is in the mortar."

They continued to drink and converse into the deep night, the issue of Tiempo's past not coming up again. But after they left Tiempo began to question himself for the first time. He knew what he had lived and knew what he knew, and he knew all that he had told them had happened and he had recounted them without a scintilla of embellishment. And yet, what if they were right and it was all an elaborate production of his imagination, an imagination that had hallucinated ghostly encounters? And if so, what if Sharifa was imaginary? But even as he considered this he concluded that it was just a wish that his past would be imagined.

Too, with war pending and relationships being mended, Tiempo was pleased to see Mansa and Fosua the next day. "We hear you have someone special you are looking for," Fosua said.

"Did Addae and Karikari tell you?"

"They said you shrouded your past in mystery in order not to say exactly what it is," said Fosua.

"That you came up with a tale about living different lives over impossibly long years," said Mansa.

"Very clever," said Mansa. "But your concoction of a love interest is really not necessary."

"Serwaa has really taken time to talk to us," said Fosua.

"What did she say?"

"She said we should respect your wishes," said Mansa.

"And do you?"

"What choice do we have?" Fosua said.

"In a time like this, we can't worry about ourselves; Serwaa told us you will be needed and that you don't need any distractions," said Mansa.

"Are you saying you are no longer interested?"

"That is not what we are saying," said Fosua, "but with time and in due course, who knows what will happen?"

"After everything is over, we will see," said Mansa. "We are very patient."

"And perhaps your friend will eventually materialize and put us all to shame."

He wasn't sure if Mansa or Serwaa said this, the sarcasm clearly intended, but he had acquired a reprieve, that at that moment they bore him no ill will. But what he did not know was how long that goodwill would last.

BENJAMIN KWAKYE

# Staring at Death

There were events and happenings that no one could fully fathom. It started with rain as heavy as blanket (and with an angry drum, pam-pam-pam, voice) that the townsfolk dubbed a rain of many skies, and though initially they enjoyed the umbrella of rain from the intense sun, they soon regretted that joy, for the rain increased to such intensity and in such volume that each bead seemed extra swollen with water and the sky looked like it was sending a message of anger, that it was trying to settle a score with the earth it punished so. Those who would otherwise stand in the rain and play, especially the stubborn children who never listened to their parents, hid behind their frightened mothers or crouched close to their shaken fathers. The rainfall, therefore, was a massive, impenetrable curtain, producing a deep darkness at noonday. And the thundering was of a voice they had never heard, even the oldest among them, as it roared with deep blasting, causing brave men and women to shudder and many to cower in the corners of their bedrooms, knees brought to the chest, hands holding knees to diminish the size of the human body as much as possible. And then the rain lifted after it had poured itself out onto the earth, and suddenly in its place there was sunlight, light so strong and with heat so intense that some feared it would singe their skins. And there was no escaping the heat, whether indoors or outdoors. That too passed when the sun dipped over distant trees like an exhausted lover after difficult exertions. And more, animals usually preparing to sleep came alive. Dogs barked, birds cheeped, and fowls crowed in unison, and whether to bid the bad weather farewell or otherwise come to welcome the more benign version was anyone's guess. As the exhausted sky lay overhead in its grey, Nana Yaa Asantewaa summoned Tiempo, Addae and Karikari. She was deeply disturbed by what she had experienced and surmised it might be a message from the gods. She wanted them to consult with the priest Fofie to see if he had heard anything from the gods that he could share. With war coming, they could not leave anything to chance.

Tiempo wondered if it was mere coincidence that he would be asked to go see the priest so soon after his own encounter with a snake (or snakes). He had never been to see Okomfo Fofie, but he had heard that the priest kept a cobra that he often fed with all kinds of nourishments, some even said with humans, and that the cobra would attack anyone who visited the priest that he did not like. It was rumored that many had lost their lives in such manner. He was therefore greatly feared, and it was also said that the priest sometimes chose to communicate with those who visited only through music, that he would sometimes sing in strange sounds and the visitor would somehow be able to understand the awkward serenade of sorts. Sometimes he would simply drum his meaning and he did not care whether his visitors understood what his drums were communicating.

The men set forth as instructed, carrying a bottle of gin for the priest. If Addae and Karikari were afraid to approach the priest, they did not show it. Perhaps they all had thoughts and other things that were inoculating them from such fears.

They had each observed the venom of rain and immediate morphing into sunlight, and they were therefore as shaken as anyone else, and were not in the mood for conversation. This suited Tiempo perfectly, for he had a lot on his mind: the impending war and how things would also all end with respect to Sharifa.

They walked long pathways, stepping over worms and millipedes that had ventured outside, wiggling on the ground, and they disregarded the strong petrichor, which many often found fragrant and soothing after rainfall. When they turned four corners, they finally arrived at the shrine and home of Okomfo Fofie. A young woman stood at the doorway to the square building, a piece of cloth wrapped around her from under her exposed breast and reaching her ankles. They heard some hissing but they did not see any snakes in sight, although an enclosed shed to the left side of the building could harbor anything.

They asked her if they could see the priest, being on a mission from Nana Yaa Asantewaa. She did not argue, as she knew Addae and Karikari and would have no reason to doubt them. She bid them enter the building, which they did. When their eyes adjusted to the dark room, they noticed Okomfo Fofie seated cross legged in the corner. He was bare chested, but wore a raffia skirt from his waist to his knees. The locks of his hair fell to his shoulders. He looked at them with eyes that appeared not to blink. They saw no musical instruments and remained hopeful that whatever he would communicate would not be through music. They greeted him and he acknowledged them with his head, a slight nod to welcome them. He asked them to sit and they each sat on the floor. In his hand, he held a fly whisk, which he shook to his left and then to his right. As if to compensate for his earlier unblinking gaze, he closed his eyes and opened them many times before asking them about their mission.

Addae explained, as he offered the bottle of gin to the priest. He asked them to give it to the young girl. Then the priest took some cowries from a big calabash next to him and threw it on the floor. He studied the thrown cowries for a while and shook his head. Then he shook the fly whisk to the left and then to the right. Okomfo Fofie shook his head again, and uttered words the men could not decipher. He closed his eyes for long moments and yelled as if in pain, then he opened his eyes. He stood up and began to dance as one possessed. His feet did such a zigzagging of movements that it was amazing he did not fall, his lean body gyrating in various directions.

Then the priest began to speak: "Sometimes the gods weep and when they weep it is because something has pricked them or is about to prick them. They are weeping and their voices are booming in their anguish. But remember that the rain does not last forever, and the sun does not shine forever. It is all a cycle. The rain will come. The rain will go. The sun will come. The sun will go. But when the sun goes to rest it will rise again; therefore, do not be afraid of the rain and do not have too much respect for the sun. Everything happens in its time."

They all looked at him, expecting more or some form of explanation that did not come.

"The gods have spoken," he said.

"But what does that mean?" Karikari asked.

"Don't be insolent!" Okomfo Fofie said. "Am I the gods? What they have said, they have said, and I cannot add any more to it."

"But..."

Addae hit Karikari on the back to hush him. "We thank the gods," Addae said. "And we thank Nana for his words of wisdom. We will let Nana Yaa Asantewaa know."

They asked permission to leave, and permission was granted. When they were out of earshot Karikari said, "If I knew I was going to hear such nonsense I would not have wasted my time."

"Listen to you, Karikari," Addae said. "This your big mouth will kill you. Don't you know that sometimes the gods speak in riddles because otherwise their words will destroy us?"

"Then why should they speak at all? If they can't talk in a manner we understand they should shut up."

"I have said it, Karikari, watch your mouth. You may not understand their words, but the wise will."

"What, Addae, are you saying I am stupid?"

"Did I say that?"

"Am I stupid I can't understand the words of the gods?"

"I don't think that is what he means," Tiempo said. "I think those with the experience of years and with more spiritual insight are able to understand things that even the wisest of people are not able to understand otherwise."

"No one asked your opinion," Karikari said.

Tiempo did not respond, nor was Addae inclined to speak, so for the rest of the journey back, they listened in silence to Karikari's mumblings about the futility of the trip. When they told Nana Yaa Asantewaa what they have heard, she was silent for a long time. Then she said, "What must be must be. The rain will fall when it will fall. The sun will rise and shine when it will rise and shine. And so, we must act when we must act."

SEASONS of FOUR FACES

# Fidgeting for Blood

When Hodgson sent more men to search for the Golden Stool, he was continuing to stoke something that he may not have realized (or perhaps was done to further provoke ire). Insult upon insult. Injury upon injury. When would this man learn? The people had been docile for too long. Who would help answer Nana Yaa Asantewaa's call? Tiempo stood up. Anane stood up. Manu stood up. Addae stood up. Karikari stood up. As did many others. A few expressed worry that they would die. Nana Yaa Asantewaa was resolute in her belief that they would not die, but if it was the fear of death that would keep them from fighting, she reminded them that the British would come after them if they retreated. So even if they thought fighting meant death, they should remember the slogan:

> If I go forward I die.
> If I go backward, I die.
> Better go forward and die.

And then they lay their siege. And they waited for the opportune time. Then lying as in ambush in the forest they saw a group of Hodgson's men pass by as they resumed the search for the Golden Stool. Within clear shot, Nana Yaa Asantewaa gave the order and the men opened fire with their "Long Dane" guns. Ra-ta-ta-ta... It was more random than targeted, for within such clear sight, there was no way the shooters would have otherwise missed their targets. Realizing they were under attack, the surprise of Hodgson's people quickly ceded to fear and they scattered into the bush and out of sight. Yaa Asantewaa's men did not pursue Hodgson's men at that time. But it was clear that the hostile search for the Golden Stool would be met with fire, and even more.

Numbering about five thousand troops now, Yaa Asantewaa's forces, including Tiempo, Addae, Karikari and Anane marched on to the British fort. The troops were animated and ready to attack, but Nana Yaa Asantewaa told them to wait. Some urged her to use surprise to their advantage, Karikari and Addae being one of the most ardent advocates for this course. But others, including Tiempo and Anane, urged her to withhold a full scale attack on the fort. There would be no surprise because the British forces must have known by then, especially after the attack on the Golden Stool searchers, that this was forthcoming. Also, how could they scale the fort without coming under severe attack from inside and suffering heavy casualties?

After listening intently, Nana Yaa Asantewaa stood firm that they ought to wait. Instead, she instructed them to form a blockade. As some kept watch, others started to construct stockades. Little by little the stakes were put into the ground, passages allowed only in certain parts. Orders were given and men went back and forth with haste and purpose until the passages were layered with bells and empty bottles. On a number of occasions, Yaa Asantewaa's troops seized the food supplies intended to reach the British fort, the suppliers often announcing themselves when the bells rang as they passed and the bottles on the passageways cut their flesh and they yelled in pain.

One night, the British must have tired of the blockade that prevented any food supplies from reaching their fort. So besieged, the British forces must have decided they ought to attack or risk starvation. But their arrival was announced as they began to advance on the passageways, the sound of boots on the bells and empty bottles announcing their advancement and giving Yaa Asantewaa's troops ample audible warning. They lined up, waiting. From his vantage point, Tiempo picked out a few of the advancing British forces and started taking them out one by one. They were falling like flies, seemingly surprised by the suddenness and heaviness of the attack. Karikari, Anane, Addae and others side by side, they fired, reloaded, and fired. At some point the British forces realized this was a futile effort and retreated to the fort.

And then it was quiet, as the voice of the won battle resounded with brief silence before Karikari lifted a war song of victory. The troops sang and they sang:

Asante Kotoko, wu Kam apem, apem beba (Asante porcupine, kill a thousand, a thousand will come... Asante Kotoko we are going... We know how to fight, we don't know how to run...

The entire camp was in a festive mood as these songs became the soundscape of the night, soon joined by drumming. And the drumming then also became a war weapon, men taking turns drumming loudly to instill fear in the British.

And then Tiempo reached way back to remember the song Apophis had once sung for a pharaoh, and he remembered the song Suleiman had once sung for Mansa Musa, and he decided that he too would sing a song and it would come from deep within him, so he reached as deep as he could and lifted a praise song:

The backbone that straightened the bent back, what praises can we offer you? We can gather all the words in the world, and they will not be sufficient, for great daughter of Asante, you have shown that you deserve to be named with the greatest. Nana Yaa Asantewaa, backbone when they fouled Prempeh and stuck their fingers in Tutu's eyes and in

Anokye's too, you are great!

You are the land that is not passable to sea, for you lead to the mysteries of the forests, where a step this way is lost unless you point that way. When a nation was suffocating with the foul air of the invader, you became the breath of the nation's clogged nostrils, passageway to its heart with the fragrance of your bravery.

Nana, come gather your praises, come gather your praises like the freshness of the air that you are.

They tried to tear your heart when they seized Prempeh, when they seized Afranie, but they did not know that your spirit is greater than your heart. When men shake at the threat of gunfire, the spitfire of Hodgson, you stood like the giant they failed to see. They wronging ones had bargained with the wrong breast. Asante Kotoko. Kum apem, apem beba. Unconquerable spirit. You are it! Nana, come gather your praises. Asante warrior, defying the color of the northern wind, braver and fiercer than the lion with wounded teeth. Nana, come gather your songs that fill our mouths with the vapors of victory that they who smell flee into shelters like frightened fowls, we sing your praises. They forgot that you catch the wind with your burp, that you are the gatherer of snails who mushrooms them into elephants, you, born on the same day as fire and fierier than fire, eating fire in your sleep as spitting it in seven directions, no ten, no thousand directions, we sing you. Defender of the Golden Stool, we say, come gather your salutes.

When death sees you in battle, he prepares a bed for the enemy and opens his mouth with the laughter of the banquet before it. Your surrounding air shudders the nose hairs of enemies.

Muted march of trampling feet, the elephant's gallop of

the evening wind, we still hear you. Step forward, Nana, royal soul, we shall pave the way for your golden feet to walk on. Teeth without which the tongue cannot chew, knee without which legs stand as one place, immobile as trees, burning blood coursing through the enemies. We praise you. Let the air unwind its journey to go tell in far lands of the treasures we wear in bejeweled praises. Nana Yaa Asantewaa, come gather your songs! You are the day that summons the sun like the talking drums calling out the dancer's sleek moves only to swallow him with the choke of the wrestler's hand. You are the night blinding the pride of the sun so that it cannot see where its power has gone, until you pick them up with your feet in the dawning light.

Your people call on you, Nana Yaa Asantewaa. Come gather your praises.

When we can count the sands of the shore then we can measure your worth. You are the knowledge of tomorrow, slouching past shadows to discern their colors. You died yesterday and lived today. You are the mystery they will never unravel because you are the color of shadows. Like He who gifted her to us, you leave no shadows, for your shadow is light; mother of multitudes who has midwifed many warriors. You quake with great intellect and charm and your seismic impact will reverberate from generation to generation. Your people call on you, Nana Yaa Asantewaa. Come gather your praises.

BENJAMIN KWAKYE

# Encircling the Python

And for a while the British lay in the fort like an overfed python, biding its time. Then they attacked again, this time apparently determined to return fire with fire. Many fell, but still some were advancing. Tiempo and others had tied pieces of plantain trunks into ropes and as the British forces advanced, Tiempo and the others began to pull on the ropes, which sent out a noise that mimicked human movement, causing the British forces to fire at the trunks, thinking that there were more human forces arrayed against them than was actually so. Once again, the British forces retreated to the fort after having suffered considerable casualties. And once again, there was great jubilation in the Asante camp, marked with song singing and praises to Yaa Asantewaa as a great general of the Asante army. And the drumming designed to instill fear in the British tore through the air like great thunder.

Under such relentless siege, Sir Frederick Hodgson's next move was somewhat unsurprising, but still surprising for a man whose impunity seemed boundless. In the light of day, a group of seven men, clearly unarmed, hands lifted up as in surrender, emerged from the British fort. Asante guns were trained at them, ready to be fired at the least provocation, but there was none, as the men indicated they had come in peace. They were led to the presence of Nana Yaa Asantewaa. They wanted peace, their message was that short and simple.

Nana Yaa Asantewaa listened to her advisers. Some asked that the men be killed to teach the white man a lesson. Kill the spider when you have it, else it will turn into a tarantula to bite you, they warned. The nature of the British was not peace. Had they not shown it by the way they treated Prempeh? This was the time for Asante to press the advantage and finish off the job before the British regained energy. Tiempo and Karikari supported this faction of thought. Peace had its place, but war when hot need not be doused by those who would otherwise mock peace for advantage. But others, including Addae and Anane, argued that they ought to accept the peace offer. Further hostilities would benefit none. Even if the Asantes prevailed this time, the white man would ultimately be able to summon more resources, including from the coast and the war would become bloodier. Nana Yaa Asantewaa was silent for a long time, pondering these conflicting thoughts. Then she announced that she had decided to pursue peace.

Her advisers counseled on the terms of peace. The list was then announced to Hodgson's emissaries, including canceling the debt imposed on Asanteman by the Fomena Treaty, the return of Nana Prempeh and the other exiled chiefs, and cessation from pursuit of the Golden Stool. The emissaries listened and went back to the fort, returning later to announce the governor's acceptance of the peace terms. There was a great deal of singing and dancing in the Asante camp that day. But not Tiempo. Nana Yaa Asantewaa called him aside to ask about his mood.

"Nana," he said. "I don't trust this man Hodgson. I fear he is only stalling, looking for time to seek an advantage."

"I hear you and I also worry that you are right. After all, the elders say the one who has been bitten by a snake fears the worm. We have reason to be wary. You and I are so much alike. I would like to finish off what we have started now that we have the advantage. But look at the men, many of them are so convinced that I worry not accepting the terms of the peace offer will weaken their resolve in this war effort. I know it's a gamble, but let's hope the gamble works."

"Nana, I respect your judgment, and you have my full support."

With that, Tiempo joined in the jubilation, although he simply put up an outward show, for he had no doubt the British would renege as soon as they felt fortified enough to do so.

And they did, as news soon reached the camp that British troops had burned down some villages around Kumasi. Tiempo refrained from telling others *I told you so*, instead joining in them in their infuriation. This time, it would be all in, all or nothing, as the opposing troops engaged again. There were gunshots and sinewy fights, deaths and escapes. Tiempo shot many, pursued a few on a number of occasions who fled, strangled some to death and plunged his sword into a few others. But both sides suffered heavy casualties, and the smell and sound of death was everywhere. As this battle raged on, a number of them received word that Sir Frederick Hodgson was fleeing the fort.

Tiempo, Anane, Addae, Karikari and others were tasked with pursuing him. But the word had reached them too late, diverted as they were with the main effort. Still they pursued through thin and thick foliage, through pathways and bushes, in the open and in forests. By the time they reached the tail end of the governor's fleeing party, he himself was way beyond pursuit. But they attacked those they could, killing many in the process.

Many British soldiers dead at their feet, Tiempo and the others surveyed the surroundings, victorious in the killings but not so much in the escape of the governor. When they returned to camp, songs hailing them as heroes greeted them, the word *victory* resounding throughout the camp. With the governor's flight, the heavy casualties of the British, the prevailing view was that the British had been defeated, and Asante had emerged victorious. This was a reasonable belief, considering also that this would not be the first defeat of the British at the hands of the Asante people.

Never had the camp seen such joy. Perhaps never had the people of Asante seen such joy since the time of the defeat of the Denkyira, which had overthrown a heavy yoke and prepared the pathway for the creation of the Asante Confederacy, or the joy that must have pervaded the land when Okomfo Anokye conjured the Golden Stool from the sky. Even more befitting and satisfying, Tiempo reasoned that this war had been fought in defending that very stool. He had never been prouder of himself to have arrived at this land and to have fought in its defense, never been prouder to have been called a son of the land, an Asante.

He also had one more reason to rejoice. Whatever had led him to remembrance and to the thought, Tiempo was thankful, for now he had fought the eighteenth war. If that was indeed a hindrance to finding Sharifa, it had been removed. All he could do was wait. He would find Sharifa or, as she had so strongly promised, she wound find him. Who found whom was irrelevant, so long as these was a finding.

These were the thoughts that filled Tiempo's mind when he returned from the pursuit of Sir Frederick Hodgson and left many dead in the wake of the battle, as he joined the rest of the camp, as victory was announced and as the celebrations commenced.

His voice rang thunderously as he sang along in the songs of victory. His arms swung even more pendulously as he danced, his feet nimble with the to and fro summoned by the incessant beat of the drummers who hit the fontomfrom with more ardor and passion than ever before. He was dancing and he was not watching others lest he be distracted; though a group celebration, it was more singular to him than anyone else could appreciate. He was singing in conjunction with the others, but his moves were also solely intended for his own soul, his own spirit, lifted higher than he could remember. When the palm wine was brought, he drank from the calabash with such relish, any keen observer would have thought this was his first and last taste of the drink. Past the drinking and the singing and the dancing, and the congratulatory words, he had only one name in the recess of his mind:

Sharifa!

SEASONS of FOUR FACES

# Foraging for More Blood

As he waited for Sharifa, somehow now convinced that, after the eighteenth war, she would find him in Asanteman, or that he would find her there, Tiempo still had at the back of his mind a foreboding he could not quite fathom, a certain discomforting restlessness that rendered his nights almost sleepless. It wasn't the stirrings of what had bothered him ante-bellum, the longings by Mansa and Fosua, who were beginning ever so subtly to signal to him that they were ready to renew their pursuit of him, nor the corresponding detection of a growing distance between himself and Anane and Karikari, he suspected on account of the abiding interest of the women. This was a post-war period when he ought to bask in the surfeiting glow of the victory he had helped win. But the worried warrior could not find that comfort after that night of celebratory abandon and as things stuttered to some semblance of normalcy.

He was therefore not totally surprised when the attack came, justifying his restlessness. He knew it, but had also pretended that the British had been defeated, when it must have occurred to all that they would return with vengeance on their minds. It was obvious the British had strong reinforcements and, having tasted defeat the other time around, were not taking any chances this time. They came with indiscriminate destruction on their minds, scorched earth in their tactics. When he was summoned to war, the war was already lost. Ejisu was defeated, with many Asante casualties, and with the British forces ubiquitous. It was no wonder that knowing the prowess of its queenmother, the British would target Ejisu in particular. But the British also suffered massive casualties.

Nana Yaa Asantewaa and her remaining troops had to retreat, and Ejisu was not safe for her. Still, she had not lost any of her confidence or defiance. Her only worry was that her troops had dwindled to only a few hundred, including the ever loyal Tiempo, Addae, Manu, Anane, and Karikari. How were they to face the British troops who, despite their losses, still seemed to have thousands of troops and whose weapons seemed vast and superior, able to fire many rounds without reloading? A frontal attack of the British was certain death, which, after a little rest, she seemed prepared to undertake rather than wallow in defeat or surrender. It took Tiempo and many others to convince her to be patient, for her death or capture would certainly kill off any remnant of resistance left and Asante would be totally defeated.

Nana Yaa Asantewaa could not find a solution, the predicament worsened by the obvious hunt for her and her remaining troops. They would hear in their depleted camp that the British were on their way and would soon arrive at their camp. There were rumors of informants all around them, and none could be trusted. So they had to move camp almost every other day to escape capture in tense moments when they did not hear and were not soothed by confident songs of warriors.

Once, as they moved on to elude capture, they came across a village where some white missionaries were leading some Asante children in doxologies, evoking a deity of peace, love and justice. Karikari readied his rifle, saying, "Look at them. What kind of hypocrisy is this? They pray to their god in one way and practice the opposite." He aimed his rifle at one of the missionaries.

"What do you think you're doing?" Addae asked.

"I will finish these hypocrites off," Karikari replied, positioning himself for better aim.

"Put the rifle down," Addae said. "What will that accomplish? Do you want to draw attention to us at a time when that is not what we want?"

Extremely pained by this but realizing the wisdom of these words, Karikari brought his gun to the side, and the group moved on.

Tiempo wept.

When he saw how this great warrior had been turned into a fugitive in her own land on account of her defense of her people and their sovereignty, he wept. When he thought of the humiliation she was facing by the dwindled support and even treachery all around her, he wept. When he thought of how the British had captured Ejisu and most of Asante, he wept. Because of this, he was sure to praise her as often as he could, do his part to show how much he loved, admired and appreciated her. She listened, though she did not seem prone to flattery or sycophancy, but she would smile and comment on his sweet tongue.

They were not sure how long this stalemate of sorts would last.

Then the British made their most painful move yet.

They received word that Serwaa and other relatives of Nana Yaa Asantewaa had been captured by the British forces. The army general almost fainted to hear this and fell silent for a long time. Almost in tears, but showing the bravery that was her hallmark, she asked if Tiempo would lead a delegation to Ejisu to talk to some of the leaders to ascertain the veracity of this. He need not embark on it, for with Ejisu in British hands, this could mean death. He would be glad to go, Tiempo said. Anan, Karikari, Addae and Manu agreed to go with him.

They left on this trip of uncertain outcome. They fought elements, insects, gnats that clung to their bodies, and inclement weather for the three days it took for them to reach Ejisu. Under stealth, they arrived at the house of Elder Amponsah, having been stopped three times on the way but without being captured. Either the British troops were incompetent or they wanted to facilitate the meeting.

It was true, Elder Amponsah confirmed. The British were holding the children captive and would not release them until Nana Yaa Asantewaa surrendered. Could they see proof? This was dangerous, but he would try. Elder Amponsah led them to the fort where the captives were being held. Tiempo counted at least a hundred British soldiers milling around. They were made to wait a distance away, and then after a while Elder Amponsah returned with Serwaa, ten British troops with them. Tiempo almost went for her, but Addae held him back, whispering in his ear not to jeopardize the purpose of the trip.

Serwaa stood gallantly with a smile. She was her mother's daughter indeed. And then she told them to tell her mother never to surrender. Asanteman needed her to continue the fight.

One of the soldiers with her told Tiempo, "Now you can see we have her. We also have other children here with us. If we don't hear from her soon, they will be transported to Accra and exiled, or worse."

Tiempo and the others stayed in Ejisu for a day and sneaked out in the middle of the night in the hope that they would not be followed by spies, but they didn't need to worry, as the British seemed content to allow them to return unimpeded with their message for the Asante war general.

Back at Nana Yaa Asantewaa's camp, the confidantes informed

her of what they had seen and what they had been told. There was begrudging consensus that the war was over, although Tiempo argued that they could still fight on. For the others, the British had won and had a massive and well-armed presence in Asante. Staying away would serve no purpose, except to bring prolonged suffering, especially on the captured offspring. Nana Yaa Asantewaa listened intently and then walked away to be by herself.

When she returned, she announced that she had decided. She would surrender. "No!" Tiempo yelled. He would fight alongside her, even if it meant death. She could not give the British this victory.

Addae intervened. "We are talking about her offspring here. If she does not surrender who knows what they will do? They have shown how ruthless they can be. And we all know that we don't have the ammunition to fight them. Nana, what good will it do if you fight and die and they keep your child and the others anyway?"

"I only worry if I can trust them," Yaa Asantewaa said.

"According to Elder Amponsah they have given us their word," Karikari said.

"Their word is not to be trusted, we all know that," Tiempo said.

"We don't have a choice," Addae replied.

Tiempo tried, but Nana Yaa Asantewaa could not be dissuaded. She would not put those captured at any more risk, which she would have been prepared to do if there was any realistic chance that it would save Asanteman.

It was like a procession to a burial for Tiempo as they left for the surrender. Nana Yaa Asantewaa thanked him, and all the others who had so faithfully fought for the land and remained at her side until this moment. They should be proud of what they had accomplished: the British may have killed them, may capture them, but they had failed to capture the Golden Stool and in this they had been victorious. As for Asanteman, it may be on its knees, but as it had risen in the days of Nana Osei Tutu and Okomfo Anokye, it would not stay down. Light that evolves, never dies.

"The sun may be setting on the Asante Empire at this moment," she said, "but it will at some point in time set on the British Empire too, and then the Asante Empire will, in its current or an evolved form, rise again."

The words of Okomfo Fofie resounded:

"…the rain does not last forever, and the sun does not shine forever. It is all a cycle. The rain will come. The rain will go. The sun will come. The sun will go."

SEASONS of FOUR FACES

# Howling for Whispers

The two camps faced each other. The British forces were lined up at one end when they arrived, Nana Yaa Asantewaa, Addae, Tiempo, Anane, Karikari, Manu, and the remainder of her troops still with her were lined up at the other end. Nana Yaa Asantewaa asked to see her children as a precondition to her surrender. Some present with her began to sob; Tiempo fought hard not to do so. She told them to stop but they did not, not in defiance but because this was beyond their ability to control. There was murmuring on the British side and then a command was given and the captives were brought outside.

Tiempo looked down, ashamed to look up, ashamed to see the woman she admired and respected so about to be humiliated and taken prisoner by the British, to be exiled or even killed. But then he decided he could not look away while his queen and general was led away. He ought to be bold enough to give her that respect. So he looked up.

And the world suddenly seemed to spin widely and things turned bleak and bleaker and then light and lighter and lighter, and his heart beat furiously and sweat broke all over him and then goose pimples fell like a blanket over his skin. He reached inside of him as he had done so many times when he thought he had no energy but had always found that reservoir that brought him back from the brink. For this occasion, he was at once enervated and energized and it was in that state that he shouted. And she shouted. Simultaneously.

Sharifa!
Tiempo!
Tiempo could not help himself as he sprinted forward

towards the woman he had been waiting for, looking for, all this while. Thoughts ran through his mind quickly. Had she finally arrived in Ejisu and been captured by the British in the mistaken belief she was a child or follower of Yaa Asantewaa? It did not matter. He was going to reach her. The moment was unreal as much as it was real. And it was a moment of profound reckoning, reminding him that all his journeys were meant to come to this one place and time and that he could not lose her again. Tiempo blinked and looked at her, stopping in a spurious moment of hesitation that would not last. And it was a moment of joy and a moment of frustration steeped in the reality that the person he had traveled so many lands looking for, the person for whom he had lived and countenanced so much abuse and pain, was standing before him, in enemy hands.

So what choice did he really have?

He started his forward run again, and this time there would be no hesitation and there would be no stopping. She was also trying to break free from the British soldier who held her back. Tiempo could hear voices, especially of Anane, Karikari and Nana Yaa Asantewaa telling him to stop. He did not listen. Tiempo continued to run towards Sharifa. Shots seared the air like fiery lightning. Bullets lifted him up, and then brought his body heavily to the ground. And Tiempo thought he saw the shadow of Aboakesie mocking him in the distance, as then the shadow faded. All else faded. And all that was left was silence.

# PART IV

# CHAPTER

# 1

*"This is my home," Tiempo said, "the only home I have."*

## Songs of the Shore

The seashore sang with the orchestral lashing of the waves, waves rising and thrusting ashore as if in search of something that needed punishing. Onshore with seeming violence and then retreating with softness. But for those used to this, it was not violent at all, as familiarity had numbed the full thrust of its ferocity, but a form of expected copulation between water and sand, sea and shore. They were used to the spurting waves that rose high from the bobbing sea for sand splattering. It was loud and it was soft. It was violent and it was soothing. But for those who knew it, familiarity had not erased the depth they perceived—even the seashells told more than what the eyes could see; they told of dubious history (distorted by those who came from afar on the seaways), of stories stolen in time to watery graves, including the trade in humans, but that was a story for another day. For now, the fishermen were dragging the nets to bring in the haul, singing mostly coarse tunes as they pulled on the nets with sinews bulging, taut as stone. Pull! Pull! Pull! They pulled, spurred on by the profane words that promised of after-work, where carnal rewards awaited, as much as they were also inspired by the smells of the seashore, a form of incense, the piscine odor mixing with other odors no one could define. They took these smells in with breaths inhaled with gusto for the task of fish hauling. They were inspired too by the brilliant show of sunlight, glorious against the hyaline heavens, suggesting that space was the roof that sheltered all with sun and azure skies.

The harvest, when it came in, was bumper, now inspiring songs about the sea as a lover with caressing hands, dexterous hands of a lover, of the sea-top and horizon in love making, such that the undulation of the sea, when at rest mimicked the soft hump of a love-maker, the sea as mat, the far horizon as the capacious room. The fishermen sang odes to the good harvest, of peace that rendered the coast itself a ground of transcendent tranquility, the shore as a form of paradise, where each seashell under noon rays glowed like rare treasure. As they bought their catch to the shore, their footprints told of muscular feet that themselves announced life stories from variations of mostly naked imprints, and here, life's salmagundis were simple in the presence of the fisherman, as they were also more complicated than many of them could envision. Nor at that moment were they aware that in the near future, the lives of a few of them would change forever, that some of them would be summoned to a different calling that offered both freedom and death.

# SEASONS of FOUR FACES

Tiempo watched as the other fishermen went to haggle with the women who had come to buy the fish. He had a sudden thirst and walked to what he considered the farm of the seashore, the coconut trees and the canopy they offered, under which he often lounged. He scaled one with such ease as simians would admire and plucked a number of coconuts, which he let fall on the dank sands. By the time he descended the tree, Sowah was waiting with a cutlass in hand. It was a fairly routine matter: his need for thirst quenching, the scaling of a tree without much forethought, the plucking, and Sowah's arrival on the scene as if it was something choreographed.

And it was, in a way, considering that Sowah had seen him many times approach with the coconut pods and ask for a cutlass to shave off the coir and break the top so he could drink the water and split the pods and eat the coconut flesh. After a number of such sequences, Sowah would anticipate Tiempo's moves and bring the cutlass to the trees so they could sit under the canopy and enjoy the coconuts together. So, as they had done numerus times before, Sowah cut off the tops of the coconuts with the cutlass, offered one to Tiempo and took one for himself. The fishermen sat with their backs to a coconut tree and drank the water, complemented by the up-down movement of their Adam's apples. They did not need much conversation, these two men, both reticent. That was perhaps what had brought them together.

When he'd appeared asking to be allowed to join the men, most had started asking questions. Where had he come from? Did he have any experience? Why did he want to be a fisherman? Tiempo had said nothing to these questions, and some of the fishermen had begun to hurl insults. Couldn't he speak? Was he a giant without a brain to supply his tongue with words? As he stood before them like an accused man, Sowah, clearly a man whose opinion carried authority (and who had remained quiet until then) intervened.

"Quiet! Enough. If the man wants to fish with us, then he will fish with us."

When Tiempo looked at Sowah, he could understand why Sowah would be deemed a man of authority. He stood tall, sinewy (with no apparent fat on his body), exuding stoicism that commanded authority. No one challenged Sowah. He called Tiempo to his side, introduced himself and asked Tiempo his name. He struggled to pronounce the name, but though he mangled it as Tempu, he did not ask Tiempo to repeat himself. He asked Tiempo to stay next to him and just observe what he, Sowah, did.

"You are a strong man," Sowah said. "I can tell just by looking at you."

And so Tiempo had done as suggested, watching and learning fishing, so well and with such agility, dexterity and strength that, even if they did not say so, the other fishermen were soon holding him in admiration. He joined them, did his work, let them do the sales and collected whatever they gave him without complaint. They began to admire even his reticence, calling him the quiet giant.

As they ate the coconut, Tiempo and Sowah looked out to the sea, where they could now see some swimmers weaving the sea with arms and bodies in and out of the great water in great displays of natation. They could see littoral inhabitants walking the shores. They could see the canoes riding the waves that had weakened. They could see a few of their fellow fishermen promenading as if in rest from the strains of their just completed task.

Tiempo recalled the days and nights he had spent on the

seashore as both workplace and resting place, for after work, when everyone else had left, he stayed and slept there. If he had time in the day, he would pick a street and go promenading. He was particularly struck by the office and store buildings, some with captions and others with shingles announcing themselves, and the electric poles that flanked the various vehicles, including trotros and taxicabs, and people. Women, some with baskets containing household accessories and toys, balanced on their heads, crossed the streets with apparent disregard for safety. Others with babies strapped to their backs, did likewise. Men complemented this ownership of the street as they zigzagged in and out of vehicles, often drawing insults from drivers, who were wont to direct their verbal abuse at their fellow drivers as well. In the distance schoolboys and schoolgirls in khaki shirts and shorts or skirts fled from kaakaamotobi, masqueraders walking on stilts, and naked madmen who uttered unintelligible words. It was a bustle of activity that reminded him that the city was alive. At night, he would walk the streets of Osu and buy a meal from one of the nighttime sellers who set up their makeshift shops by the streetside, usually hot kenkey and fried fish with hot pepper and kelewele. Sometimes he sat on a nearby bench and ate in the relative darkness, the few lit lamps of the sellers as soft illumination, especially on days when the moonglow was weak. Sometimes, he took the food with him to the seashore and ate under the coconut trees.

 He would watch the night thicken in darkness, the moonglow for light, and wait for sleep. Usually, he slept without interruption; sometimes someone would pass by and inadvertently disturb his sleep. Spirits had visited him, for sometimes in the middle of the night he sensed a presence or multiple presences, though he could not see anyone. Once or twice he heard voices he could not attribute to any particular source, and sometimes of such strange intonation as he had never heard before that he concluded they could only belong to supernatural beings. But here was a man who had seen much, both natural and unnatural, so these did not faze him. Nor did it intimidate him when one night he heard a voice, purportedly belonging to Maame Water, the mermaid of the seas, asking him why he was invading her space and warning him of harm unless he embraced the sea by allowing himself to drown in it or otherwise by leaving the place under the coconut trees that had become his nocturnal abode. He did not respond, nor did he follow the limits the voice sought to impose, and he always thought he had unfinished business with Maame Water. He had gone for the occasional swims at night and though the waves buffeted at times, he had swum without surrender, not letting the sea drown him. He did not be leave his habitation under the coconut trees until later, but not as commanded by Maame Water.

Of all his nights at the beach, one remained most vivid. One night a man approached him and asked if he could sit with Tiempo for a while. This place belongs to me as much as you, Tiempo said. You may sit. Tiempo had never seen a man of such appearance and countenance, dressed in a black gown that reached to his feet and seemed to sparkle, just like his face, with the radiance of the sun, his beard full like a great boffin with little time for grooming. He reminded Tiempo of Griot Ibrahim. Tiempo asked him his name. The Poet, he said. He would not sit for long, he said, as he was on a journey.

"Yours is a story of many loose ends, isn't it?" he asked.
"How do you mean?" Tiempo replied.
"Don't worry about loose ends," he said.
"Why not?"

# SEASONS of FOUR FACES

"That is life."

He had a word to share with Tiempo, he said, and it would be said in the form of a poem because he was, after all, the Poet. He would do so and be on his way. Before Tiempo could reply, he continued:

> From Coast of Gold
>     the castle still speaks
>     past erosions of history
> echoes of guttural protests of pain
>     talons scrawling protest eaten
> by cramping walls
>     where they shackled them as beasts for
>     the slaughter of spirit
> blinded as darkness
>     in dungeons of no return
> shadows simulations of death to sleep sitting
> to sleep head-bowed
>     between strangers' legs
>     spirit-stripped and lashed
> to yielding wombs
>     rape an escape
>     this or death for even death wept
> at the sight
>     it could not behold
>     and took souls with trembling hands
> with face turned away
>     with those living becoming ghosts
>     in the bestial wallow of
>     vomit
>     blood
>     sweat

# BENJAMIN KWAKYE

    tears
    feces
soup for the devil
    above them rose Sunday's prayers
but the ghosts were in gestation
    to beget living lions who roared
through bestial burdens
    acts offensive to nature
but the lions lived
    years have sojourned
    and returned aged
and still the walls utter guttural moans
    there is no sangfroid here
every spirit that visits weeps
    it calls forth
    I am your castle
from walls of stone
    the voice of death
    outlasts the facades
of ageless walls
    the dead stand to remind you
    you who became ghosts across
aqueous graveyards of the Atlantic
    now in your leonine season
you can live again
    you borne of living ghosts
    whose spirits live
in the crucible of wounded blood
    I call you
    you whose lawns bore
the fiery cross
    whose eyes witnessed

# SEASONS of FOUR FACES

        hoods sporting the hangman's rope
I call you
        the spirit of the survivors
        speaking from my walls call you
dip desiccated tongues in the troughs
        that have widened to full ocean
instead of bread of sorrows
        make bread from sorrow

Stand Stand Stand

the door of no return
        is the door of return
Amistad is liaison of punctuated times
        not their chasm
the oceanic tombstones
        carry the pilgrims back
        bearing them over sea and cloud
the children swim gyrating welcome motions
        groaning shadows have begat lions
screams from the walls
        give roaring voice to lions
        and living ghosts have begat lions
roaring and roaring
        with the voice of the Atlantic.

And then he thanked Tiempo for the time and company and walked away. And Tiempo would see him only one more time.

BENJAMIN KWAKYE

# A Homecoming

One night, while he slept, he heard a voice calling out his name. As he left that opaque space of sleep into half awareness, he began to fear that he was drowning in the throes of death, not because he was afraid, but because this time, even before he gained full consciousness, the voice was real, a voice he knew, a voice that could direct him and he would follow. It said his name, and as he became more aware of himself, he realized that the pronunciation of his name was mangled. And it was only in the recognition of that butchered version of his name (Tempu) that he lost his worry, as the voice became clearer with recognition. But even then, he had heard of spirits that sometimes mimicked human voices, as he himself had experienced with the dwarfs of the Asante forests. So he fully opened his eyes for better verification. A body stood next to him with its majestic height and impressive muscular silhouette. He reached out to touch the leg. It was physical. Still, he wanted one more proof.

"Is that you?" Tiempo asked.

"Yes, it is I, your friend Sowah."

Tiempo sat up, turning his sleeping space into his seat. "Sowah," he said, "why are you out here so late?"

Sowah sat next to him. "That is the question I wanted to ask you. Why are you sleeping here? Don't you have any home to go to?"

"This is my home," Tiempo said, "the only home I have."

"You are a very mysterious man, my brother. You don't say much. I thought I was quiet, but you are even more so. I sense a great mystery behind the silence. I sense that you have experienced or seen events of such depth that you have moved past ordinary things. I have wondered what it is, but I did not want to pry, so I have kept quiet and just watched you. And you seem to do things with a purpose. Your focus when you work, your preference for solitude… I have wondered but not asked. But, brother, let me ask you this one time. I will only ask you this one time, and I will respect your decision not to answer. But I will also be pleased if you will answer. Tempu, where are you from? Where is your family?"

Tiempo's breath came heavily, even ominously in the quiet of the night, the swooshing sounds from sea the only soundscape. "Sowah," he said, "you have been a brother to me. And I have come to admire you and to love you. The way you carry yourself with such dignity, rising above the profanity and mundaneness of the others. Your quiet, your friendliness… Sowah, you are a good man. You are a great man. But my story is very personal and deep. I have scarcely told anyone, and everyone I have told it to has not believed me. So, if I may, please let me keep it to myself."

"Very well, my brother. I respect your decision."

"Thank you."

"But there is one more thing I want to discuss with you. In fact, it is the reason I came to find you tonight."

"Anything you would like to discuss, Sowah."

"Anything but who you are," Sowah said chuckling, drawing Tiempo into his mirth with an echoed chuckle. He continued, "I don't like it that you are sleeping here by yourself. It is not good."

"It is well. I am perfectly comfortable. I have slept in worse places."

"But this is my backyard and I can't have you sleeping here."

"What are you saying?"

"Come home with me."

"What?"

"Come home with me. There's a room outside the family home that is not currently occupied. You can stay there until we find another place for you."

"Sowah, please, I can't accept this. It is a very generous offer, but I can't accept it."

"Why?"

"I don't want to impose."

"Did you ask me for a room?"

"No."

"Then if I, on my own volition, have invited you in, that cannot be an imposition!"

"But your family…"

"I have spoken with my family and they are comfortable with it. My wife says the way I speak of you she will be disappointed if I don't bring you to stay with us. Don't insult her."

"Sowah…"

"This is settled. It is not a matter for negotiation or argument. Come, let us go home."

And home they went.

# SEASONS of FOUR FACES

## The Heart of Embrace

He was convinced he had made the right decision when he met Sowah's wife. Even in the middle of the night, her warmth was like ambient air, present and easily detectable, if subtle. They did not speak much that night. She smiled and asked if he wanted something to eat. He had already eaten, he said. Then Sowah took him to his room. It was stuck on the outside of the main house of three buildings that formed a semicircle with an open compound in the middle. The building given to Tiempo looked like an afterthought, a small square structure, the blue paint peeling off the walls. The room itself was totally bare, except for a raffia mat laid out in the middle with a pillow atop. There were also a pile of clothes nicely wrapped up in the corner. They had been picked up for him, Sowah explained. And then there was a flickering kerosene lamp and an almost burned out mosquito coil. But the room was full of energy, a welcoming presence.

Tiempo had not slept so soundly for a long time as he did that night.

The following morning was a time of introductions. That morning being a Saturday, he met all of the inhabitants before they set out relatively late on account of the leisured weekend to various pursuits. Tiempo saw Sowah's wife in the clarity of the rising sun. Adjele: deeply dark in color and slim. Their only child, Boi, was five years old and polite and seemingly shy, hiding behind his mother's skirts. Adjele sold porridge in the morning (and whatever foodstuff she could find in the market) to those in the neighborhood. Sowah, Adjele and Boi occupied the left building of the compound house. Sowah's brother, Tetteh, the second born, occupied the middle building with his wife Fofo and their twins Akwele and Akuoko. Tetteh was a bit more on the stout side, his wife also a beauty in Tiempo's view, more rotund than Adjele. Armah, the third and youngest, occupied the third building. He was the shortest and stoutest. Unmarried and without children, he was a pastor at a nearby church. Every member of the extended family was welcoming and polite, although Armah was a bit more reserved and less profuse in his welcoming words.

Immediately evident to Tiempo was that the compound was almost always busy, either with the children at play or when some came out to sit, relax and engage in repartee that sometimes lasted deep into the night.

In the ensuing days, this sense of welcome became even more entrenched, as the congeniality continued and as Adjele sent him food in the mornings and evenings, occasionally by herself but usually through Boi who, even for a small boy, carried out his duties with distinction. Once in a while, Fofo would also send him food, through Akwele or Akuoko, her teenage daughters. Tiempo offered to pay for the food, but Sowah and Tetteh declined the offer; he offered to pay rent and the brothers rejected this offer until he threatened to leave the house. They proposed a modest rent that Tiempo knew was way below market value. To feel like he was not abusing his welcome, he would periodically go shopping and bring the food items to Adjele and Fofo. He'd never seen such profuse expression of thanks as from them.

It was difficult for Tiempo to fathom their kindness and generosity, so one night after everyone had gone to sleep, he knocked on Sowah's door. "Is something wrong?" Sowah asked when he opened the door.

"Can you spare a few minutes to talk?" Tiempo asked.

Sowah brought out two stools and the men sat in the open

compound, the starred sky above them, a moment reminiscent of the night when Sowah had convinced him to leave his seashore abode.

"Sowah," Tiempo said, "you have been more than a brother to me, from the moment you saw me. I know you are doing this from your heart. If have said it before, then let me say it again: You are a good man and you are a great man."

"Those are kind words, but I am neither. I am just a man, a fisherman."

"And humble too... But that is not why I asked to speak with you… to talk about your virtues. It's just that as much as I think about it, as much as I know you are a good man, I still cannot understand why you are so good to me. You didn't even want me to pay rent and you won't take any cash payment for all the food you give me."

Sowah wiped his palm over his face, as though to rub away sleep. "This question you ask, Tempu, I don't know how to begin. It's not something I wanted to share with you, but I might as well. You say I have been more than a brother to you, but you also have been a brother to me and the rest of the family, more than you know. Do you think the moments I share with you under the coconut trees or in a promenade here and there are entirely selfless? No, they are not. Don't you see how much calm and spiritual fortification you provide, such as we have not had since Oko passed away?"

"Oko?"

"Yes, my twin brother."

"You are a twin?"

"Yes, I am Ate. Oko and I were born twins. He was the elder. Since infancy, I felt a sense of protection over him. You see, Oko never managed to speak. He would never respond when people spoke to him. I was the only one who could communicate with him, not by speaking but through signs. Over time, people began to think he was mad. Sometimes, he would strip and walk around naked until I talked to him. Sometimes he would throw himself on the floor and bathe in the dust, and run here and there without any purpose. In short, he engaged in all sorts of weird behaviors, so much so that people were always insulting him, at times even beating him up. I tried my best to protect him, but at some point he developed a tendency to disappear for days and even weeks, returning home dirtied and bruised and sometimes naked.

"Our parents got fed up with him and thought he would be a bad influence on the rest of their children, especially in our late teenage years. They built the building where you are now for him. They wanted him isolated from the rest of the family. That way, he could go and come as he wished. But I insisted I would not let him sleep there by himself. As much as they didn't like it, my parents allowed me to sleep in that room as well. And this seemed to calm him down and he spent less time roaming aimlessly. Then one day he left for weeks and next thing we knew his dead body had been washed ashore. That was a very difficult loss for me and my brothers, but over the years, with Adjele and Boi and the rest of the family, I have managed to cope. We rented the room to people, but they would come and go and none stayed for long.

"In any case the first time I saw you at the beach, I thought I was seeing Oko again. You look quite like him—not exactly, but quite close, like an older and taller version of him. And the way you listened to the others without responding reminded me so much of him, his reserve and refusal to speak, that I felt my brother had returned in another form. And the following days only confirmed this, how easily we got along, even without having to speak much, as if already deeply connected and I vowed that so long as I am capable, I will take care of you. I hope you can forgive me, now knowing that my reason for all this has been a selfish one."

"My brother," said Tiempo, "I am the one who should be thanking you. No matter the reason, you have been so, so gracious."

"Tempu, I know you are not Oko, but there is a connection between us. It's no wonder the other members of my family have so easily accepted you. It can't be that they are just nice people. I think they recognize that we share more than meets the eye, even if we can't fully explain it. So that day when I asked for more details about yourself, I was hoping that you might be able to reveal something that would help explain all this."

Tiempo's sigh was one of depth and confusion over what to do. "I have told very few of my past and they did not believe me. I will tell you and I will not blame you if you don't believe me or if you think me mad."

"You don't have to tell me, Tempu. I don't want you to feel compelled."

"It is proper that I tell you, Sowah. The last time I told my story, I was inebriated and seeking friendship. Now I will tell you sober and seeking brotherhood. It will seal our brotherhood tonight. All I ask is your word that you will keep it to yourself."

"You have my word, brother," Sowah said.

Tiempo retold the story of Pharaoh, Adom and Sharifa; of Mali, Mansa Musa, Kouyate and the dyeli; of Asante, Nana Yaa Asantewaa and Karikari, Addae, Anan, Manu, Fosua and Mansa. He told of blurred times in between these epic situations, of his ongoing search for Sharifa.

When he was done, Sowah sighed and said, "You are

right. Your story is hard to believe and at the same time impossible to dismiss. If true, you are ageless like a spirit; if false, you are either a liar or mad, or somehow delusional. I will not second guess you. I do not see you as mad or as a dissembler. Besides, all stories are true, even those that are made up, so long as you believe them. So I will not ask if it's true or not, only believe if you believe. I accept your story as you have told me."

"I will accept your acceptance. It is more than anyone has gone with me."

"So, then, the question is: Where is Sharifa?"

"Indeed, that is the question. When the British left me for dead in Asante, they took her with them, I was told, but where, I do not know. Was she sent to the Seychelles? I doubt it. If they'd found out she wasn't Asante royalty, they would not exile her with Nana Yaa Asantewaa and the rest. Did they kill her? That is possible, but in my heart I believe she is alive. As patient as I have been all this while, I can only continue to be patient."

"So you are here in Accra hoping to find her?"

"Yes, or that she will find me. That was her promise to me."

"Then we have to make sure you are well when she finds you."

The men had exposed each to the other in a way that they had not thought they ever would. When Tiempo recounted his story to Addae and Karikari, he knew with certainty they would not believe him. This time, even though he had wondered if Sowah would believe him, Tiempo trusted Sowah would—if not totally believe, at least genuinely wonder about its veracity in a way that veered more toward belief than unbelief. He had felt the same way with some of his ghostly encounters, when he thought and believed he had seen ghosts but then wondered whether he had actually seen them or whether they were subjects of his hallucinations, leaving him believing but with some unbelief always lingering. And he was sure Sowah had told stories of Oko to many, but never in this intimate way to reestablish a connection to the past that on the one part was dead but on the other resurrected.

Nothing was simple, Tiempo concluded, especially in this situation, and definitely not his ongoing search for Sharifa. Had there ever been such a complicated love story, as complicated (in the nuances of searching across times and generations) as it was simple (a poignant search for love)? A story in which he could hear the abundance of rain, but with the rainfall not falling, leaving him in painful expectation.

As he walked over to his room, he looked up at the stars. They continued to glitter against the dark skies that seemed to fondle them, worship them as though in silent astrolatry, and he began to wonder why he had often seen the night's darkness as so impenetrable that he had to tackle it with boldness in order to overcome it. He was looking at it anew, looking at the stars anew, thinking anew of the many stars that glittered despite the backdrop of darkness, or perhaps because of it. Why had he not thought of it this way previously? Why had he thought of the night as something to be mastered rather than as something to be outshone?

He dreamt that night of Sharifa.

They were seated on the beach and the world was bright and sunlit and many people were coming towards them, each one carrying a congratulatory song, urging them on to the finish line, telling them that it was worth it, that all things would work out for the better in the valley of doubts and would and must be exalted onto mountaintops of certainty and the surfeiting of the light of love. In the dream, it rained and rained. And though his night was occupied with dreams, he slept peacefully, never once stirring.

He ate the porridge Adjele provided and the bread Fofo supplied him the next day with much more relish than ever before, believing there was something oldish about the breakfast even through it was fresh. And when Sowah came to fetch him to go to the shore, Tiempo responded with more enthusiasm of voice than ever before, and when he joined Sowah, he walked on with much more aplomb.

# CHAPTER 2

*"But if they are spirit, so am I," Tiempo said.*

## Hooting at Hunger

The days that followed were full of purpose, or renewed purpose, and moments of relish. Tiempo had found someone who did not mock his story or dismiss it outright leading to: Moments when the porridge tasted a little sweeter, the bread softer, when the sun shone brighter, the ground was more pliant to the feet, the moon glowed softer and everything acquired higher incandescence, no less in the belief that Sharifa was closer and that the distance between them would soon close, if he could even call it distance. Tiempo loved the morning walks to the seashore, with creaking tree branches, croaking frogs, and chirping birds, and even the wiggling gogomi worms on wet soils, the times and moments under the coconut trees sharing a drink with Sowah, the evening promenades, the nighttime storytelling with the family gathered in a stool-sitting circle on the compound, bodies emitting whiffs of fragrant soaps used in the evening baths, when each family member took a turn, although usually without Armah, who spent many a night in prayer vigils at his church, ignoring all distractions, even the often loud ringing from its belfry. These were hopeful and refreshing moments that Tiempo wished would never end, or would only end when Sharifa found him or he found her and they went on their own to continue their lives.

The only worry was a dry patch they faced at sea.

The Homowo Festival was upon them anyway, "homo" meaning hunger and "wo" meaning hooting. With the constant flip flops of their slippers a soundscape of their business, Tetteh and his wife Fofo were feverish in their preparation for the festival, Sowah and Armah less so; in fact, Armah seemed indifferent, even hostile to the festival. Tetteh explained to Tiempo how important Homowo was to the Ga people, the hooting at hunger that had begun years ago after the Ga people had gone through famine and overcome it with defiant tilling of the land and planting and with fasting and prayer, which was annually celebrated to mark the beginning or harvesting of maize.

Tiempo took in the various activities as if he was watching episodes of a great event that eventually cohered.

Tiempo was informed that a ban was placed on any form of noise making, as there was a fear that the noise would negatively impact the crops in addition to scaring the spirits of the ancestors away. Armah in particular bemoaned the forbidding of playing drums in churches, an unnecessary edict in his view. The drumming and singing that Tiempo had gotten accustomed to all around him that were sources of diurnal joy ceased, and even funerals were delayed in response to the ban. But even more impactful to him was the ban on fishing also, depriving him of the one physical activity that occupied his time and gave him fulfilment, and he roamed around the streets thinking his days were as good as dross and itching for some form of action. In such moments, Tiempo would take in sights (mostly buildings and bodies in motion) without sounds, and in a way life itself had been forced to stand down from expression.

Then thirty days later, on a Monday, the ban was lifted and Tiempo rejoiced.

He understood how enthused Tetteh was about his twin daughters' participation in the festival, when Tiempo overhead him arguing with Armah, who kept insisting that Akwele and Akuoko should not be exposed to any bad spiritual forces. But Tetteh contended that and he was tired of this argument, that it was part of his culture and he was glad to have his twins participate in the celebration of the twin festival. Tetteh would explain to Tiempo how much the Ga people revered twins as a blessing from the gods, as a symbol of fertility. He was not about to invoke the wrath of the gods by withholding them from the celebration.

So the following Friday morning, Akwele and Akuoko woke up to take their baths and wear the white calico cloth laid aside for them. Then their skins were smeared in places with white clay and they would later eat a special meal of eto (eggs and mashed yams). And Fofo prayed for protection for all the children of the household and in appreciation of the gift of their birth.

Tiempo saw the mixing of leaves, including the hiatsobaa and other herbs, in a wooden basin of seawater and ordinary water. The horns of a ram were then washed with this water. Some elders poured libation and the blood of a slaughtered lamb was poured into the water. Many people came forward to drop coins into the water, take some of the water in the bowl for bathing and for petitioning the gods.

Tiempo joined a procession on the streets, in which Akwele and Akuoko participated. As they marched the streets, the procession broke into song, and then suddenly the twins seemed possessed and they lost control of themselves, staggering to one side of the street and then another. The pupils of their eyes vanished, so that only the whites showed. And at that time, Tiempo feared them, for they were not Akwele and Akuoko, but were instead possessed by something spiritual that was not to be trifled with.

Later, Tiempo accompanied Tetteh to a gathering of various chiefs and wulomei, and then they walked to Okaikoi in Ofankor, the death place of Okaikoi, once a Ga king. They performed a few rites, then had a procession through some principal streets, singing and firing guns into the air.

On Saturday, the women cooked some kpoikpoi (or kpekple), made from fermented corn with palm oil and fish. On Tetteh's prompting, Tiempo went outside to observe the king and his people sprinkling the kpoikpoi in various houses and junctions to feed the gods, a drummer drumming as women sang. The procession arrived at their household, sprinkled some kpoikpoi and collected some from Adjele and Fofo for further sprinkling in other houses ahead.

All members of the household, except Armah, ate from one giant bowl of kpoikpoi, to demonstrate their oneness. After the feast, they painted their faces and marched down the roads, dancing and singing celebratory songs. That Sunday, the entire family gathered, again without Armah. Sowah and

# SEASONS of FOUR FACES

Tetteh remembered the dead and then blessed the young ones in the household.

Tiempo observed the parties thrown for the twins, how they were feted, even to the point of reverence. He smiled at the undeniable joy that permeated the household, even if Armah was wont to protest.

# BENJAMIN KWAKYE

# A Battle with the Sea

But even after this, the drought they had faced at sea did not end. They had not caught much fish in a long time and they were all anxious. They had hooted at hunger but hunger seemed to be hooting back at them with great vengeance. Sowah decided then that they needed to go deeper into the sea. And they would go at night. A few of the men demurred, for one reason or another; but one of the fishermen in particular, Ayittey, decided to go along. Considering that a few still insisted on not joining the special call, only six of them went, Sowah as leader, Tiempo with him. Their nets gathered in the canoe, they left as the sun set and before full darkness, paddling the canoe to outer sea. The canoe floated like an object of singular importance, the sea still reflecting the remnant of the shimmer of the earlier sunlight, the water calm in almost seamless flow. The sky was also calm, cloudless, the glow of moonlight ample in the quiet lunar moments.

They moved deeper yet into the mighty waters, and now they lost that singular focus of importance, for the canoe floated like jetsam, as if it had no importance in that vastness of the sea that carried it as it did many things, especially those hidden in its bellies. Of the hidden parts, the fishermen were well aware, and many had witnessed the sea's fierceness, its strangeness and its seeming caprices. Deeper and deeper still they went. For a while it appeared their venture would be without fruitful result, for Sowah's trained eyes could not spot any fish. But he asked Tiempo to be patient when the Tiempo asked if they should cast their nets when he saw a fish leap out of the waters into the air briefly before falling back into its familiar aqueous habitat.

# SEASONS of FOUR FACES

And then moments later Sowah asked the men to cast their nets after a short period of study, when he had looked into the waters with an unwavering intensity worthy of ovation: the calm yet fierce gaze of unblinking eyes and measured breathing, and of furrowed brow and pursed lips—the markings of a guru of sea matters. When he spoke, they knew it was time to obey, and obey they did. The nets went into the waters, opening their orifices to gather fish, and more fish, and even more fish. It took every bit of energy to pull the nets in, on account of the fat haul. The men sang as they pulled in the haul, voices hoarse yet hearty. Pull! Pull! Pull! The nets came back into the canoe and for a while it even seemed their weight would sink the canoe, though the wavering canoe became steady, bearing the added weight well. The men continued to sing, now eyeing the return home, the triumph of the haul and the monetary reward it would bring. Their songs turned from triumph to jubilation and cheering. In such a hearty mood, they had not noticed the air around them darken, ever so slightly.

It was only when the sound of something hiss-like, but more ominous, pierced the air that they became conscious of the change in atmosphere, the darkness deeper now that the horizon seemed swallowed by it, and it was as if they were in a different dimension altogether, where there was no end, or beginning for that matter. The men stopped singing, something was afoot, something unusual, perhaps dangerous. Then, when they lifted their eyes to accommodate the overshadowing, weighty darkness, they saw an apparition before them, with the head of a buck, resplendent with a well groomed goatee, at first appearing bipedal when in fact it had the body of a fish, a form none of them had ever seen. And shivers covered all of them.

Sowah took a deep breath and said, "If any one of us has offended you, we beg you to forgive us." Tiempo attempted to stand up and even jump into the water, but Sowah pushed him down. The creature in front of them made the sound of a bleating goat, and then vanished. Sowah turned to Tiempo and warned, "This is not a physical fight. These are spiritual beings."

"But if they are spirit, so am I," Tiempo said.

"Don't be foolish," Ayittey said. "These gods of the seas are not to be taken lightly."

"Has any one of you committed any sin against these gods?" Sowah asked, as at that very moment they heard another sound none of them could have described, as if it was an amalgam of hissing, bleating, neighing and human voice. "If you have," Sowah spoke, "confess now so that we may ask for forgiveness and perform whatever rites we need to perform when we return to land."

Ayittey, who had bowed his head, spoke. He had had carnal relations right before the trip and had not had time to wash. "You know the gods of the seas don't like this," Sowah said. "To them this is filth. Ayittey, you know this!"

"I am sorry," Ayittey said. "I did not know we would come this deep."

"It doesn't matter how deep or shallow we come, you know you must cleanse yourself before you come to sea."

"I am sorry," Ayittey said again.

And then the mixture of the sounds they had heard earlier came again, this time louder, and before they could recover from it, they saw a creature begin to materialize before them, and as they sat shivering in the canoe, the creature took shape, and they realized it was Maame Water. Her face and upper body was human, pale as febrile moonglow, and as it rose higher in the sea, they saw that its hind parts were that of a fish. Once again, Sowah begged for forgiveness, this time aware of what he believed was the source of displeasure of the gods of the sea. The creature dove into the water, displacing a thick mass of water, bringing into the canoe a shower of seawater and with it a strong piscine odor. Ayittey vomited into the sea. Maame Water rose again from the sea, making strange sounds.

"Let me jump into the sea and fight this creature," Tiempo said, assured that the unfinished business with Maame Water he had suspected on land under the coconut trees needed to be finished there and then.

"No!" Sowah said. "This is not your fight."

As if Maame Water had heard this conversation, the creature made sounds again and the men cowered in fear. Tiempo would not be restrained this time as he jumped into the sea amid the gasps of his compatriots. "No!" Sowah yelled, but it was too late, as Tiempo swam towards Maame Water. This frontal challenge infuriated the creature even more, with a countenance that changed into a grotesque mixture of indescribable colors and shapes, and impossible contortions, and the statuesque upper body lost its contours and became fluid as the sea itself. And yet, Tiempo swam on. There was going to be a battle of Maame Water and Tiempo as he got closer and closer. But just as Tiempo was within his body distance from the creature, the creature let out one loud shriek and sank into the sea without further ceremony. And all grew quiet around them, and the moon glow returned, and the horizon appeared, no longer as a place of unknown beckoning. Tiempo got out of the water and went back in the canoe. Then Ayittey vomited one more time and his body convulsed and then he fell into the sea, motionless, his body sinking. Tiempo jumped back into the water and took hold of Ayittey, bringing him back to the canoe. For a moment he seemed dead, but Tiempo slapped his face four times and called his name four times, and then Ayittey coughed water and opened his eyes slowly, sitting up.

The canoe, with fish and men, drifted on the sea, but the men paddled hard to bring it ashore, and they had not realized that they had spent the entire night at sea, as time had become lost to them. And when they noticed it, the sun was rising, sitting half-body on the horizon, beginning to bring its shimmer.

# SEASONS of FOUR FACES

## Song of Wrestlers

Ayittey invited Tiempo to an event, as his way of expressing gratitude. The errant fisherman said he had gone to see a priest and performed some purification rites to appease the gods of the sea. He had had to pay a hefty sum of money and make other offerings, including a bottle of schnapps, two lizards, a frog, cola nuts, and a fowl, to be used for necessary rituals. He was now free to return to the sea and, despite the heavy price, he was relieved, so relieved that he was participating in an annual wrestling match at the seashore as his form of celebration. He had come in second the previous year, having lost to the man he referred to as Ankrah, who had won each of the past five years' contests.

Although not inclined to witness the wrestling competition, Tiempo had nothing else to do that afternoon, bright but not unusually hot, the sky clear and blue like the sea itself. So he went with Ayittey. They arrived at just about the right time, as the first bout was about to begin. There were about one hundred people gathered in a circle, equally composed of men and women and a few boys and girls, even some babies carried on the backs of their mothers. A couple of acrobats were performing somersaults and other body gyrations as the opening act.

Then the competition started, two wrestlers at a time clad in their shorts only, sinewy in every part of their bodies: muscled arms and chests, triceps and biceps bulging, bellies crisscrossed with strips of muscles, calves firm and protruding. In such angular appearance, under the supervision of a referee content not to interfere, the combatants were barely distinguishable and it seemed to Tiempo, after watching the first few bouts, that what separated the victors was technique, perhaps learned from experience, and sometimes luck. Ankrah was no different, as Ayittey pointed him out to Tiempo when the antagonist went to the center, the crowd watching and cheering. Ankrah dispatched his first opponent with ease, bringing the latter's body to the ground in no time. And likewise, Ayittey, whose first few bouts were won with little effort. One by one, many of the contestants were eliminated and both Ankrah and Ayittey progressed, if with a little more effort in the latter bouts. And then came the moment of reckoning: the rematch between Ankrah and Ayittey. Tiempo whispered a few words of encouragement to his seafaring colleague and Ayittey rushed to the center, overdoing his entry in a manner that suggested false bravado.

Standing there, body slightly bent, it was hard for Tiempo to imagine that this was the same man who had cowered in fear at sea and almost drowned in the deep waters. He smiled in the knowledge that he had helped rescue this man who now looked so statuesque, almost drawing reverence in the bold pose, a section of the crowd for a singing backdrop, the sea in its murmurings and the wind as chorus. The men went at each other, limb under limb, leg behind leg trying to gain advantage, bodies intertwined and continuously motional. On and on this went, the crowd cheering, clapping and gesticulating when people thought one man had performed a great maneuver. At one time it seemed Ankrah was going to fall, his body going to the ground, until at the last moment he bought one foot out to balance himself and bounced back up before touching the ground. And then at one moment Ankrah had to do a backward somersault to stop his back from touching the ground. The stalemate continued, the men sweaty but seemingly tireless. And on they continued and then the referee for the occasion stepped forward and declared the fight a draw, to the disappointment of the jeering crowd. The referee declared that they would each be deemed champions until the next year, which meant that no one had defeated Ankrah, which meant that he was the senior champion of the two winners.

"I have said it," Ankrah said, "that no one can beat me."

"You can be beaten," Ayittey said.

"The referee saved you. No one can beat me. I am the best, the greatest!"

"I know someone who can beat you," Ayittey countered.

"You? How come you did not do so?"

"Him," Ayittey said, pointing to Tiempo.

Ankrah looked at Tiempo, who was shaking his head in disapproval.

"I can see he is a big man," Ankrah said, "but here, I am king." He pointed to Tiempo and said, "Come, if you are a man."

"Put this man in his place," Ayittey said to Tiempo.

"I am not a wrestler," Tiempo said. "I only came to watch, not to participate."

By now, the crowd was calling for Tiempo to step into the circle: Fight! Fight! Fight!

"Afraid-man!" Ankrah taunted him. "He carries his bullocks for mosquitoes to feast on, not for any other use."

"I will not fight," said Tiempo.

"Coward!" Ankrah continued to taunt.

Some in the crowd tried to push Tiempo forward.

"Brother," said Ayittey, "Come and fight."

The crowd continued calling for Tiempo to fight, even as more tried to push him forward. In frustration, Tiempo stepped forward, as the referee and Ayittey (with a smile) stepped aside. Ankrah moved to his side and then to his other side. Tiempo bent his body ever so slightly. And then in one quick move, Ankrah leapt forward like a cat and reached for Tiempo's legs around the knees, and with the full force of his weight simultaneously pushed against those legs as he pulled them. Tiempo fell on his back and stayed there. And the crowd went into a frenzy, cheering their hero, without waiting for the referee's official verdict, lifting him on their shoulders and moving across the shores in songs of hilarity and lewdness.

As the crowd left, Ayittey came to Tiempo, now seated. "Why didn't you fight?" Ayittey asked.

"But I did."

"No," Ayittey said, "You allowed him to win. There's no way that man could have put you on the ground unless you wanted him to win."

"Ayittey," Tiempo said, "People need their heroes. I don't know what good it would serve if I beat Ankrah up. I could tell that the people have emotionally invested a lot in him. It would not be wise for me to try to ruin that investment."

Ayittey sat by Tiempo and was quiet for a long time. "You have spoken with the wisdom of the sages," he said finally. "You were ready to fight a more threatening force on the seas, and yet not this one. You approached this with a bigger heart and bigger eyes than mine."

Then the men stood up and, side by side, each went home with a mystifying satisfaction.

# CHAPTER

# 3

*"The story behind it is very long and personal, so let's not go into it," Tiempo said.*

## Stirring Time Awake

Tiempo was cruising in a period of tranquility, harmony and respect at his new home and in the workplace, and even enjoying long periods of leisure without the usual itch for action. No one brought up the loss to Ankrah, perhaps knowing intuitively that he had lost on purpose, perhaps even grateful to him for that exercise of wisdom. He was hoping that the days had ended (or been suspended) when the earth seemed in a thanatology of the many war dead, and that his quest would be for his one love. But as water likes to find fire, all good things do indeed end, or are punctured. That was it, a puncturing of the tranquility in which he had so ensconced himself. He had defeated ghosts, demons, and serpents, even the poisonous wind, the simoon. He had fought his eighteenth war; he had learned the gloss of light and he had nothing to prove to himself or anyone.

But a puncturing would begin the day when the man named Aryee visited. He greeted that Saturday afternoon and then went on to speak with Sowah in soft tones. Then Sowah invited him indoors for what appeared a very secretive matter. Tiempo admired the man immediately he saw him. His voice was soft, a bit raspy, like a voice that had learned to assume a lower tone under severe strain. Still, it was deep and authoritative. His hair, peppered with gray, was fairly bushy but patted neatly into place. His goatee, totally gray, suggested intellectualism to Tiempo, or deep thinking at the least. His muscles were poorly hidden by the loose T-shirt he wore over faded jeans, his feet in Afro-Moses sandals.

After he left, Sowah explained that Aryee was an ex-serviceman. He had fought in Burma (later to be called Myanmar) in the Second World War at the behest of the British colonizers. Aryee had decided to join the conscription on the promise of jobs and pensions when they returned from the war effort. Aryee, like his fellow servicemen, had done his part and fought gallantly. But ever since their return, he and many similarly situated ex-servicemen had not received their promised pensions or jobs. They had tried unsuccessfully to petition the Colonial government for redress and Aryee was growing in desperation, Sowah explained, and he now had to rely on friends and family for support.

"He is a proud man," Sowah explained, "and it's very difficult for him to come asking me for help. But he has no choice. You see, he can barely undertake any form of labor now, as he was wounded in the war. He hides all this with dignity and strength and you would think him physically strong, but he can no longer do manual work. And he is not educated enough to get an office job. Even for his compatriots who are able and willing to work, the British have refused to find them work and for those like Aryee who need a pension the British have reneged on their promise to pay them the promised pensions. So he keeps hoping and waiting, and they keep refusing, and his dignity keeps getting eroded. The man I once knew is not the man you saw. Aryee was gregarious and boisterous; now he's withdrawn and taunted by a dream that keeps fading."

"He still looks so dignified."

"Yes, that is part of the man. He was born to lead, in my opinion, and I hear that he was very brave in war, that the British put him in a platoon of brave warriors. But after his injury they want to discard him like rubbish."

"This is so unfair. Sometimes I wonder what they take us for."

"I know—the injustice of it. Something must be done about it."

"Yes, but what?"

Tiempo's question hovered over them for a while, unanswered and the men even forgot it had been asked until later. In the interim, they were occupied by quotidian concerns.

But a little afterwards, Aryee came to see Sowah again and whispered to him, although this time with wild gestures unbecoming his otherwise calm demeanor. As before, they went indoors for a while. After Aryee left, Sowah informed Tiempo that Aryee and a few other servicemen were trying to organize a larger group to petition the colonial government for redress.

"Haven't they tried before?"

"Not in an organized way as they are planning now."

And days later, Aryee returned, this time with another

man he introduced as Adjetey, who had fought with him in Burma. Then a few days later, Aryee and Adjetey returned with yet another ex-serviceman, Attipoe, and then later with another, Odartey-Lamptey. Then on one of the visits they asked Tiempo to join their conversation, formally introducing themselves: Sergeant Adjetey, Corporal Attipoe, Private Odartey-Lamptey and, of course, Sergeant Aryee. They had heard of him from Sowah and wanted him to join them as they planned a march to the seat of the British Government at the Christiansborg Castle in Osu. Others had agreed to join them, and they wanted to present a show of force to the governor so that in the strength of their numbers and in the formal march, he would be compelled to hear them and grant them redress. Sowah had told them Tiempo would be good to include in the march, that he was a man of great strength.

"Your physical stature and demeanor draws attention and admiration," Sowah said to Tiempo. "These noble men see you and are impressed."

Tiempo did not hesitate to agree to join the march. He remembered the moment when he had seen Sharifa as she was held by the British and how he'd been shot, Sharifa once again snatched from him. He recalled the injustice he had experienced under the British takeover of Asante, the pillaging and arrogant request for the Golden Stool, the cruel exile of Prempeh and Yaa Asantewaa and other chiefs. And now this. When would it end?

At that moment, the voice of the Poet returned to him, snippets urging him:

> now in your leonine season
> you can live again
> I call you

instead of bread of sorrows make bread from sorrow
Stand Stand Stand

He would stand with the ex-servicemen, wring bread from their sorrows.

He knew the British could resort to violent means to counter anything they perceived as insubordinate, but to cower would be to surrender not just the current generation but future generations as well. And the ongoing erosion of dignity. A stand had to be taken, and he was prepared to standfast for freedom and justice. Again. Yes, he would be glad to take part in the march. The ex-servicemen shook his hand and intimated they would be sending men to the seashore the next day to help recruit more people.

Tiempo wished that these four dignified men had come themselves to the shore the next day, instead of sending incompetent emissaries. They were at seaside, having finished the day's work, many already transiting, through drinking, into the expected coarseness of the coming events of latter day and night, and so many mouths were reeking of alcohol and singing profane songs. It was an atmosphere rife with carnal instincts and they had little appetite for lofty goals at that time, let alone to participate in them. And yet, it was into this atmosphere that the recruiters came, with tocsins of serious intent, their eyes red, their tunes as they approached full of bellicose words. There were ten of them, a motley group of young, rowdy men announcing, without any tactical buildup, their need for the fishermen to support the intended march on the castle to petition the governor on behalf of their fellow brothers, the ex-servicemen and other workers the British had so cruelly fooled.

"It is their folly," said one fisherman. "They should have

known whom they were dealing with. Why will any sane man leave his home to fight for the British? They deserve what they've got."

"Don't speak like that," Sowah intervened. "These are our brothers. We should stand with them in time of need."

Sowah may have overestimated his influence over men who were not sober.

"Sowah," the fisherman who had spoken earlier replied, "we respect you, so please respect yourself."

"How am I disrespecting anyone?" Sowah asked.

Another fisherman said, "We usually listen to you, Sowah, but this fight is not our fight. If you want to go march, do so but leave us alone."

"I am going to see my lover," another said, "I don't have time for this."

He did a little dance, moving his waist sideways and thrusting it forward. He did not wait for further persuasion as he left, taking about a quarter of the fishermen with him, who chorused a love song he started as they left the seashore. The recruiters were now arguing among themselves, debating whether this whole recruiting effort was even necessary. They could do it themselves, said some. Then why did we come? asked others. Because Adjetey and the rest asked us to come; they want numbers. As they argued among themselves, about another quarter of the fishermen left.

Ayittey then said, "Brothers, I am begging those of you who can join this effort to do so. It may be another today, but tomorrow, it will be you or me."

There were murmurings among the remaining fishermen. But their murmurings did not prevent another large number from leaving. With only ten men left, Tiempo realized they could not afford to lose any more men. He raised his hand, signaling he wanted to address the remnant. The surprise of seeing this seized attention. The man who rarely spoke to anyone, except Sowah, wanted to talk to them? Whatever this quiet, mysterious man had to say was worth listening to. Everyone fell quiet.

By now, the sun was setting, and the abiding light was weak, so that when Tiempo stood in front of the group, many shadows shaded parts of his body, creating an intriguing image that connotated power, if hidden power. The sea murmured and the wind blowing from sea chilled the air.

"Brothers," Tiempo began, "I know most of you don't know me, even though I have been with you for some time now. The point I want to make is, even I, a relative stranger to these parts, feel a strong sense of brotherhood, a fraternity, not of blood, but of our abused humanity. I tell you that I have seen many things in my life, but none has galled me more that this blatant inhumanity towards us and the abuse of our dignity. These people have done so in the past, and they are doing so now, and they will continue to do so if we don't signal to them that we won't take it. But here, we are not talking about taking up arms, though it will be well within our rights to do so. We are not talking about any acts of hooliganism, though who can blame us if we did? All we are asking is that you support our brothers in numbers to march to the castle to present a petition for redress. Please, brothers, let us not reject this fraternal call."

A hush engulfed the crowd and Ayittey said, "If he, a stranger among us, can make such a call, how much more those of us who have lived with these men who were calling for our help?"

One by one, the men began to vocalize their support for the march and to indicate their intention to participate. And one by one, they came forward to shake Tiempo's hand and to indicate that he had spoken well; one by one, including the recruiters. One by one they left the seashore until only Sowah and Tiempo were left. Sowah looked at Tiempo for a long while, then grinned and stepped forward and embraced him. And when they arrived home that night, Sowah told his brothers of what had happened at the seashore. And they all praised Tiempo to the point of embarrassment.

Tetteh turned to Armah and asked, "You have no problem with this, do you?"

"Of course not; why would I?"

"I have heard you say from your book that we should turn the other cheek."

"Not to the point of foolishness. Our brothers are merely asking for what has been promised them. Our God is a God of peace, but He is also a God of justice. They can't have one without the other."

That evening, Sowah asked Tiempo to dine with him on the family compound, and when the men sat down to eat, Tiempo noticed that he had extra fish with his kenkey. Adjele and Boi came and sat next to them for a while. Then Tetteh and Adjele and Akwele and Akuoko joined them. And then in a short while Armah also came outside and joined the rest of the family.

SEASONS of FOUR FACES

# Positive Action

A confluence of events conjoining almost haphazardly towards one purpose: a form of rebellion, even if muted, against European heavy handedness. The locals began to object to the high prices of European goods. This would not have been a problem but for the fact that the locals had developed a taste for such goods. Put a different way, after having created a local taste for European goods, the Europeans could now charge high prices. And the locals who had survived a long time before European contact and penetration without such tastes, now found cause to complain.

    Regardless of the basis for their discontent, it had become a matter of such urgency that the Ga Mantse himself, Nii Kwabena Bonne II, called for a boycott of all European goods. Not that this was of much concern to Tiempo, in that he was, and had been, content to consume local foods and goods. He loved kenkey and he loved fried fish from the sea; he loved fufu pounded from cassava and he loved palm oil soup with bush meat; he loved his kelewele and he loved his morning porridge and boflot, not caring to lace it with either sugar or milk. He loved his batakari and he loved his joromi and jokoto, and he loved his kente cloth. But he was sympathetic to those who had developed a taste for European goods, and pitied those who felt compelled to defy the boycott.

As the boycott calendar dwindled to its last day, the ex-servicemen concretized their plans for a march to the Osu castle. The call had gone out and many had responded, including some of the fishermen. So on a January afternoon designated for the march, Tiempo and Sowah were among the first to arrive at a white house designated for the congregation. At first, there was only a paltry number of six or so and Tiempo began to think the march would fail. But, as stream flows into river or river flows into river, more began to arrive. One by one, they came; two by two, they came; and, three by three, they came. Until there were about a hundred ex-servicemen and a few of their supporters. They milled around for a while until they were sure their numbers would swell no more. Whisper from ear to ear: they were to march peacefully; under no circumstance were they to cause any commotion. As leaders, Corporal Attipoe, Sergeant Adjetey, Private Odartey-Lamptey, Sergeant Aryee and a few others were at the front of the group as they began the march. Tiempo and Sowah were in the second row, Ayittey behind them.

Tiempo recalled the night before. Adjele had come to his room, fidgeting, brow furrowed. "I have a bad feeling about tomorrow," she said. "I have a feeling something bad will happen, and I am very worried for my husband."

"That is understandable," Tiempo said, "but he is a part of a just cause."

"I understand that," Adjele said, "but when has a just cause stopped them from hurting us?"

She might as well have taken his thoughts and articulated them. He wanted to assure her that nothing untoward would happen, but as much as he hoped for that, he would be foolish to guarantee anything. He could not deceive her so, repay all her kindness to him with false assurances.

Because he could not bring himself to deceive her, Tiempo provided the next best thing he could offer: "I will be sure to be by Sowah's side all the time and I will do all that I can to make sure he comes home safely to you."

She pursed her lips, sweat forming above them. She licked

her lips, looked down and then looked up at him, and then she said a soft "Thank you," and left the room.

The image of her, sweat forming a wet moustache over her upper lip and then dripping down, her face furrowed with worry; the image of her, worry sitting like needles in her eyes; the image of her, leaving the room slowly as if she wanted to return to hunt for greater assurance… all those images stayed with Tiempo as they began the march forward, two thoughts on his mind: be peaceful, no matter the provocation, and protect Sowah, no matter the cost.

They marched slowly. The mood was bright as was the sun, optimistic, even if laced with caution. This pleased Tiempo because as much as he would have liked to urge the marchers on to violence, and he would consider any violence at the colonial apparatus (human or property) justified, this was not the time. What would unarmed men bring to any attack by the other side? Let peace prevail when peace was needed. He envisaged a time, perhaps soon, when war and blood would be necessary to purchase freedom, but let that time come when it would come.

They chatted among themselves in some instances, Tiempo surmised, to ward off fear that must have tugged at the nerves of many. But what did he feel on the fear spectrum? He was agnostic, a neither here nor there-ness, short of full boldness because in his mind was Adjele's sense of foreboding, urging caution, at the same time as he was emboldened by the justness of the cause, a tension that put things in a curious equipoise.

When they got closer to the crucial Christiansborg Castle crossroads they could see a number of people ahead of them, an unmoving phalanx, which came into clearer view, not as a motley group, but as an organized force: the members of the colonial police. It was clear then that the colonial police force was standing to prevent the ambulatory group at the fork from taking the road that would take them to the Christiansborg Castle. Clearly, either by tipoff before the march or during the course of the march, someone had informed the Castle that the group of ex-servicemen was on the way.

And as the group got closer to the crossroads, the tension within it got deeper and the chatter of the men became more muted. Tiempo tried to survey the men as best as he could see. From his many years of battle, he could detect shifting moods, when troops moved forward with boldness or when fear caused them to slow down. He did not read mass fear, but he could detect concern. And the ocean breeze seemed not as generous as it had been before and the sun seemed to burn a little too violently and the crows that flew overhead looked like vicious raptors. Tiempo wanted to yell above everyone that they should hold their resolve, that they should not let the enemy smell fear, which, he soon sensed was beginning to seize large sections of the group. But none among them stopped or turned around, and they continued to move forward, and forward, and forward. Tiempo looked to his side at Sowah. The man moved on, and if in fear, then also in boldness because he did not let any such fear deter him. Tiempo was so proud of his adopted brother that he was even more assured that he would be willing to take multiple bullets for him; and the beauty of this was that he did not expect Sowah to reciprocate. When he looked beside him, he saw Ayittey smiling, nodding encouragement.

A few more steps forward and the group had to slow down considerably because their leaders had done so. There was no doubt that the force standing before them was armed with rifles. But still they moved forward. Slowly.

Then, like thunder coming with the sound of rain, expected but still jarring, they heard an order to disperse. They did not, although they slowed down even more. The order to disperse came again. The group of ex-servicemen and their supporters were not inclined to obey the command of another colonial voice, for they could now tell that the voice came from a white man, who was evidently in command of the forces. He seemed frantic now, issuing his orders with more loudness, but with less authority, perhaps realizing that the marching group would not listen to his request. So he turned his attention to his armed men. And he ordered his men to fire on the advancing men. His men did not. Tiempo observed his men and tried to occupy their minds, and he understood that they were reluctant to fire into a group of unarmed men who were only walking forward, their only act of violence being that: walking.

If he had been frantic before, the man was even more so now that his own men disobeyed his command. He issued the same order again. Tiempo could hear one of the men shout back in an act of unexpected boldness, "But Superintendent Imray, they are not armed." Superintendent Imray turned red, infuriated by what he must have deemed an act of insubordination. The image of Adjele in Tiempo's room the night before came haunting his mind's eye. He moved forward in order to walk in front of Sowah.

"What are you doing?" he heard Sowah ask.

Tiempo did not answer, nor did he have much time to do so. When he looked up, it was like an action enacted in a surreal realm that was unbelievable, though at the moment Superintendent Imray had begun speaking, Tiempo expected something like that was inevitable. As he watched, Superintendent

Imray reached out to one of his men and as though demonstrating bravery when in fact it was the utmost show of cowardice, pulled the man's rifle out of unwilling hands, and then held the gun to his chest and aimed it at the group. And fired.

Once.

Twice.

Thrice.

There may have been two more shots after that.

Tiempo looked in front of him and realized that at least two of the ex-servicemen had been shot. And his first instinct was to reach out to them to see what aid he could provide. But the other instinct was to make sure Sowah was safe, so he looked around and behind him, but he could not locate Sowah. Then Tiempo looked down to his right. And he almost collapsed with convulsing heartbeats as he saw Sowah on the ground. All Tiempo could think about was Adjele. And Boi. And he decided his first duty was to the family he had come to know. The rest were capable of taking care of themselves. And it would have been a fight worth fighting further at that moment if the others with him were willing to fight on. But he noticed that the crowd was dispersing, some running from the scene. He was loathe to abandon the former servicemen who had been shot, but he could never forgive himself if he did not assist Sowah. It would be the more egregious sin. So he reached down and gathered the shot man in his arms, and then he noticed that Ayittey was by his side, and the men knew what they must do. With all the energy they could summon, they ran like mad men to the nearest clinic they could find, everything else at the moment a backdrop of irrelevance.

SEASONS of FOUR FACES

# Wounds of Freedom

Luckily Sowah's wound was not fatal. In fact, it was superficial. And in hindsight Tiempo wondered what boldness had caused him and Ayittey to enter that clinic unannounced, asking for treatment for Sowah, and what had caused their request to be granted. Was it the sheer audacity, the way they had rushed in and demanded of the nurse at the reception desk that Sowah be treated? He had spoken boldly and loudly, as a man who did not expect to be disobeyed. He had detected a moment of hesitation as the nurse's eyes widened to seize him up, and then without asking any questions she admitted Sowah and then hurried to get the doctor. The doctor had not questioned them either, perhaps his form of solidarity with their cause, or his way of defying the system. He inspected the wound on the lower right side of Sowah's abdomen, the torn skin where the bullet had hit him. He treated Sowah and discharged them, after giving them instructions on ongoing treatment of the wound.

Sowah wanted to walk with their support, but Tiempo and Ayittey rejected the suggestion and instead carried Sowah home. By then, it was getting dark and the evening shadows teased around them like lurking fugitives. All the way home, Tiempo's chest heaved with anticipation and angst over how Adjele would react to his failure to prevent the bullet from wounding Sowah, but also with relief that the wound had not been fatal.

The wailing that greeted them as they entered the family compound unsettled both Tiempo and Ayittey, and they stopped for a moment as Adjele, Boi, Tetteh, Fofo, Akwele, Akuoko, and Armah, all gathered on the compound, rushed towards Tiempo, Ayittey and Sowah, Sowah still carried by the other two. Then Tiempo heard Adjele yell, "O, so it is true. They have killed my husband... O Sowah ooo..." This was followed by a deep wail, accompanied by flailing arms as Adjele moved towards them, tears jerking out of her eyes, phlegm dripping from her nostrils.

Sowah disabused her of this belief of death, almost jumping down from the arms of Tiempo and Ayittey to stand on his feet as he declared, "I am not dead."

But the effort must have been too much as Sowah bellowed in pain, wincing and holding the part of his now bandaged abdomen. Adjele and just about everyone present rushed to help him, but as they surrounded him, they ceded eminence to Adjele and she was the one who held her husband, and he leaned on her with the fullness of his weight, which did not daunt her. Tiempo's heart beat badly, expecting her to lambaste him for failing to protect Sowah. She had not looked directly at him since they entered the compound, and he stood helpless in the darkening space as Adjele helped Sowah to their part of the homestead. Tiempo was about to turn and leave for his room, when Adjele turned her head and looked at him and then at Ayittey, and through the moistness of eyes and cheeks just recently running with tears, smiled faintly at them and said above the cacophony of Sowah's brother's voices who were beginning to question Tiempo, "Thank you." And with that she entered the room with her husband.

And then the brothers and the rest of the family started earnestly asking Sowah and Ayittey what had happened, as they had heard that a few of the marchers had been shot dead. When they had not seen or heard from Sowah and Tiempo in a while, they had assumed that the two were among the fallen dead. They had even gone to search for Ayittey and obviously and not found him either. As if they were listening to a war hero, they perked their ears and drew closer to Tiempo as he recounted what had happened and, though he could not confirm any deaths, he had seen at least three people, perhaps four, fall as the bullets were fired, but things had happened so fast, especially as he was trying to get Sowah help and to safety that he had not stayed to confirm deaths and injuries. Ayittey could not add much more to this.

But what they could not confirm then was soon confirmed by rumor and media. By the next day, it was clear that three men had died: Corporal Attipoe, Sergeant Adjetey and Private Odartey-Lamptey. When Tiempo heard this, he realized that the dead were the three he had seen fall, that he had hoped his sight was faulty from anxiety and also hoped that he would hear that they had in fact not been shot at all or, if shot, that they had not died. Verklempt swept over the household, especially considering a later confirmation that Sergeant Aryee was also among the dead. In their soured moods, the brothers refused to eat for hours.

Later, Tiempo knocked on Sowah's door and asked Adjele if he could see her husband. Sowah was lying in bed when Adjele let him in. He was feeling well and, with Adjele nursing his wound, he expected to be back on his feet soon. He thanked Tiempo for helping him. He would forever be indebted. No need, Tiempo said, as he left.

Adjele followed him to the compound. "You have been a great blessing to us," she said. "I can't thank you enough. Sowah has told me all that you did, with Ayittey's help. He said when you realized there might be shooting, you even moved in front of him and if he had stayed behind you he would not have been hit."

"Thank you!" Tiempo replied. "Now we need to make sure he comes back better. We have a lot of fish to catch."

SEASONS of FOUR FACES

# A Fight

So Sowah stayed at home healing, and Ayittey came to check on him from time to time. But while he healed, the city was being wounded. If the Sowah household was a microcosm, the sadness that had encroached upon the city (and perhaps most of the Gold Coast) hardened and morphed into anger. A stream of sadness flowing everywhere. The just cause of the unarmed, peaceful marchers juxtaposed with the unjust, mean-spirited response of the armed colonial power, epitomized by Superintendent Imray and the callous disregard for human life (or some human life) was a potent catalyst for a violent reaction. And so the people hit back at the targets they associated with colonial power. In the streets of Accra, war songs erupted in anger like lava; men joined other men and women and women joined other men and women rampaging through the streets, finding shops owned by Europeans and Asians, and looting them.

Their brother had been shot and could have been killed, their relative had been shot and killed, as had their friends. Tetteh resolved to go on the looting rampage too. When Tetteh asked Tiempo to join him, Tiempo tried to dissuade the angered brother from going. Tiempo's first instinct was to join in the action, but he thought of the harm inflicted on Sowah and counseled otherwise. He could understand the pain and anger, but the response needed to be planned and targeted, not this spontaneous reaction that was fraught with danger and the potential loss of lives, including innocent lives. Even as he took this view, Tiempo murmured to himself that he was becoming soft, that a new version of himself was emerging more and more. What was it: Age? Time? Love?

But Tetteh was too angry and determined. He would join the looters, whether Tiempo came along or not, whether he agreed with the choice of response or not. He should have been there when they fired at Sowah, Tetteh said. He had failed his brother by not joining in the earlier protest of the ex-servicemen. This was his chance to make amends. Armah was insisting on prayer, Tetteh bemoaned, when what they needed was a hard punch in the eye of the Europeans. Fair enough, but he could not join them, Tiempo said.

But Tiempo reconsidered. He was too close to this family to let Tetteh go on this venture, however flawed (or noble) without him. So minutes after Tetteh left, Tiempo followed, but soon realized that Tetteh had been swallowed by a larger crowd, marching the streets, smashing the doors of stores and businesses they identified as European or Asian and ransacking and looting them. Tiempo was also swallowed by the crowd and as much as he wished to leave and extricate himself, he found that the affinity was too alluring, the power of inflicting pain on the enemy, whether real or imagined, intoxicating. And indeed the people were riding high on momentary power, which had to be deployed sharply and quickly before it dissipated.

And so Tiempo moved along with the crowd, but refused to enter any store, although the urge was overwhelming when he thought of Hodgson and Imray, when he thought of Nana Yaa Asantewaa, Nana Prempeh, when he thought of Attipoe, Adjetey and Odartey-Lamptey and Aryee. When he thought of the wounded Sowah. When he thought of the countless others who had faced the brunt of colonial violence. But he mustered enough self-restraint and only watched as he marched along. And he would have forged a begrudging contentment to participate this way, if only to placate his conscience, until looking farther ahead, he thought he saw Tetteh running into a store with windows that had been smashed open. Instinct or a sense of protection prodded Tiempo to ran in that direction until he was standing in front of the store.

The moment of decision.

As he stood there, undecided, he saw those that had entered coming out, some with television and radio sets. He expected Tetteh to exit the store too. But he waited, and he waited. Tetteh was not coming out. And the rest of the crowd was moving on. Had he not seen Tetteh enter the store as he had thought? That must be it: he must have mistaken someone else for Tetteh.

Tiempo started to walk away to join the group when a nudging instinct tugged at him to check, just to be sure. He went back and this time entered the store without hesitation. It looked like the scene of a brawl, a forgotten cemetery of goods with the unburied scattered all over: broken parts, sets and goods on a minefield of debris. But he could hear nothing... wait, nothing except some grunts and groans. Tiempo moved slowly in the direction of the noises... slowly the noises led him to the backroom of the store.

And he saw Tetteh and another man, white, tussling on the floor. In one moment, Tetteh was on top, strangling the man, then in the next instant the man had gained the upper hand, chocking Tetteh. It was a scene Tiempo had seen many times before, and most times there had been a fatal victim. It was not clear who would prevail but in a short while the man seemed to be tiring and Tetteh pinned him down and began to strangle him. The man was writhing, but then Tiempo noticed that he was reaching out with his hand, as if groping for something. Then Tiempo realized that the man was reaching for a pistol lying on the floor, and unless Tetteh realized this or managed to incapacitate him it was only a matter of time before the man grabbed the pistol. Tiempo lunged forward and grabbed the pistol, and it was at that time that both men noticed him, and the distraction caused Tetteh to lose concentration for a second and with that his grip as well, enough for the man to extricate himself and stagger towards the back wall, where Tiempo observed a number of hanging rifles.

"Stop!" Tiempo said. But the man did not stop, gambling his advantage as he reached for a rifle on the wall. "Stop!" Tiempo yelled one more time, but the man did not stop.

Tiempo saw Superintendent Imray snatching a rifle from one of the colonial officers, and he saw Superintendent Imray aiming the rifle at the unarmed ex-servicemen, and he saw Superintendent Imray shooting at them. Tiempo saw the man snatching a rifle from the wall. Tiempo saw the man aiming the rifle at him. Tiempo fired the pistol.

Once.

Twice.

Thrice.

And he saw the man stagger for a few seconds and then fall to the floor.

Tiempo looked at Tetteh; Tetteh looked at Tiempo. They did not need to be told. They bolted from the store.

It was quiet outside. And getting darker. The crowd they had been with had moved on and was much farther away from them, or perhaps even dispersed for the day. The men began to hurry home. But then, as if materializing from space, they heard the words, "You two, stop!"

Tiempo looked behind him and saw two colonial policemen. "Tetteh," he said, "run with me."

And they ran, first in a zigzagged manner, trying to outwit

what they believed was a chase and the possibility that they might be shot at. Then, taking the lead, Tiempo run off the street, between two buildings, Tetteh closely behind him. They could still hear the sound of running on the ground behind them as they went on a path full of mewing alley cats, whose increased mewing betrayed the running men. And then they came to a dead end with a wall in front of them. These was no choice but to scale the wall, landing them in a backyard. An European couple were seated on the verandah of the bungalow, a car parked outside. The startled man and woman looked at Tiempo and Tetteh with wide eyes. Tiempo and Tetteh did not wait to be interrogated (or worse) as they ran on and scaled the wall on the opposite end that would land them on a backroad.

But as Tiempo crouched on top of the wall and was about to land on the other side, he looked back and saw the policemen now on the compound of the house they were leaving (still in pursuit) and he saw the European couple holding each other, and then behind them he saw someone bringing them tea. And Tiempo gasped. And he wanted to go back even at great risk. But Tetteh sensed his hesitation and pushed him so that he almost fell forward from the top of the wall, landing on the backroad. From then on, through narrow alleyways and paths and backroads, Tiempo and Tetteh ran and eluded their pursuers. But Tiempo had become reluctant a runner, for all he could think of was the woman he had seen.

# BENJAMIN KWAKYE

# The Battle Past Silence

The killing of a man (even if in perceived self-defense) was an experience few shared in civilian life. But what affirmed their relationship went even deeper than death, went deeper than the solidarity they experienced when fleeing from the police. At that moment on top of the wall, that moment when Tiempo had looked back and hesitated. It was not lost on Tetteh that the hesitation was not from looking at the European couple nor the pursuing policemen. That woman who had appeared on the verandah, barely visible from where the two men crouched. Why had Tiempo hesitated? Tetteh came to Tiempo's room the next night to inquire. They both pledged not to divulge the secret of the shooting to anyone, the jeopardy in which this could place them was obvious to both men, especially Tiempo who had pulled the trigger.

After fidgeting for a while, Tetteh said, "There is something that I have been thinking about all day, Tempu... That woman on the verandah. Who is she?"

"That was a brief moment, Tetteh. So very brief. I'm surprised you noticed."

"Your pause as the moment of danger was enough for me to notice."

Tiempo sighed as he peered hard at Tetteh and then said, "She is a woman from the past."

"Just a woman from the past?"

"A woman I love."

"When a man's life is in danger, his only goal is to escape that danger. But when you hesitated on top of that wall, when you seemed like someone in a trance, I thought you were even about to jump pack to the compound, to return to danger. And the only thing I could tell that was different was the woman. I wondered, was it a gripping beauty you noticed about her that so entranced you? But then I concluded it couldn't be. We could barely see her. It must have been something else, something either familiar or extraordinarily gripping. If it was something gripping, then what had I missed? Why had I not been equally gripped? I began to think that you knew her, knew her so well that you noticed her even in the distance. So now that you say you love her, I am curious—who is she?"

"The story is very long and personal, so let's not go into it," Tiempo said.

"Broken heart? Too much pain?"

"Yes, something like that."

"If you still want her, let's go get her."

"That's what I intend to do. I can't wait to return to the house, and it kills me to wait, but I want things to calm down a little. Under the circumstances, we could come under suspicion. The police may be looking for us."

Tetteh nodded and left the room. And Tiempo continued to plot how he would return, as he had been doing since the moment he started running from that house. The danger of returning immediately was fraught with risk, but that is what he decided he should do. Now that he knew where she was, how could he wait and suffer even more deeply?

But the complexity would be compounded the next day when they learned that the governor had imposed a state of emergency, which meant the forces would be out and about and would not hesitate to shoot on little to no suspicion, shoot without forethought and without asking questions. And if the policemen had managed to get a good view of him, who knew what word was out about him? As much as it pained him, Tiempo had to wait, no less when he heard that the legislature had passed an emergency Riot Acts, forbidding rioting. That meant that the government was shaken, which made the situation even more precarious.

But only a week later Tetteh came to him with news: he had scoped the bungalow and noticed that the European couple left the house in the mornings by 9 a.m. He had seen them get into their car and leave. When he checked at noon, they had not returned. For days, when he checked at 6 p.m., the car was parked outside. This meant they left home by 9 a.m. and returned after noon and sometime before 6 p.m. That was the open window for Tiempo to go find his love, Tetteh advised. But in all the days of scoping, he had not seen anyone come out of the house and his only conclusion was that Tiempo's love preferred to stay indoors, or perhaps she was so busy with chores that she had no time to come out of the house.

This information was just too valuable for Tiempo to let slip under the weight of fear that he might be caught. Although he acknowledged he had become more circumspect, since when had he succumbed to fear? Besides, Tetteh noted that he had not seen policemen in the vicinity and it looked safe. And now that Sowah had virtually recovered, Tiempo had gone fishing with him, although Sowah mostly observed rather than participated. In the walk abroad, he had not once been accosted. Perhaps the policemen had not observed him well and not linked the death in the store to him or Tetteh. There had been so many people rioting that it could have been anyone.

A little after 9 a.m. a few days later, he went to the house, sure to check that the car was gone by peeking over the house gate. Then he walked to the front door, sweat bathing him, and with heart pounding and knees weakened. He knocked on the door. And knocked and knocked. Hearing no response he tried the door. It was locked. He called out to see if there was anyone home. There was no response. He even shouted Sharifa's name, and still he received no response. There was no one home, Tiempo concluded, as he left forlorn. Tetteh told him to pick the lock if he got no response the next day, giving him a small nail for the purpose and showing him how it was done. And that is what he did the next day, brushing the danger aside with the hope of a glorious moment of seeing Sharifa. The curtains were drawn and the room he entered was dark. He was about to turn on the light but stopped when he thought he saw Sharifa standing in front of him, illuminated as a glow that stood out in the darkness. "Sharifa," he whispered with fast pounding heart, but then there was no response and when he looked harder, where Sharifa had stood he saw darkness. He cursed his imagination for the vivid projection of Sharifa and moved on, searching the rest of the house, whispering Sharifa's name to no avail.

It was a three bedroom bungalow and he could tell one of them was the bedroom of the European couple and one was unused, but he guessed that the third was Sharifa's room. There were no telltale signs. She might not be there in person, but there is a way a man call tell the spiritual presence of one he loves and loves totally.

But if she wasn't these is physical presence, where was she?

# BENJAMIN KWAKYE

# A Time for Everything

On account of his recovery, even amid the uncertainties of the times, Sowah called for a celebration, his justification being that even though they had lost much, they had not lost everything and they needed to celebrate that which they had not lost. Therefore, for this party of the "not lost," he wanted the entire household to suppress the past and focus on the future. The family prepared feverishly for the party. Adjele in particular spent the bulk of the morning cooking, while the young ones in the household cleaned the compound and brought out a few chairs. When the guests arrived, including some of the fishermen, the food was ready to be served: kenkey, fish and shito; white rice and chicken stew; jollof rice. Ayittey was treated as a special guest, on account of his part in rescuing Sowah on the day of the shooting. The feasting began in no time, filling the compound with the sound of munching and conversation. For drinks, the family served pito, akpeteshie and palm wine for the adults, and Fanta for the children, who enjoyed their soft beverages with boflot. Tetteh served as the unofficial master of the banquet, praying a prayer of thanks, thanking the guests, issuing instructions for more food to be brought when it was running out, and urging people to eat.

Then Tetteh brought out a guitar and Sowah drums, and they began to play. Adjele started singing. He had heard many a renowned singer sing, most recently highlife tunes. He had thought they could sing, but this voice was something else. When she began to tire, Fofo, Akwele and Akuoko took over, singing beautifully, if not as sweetly as Adjele. And then the men joined in from time to time as well.

# SEASONS of FOUR FACES

The women and men began to dance the kpanglogo. What a wow! Hands by the sides moving to and fro in quick movements, palm turned upward and then downward, legs moving backward and forward, waists gyrating left and right and then moving lower before coming back up, all well-coordinated, harmonized with the drumbeats, as the singing rose higher in tempo: "… adzo palogo, logo, ligi, mawo, mawo, palogo..." It was both sensual and divine, Tiempo concluded. He needed no prompting to join in the dance. His movements were not as elegant, but it did not matter, for he was among family that he loved and that loved him. And then he noticed that Ankrah, the wrestling champion, had come also, although he had not seen him before that moment, and he was dancing the kpanglogo as well, full of verve. Then Ayittey moved close to Ankrah, facing him, and for a moment Tiempo thought the men were about to engage in a wrestling match and he was sad to think that they would choose this occasion for that. But false alarm—rather than wrestle, the wrestlers embraced, and Tiempo believed this was done in honor of Sowah, and then they were both dancing. And seeing this, Tiempo continued to dance. He was dancing for Sowah's recovery, for himself and the others at the party, but above everything else, he was dancing for Sharifa and the promise of a reunion. And so, as if seized by tarantism, he danced and he danced and he danced, ignoring the sweat that bathed him in the setting sun that would soon yield to moon that would then yield to sun, assured in the knowledge that light never dies, only takes different forms, and that from the strong, it could morph into the weak, but that the weak would not last and that a new day would hold a brighter and stronger light.

# CHAPTER

# 4

*"Freedom is beautiful but treacherous," she said.*

## Afternoon Delight

They had heard of the call by many politicians for independence from British rule. But they heard that one of them was rising: Boniface Popolampo, renowned for his wealth, some said by association with some rich Europeans. They heard that he was a redeemer, a man of great intelligence and wit, able to match the Europeans in eloquence in their own language. When he spoke their language, the Europeans nodded their heads in admiration. It was with hope that they gathered just about the entire family to go see him. With the death of the ex-servicemen still open as fresh wounds, they needed the medicine of hope that freedom was imminent.

## SEASONS of FOUR FACES

It was a hot day of blazing sun waves that pierced to draw sweat. It became clear to Tiempo how special Boniface Popolampo must be because, despite this heat, the crowd at the park was unbelievably large. They had to wait for him for three hours (of heat and sweat), which caused improperly washed armpits to emit offensive smells. But as this was "the one," he suffered patiently.

A motorcade preceded his arrival, unusual for a native politician at that time, prompting a truant thought in Tiempo's mind that he was perhaps a sign of the future, an ostentation that belied the reality of the masses, but this was such a troubling thought that he dismissed it outright. He strained his neck to try and see Boniface Popolampo as ten men dressed in red suits stepped out of three cars, with two motorbikes on the side.

"I don't see him," Tetteh said to Sowah.

It turned out that this was just the first battalion of his entourage. Two more motorcades of identical composition—except one brought gold-dressed men and the carried green-dressed men—arrived before his appearance. Those in his motorcade, when it arrived, were dressed in myriad forms of red, gold and green. Even though Tiempo had never seen him before, he could distinguish Boniface Popolampo from the others when he stepped out of his car. He was the only one dressed in a black suit. His entourage quickly formed two long lines from his car to the center of the park so that he was well flanked as he made his way there. And what a figure he cut as he strolled on slowly, taller than any in his entourage, all this while with his entourage, a claque of praise singers, extolling his greatness.

Boniface Popolampo took the spotlight after a long introduction that lasted almost an hour, which mentioned his degrees (all honorary) and the long organizations to which he belonged (no less than twenty). If there were any remnants of doubt left, the catalogue of accolades erased them. "This man is a god," Sowah whispered to Tiempo.

They were all cheering loud and hard when it came Boniface Popolampo's turn to speak. He took his time, smiling and nodding as the applause rose, fell and rose. And then there was total silence (except for his voice) when he started speaking. Even bleating goats stopped bleating and barking dogs turned quiet when the boom of his voice sounded. If there'd been any lions there, they would have stifled their roars.

"The greatness of the ssendnilbism shall set us free," he announced. "Our ssendnilbism shall equate progress. If you believe in ssendnilbism let me hear you say yes."

"Yes!!!"

The crowd was agog, each one trying to outdo the other with enthusiasm.

"Let me hear you say ssendnilbism."

The crowd yelled: "Ssendnilbism!!!"

The next half-hour was a continual chant of "yes" and "ssendnilbism."

The crowd was full of his sweet fever. He deserved more than applause, someone decided. As they were already standing, he was disappointed they couldn't give him a standing ovation. To remedy this, that person started jumping and clapping and soon the entire crowd had joined him in offering him their jumping ovation. Even as he left, they were still yelling "ssendnilbism," his parade of cars and motors vanishing from view in the horizon and then swallowed within the sunset.

"What a great man," they were all saying as they headed

back to their homes.

When Tiempo was alone with Sowah and Tetteh, he said to them, "That was some display."

"Indeed," Tetteh concurred.

"The only thing I need to understand is ssendnilbism. What does it mean?"

With a frown, Sowah asked, "You mean you don't understand it either? I thought you knew what it meant."

"No, I thought *you* knew what it meant."

They looked at one other, now a notch wiser, and in every home, they could imagine a similar conversation unfolding. Sowah shook his head. "Well," he said, "even if we don't understand what it means, we can rest assured that when tomorrow comes, the sun will rise again. I only hope we are alive tomorrow."

BENJAMIN KWAKYE

# Embracing the Time

Tetteh next informed him that there was a recruiting effort for the United Gold Coast Convention or UGCC, a political party that was advocating for independence from British rule at the earliest possible time. The excitement of the moment had caught all of them in its clutches, but Tetteh seemed the most enthused, perhaps his reaction to an organization that would end the system that had shot his brother. After much thought, Tiempo had become deeply unsatisfied with Boniface Popolampo's performance that he doubted the usefulness of the various political activities, but Tetteh assured him that these crop of UGCC politicians was different. They were holding a meeting the next day to recruit more members and he wanted to attend and wished Tiempo would come along. The notion of independence from British rule touched a sensitive part of him and Tiempo eventually felt compelled to go along, although they all knew that under the state of emergency, this was a risky gathering. But the cause tugged and tugged and drove them to defy the risk. And so they (Sowah, Tetteh, and Tiempo) went and heard short speeches from the leaders of the UGCC, particularly J. B. Danquah and Kwame Nkrumah. After the meeting, which had been incident free, was over, one of the men with the leaders introduced himself to Tiempo as Adofo and asked Tiempo to follow him. Tiempo did, obedient to the suspected adventure he believed this summons would bring. Adofo introduced him to J.B. Danquah and Kwame Nkrumah and he was drawn to Danquah's affability and Nkrumah's charisma. The two said they were looking for strong men, not only as foot soldiers, but to help with protecting the leaders. They had been receiving threats. Would Tiempo be willing to be a foot soldier as well as a guard? He was honored (and surprised and said so, but said he would think about it. That was understandable. When Adofo returned with Tiempo to Tetteh and Sowah, Adofo said, "I will be in touch, so think about whether you want to be a part."

As Adofo left, Tiempo turned to look at Tetteh with suspicion.

"I met Adofo through a mutual friend and told him about your bravery and your part in the march of the ex-servicemen and suggested that you might be a strong asset in this noble effort," Tetteh said.

Tiempo turned to Sowah and asked, "You knew about this?"

"Yes," Sowah said, "Tetteh and I both think this movement could use you. I hope you are not angry with us."

"I am not; I just wish I'd known."

"Sorry," Tetteh said, "but we were afraid you would not be up to it until you saw the leaders for yourself."

"Just think about it," Sowah said. "Next time we come, we can give them an answer."

But the next time would be delayed, for the next day they heard that six local political leaders had been arrested, accused of instigating the riots in the streets: JB Danquah, Kwame Nkrumah, Edward Akufo-Addo, Ebenezer Ako-Adjei, William Ofori-Atta, and Obetsebi Lamptey. Men who would be dubbed the Big Six. The arrest infuriated Tiempo. Would these people stop at nothing? Did they have no scruples? How dare they imprison these dignified sons of the land. He would certainly join the effort. And while he waited to see how the Big Six would be treated, Tiempo continued his search for Sharifa.

BENJAMIN KWAKYE

# Water Droplets

He returned three more times to the bungalow of the European couple, but the building was empty each time. And he began to question his memory. Perhaps he was trying too hard, perhaps he had not seen Sharifa on that day of the pursuit. Had he gone on a soothing mental pursuit and hallucinated Sharifa to escape the actual pursuit? Had he in emotional desperation conjured her spiritual presence in the house when in fact she had never been there? It must all be an illusion because how could he otherwise explain not having seen her after so many visits? So he fought two pulls of emotion: the elation of connecting, or soon to connect, with the independence movement and the depression of the imprisonment of the Big Six as well as the deflating concern that he had not seen Sharifa.

But the next day when he returned from the shore, Adjele called him and said someone had come looking for him, adding, "It looks like you have been busy, my brother," she teased.

Tiempo began to sweat, almost panting. "Did she tell you her name?"

"Yes… she said I should tell you that her name is Sharifa."

"Sharifa?" Tiempo said, wide eyed.

"Yes, Sharifa is what she said."

"Where is she?"

"She left."

"When?"

"When you were still at sea."

"But where can I find her?"

"She didn't say."

"She didn't say? How could she not say?"
"She said she will come back."
"When?"
"She didn't say."
"What did she say? Please, Adjele, tell me something more."
"Sorry, Tempu, she didn't say much. I asked her to wait but she said she had to leave; but, as I said, she said she will come back even though she didn't say when."

Sharifa!

As she had come looking for him, Tiempo decided to return to the European's bungalow. But this time, defying caution, he went at night. If she lived in that house, surely she would be there at night. He left the house dressed in all black, hoping to blend in with the darkness of the hour. He moved with the furtiveness of a cat, and with as much stealth as he could, walking close to trees, under their canopies, away from any streetlamps, avoiding main streets, using backways and pathways.

He stood outside the house, catching his breath, the semaphores providing little sparks of encouragement. And then, heart hitting hard, he scaled the wall of the house, looked about for life and, finding none, landed with a thud on the compound. He looked to his left and his right, grateful that the couple had no dogs. Then he approached the house slowly, almost crouching. Rather than enter through the main door, he decided to climb to the window of the room on the side he believed to be Sharifa's, using the ledge of the lower window as lever. But as he stepped on the ledge, he heard a sound below and when he looked down a man was standing like a ghostly shadow amid the darkness of the night with a rifle pointed at him.

"Get down now!" The man said firmly.

Tiempo jumped down.

"Hands up," the man said. Tiempo complied, under no illusion that the man would hesitate to employ the gun. The man approached him until the muzzle of the gun was touching Tiempo's chest. "What do you want?" the man asked

"I am sorry," Tiempo said.

"Haven't I seen you somewhere before?" the man asked.

"No, sir," Tiempo said.

"You picked the wrong house to rob," the man said. "I could turn you in to the police, but I won't. Prepare to meet your maker."

With every warrior instinct he had, Tiempo moved to the side in a fast motion and then forward, reaching quickly to dispossess the man of the rifle. The temptation to shoot the man ran through him like his own blood, but he decided against it. He would not complicate matters or implicate Sharifa. So he knocked the man down with the butt of the gun and fled, leaving the rifle behind. The run back home was full of regret and a sense of sinking in a berserk sea.

## SEASONS of FOUR FACES

# Walking the Chasm

For a long time afterwards, Tiempo had a sense of a shadow following him, at times mocking him for his ineffectual efforts, at times trying to attack him, reminding him that he had killed a defenseless man in cold blood in his own store (and the falsehood of this did not diminish the grating impact of the taunt, at times mocking him that he was nothing but a trespasser, and often telling him that he would never find Sharifa). And he did not know how to get out of the stalemate he had created out of his impatience, for no doubt the European couple would be more diligent now and may even have guards at the house and most likely would have informed the police. To venture near the neighborhood was therefore out of the question. His only hope was that Sharifa would return to him as she had promised, and though he believed her, the itch of longing and the concern that her circumstances might change and put her in a position where she could not come to him, made him a very unhappy man. And though he said nothing, he was not amused that Adjele tease him every now and then about his love and promising him if she did not come to him she would find him a better woman.

If Tiempo found any solace in his circumstances, it was that the Big Six that had been incarcerated for inciting the Accra riots were released. And with their release he was pulled once again into politics, and more so than he would have liked.

Not long after he agreed to join the UGCC, Kwame Nkrumah, its secretary, left the party and formed his own, the Convention Peoples Party or CPP, and this split also drew a fault line in the household, with Sowah still supporting the UGCC and Tetteh switching his allegiance to the new CPP. Tetteh would sing Kwame Nkrumah's praises, referring to his new cognomen, "Kwame Nkrumah Showboy" whenever he heard Nkrumah give a fiery speech.

Tiempo listened as the brothers debated which party was better for the people.

"We need radical leadership," Tetteh said. "Dr. Nkrumah is calling for independence now. That is what we need, not the weak call for independence within the shortest possible time as the UGCC has been advocating."

"He has it all wrong, your Osagyefo Dr. Nkrumah," Sowah replied. "These people are not going to grant independence to us now. You have seen their heavy handed tactics. Do you think these are people who will hand you independence?"

"Exactly why it must be wrestled from them, even if it takes violence."

"If they have to murder us to hold on to power, that is what they will do. That is why we must take our time and pick our battles carefully. I am worried Nkrumah will only throw the country into a bloodbath."

"Sowah, why this fear after what they have done to us, to Corporal Aryee and the rest, to you? I would expect you to want a more forceful approach."

"Where will that lead us? We need men with tact to negotiate with the British, even if that means we need to be patient."

"And that is the one thing I don't like about Danquah and the others They are too tactful, too diplomatic, too elitist."

"Elitist?"

"Yes, they are at the top of the educated elite in the Gold

Coast, and they are closer to the white man than to the ordinary people, the fishermen like us. For them, even if we should become independent, they will behave like the white man if they get power. They are like Boniface Popolampo."

"You are being totally unfair, Tetteh. They are not in any way like Boniface Popolampo."

"But it is true, Sowah. Compare them to Nkrumah. He is a man of the people. He calls us to positive action. He identifies with the common man, with us."

"Don't be fooled by the cheap popularity and demagoguery."

Sowah turned to Tiempo. "What do you think?" he asked.

"I see this crack continuing into the future, and I wish it were not so."

"Who knows, maybe the parties will patch things up and present a united front," Sowah said.

It was a wish that did not materialize and it soon became clear to Tiempo that if he wanted to be involved in the fight for independence, then he had to be on one side or the other. He attended the rallies and meetings of both parties, he listened to speeches by their leaders, and sympathized with both parties. He liked the appeal to calm, that calculated walk to independence and navigating the tightrope of dealing with the British and the danger that one false step could cause the walker to tumble into a precipice of no return. But at the same time he found the call to immediate action fierily appealing. He was a man of action and action he wanted. And he was not so sure that the British would cede any space unless strong pressure was brought to bear on them to a point where they were so uncomfortable they would have no choice but to leave.

"Self-government now!" Nkrumah declared.

There was something about the urgency, the self-assurance and self-belief of the phrase that found a poetic portion of him, and worked that tense part that held both the bellicose and the poetic. So he sympathized with the UGCC but left to work for the CPP, attending more of the CPP's rallies and canvassing for the new party. On occasion, he was made to guard Nkrumah, Adofo telling Tiempo that several threats had been made on Nkrumah's life by certain political brigands.

On one occasion, he had stood behind Nkrumah after he gave a rousing speech. When it was over and the crowd was dispersing, a group of men approached them and one of them pointed to Tiempo, and said they wanted to talk to him in private. Suddenly wary, he was about to decline when Adofo assured him he knew the men and that Tiempo should pay heed to whatever they had to say. Then they took him aside, and told him he had been fingered as responsible for the shooting of an European store owner (on account of the report of two policemen) and that he had trespassed on the property of another and assaulted him (on account of a complaint filed by the victim). The suspect in both reports matched Tiempo's description. If they were to take him in and fingerprint him, they could match him with the prints taken at both scenes, particularly on the guns used. As Tiempo began to contemplate how he would escape from them, they added that he was not to worry. They would see to it that the fingerprint evidence was destroyed. They were doing this because they knew Adofo and were secret admirers of the CPP and they had seen Tiempo's involvement and the high praises Adofo had provided. But if he got into trouble again, they may not be able to help him.

It was not the fear of danger to himself that dampened Tiempo's spirit when he heard this, but the reinforcement of the reality that there was little to nothing he could do to find Sharifa, now that he knew that his description had made it into official records and but for the police's busy schedule with other matters, he would probably have been apprehended before he was warned. As it was, Adofo advised that while they could still use him, it was overly risky for him to be too close to Dr. Nkrumah, that the visibility could render Tiempo vulnerable to recognition and police harassment.

So Tiempo left.

But within days, the itch that had not been fully scratched, to be a part of the independence movement would not leave him and he begged Adofo for a role. It was dangerous, Adofo warned, but if he was willing to take the risk, then he could become a campaigner, one of those who went from door to door, knocking on doors, distributing CPP campaign paraphernalia in the upcoming election that pitched the CPP against the UGCC. As unwilling as he was to so frontally campaign for one party over the other, this was what he needed. Action. Plus, Adofo promised most of the work would be outside of Accra, where it would be safer for Tiempo. The party needed more work done in the hinterlands, which suited Tiempo well, especially because he needed to keep trying to get his mind off his failure to find Sharifa. He was concerned she would come looking for him when he was on a trip outside of Accra, but what were the chances that would happen soon? Tiempo asked himself, considering that it had been a long time and she had not returned to find him. So busy he became. With a little stipend, Tiempo and Tetteh and a few others left Accra and went to the hinterlands, buoyed by the knowledge that they were not alone in this effort, that Dr Nkrumah himself was canvassing hard, reportedly sleeping on verandahs; hence, together with the rest of his followers, earning the nickname "verandah boys." It was such a great adventure to see other parts of the Gold Coast, from the Eastern to the Western, Central to the Northern, the Asante part being the region Tiempo was mainly familiar with. They passed out literature and they spoke to whomever would listen to them about the need for immediate independence from British rule. They were welcomed and they were rejected. They were fed and they were swindled. They slept on people's verandahs and the makeshift bedrooms of the more sympathetic. They slept in open spaces, with groping wind as their friend, sometimes as stargazers until sleep came, and they slept in closed spaces where darkness was their companion. They were burned by the sun and they were washed by the rain.

In the east, after a hard day of campaigning near Wli, they went to the Agumatsa waterfalls, awed by the height of the falls and the way the sheet of water fell. They took a swim in the pools at the base, Tiempo overwhelmed with a sense of belonging, not only to those with him, but to the place, the water that spoke power and peace and something ancient that offered great rest. Even the fruit bats nesting in the cliffs nearby appeared friendly, willing to offer fruits if asked. Allow me to flow, Agumatsa Waterfall. Tiempo believed from then on his spirit would flow even more freely. This offered enough energy for them to climb Mount Afadja in its biodiverse environs. This experience was in his mind when after campaigning in Koforidua, they traveled a little northeast to the Boti waterfalls, specifically the twin male and female waterfalls, two waterfalls meeting where the splashing of the waters created a rainbow. "The heavens have come to meet us here," Tetteh remarked as they observed the beauty of the scenery, the aqueous lovemaking that birthed the rainbow.

# SEASONS of FOUR FACES

"Salivate at the gods making love," he added.

It was like that, with days of hard campaigning, when they would even fear for their lives, and moments when they were at great peace, as if the heavens were ready to refresh them and confirm their efforts as worthwhile. It was like that when they were chased in Asante and found temporary refuge in a large cocoa plantation that seemed unending in its sheer vastness, until the owner found them and offered them a resting place in one of his mansions, expressing sympathy for their cause.

They found joy in the west, when they went to Nzulezu and were invited to the homes of the village that consisted entirely of stilts and platforms constructed in Lake Tadane—a floating town of sorts. They moved from one structure to another, over wooden planks, talking to the inhabitants, sometimes with the floors creaking, giving the impression that they would give way and plunge the people into the waters below, but they all knew this would not happen, that the structures were well constructed and that the fear was foreign to the natives who had lived on the stilt supporting structures for generations. A man named Blay danced on the planks, rejoicing that the campaigners had come to see them, and then he looked at Tiempo and smiled, revealing a mouth with all front teeth missing.

"You are a tall man," Blay said without expecting a response. He danced a little more and pointed to the top of his head, bald at the top with bushy hair on the sides, and said, "This is a mosquito airport, and mosquitoes use it more than Attuquaye Quayson's forehead. Then he asked Tiempo, "Do you know Attuquaye Quayson?"

"No," Tiempo said. "Who is Attuquaye Quayson?"

"I don't know; that is why I am asking you," Blay said as

he continued to dance, proclaiming that he was dancing in celebration of the change coming and that Tempo and the rest of the campaigners were helping bring about the change. It was a strange episode in the campaign, but it was a strange sweetness, rooted in the assurance that many, including some strange people, were expecting and hoping for change, for freedom from colonial shackles.

    They would go up the Kwahu mountains, where some threatened to throw them down to their deaths while others offered them protection and nourishment. In the north, they would go to Paga and find a crocodile pond and sit on the back of crocodiles that would not bite them, after they had been chased away with stones at a nearby town. In Mole, they would marvel at the sheer beauty of nature amid the company of warthogs, buffaloes, elephants and others, only to be threatened by a rifle toting man who claimed to be the god of the land. At one point, they would find refuge at the Larabanga Mosque, the triangular structures with spikes jutting out, a thing of beauty, a sight refreshing to look out without any spiritual affiliation needed, complemented by the nearby Larabanga Stone that stood mushroom-like from the soil and which they had been told returned to its original position whenever it was moved; likewise the Zayaa mud shrine in Wulugu, a symmetrical four story mud building with openings at the top that looked like little clerestories and that triggered the impression of something dropped from the sky after been divinely architecturally designed. These and many more formed their days, a zigzagging through the land without any design but to campaign, sometimes treated as heroes and sometimes as villains; emotions now inflated, now deflated; now buoyant, now flat.

# SEASONS of FOUR FACES

# Song of Heroes

And one day, Tiempo did not know exactly what prompted him, he began to think of the future and how those who had fought and were fighting for freedom would be remembered. And as he had sung for some heroes before, he began to sing for them too. It was unplanned and perhaps even incoherent, but it did not matter to him because it was coming from a genuine and pure part of himself. He gathered a few of his fellow campaigners, and with the heat bearing down on him, sweat trickling down his face, Tetteh in admiration, Tiempo said, "I sing this song so it can be written on tongues; obviously, a song to be sang not from the mouths of carcasses and corpses but the living." And then he sang his song:

What shall I say of these heroes? I fear they will be unsung and their children and their children's children will forget, someday when they take their freedoms for granted, not realizing the price their forebears paid for them or, even if they may occasionally remember, the passage of time will cause the remembrance to be perfunctory, perhaps on some holiday, when instead of celebrating their heroes, they will gather at beaches or in the comfort of backyards to enjoy parties of music, drinking and dancing, forgetting how history punishes those who forget or diminish it, with its vilest vomits, regurgitating what they would have thought forever swallowed in the bellies of time.

Therefore, let me sing them a song. If by chance someone comes across it, then let him or her sing it and perhaps another will hear it too and sing it and another and another, until the land is filled with a song for our heroes and the ever echoing echoes of that song.

They are the blood that flowed in the sacrifice of limb and life, asking big questions of those who had come to their shores, saying we shall be your lords. They heard it and for a while many of them became the sleeping cat. Yes they are the cat that slept. But when the lion sleeps no longer, its roar is the thunderclap of the forest that shakes the arrogant snake. Lions, I sing you this song. Thank you for that roar you found, and emerging from the shrouds of the forests to show that freedom delayed is not freedom forgotten, not in the lair of the lion. Lions, hear your song. When the streets and avenues of the city were lined with the foreign voice that boomed over bent backs, you were the stampeding feet that bit ankles. You are the sea rising in waves with fierce thrust over the lizards sunning on your beaches in the arrogance of their leisure.

You became our eyes when the night had grown thick like death, our ears when the discord of their songs caused us to dance the strange dance of despair, the voice that thundered when their voice hissed over the people in that place of bleakness, the future filled with hopelessness. You are our heroes! And we will sing you praise songs. Those whose names we will recall and those we won't, who walked and marched and protested, who faced death and other degradations with the dignity of your purpose.

You are the anthill on which the modern movements were born, those who now speak the language of the foreigner without stut ter and wear suit and tie and argue with him word for word, pointing out his hypocrisy. They too are

## SEASONS of FOUR FACES

heroes and I sing their praise songs. Whether with patience or urgency, they have found the hiding place of the occupier and called him out, and they have outshone sunlight. And he squirms like a worm. You have become the people's voice, if only for a purpose. I sing your praises.

Hero falling under the gun, this praise song is for you. Hero perishing in that cell, this praise song is for you. Hero with bent back from humiliation, this praise song is for you. Hero unsung, this praise song is for you.

The listeners applauded this impromptu praise song, even if some of them deemed it out of place for the forum, others saying it was like a bolt of lightning on a cloudless day, while a number of them marked him down as a potential leader for the party.

Through it all, they kept working. On a few occasions, there were skirmishes with members of the UGCC. Tiempo tried to convince some that at the end of it all, it did not matter who won, so long as one of them won and the people were liberated from the tyranny of European colonialism. He said this in the hope of bringing peace when the tension between the CPP and UGCC supporters got tense. But neither side was pleased with this message. If it didn't matter who won, why was he campaigning for the CPP? The UGCC supporters asked. He had to campaign for one side, he explained, given that the leadership had split and someone had to win. What kind of diluted message was he sending? His CPP compatriots asked him. The UGCC was not the enemy, he tried to explain. This is exactly what the British wanted: that they would be so divided that the British would deem them not ready for independence, or even if ready, so they could exploit the divisions to their own benefit. What chaos might ensue if such divisions were to get out of hand, he warned. He was talking nonsense, they retorted. But he would not listen, and though he campaigned for the CPP, he was ready to embrace the UGCC. This, however, became untenable.

One night, after some of them had left the home of a wealthy merchant in Cape Coast, a group accosted them and threatened violence. Tiempo urged calm and called them his brothers and begged them not to incite violence against their brothers. They listened to him and went their way, but not long afterwards, while he was resting with Tetteh at a bus station, a bunch of men, numbering six, descended on him, raining blows on him, identifying themselves as representatives of Boniface Popolampo, who had noticed that he was working for the enemy. Boniface Popolampo, whose name had almost become forgotten? For a while, Tiempo took in the assault without fighting back as he pleaded for them to stop. Tiempo continued to take in the assault until Tetteh's call for help brought the intention of others.

That night, he saw the Poet again. The Poet hushed him, simply saying he too was a form of itinerant and telling Tiempo to put everything in context with these words:

It is all about power. The powerful lord it over the less powerful and the powerless. It is all the same. It's just that some are more wicked than others and some are kinder than others. Even the powerful among the powerless exhibit this trait. So when you pray, pray for the kinder to gain power and that the foul fragrance of power does not turn them wicked.

# SEASONS of FOUR FACES

"I leave you now," the Poet said.
"When will I see you again?"
"I am with you always, always in words."
And the Poet left.

At that moment, Tiempo decided that a phase of his involvement in the campaign was over. He had done his part and he was no longer sure there was much more left for him to do that others more partisan could not do. Therefore, he told Tetteh, it was time for him to return full time to Accra and to fishing. He had been absent for too long and he had to go and allow Sharifa to find him.

Tetteh agreed, saying, "Go get closer to your love and finally find her."

# BENJAMIN KWAKYE

# Another Look at Time

A day after he returned to Accra, Armah invited Tiempo into his part of the building for the first time. The inner chamber boasted a sofa, a coffee table with a couple of large bibles and religious paraphernalia on it, and a small transistor radio. The men faced each other, but with more unfamiliarity than familiarity, for a moment studying each other in gazes intense but friendly. Then Armah asked Tiempo to sit on the sofa as he did the same. Now side by side, Armah said an unsolicited prayer for Tiempo, ending by thanking Jesus, through whom he had prayed.

"My brothers have taken kindly to you," Armah said.

"I hope you do too."

"I have no cause not to," Armah replied. "I have been busy with church matters, so I have not taken the time to get to know you better. You seem to be a good person."

"I like to think so, although many will not agree."

"Why wouldn't they?"

"I have done much in my life."

"No one is perfect," said Armah. "Even the best among us is deeply flawed. It is for this reason that we need the saving grace of our Lord Jesus Christ."

"So you also believe in that stuff?"

"I would not be a pastor if I did not believe."

"There are many pretenders."

"You are very perceptive, I must say."

"You have no doubt?"

"In the interstices of faith, there is doubt, but it is the doubt of the mind, never the doubt of the heart. The heart always wins. But in this day, we think we know too much. I lament that the end of innocence is the beginning of folly. When people think they know too much they begin to deify themselves."

"That's an interesting way to put things. In any case, it has never made sense to me why a man should die for our sins."

"Well, you will agree with me that we are imperfect. If so, we can't soil God's presence with our imperfections unless something cleanses us to allow us to obtain the right standing with God. It is the blood of Jesus that cleanses us."

"Let us assume that you are right, but why do we need bloodshed to be cleansed?"

"Good question. There are many gods, but only one God and, while few see it this way, I believe every god needs the pacification of blood. Think about it—all the animal sacrifices that are made at various shrines. Ask yourself why. And then there are those we don't think of as sacrifices. When we go to war and shed blood. When a man kills another because of a different race or ethnicity. It is not senseless at all. Their gods need the blood. So, what am I saying? We sacrifice animals and humans through bloodshed to various gods. For these lesser gods, they need the blood to thrive; otherwise they are rendered weak. In the case of the great God, human sacrifice will not do, and animal sacrifice is nothing. He had to sacrifice of Himself, by creating human flesh out of His Word. That is Jesus, the begotten, whose bloodshed reconciled us to God. This is the Jesus I worship, the God I worship. The God of Abraham, Isaac and Jacob, the God of Moses that set the captives free from Egypt, the God of perfection."

The mention of Moses and Egypt struck Tiempo. "Your God is the God of Moses?"

"Yes, and of you, if you will let him by confessing Jesus as your lord and savior."

## BENJAMIN KWAKYE

Tiempo was quiet, recollecting the encounter with Moses, who had claimed to act on behalf of God, whose people had been set free, of whom he later learned had crossed the Red Sea, which parted to let them through, but then had closed to drown Pharaoh's pursuing soldiers, of whom he would have been one if he had not fled Egypt. "But isn't this Christianity a religion of the white man? They are after all the ones who brought us the Bible in exchange for our land."

"I have heard that said many times. First, just because something comes from outside, even if from an oppressor, does not automatically render it bad. We must assess it for ourselves. Second, it is not true that it is the religion of the white man. Moses was not a white man. Jesus was not a white man, although many have depicted him as such. Ethiopia has had Christianity, even before it spread in parts of Europe, when king Ezana adopted it during the Aksumite Empire. You should study the Lalibela. So it is true that in recent times Europeans have been influential in spreading the faith, but it is false that it belongs to them or should be viewed exclusively as theirs. Now, I agree that in their zealousness, they have made many of us reject our cultural practices in embracing European cultures, and many of our good practices we have are banished to heathendom. They have also sometimes preached a false pacifism that has made it easier for us to be conquered. And then there are those other charlatans who have misused God's word to deceive many. But each of us is called to make a personal decision that seeks God, that seeks that personal relationship, free from the foibles of humans."

"There is a lot in what you have spoken."

"What do you say?"

"A lot doesn't make sense to me."

"Nor to me. If it all made sense to me, then I would be

## SEASONS of FOUR FACES

God. There's a lot I don't know and will never now; otherwise, I would be God, all knowing."

"And you are comfortable with that?"

"I am comfortable with accepting that, despite the incredible capacity of the human mind, there are dimensions outside of its natural capability. I know I've said a lot, so take time to think about what I have said. That is all I ask.

"I will."

"But before you leave , there is one more thing."

"Yes?"

"Where are you from? I have wondered about this for a long time and I haven't been able to satisfy my curiosity."

The secret, selectively revealed to others, should he tell Armah? He remembered the incredulous reaction of Manu and Addae and the more tampered responses of Sowah and Tetteh. He was now not inclined to tell Armah. But when he looked at the man, he detected such earnestness and a certain trustworthiness. He could not explain what it was about the man, but he decided to divulge his history. Perhaps his God would help just as he had helped Moses? So, drawing closer to whispering range, he told it one more time. Armah listened attentively without interruption, sometimes closing his eyes as if imagining what Tiempo narrated.

When Tiempo finished, Armah pursed his lips and then said, "That is a very strange story."

"I was afraid you would say something like that."

"Of all the journeys you have described, I note that you highlight four: Egypt, Mali, Asante and now the Gold Coast. Four. The number of completeness. And you know, some believe that my people the Gas migrated from Israel to Egypt and then Ethiopia, where they settled near where the Blue Nile originates, hence the name Nai Wulomo, which could be interpreted as High Priest of the Nile. From there, they went to Sudan, then Nigeria and so on. So your story about being in Egypt resonates with me."

"So you believe me?"

"You describe things so vividly that I can't say your account is false. But I think it happened in a different way."

"How so?"

"I don't think you are the Tiempo of Egypt or Mali or Asante. You are just the Tiempo of the now."

"I don't understand."

"Your story has been passed on from generation to generation, told from one Tiempo to the next Tiempo with such vividness that the Tiempo of each generation carried the Tiempos of previous generations with him. You are not a polyglot. Each Tiempo grows up quietly learning the language of the place where he finds himself and then he asserts himself and continues the legacy. And at some time, you will also pass it on to the next generation. You are the Tiempo of the Gold Coast, but you are not the Tiempo of Egypt, or the Tiempo of Mali or the Tiempo of Asante."

"Interesting perspective, even if I disagree with you. And what of Sharifa?"

"It's the same with her."

"That would be strange, don't you think? Tiempos replicating a story as well as Sharifas, in search of one another over time."

"It's no stranger than your version."

"And why don't I remember my childhood here in Accra. If your explanation is true, I would remember that, wouldn't I?"

"I can't fully explain that, but you possibly suffer from some congenital form of amnesia that makes you forget portions of your past."

"That'd be bizarre, but thank you for your time," Tiempo said, as he stood to leave.

"I will pray for you," Armah said. "And Sharifa."

BENJAMIN KWAKYE

# Shackling the Unshackled

Four days after his return to Accra, Tiempo was rested enough to return to work, and had reflected on the events of the past few weeks, content that he had done his part, at least for the moment. He would watch how matters evolved and then decide in the future whether to campaign at the behest of any party or stay out of the fray and instead urge unity. His greatest regret was that in his absence, Sharifa had not come looking for him, which was also his great relief in that he would have been pained if she had come in his absence. His comfort was in the hope that she would fulfill her promise. And, whenever that day of her return was, it was certainly closer now than when she had made it. He would have to tame his impatience by staying as busy as he could. And so it was in the relief found from work where he put all his energy. And he continued to sit under coconut trees and enjoy coconuts with Sowah, just like the good old times.

They had stayed at the shore a long time one day, and evening was approaching when they set out to return home. Tiempo was fatigued from the day's work and his hope was to eat a good meal and go to bed. But just as they turned a street corner they found themselves facing three policemen. Tiempo recognized two of them right away. Two of the ones he recognized were armed with batons, the other with a pistol. "You there," the pistol toting one said. "Hands up, and don't get any ideas about running away, or I will not hesitate to shoot."

Tiempo complied, but Sowah was stunned. "What is the problem, Chief?" he asked.

"You are not the one we are looking for," the man said.

"Your friend here is the one we want." Turning to Tiempo, he said, "You are under arrest."

"For what?" Sowah asked.

"He is under arrest for the murder of John Oldsman, for criminal trespassing and for assault."

"You have the wrong man," Sowah said, "this is a mistake."

"We know what we are doing and you better keep quiet before we arrest you too."

The policeman turned to his compatriots and nodded at them, and they then moved forward towards Tiempo and handcuffed him.

"Say something," Sowah urged him, but Tiempo remained silent.

The policemen prodded Tiempo along to the Osu police station, where he was put in a cell where the wall painting's craquelure suggested a serious need for refurbishment and the pungent smell of urine and feces stressed Tiempo's nostrils. He was left by himself until later that night. Then three policemen entered the room and told him to step forward. They asked him to turn around. At that moment, Tiempo considered overcoming them, which he easily could, and making his escape. But then he thought better of it and decided against that course. What good would it do? Did he want to become a fugitive, always on the run? At what cost, especially knowing that Sharifa was close. He complied as they tied his hands. And then the beating began. All three men hit him, with fists and truncheons. They hit him randomly, in the face, abdomen, arms, back, calves, feet. And on and on. But aside from a few grunts, Tiempo refused to cry out, doubling over instead of falling as they had expected. A rising urge to undo the ligature fell when they stopped after they started huffing and puffing.

One of them asked, "Are you ready to confess?"

"To what?"

"To your crimes, what else?"

"I have no confession to make."

"Do you want to undergo more beatings?"

"You can kill me if you want."

"You think you are a tough guy, don't you? Confess, you will."

They would confront him further with hard sayings, cursing him and his ancestors, and left promising that they would return the next day, which they did, announcing their importance with another round of beatings, though less intense than the previous night's. They asked him if he was ready to confess, and he declined to do so. After many days of similar treatment, Tiempo asked, "Are you not supposed to arraign me before a judge?"

"You think you know book, eh? We can kill you and no one will know where you are, so if you know what's good for you, you will cooperate and tell us what you did."

"What did I do?"

"Look, my friend, stop wasting our time. Our police brothers chased you on that day of the riots. They found the dead John Oldsman in the store you had just left. Not knowing that you would later return to one of the houses you had run through to assault the owner, for what reason none of us can fathom. He was wise enough to preserve the gun so we have your fingerprints as we do on the gun you used to kill Mr. Oldsman. We have informed Peter Boyle and he is on his way here to make an identification. Mr. Boyle is very angry that you trespassed on his property and on top of that assaulted him. You will hang to death, idiot."

Tiempo said nothing as they pestered him to confess and

save everyone's time. They left him for a while and returned seemingly even more agitated and almost desperate to get him to confess, at one point almost begging him to do so. One of the policemen let out, "If only Mr. Doyle had not died so abruptly." His compatriot hushed him. Recognizing his error, the errant policemen smiled and said, "I am playing with your mind. Mr. Doyle will be here any minute now and then you can tell us whether he is lying or you're the one not speaking the truth."

Tiempo said again that he had no confession to make and they left him, leading him to two conclusions. For some reason, their star witness, Mr. Doyle, had died and so he could not come to the station to identify him, which would leave them with the fingerprint evidence. But if Adofo's friends were true, then they would have destroyed that evidence. If so, the only witnesses they had were the two officers. It would then come down to his word against theirs. That might be good enough, so why had they not moved forward?

One night before he slept, he overheard the policemen talking outside of the jail cell about Kwame Nkrumah's victory in the election and his being named leader of government business or the equivalent of prime minister. Though Tiempo had many things preoccupying him, he took a moment to take this in, gladdened that a native son would run the government. If he died in jail, he would have two main regrets: that he had not had the chance to see Sharifa one more time and that he had not experienced the joy of living freely in a land ran by one of his own.

And the policemen were right. They could have killed him and no one would care. So why hadn't they?

They fed him little and sometimes they beat him up and sometimes they did not. He heard them talking about a writ of mittimus that would keep him in jail for a long time. In all this, there were moments of their carelessness that he could exploit to escape. But he was resolved to see this part of his life to its organic conclusion. He would never again become a fugitive, run away from the law or, as in the past, powerful people.

The nights and days became almost indistinguishable as time ceased to matter in the repetition of thought and little motion that tormented Tiempo.

Then one day a man who identified himself as Amidu came to visit Tiempo. From Amidu's smile and friendly demeanor, Tiempo concluded he had benign intentions. He told Tiempo that he was a friend of Adofo's. The only reason Tiempo was alive was that Sowah had gone to see Adofo when Tiempo was arrested. Adofo had contacted officers he knew, hoping to negotiate Tiempo's release. But this was a delicate matter, the police said, because it involved the killing of one white man and the assault of another.

But the matter was made a bit easier when the white man died, apparently of natural causes. They thought that would pave the way for Tiempo's release but his wife had intervened. She did not want Tiempo released and claimed she too had seen Tiempo and could make a positive identification. But just when she was poised to come to the police station, she too had fallen into a coma. And she also died and now there was no obstruction to Tiempo's release, except the two police officers who had identified him. But all of a sudden they had gone quiet, changed their story, saying they were mistaken about the situation, and that Tiempo was indeed an innocent man.

So what was the Amidu saying?

## SEASONS of FOUR FACES

Amidu smiled. "After all this time, you may have given up hope in yourself, but there are those who haven't. Sowah, Tetteh... they have been paying some people to keep quiet. And then there's a lady who has also become interested in your case. She has been coming to the police station almost every day, but no matter how much she paid, they would not let her see you. But today being your day of freedom, she too is waiting for you outside."

"Adjele is such a kind woman," Tiempo said as he breathed deeply on hearing of his imminent release.

"She is," the man said, smiling. "Now let's go outside and meet your waiting family."

The sunlight, when it hit him on this day of freedom, was a little different, brilliant in a way that almost blinded him as he stepped outside of the cell into freedom. And then the figures became less glaring and more recognizable. He saw Sowah. He saw Adjele. He saw Boi. He saw Tetteh. He saw Fofo. He saw Akwele and Akuoko. He saw Armah. And then he smiled. And then the world came to a full stop.

The sun was not shining at all. It was doing something indescribable. As if it was twirling and in the twirling it set the bright clouds on fire and the blue of the sky became as fiery as an inferno, only it was a sweet inferno, and a number of doves flew across the sky singing in sweet chirps in a manner more elaborate than a well conducted orchestra. And the air stopped and became a wild wind that, instead of moving, thrust out a force of heat that was like a sweet balm of fragrant air. And the trees were being uprooted and their roots were like rivers of songs that went deep but sang like they had the sweet voice of humans.

All this is to say that a promise had been fulfilled and

Tiempo was witness to its fulfillment, and although he had not really doubted that it would be fulfilled, he had still doubted—I believe; help my unbelief. All this is to say, as real as it was, it seemed so unreal. He had been told that his family was waiting for him and this was more than he had imagined. His most recent family was indeed waiting for him. But the family that counted the most, the family for which he had ran from kingdoms and to kingdoms, the family for which he had endured all manner of pains, the family that was a family of one (two if you included him), that was the family that was also outside of the station waiting for him. This time, he had an inner assurance about the longevity of the matter, that he need not worry that all would be lost unless he moved quickly, or that he was in competition with anyone else, assured that all preconditions had been satisfied and that this time, it would be forever.

Sharifa, he cried with a voice that shattered the confines of human joy!

Tiempo, she cried with a voice that shattered the confines of human joy!

# SEASONS of FOUR FACES

## Heart-washing

At long last...

As he held Sharifa's hand and ignored complaints about their public display of affection, Tiempo listened to the words of the leader of the newly independent nation that was no longer the Gold Coast, but Ghana (land of warriors) named after another mighty kingdom. This time the people had elected their own king to lead the first nation south of the Sahara to gain independence from British rule. Tiempo thought about how far the nation had come, the force with which the British had overtaken the land, in some cases, the killing that had accompanied the land grab. He thought of past leaders who had sacrificed so much, including Nana Yaa Asantewaa who had died in exile in the Seychelles. He thought of the more recent sacrifices, including those of the ex-servicemen and he breathed heavily and whispered, "I love you."

It was meant for the new Ghana.

And it was also meant for Sharifa.

He had patiently taken in her story, in many ways more heroic than his. She had told him of how she had escaped from the palace of Oumar with the help of some of her palace maids, moving from village to village, staying in dark shadows for fear that she might be captured. She had traveled stealthily and steadily, not sure of her final destination, just moving on and on, finding work of all sorts wherever she went. Eventually she had arrived in Ghana, and traveled to the Asante nation, led by instinct. "Love goes towards love." There was nothing contrived about that. It just was. And then she had heard that there was a Tiempo fighting with Yaa Asantewaa to protect the Asante Golden Stool. So she had made it to Ejisu to find out what she could about him. When the British captured Serwaa, they had included her as well, thinking she was also one of Nana Yaa Asantewaa's children or grandchildren. The brought her to Accra, but when they realized she wasn't related to the queenmother, they had released her. She had returned to Asanteman but was told Tiempo had recovered from his wounds and left, but they did not know where. Sharifa had stayed in Asante for a while and then left.

Again, by instinct she came to Accra, hoping, in fact, believing she would find him there. Again, she had survived through whatever means she could. Eventually, she had found employment with the Doyles, the British civil servants who offered her a job as a maid. They paid her a pittance, but gave her a place in their home. Whenever she had the chance, she would leave the home and find other jobs. Sometimes in the day and sometimes at night. Tiempo now understood why she had not been in the house the many times when he had gone looking for her.

She had no idea Tiempo was looking for her until one day Tetteh sneaked in to tell her that Tiempo had been looking for her all this while. She had come looking for him. And she wanted to return immediately afterward, but the Doyle's had taken her on a trek to the North, a break they said from the capital after what they deemed an attack on their house the day Tiempo hit Mr. Doyle. Then after a while they heard that that the man had been arrested. When they returned to Accra, Sharifa overheard a conversation between Peter Doyle and a policeman who had come to the house to ask him to identify the man. He mentioned the name Tiempo. And then Sharifa knew he was in trouble. She had gone to see Tetteh, who confirmed that Tiempo had been with Sowah when he was arrested and they had been paying bribes to keep him alive. She added what she could to the bribes to keep him alive, but knew that she must do all she could to stop Peter Doyle from identifying Tiempo or pursuing the matter any further.

Sharifa did not specify what she did and Tiempo did not ask. All she said was that, "I am a healer, after all, and I still know what plants can be put in food that can make things happen without trace."

Then after Peter Doyle died, his wife Joyce Doyle decided to take over the matter. She also had to be stopped. Although she had proved more resilient than her husband, she was also vulnerable. Eventually, she died. With Sowah and Tetteh, and with the help of Adofo, and his lawyer Amidu, they had ensured that the two policemen who had pursued Tiempo were well taken care of.

This was something more than an ending; it was something past epilogue, for they expected this one to last, and it therefore meant more than any of their previous encounters or reunions. And it was not a beginning either. How many beginnings made a beginning no longer count as a beginning? It was therefore not prologue. Neither a beginning nor an end; therefore it was past beginning and end. It just was. They could search all the earth for all the words of every language and they knew they would not be able to find the right word or combination of words to describe this. They had to be content that it was.

It just was!

So even at night they would admire themselves through the organza clothes they wore to bed, so that if one were to wake up in the middle of the night, he or she could gaze in awe at the beauty of the other. In the morning, when the dew still sat on grass and soil, two figures walked the Accra pathways as they avoided the busy roads and streets. They walked side by side, shoulder to shoulder, the rhythm of their presence creating an aura of joy, their breaths, newly collected from the fresh air, unpolluted with their inhalations and exhalations. In those hours, they were part of the landscape bringing morning to Accra. They heard the morning wake up calls of the fowls—cock-cocko-crow-crow—the sound of easy hours that called to the sleepy eyes of inhabitants to open. Sharifa imitated them but softly, so as not to disturb the fauna-call, prompting Tiempo to do the same. Voice for voice, one in this imitation, they would listen to all other sounds, in a form of unexpressed love-call to the city, even as a sheep bleated, and waking mothers made waking calls to their children to precede the clash of utensils striking other utensils in the beginning of the preparation of breakfast. It was soothing but taxing also, considering the attention to detail the moments required. And tired, they would lean against a tree, any tree they could find, side by side, to catch their breath. But sometimes the attraction was too much and they would embrace and neck, using overgrown leaves as shield, hopefully, from any eyes that might pry.

These were moments they found very difficult to disentangle from, for if everything ended there and then, they would be content. But when they managed to decouple their bodies, they continued their walk to the beach. And at the seaside, hand in hand, they watched the morning sea, its mellow waves dancing with the aqueous elegance of its softness when at rest, the infant sun weak in glow but rising over the horizon like an ancient, golden artifact whose luster was only momentarily dull, but beautiful in the matutinal context. The smell of the sea reminded them of open wounds that they were closing, and they would often dip into the sea with their toes for its soothing coolness, and they would sit by the water side, one head on a shoulder of the other. They would swim at times, enjoying the vastness of which they were a part, always close to each other, overcoming the coldness with their vigor and their enthusiasm. And when they left, the shore's white sands and swaying coconut trees were a front canvass to the rising sun piercing the horizon in the far distance. She would say to him:

> I will never tire of singing you songs, for in the abundance of the heart, words never dry up, flowing as waters of the oceans, ever fertile with the love the feeds them day and night. Your see through heart shows nothing but love; Our love, it is more than everything: Sheltering as the tortoise's carapace, it is capable of burning the sun and has the power to freeze ice.

And then she would complain when he was silent, and then he would say:

> When you see me looking in silence, words have failed me, so do not fret, in these moments when I do not sing you a song, for in my silence, it is my heart that sings, and my song is my heartbeat, like the talking drum that can't find the words to reduce my love to letters, love that is as timeless as air.

Other times, they would sing songs to each other, embracing every cliche they had heard and repeating them in jovial playmaking like schoolchildren authoring awkward billet doux: You are my harmattan pawpaw, my only fish in the ocean, my only air in the wind, my only coconut on the coconut trees.

# BENJAMIN KWAKYE

You are the only sweat on my skin, the only saliva in my mouth. You are my only star in the sky, my only goal in the net. Take me to Afadjato and I will fall down for you.

But when they moved from the jovial to the serious, then the poetry of their song changed and the words they spoke mingled, and their voices became interchangeable, and what he said was like what she said and what she said was like what he said, and it did not matter who was saying what, for they very well may have been speaking the same words and it would sound true for her as it would for him:

> You are the fresh wind of the heated after noon, your passion burning with the power of your sun, your embrace ebbing the heat with the softness of your moonglow. If you did not exist, I would not exist: This is the essence of our love. You are the one that moves in me, gorging me with living wine. I can always hear you, even a thousand distances away. Your fingers unwind the mysteries of pleasures, your lips are a flute of many voices. Unfurl yourself, your full self, for on it and from it, we are uplifted from the shroud of the mangrove to the tops of the mountain. And in you, all that must exist exists.

"Why do we sing songs?" he asked.

"Because beautiful songs don't sing themselves," she said. "We have to sing them or they are of no value." She sang him one more song, a summary of all else she could have said:

> With the water of your words,
> you have totally washed my heart,

# SEASONS of FOUR FACES

> with your tongue you launder
> and with your heart you gather
> where the heart-washing finds
> its receiving oceans for our mutual wash,
> for love is a cannibal that eats its own.

"Until now I have been running but at standstill," he said, "married to death, with life as a paramour, death engaged with passion, love to be enticed. Now it is the opposite."

"Then I will help you, as you will help me, to the place where death is not even a paramour and our marriage to life is complete and total."

The afternoons were hours of steamy oneness, where they would embrace themselves in the heat, as if in defiance of the sun's unrelenting heat. Eye to eye, they climbed the scales of what had become familiar mountain ranges, easy to negotiate on the familiarity and rising comfort. Protrusions held in clefts, harmony was a song of motions and motionlessness, trot and sprint, sprint and marathon. It did not matter. They were in a hurry and they had no hurry. Time we like the air, essential but taken for granted.

When they stepped outside, it was as if they had conquered the heat and the sun was nothing more than a light giver, the illuminant with which they walked to the marketplace, friend of hawk and vulture, hovering raptors and foraging scavengers alike, that flew overhead or perched on rubbish heaps. They would buy a meal, her favorite the red-red of fried plantains and beans. They would drink alasa and walk at leisurely pace back to the seashore, apart only when he had to go to sea with the other fishermen.

She would be waiting, though assured he would return,

still anxious that the sea word want to keep him, especially the Maame Water who had once challenged him. But there was no duel for his affections and he came to her embrace with his own embrace.

And into the night they went, the hour of entertainment for some and of rest for others, and both for them. For if the one was tired, the other lent energy and neither of them seemed to tire from taking from the other, recognizing that there was nothing selfish about the taking, for it would be returned and in fact it was given in joy. The moon glow as their muse for more love songs, sang by voice and with body. Even if a bat was on tree nearby, they were not bothered by the curious view of the birds hanging upside down. The night was theirs, the stars, each an orating illuminant, urging them on. And they listened to the summons. Exertions led to exhaustions, which led to energies, which led to exertions, which led to exhaustion and then energies. And the mornings came to find two bodies, no spirits, that had become as one, even if in their heavily trafficked bodies.

What more could they say to each other? They had found each other, after love had been honed to perfection in the time apart. And joy is a form of memory thief, for they would remember the past, not as struggle but as preparation for this moment. And their love had become a frequent thought smuggler, identifying for each the other's thoughts before they were spoken. In the beginning was not a nothingness, but a somethingness. And they had found a somethingness that had blossomed. They had lost each other, lived for each other and died for each other, and had found each other. And they were in such a place of harmony where things were coming together, where the rhythms of their footsteps, like the rhythms of their snores, were becoming more coordinated, acquiring a spiritual musicality. What more could they say to each other? They did not need to say it, for they knew it. But for the wind's ears that carried messages to its mouth for the world, in case anyone wanted to hear them say so, they said it as simple and overused as those words were, more powerful than any combination of words known: I LOVE YOU.

BENJAMIN KWAKYE

# The Brink

That she of all people would fall ill at the time was never part of the calculus, not anything he would even have ever contemplated to breach his joy, not at that time when they were riding so high on the joys of their reunion. So it was shocking to Tiempo when one day, without any warning, her breath loud and strained, Sharifa would not get out of bed, pulling the sheets close to cover her body up to her chin, shivering and sweating at the same time and complaining that she was cold and that it felt someone had taken an axe to her head, not once or twice, but with persistent hammering. She slipped in and out of consciousness at the time when Tiempo asked her what medicine she would prescribe for herself. No matter where it was, he would travel to get it; no matter how much it cost, if there was a price attached to it, he would find a way to pay the price. But whenever she opened her eyes, she would close them before she uttered anything coherent.

Tiempo asked his new family for help and they each had different suggestions. The one that held sway was for him to treat her with the neem. After much discussion, Sowah and Tetteh helped carry Sharifa out to the compound in one of her states of semi-consciousness, put her on a stool and, with Tiempo kneeling behind her and holding her as upright as he could, placed a bucket of hot water with neem leaves in it and draped a thick blanket over Tempo and Sharifa. It was hot under the blanket, with the neem-full hot water stirred from time to time by either Tetteh or Sowah, who would enter the blanket covering to perform this task and then get out. Holding her over the bucket, Tiempo could hear Sharifa's strained breathing as the vapor entered her nostrils, the heat squeezing

# SEASONS of FOUR FACES

out copious sweat. In such close proximity, both Tiempo and Sharifa were drenched in sweat. Tiempo held on tight, body to body, sweat intermingling with sweat, saying, "We are one sweat, Sharifa; we are one body. We live or die together."

After a while, Sowah and Tetteh helped carry Sharifa back to bed. She slept quietly, her breath more subdued. That night, Armah came to the room, apologizing for not being present when Tiempo needed him. He looked at the sleeping Sharifa for a long time. Then he knelt next to her and prayed for the restoration of her health, saying she was fearfully and wonderfully made and that by the stripes of Jesus she was healed. It would take a few more days for Sharifa to regain full consciousness and coherence and, in between, Tiempo gave her water from boiled neem leaves to drink. She would spill most of it, but managed to swallow a little. It would take even more days before she was strong enough to stand on her feet. And all this while, Tiempo remembered a time when she had healed him, knowing that it was not just the neem or whatever medicine was administered, that she and now he was the real roborant.

The first time she walked to the compound after her illness, Sowah and Tetteh noted that the neem treatment had worked; Armah thanked Jesus for the healing. Sharifa smiled and thanked the family. Tiempo would later hold her tightly for a long time and say, "Next time, give me warning if you are going to get sick, so I can get sick with you. Next time allow me time to prepare."

# BENJAMIN KWAKYE

## Canoeing Freedom

"At long last the battle has ended," Kwame Nkrumah said to rapturous applause.

Tiempo looked around him at the teeming crowd cheering and cheering as the men of independence stood at the podium in their batakaris. And yet, amid the people and the cheering, his mind and the bulk of his concentration was on Sharifa. He tightened his grip on her hand, though sure he would never lose her again, thinking of her promise long ago that she would find him. And she had. He recounted the moments they had spent after his release. Never had there been such sweet moments when they expressed their love for each other. And they had hugged and continued to seek the highest meanings of love in each other's company, sometimes even in the intensity of the silence of their staring at each other, naked eyes that looked into naked eyes with nothing but the purest emotion of love and deep admiration. And the rest of the household had allowed them their space to grow deeper into each other, even happier on the news that Adjele would become a mother for the second time.

And the reality of independence from British rule only added to the buoyancy. It was as if a new air had been breathed upon the country from the heavens and the future was bright in the pregnancy of hope and expectation and the sheer fulfillment of freedom from foreign rule and the audacity of belief in self: "At long last the battle has ended and Ghana your beloved..."

Ghana the beloved. North, South, East, West. Beloved and

SEASONS of FOUR FACES

loved by those who dared to believe in all that was possible.

The crowd cheered even before Nkrumah finished his sentence. Tiempo took the words apart.

"At long last." And how long it had been, from arrival at the coasts, to their incursions into the hinterlands, to their conquests, to their wanton partitioning of the continent, to their rule, to the resistance and the crashing of it to the indefatigable nature of the thirst for freedom. "The battle," oh, yes, the battle, some of which he had experienced firsthand and the bloodshed for the newly born nation, the blood spillers without any bloodguilt on their conscience. He looked at the many who held the flag of Ghana: the red symbolizing the blood shed from the battle; the gold for the mineral wreath of the country; and the green for its natural wealth. Three bold horizontal colors with a black star in the middle, the lodestar of Africa, its people's skin color shining as the new African.

"At long last, the battle has ended and Ghana your beloved country is free forever!"

Freedom!

"Freedom!" Sharifa affirmed. "Freedom is beautiful but treacherous," she said. But no one was listening.

The weight was lifted off as Tiempo and Sharifa left the Polo Grounds, where the rally had just taken place and the batakari clad Dr. Kwame Nkrumah, flanked by his compatriots Kojo Botsio, Komla Gbedemah, Archie Casely Hayford and Krobo Edusei, had just proclaimed the independence of Ghana, its freedom and the local as the new national custodian of justice for the people. That promise of freedom propelled them into dancing on the way back home. Tiempo danced and Sharifa danced. And the people around them danced. And some sucked in the intoxicating liquor of independence and some the intoxication of spirited beverages. And some winebibbers staggered here and there, worsening the foot traffic, and some fell on the streets and some fell into gutters. Here and there, people called to one another sometimes with sweet words and sometimes with profane and vulgar words, in their version of humor. Tiempo and Sharifa sailed on these and even if anyone would have any inclination for doubt or sadness, the atmosphere itself would not let them. So they walked home, and they danced home and they sang home: God bless our homeland Ghana!

# SEASONS of FOUR FACES

## Fresh Air

They were about to enter the room that had housed Tiempo all this while and recently Tiempo and Sharifa, when Sowah came out of the main house, shirtless. He was on his way to call a midwife, for Adjele was in labor. He was so frantic one would have thought this was his first child. Tetteh and the rest of the family were out on this independence eve, and so the homestead was almost empty.

"I will take care of this," Sharifa said.

"You?" Sowah said with worry.

"Trust her, brother," Tiempo said. "She knows this more than any midwife or doctor."

The words were too bold to admit any doubt. They went to the Sowah's, where Adjele was panting profusely and pacing and moaning. Sharifa held her hand and then wiped away her sweat with her scarf. "Let's get you ready," she said. Seeing creeping doubt in Adjele's face, she added, "I am a midwife."

Then Sharifa began to issue orders to the men to get a bucket of water, hot water, towels, this and that. And after they gathered these things, Tiempo took Sowah with him to sit in the compound. But Sharifa asked Tiempo to join him. Sowah hesitated but agreed.

# BENJAMIN KWAKYE

# Time and Space

Adjele lies on her back, legs apart, sweat covering her face. Sharifa and Tiempo each bow down on the floor, their faces between their knees. Then Sharifa looks at Tiempo, and they do not have to speak, each knowing his and her part. Between them, there is much to remember and cherish and bring to bear at this moment. A most awesome responsibility, greater than wars, for this is a war for a life in which even one death is a defeat.

They begin to massage Adjele's belly, kneading and coaxing the baby into the right place for delivery, Sharifa speaking words of encouragement to both mother and fetus, full of belief that words have glorious shadows that will continue to edify after they are spoken. The mother is straining, as they encourage her to push. Sowah pops his head inside and quickly leaves. The pair continue. Sharifa leaves the massaging to Tiempo and he is moving his hands over Adjele's belly and Sharifa moves higher to gather Adjele's head on her lap, wiping away her sweat and whispering into her ears.

Adjele moans as she pushes, all the while with Sharifa encouraging her with words and Tiempo with his hands. And she pushes and she pushes. She is in obvious pain, but the pair is helping her manage it, assuring her it will be well. And then the head of the baby appears and now Tiempo speaks, encouraging Adjele that it is almost over. One more push and another. Adjele yells, a sound that mixes pain with hope and anxiety. And then her body relaxes.

And they are all in anticipation, knowing that the moment is now when life produces life and so much hope is wrapped in the presence of a newborn baby, a moment of hope and joy and anticipation, but also, for those who are more skeptical, an angsty moment, for there is always that fear of failure and that crucible of hope in which many disappoint or are disappointed. But if that skepticism crosses any mind, it is quickly pushed aside, for it will have its moment, and that is for another day, and the moment of birth is not to be maculated with such negativity. And so they hold on to that hope as Adjele pushes new life outside of her into the waiting hands of Tiempo. About an hour after they return from the rally at the Polo Grounds, Tiempo and Sharifa hear the shrill cry of a newborn baby. As Sharifa wipes the baby and hands her over to Adjele, Tiempo asks Sowah to come into the room. When Sowah enters, Adjele is holding the newly born at her bosom, and with a weak smile, she says, here is our new daughter, from whom will spring many. Past is present and present is past and present and past give birth to the future. And the baby begins to cry, signaling life. And without anyone asking, the parents announce that the child's name is Sharifa.

∞

# AUTHOR'S NOTE

This novel is a work of fiction. While it relies on historical facts and events as a backdrop, and invokes historical figures, it should not be necessarily read for historical accuracy. In certain instances, I have deliberately tampered with historical accuracy in order to accommodate the fictional project, including manipulation of the times when certain events may have occurred. I have relied sometimes on others' accounts, including quotes without attribution, in order not to disrupt the narrative flow. Some of the quotes in the portion about Mali are taken from P. James Oliver's *Mansa Musa and the Empire of Mali: A True Story of Gold and Greatness from Africa* (2013) and D.T. Niane's *Sundiata An Epic of Mali* (translated by G.D. Pickett) (2006). Additionally, among other sources, Stephen Manning's *Britain at War with the Asante Nation 1823-1900 – The White Man's Grave* (2021) and Kwasi Konadu and Clifford C. Campbell's *The Ghana Reader: History, Culture, Politics* (2016) were particularly helpful. Small portions of the novel contain excerpts from previous poetry collections and from a previously published short story, *Afternoon Delight* (*The Executioner's Confession*, 2015).

# ABOUT the AUTHOR

Born in Accra, Ghana, Benjamin Kwakye attended the Presbyterian Secondary School in Ghana, and holds a bachelor's degree from Dartmouth College, where he majored in Government (with an emphasis in international relations). He wrote and published poetry while in college, served as editor of Spirit, a literary journal, and received a 1990 Senior Honor Roll for outstanding leadership, distinguished service and intellectual and artistic creativity. Kwakye also holds a Juris Doctor degree from Harvard Law School.

He is the winner of two Commonwealth Writers Prize awards, for Best First Book and Best Book (Africa region). His other awards include the African Literature Association's Book of the Year Award for Creative Writing, the IPPY Gold Award for Adult Multicultural Fiction, and the Illumination Book Award for Poetry (Bronze). He was a finalist for the 2019 Snyder Poetry Prize and for Greece's 2023 Eyelands Book Awards. His novel, *The Clothes of Nakedness*, has been adapted for radio as a BBC Play of the Week and was selected as a Pan African Writers Association Book of the Week. Kwakye's poetry has appeared in numerous publications and anthologies.

Kwakye is legal counsel in the Michigan area, where he lives with his family, Margaret, Nana, Jeede, and Kristodia. He is a Director of the Africa Education Initiative and Resident Novelist of the The African Novel (Digital Newsletter). You can find out more at www.benjaminkwakye.com.